The Marigold Trail

The Marigold Trail

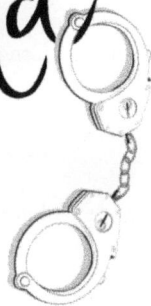

Cover design by Rena Violet
Reversible dust jacket design by Jin Shin @ Dear Marilla
Book Formatting by Authortree
Interior art: Handcuffs © KoDu Art / Shutterstock.com
Marigold © Caraulan Art / Shutterstock.com

Identifiers: ISBN 979-8-218-51098-5 (paperback) |
ISBN 979-8-218-51100-5 (hardcover)
Subjects: LCGFT: Time-Travel fiction. | Novels.

Printed in USA
1st Printing 2024

To my grandparents, who fed my imagination and blessed me with many opportunities. I find lots of hidden rooms and Irish coasts in my dreams thanks to you.
Alice, Jim, and Shirley
And to Glennifer. You are my rock.

Prologue

Behind the city, tucked in the front pocket of the Rocky Mountains, lie the playful secrets dreamt up in my childhood. Back then, living in Golden, Colorado, at the foot of the mountain, I thought the mountains held all kinds of secrets. How could they not with such enchanting scenic loops laid with folksy mountain towns deep in the rolls of the hills? But as I grew, I came to understand the hills behind me held no such thing, just otherworldly mountain views at my backdoor. The magic of it all became less fantastical and just something I began to appreciate.

My appreciation has grown since moving to a Denver apartment where the sun rises minutes earlier than it does in Golden, blasting the eastern high rolling plains with dramatic sunbeams that illuminate every inch of earth's surface. It's mesmerizing. And if you ask me, I even prefer watching the sun set from Denver, witnessing the light fade behind my hometown, like a little gift reminding me of the log buildings, rutted railways, switchback roads and glittering ghosts of old mines that lay tucked beyond the trees.

I long to spend more time there and taste the sweet drug of dopamine just like the rest of outdoorsy Denver, who flock there on weekends like it's the peak of the Gold Rush, making traffic crawl rather than flow. But my current Bureau assignment only draws me farther away, investigating a chemical plant explosion on the other side of town, so far East I question if I was fully sane when I volunteered to take it on.

I do get at least a short week of closer proximity now that the investigation's on pause. Complications arose last Friday when Agent Ben Brown, the best man anyone could ever work with—methodical and even-tempered to the max—crashed the site of my ongoing investigation during a high-speed chase on his motorcycle. His chase led to a successful arrest while simultaneously blasting through my location's crime scene and altering the chemical evidence of my examination.

And though the damage to the scene looks to be minimal, the discovery just outside the scene made for complicating matters. Ben had uncovered a freshly mutilated body thanks to the rocket-like force of his tires and my investigation now called for wider crime scene parameters.

Chapter One

I look at the time on my phone. I need to be out the door, like now.

"Atta, what's the punishment for tardiness at the Bureau? Will they dock your pay? Make you run laps?"

My sweet, naive-when-it-comes-to-anything-FBI-related mother probes me from the other line. She calls me on her morning commute to work, not missing a call since moving an hour away to Fort Collins. It's usually a quick call, but now that she's caught on to the fact that I haven't even made it out the front door yet, I get to entertain her budding questions. It's like I'm back in high school and she's still the overbearing mother-figure who will take away my Friday night if I do wrong, yet force me to watch a movie with her snuggled up on the living room couch—back then, a punishment I enjoyed.

"I won't be late. I missed my first alarm but I have dry shampoo," I say it like it's the solution to all of life's minor problems. Luckily, I make do with my hair resting in a low ponytail, putting effort into a sleek part down the middle and though only a few long strands have escaped, my highlights frame my face like wild vines—the only sign that I didn't take the necessary time this morning to wash or properly tame my hair.

"You never miss alarms. Were you up late last night? Won't you smell?" She laughs, content with her jab. Her soul demanded to keep me humble on many occasions—this morning being no exception.

"I'm not gross," I say flatly, doing a quick smell check at which I promptly pop open a bottle of sweet smelling lavender lotion. I rub a few circles on my arms. "I stayed at Ben's apartment until late last night." When I say it I try to leave out any romantic connotation in my tone to avoid misinterpretation. If anyone was going to miscon-strue my relationship with Ben it was Mom, and I didn't need to find my way down that rabbit hole this morning. The only rabbit passageway vital to this particular moment is the one White Rabbit utilizes when he's running around Wonderland yelling "I'm late, I'm late, for a very important date!" Hastily, I toss the lotion bottle on the couch and jog on over to my kitchen in search of breakfast.

"You were out late with Ben last night?" Mom replies. She asks the question with an expectant tone. A tone that bleeds a bit too hopeful.

It's not common for me to stay out late with Ben but last night he convinced our game night group—Ben and I's quick-witted jiu-jitsu buddies, Jessica and Cam, plus a Bureau IT guy Ben's known forever—to start a game of Risk after Settlers of Catan wrapped up in record breaking time—like groundbreakingly fast. Ben initiated the game of Risk, setting out the board pieces across the thick slab of wood—his modern block coffee table the size of a small iceberg—while the rest of us googled 'record time for playing a game of Catan' to no avail.

"Are we all in this round? This game can play six. If you don't want to play you'll want to watch because one of us is going to destroy Atta. She's currently undefeated," Ben said, riling up everyone in the room, including Jessica's friend—our blonde vixen of a guest. "Jessica, Cam, Adam, put the pressure on her. Atta said you both sucked during last week's game so use that as the fuel for your fire," he'd continued, proving to me once again, that his loyalty was only legitimate outside the domain of game night territory. With my mouth agape at his audacious lies and a backtrack of our friends parrying laughter, he'd comfortably sown a competitive desire in everyone's hearts for the rest of the night.

Despite Ben's attempt to start our game with a group of people holding pitchforks at my throat, I still offered my loyalty to him after walking back into the room to find him staring at the wall with absent-minded eyes, his top collar unbuttoned enough for my eyes to sample a smidgen of his firm, dark upper chest.

He perked up when I entered the room—party snack tray in hand. And I went along with it when his eyes, now dark as oil, leaked his ill-natured plan to boot Jessica's guest—the aggressive blonde sitting on the couch next to him—to the curb.

Whether it was the sight of food in my possession or the fact that he found me the solution to his current predicament, he began waving me down, the way an officer would go about directing traffic. Then he'd grabbed my waist and swapped me with the woman seated next to him, rearranging the room as if he were parking cars.

"Okay let's get started," he'd said with a sigh of relief. He began chewing a snack from my tray and smiled pleasantly at the woman so as not to offend her after parking her next to Alex on the opposite side of the table.

The truth is, Ben leaving a comfortable distance in the couch space between us until it was time to turn in at 2:00 a.m., was proof that although he'd prefer to sit by me, that woman and I were one and the same. Ben wasn't interested in either of us.

Therefore, Mom thinking our relationship was anything more than brotherly—was merely speculative. The sequence of words 'I stayed with Ben until 2:00 a.m.' didn't mean anything. Especially not to him.

Her optimism came from my long history with Ben. Ben was my childhood best friend Diana's brother. But he was also Agent Brown, the man I saw daily working at the Bureau, who just last week opened up Pandora's box by running over and making absolutely permanent the death of an already mutilated body, giving potential motivation to my case. It was one of those situations I could've jointly scolded and thanked him for.

More often than not, I refer to Ben as my partner agent since we basically work around the clock together, assigned to the same criminal and cyber department and all. Our desks lie just a few yards away. It's safe to say I spend a lot more time with him than I have with his sister since I started this job.

"You know we were just out late for our weekly game night... What's with the expectant tone? We both know Ben's not interested in me that way. You know, 'I'm just his little sister's best friend,'" I quote the words as if he's saying them himself. Then I close the kitchen cupboard void of breakfast bars just to move on to the next cupboard with a sigh.

"And yet by the sound of that sigh, you still have a crush on him," she chuckles again. She's not wrong. Unfortunately for me, the crush is still very much there. "You've got your weekly game night but you don't have any game."

I glance out the kitchen window at the early morning tangerine sky and smile with my tongue touching my cheek. She would say something like that.

"Yes, that's correct. I have no game," I laugh.

"Isn't your high school class reunion this weekend? Maybe you can meet someone there. Diana, Tyler, and Evan should be there right?" she says, momentarily giving up on Ben as the subject of matchmaking potential.

As I approach my thirtieth birthday, my love life has become a regular topic of conversation for Mom. As if she's actively hoping for me to find someone, so that I can experience the same kind of love she had in those few short years with my father—cut short due to his early death. All it took for her to find him was a trip to Spain, but I don't have enough time off to look for love in another country, let alone outside of the office.

"Diana will be there but I haven't heard from those other two in years. Who meets the love of their life at a class reunion. I mean, seriously?"

"You never know." Her tone remains hopeful.

"I'm pretty sure Ben was the best thing that came out of Golden High." I rummage through another cupboard, hoping for a protein shake. "And wouldn't I have picked up on it back then, if the love of my life was waiting for me in the Class of 2011?"

"Well then, maybe you need to get Ben's attention another way. What about longer eye contact and a top that shows off your cute figure? You're always wearing those white-collared, button-down work shirts," says the woman who's always trying to dress me.

Settling, I snatch a Pop-Tart from a box in the back of the cupboard. I'm not sure how close they are to the expiration date since I don't remember buying them.

"I dress like that because I'm always working and it's my job to investigate hard criminal threats. Not to look cute."

"Yeah, well what about game night?"

"The button-downs are comfortable," I say defensively. This time my mother chuckles. I set the phone down on the coffee table, missing whatever she says after criticizing my shirt choices. I don't mind putting the distance between me and her on the phone as I grab my camel-colored coat hanging on the door hook and throw it over my shoulders all while naturally humming my favorite tune—a habit I'd had for years.

"I hope you're putting on the coat I gave you. At least that's charming," Mom says when I pick up the phone again.

I pause for a second. "Wait, how'd you know I put on my coat? Have I been on video chat this whole time?"

"You're humming that Chris Farley song. You always hum that when you're putting on your coat." She's right. It's so much of a habit, I forget I do it at this point. When I'm really feeling myself I even add a sway, arms stretched out, the exact same way Chris Farley does in *Tommy Boy*.

"That's because 'Fat Guy in a Little Coat' is a classic."

Mom's sigh is blatantly obvious over the phone. "How many Chris Farley quotes did you do last night at game night?"

"A few," I say, grabbing my planner off of the coffee table.

"And you still think a skinny Spanish girl quoting fat white guy jokes works?"

"Yup," I say.

"Oh, Atta." Mom chuckles. "Don't ever change. Okay?"

"No worries there, Mom," I say, grabbing my keys off of the entryway table.

"Oh, can you call your grandpa and make sure he's still on for dinner next week?"

"Yeah. I'll check in with Pops," I quickly scribble a note in my planner. *Check-in with Pops* on today's bottom half of the square. "I'm heading out now. Gotta go, Mom," I say rushing out the door.

"Oh Atta, before you go, remember even if you don't have Ben's love or any man's love for that matter, you'll always have my love." And with that verbal love-pat, she hangs up, her featured contact information dissolving the way food coloring diffuses in a tornado of water.

※

FIRST THING AT THE OFFICE, I AM GREETED BY BEN, THE HUMAN equivalent of an artillery vehicle. Loyal. Deadly. Cooks appetizers well. He's still walking around the office like the responsible big brother he thinks he is, acting as if he'd done me a favor by uncovering a dead body blasting through my crime scene, though we all know it was unintentional. I pass up the chance to call him out on it, though if I wanted to I could bend his iron facade with a pinch at his waist.

My partner agent over the last five years and the one I can thank for the "Agent Suarez" nameplate that sits atop my office desk. He hands me a green-lidded, paper cup punctured with a twig-sized straw and tells me to meet him in the conference room for a morning debrief. His slight smile showing off his full wide lips. Partner or caretaker? Sometimes it was hard to tell.

I slap a baseball cap, FBI standard, over my unwashed hair and follow after Ben, who's just passed through the conference room doors. When I enter, I find him leaning over a chair, his eyes are laser beams of concern aiming to fry the screen in front of him. His arms tense like my mood on a ruined day, and I wonder if it was possible for them to collapse the same way legs do when they lock up for too long.

"Atta, come here for a sec," he says, releasing his arms from the office chairs. For the second day in a row I admire his noticeably shorter trimmed crew cut which somehow makes him look even more like a young Denzel Washington than I previously thought. My pulse races. The resemblance is quite comparable.

"Sarah called into the office this morning." Ben says.

"Sarah?" I ask, not sure who Ben is talking about.

"Sarah Carter rang today," Ben says. "You know, the part-time comedian who nearly sat on me after trying to hit on me with a Koala joke last night?"

I chuckle at the memory of Ben playing a game of human dodge-ball all evening. I remember now. He'd strategically made that initial swap thanks to my generous service. But really, Sarah performed all on her own. Forget multiple players and hard rubber balls, she proved to be a force, throwing herself at him.

"Oh stop with the laughs. I know you enjoy watching me suffer, but this is a serious matter. Wipe that smile off your face." He smiles through the words, letting me know he kind of likes it.

I deadpan. Hinting mockery was my preferred response in all Ben-related cases.

"She's an assistant at a law firm. Her boss has something for us. I'm dealing with a cybercrime case. Planning on wrapping it up today, so I told her you'd handle it."

"Did you feel her disappointment through the phone?" My pupils dance with delight. I'll claim any opportunity to give him a hard time.

"Here." He forces the phone into my hands, feigning annoyance.

I take note of Sarah's request and ask around the department to see who can accompany me to the Hampton & Burrow Law Firm in

Denver. It's not far from here and a lawyer by the name of Brian Hampton has asked us to pick up a USB from his office. I review the untidy ink marks from my planner over again in my head: *USB device contains incriminating information. A set of videos. United States Senator.* He wouldn't say much else other than that his qualifications as a lawyer are well beneath the gravity of this, besides he's now a witness.

Gathering from the details, we'd need to compile evidence as quickly as possible. Due to the potential involvement of a governmental official, we will have to actualize the lawyer's claims and make sure the information isn't spread in any unwanted circles.

I take a lap around the office area looking for an agent to accompany me, before trying the conference room one more time. I find Ben grabbing a mint from the snack dish in the middle of the table as he's packing up his things.

"You sure you don't want to ride along with me on this one?" I ask, hoping he'll delay his cybercrime case and join me today.

"Nah. You don't need me. You got this one." He looks me over and smiles—he's probably noticing my barely-thrown together state. "Glad you made it home safe after having such a rough time last night," Ben says.

I stick my tongue out at him. "Like your apartment is so far away from mine."

"Knock, knock."

Ben and I both turn to see Agent Kenny Maser standing in the doorway. He wears a little grin on his face like he just heard something he wasn't supposed to.

My cheeks burn red. I've had limited interaction with Agent Maser. He's a golden boy with the director's ear and not someone I need misconstruing my work relationships.

"Sorry to interrupt, Agent Brown, I can come back later," he says.

"No worries, Agent Suarez and I were just discussing game night. Something our group of old friends does. And we're just friends, nothing more. She's looking at a major loss next week despite having never lost at Risk. It's not looking good for you, Agent Suarez. You might need to buy some luck if you plan on reclaiming a win next week," Ben finishes.

I give him a slight jab with my elbow, thankful for the clarification, regretful it comes with a friend zone explanation.

Ben waves at both of us, signaling his departure, as Agent Maser makes his way past the snack dish. I sigh and turn to face the leather chairs lined up against the room's giant half moon desk where Agent Maser now hovers over a computer. He's the only agent left in the room. Overconfident and basking in the sunny computer glow, his Google searches likely range anywhere from "cleanest shave for stone cut jawline" and "best protein, water ratio for ultimate gains."

He types, giving his fingers a short exercise and then looks up from his gaze on the computer. "Sounds like you need a partner," he says, exiting out of whatever he was working on, then swings his leather bag over his shoulder before adjusting his posture.

He peacocks toward me.

Great. It'll have to be him today.

I'd considered myself one of the lucky ones, thanks to Ben recruiting me straight out of college, where majoring heavily in strategic analysis and game theory with a minor in forensic investigation seemed like the appropriate choice for a girl who carries miniature crossword puzzles in her back pocket. I'd always been a mad woman with a "solving" obsession and my childhood best friend's brother luckily found use for me, eventually snatching me an ultimate dream job at the Bureau. Missing child cases, Russian hackers, chemical plant explosions—the most recent case I was knee-deep in—were all challenging puzzles that made my heart leap into action at the chance to solve them. Pinch me moments are still required, and yet days where I have to be around agents like Agent Kenny Maser bring me back to reality. Sometimes my job isn't just a fun crime-themed puzzle to solve.

Chapter Two

gent Maser starts the SUV and blasts the AC. I brace against the immediate cold and it only increases the already awkward chill in the car. His gaze meets mine as our seat-belts click in unison. It seems Mr. Maser and his self-aggrandized ego —he's directly under the deputy director and all—was going to attempt small talk the rest of the drive.

"You get to enjoy the nightlife much while living downtown?" His lips congratulate themselves at the break of his question. Then his eyes trail down my face; from my soft angled eyebrows to the extra coat of eyeliner plastered over yesterday's eye makeup, finally landing on my patchy ivory cheeks thanks to my lack of foundation. He's noticed the difference; my hazel eyes probably look extra smoky since I didn't have time to go through the process of washing yesterday's eye makeup off of my dark Spanish lashes—a gift from my father's side.

"Occasionally," I say, purposely sticking to one-word answers. I was still bothered by the fact that he had to present himself in a way that made me question my own ranking within the department.

We shuffle out of the vehicle; both of our hands reach for the holsters on our hips, synchronized like a line dance we've both known forever but only performed together a handful of times. The pathway to the law firm worms along a nicely architected lawn of flower borders and green shrubbery meticulously spaced between the mulch. My steps become weighted with lingering thoughts of Agent Maser's failed car conversation and my own clunky HI-TEC brand hiking boots as we approach the russet red brick building held up by modern Doric columns and burnt orange trim.

THE LAWYER, BRIAN HAMPTON, GREETS US AT THE DOOR. He looks as if we couldn't rip the USB out of his hands soon enough and guides us to his office before locking the door behind him. Game face. Agent Maser and I are partners today. I must wipe the dense coat of annoyance off my face and apply cordial, team-player, professional face paint to it. I can do hard things.

I have to repress the urge to roll my eyes every time the words "special counsel review" come out of Agent Maser's mouth in whispers.

The lawyer begins sharing his background with us and his connection to the USB. His client, the US Senator, had dropped the USB unknowingly and Brian happened to pick it up, out from under the oak chairs facing his desk, late yesterday evening. This morning he popped the device into his computer to crack the mystery of who it belonged to, receiving an answer after just a few clicks, finding his client, the US Senator, appearing in a video onscreen.

Agent Maser turns in toward my ear, invading my personal space. "They really could appoint a special counsel. He's a government official and they can deem it a conflict of interest." He mutters the sentence as if the anticipation of a US Senator's involvement was a positive thing.

This guy. Good thing Mr. Hampton is out of earshot, gathering his files for us on the Senator, or he might have sensed my urgency to forgo my professionalism and swat Agent Maser right then and there with my arm.

Partnering with him was already starting to match a level of irritation akin to someone snapping their gum in my ear! Unreasonable rage, the kind that either carves a path for passionate action or forces you to quit that person altogether, is getting the best of me.

Ben was much easier to work with. Our cohesion and love, the sibling kind of love—his preference, not mine—was directly proportional to Agent Maser and I's discord and mutual irritation for each other. Ben was professional, a bit intimidating, and very personal when it came to interacting with the general public. He was a natural. I, on the other hand, had to "fake-it-till-you-make-it" and usher in an aura of intimidation, while I chased away the silly, uncomfortable feelings that come from approaching citizens with, oftentimes, difficult subjects.

I've managed public professionalism every day for the last five years somehow, but everyone knew I was most useful outside of the scene, when the office analysis began and I could apply game theory or map out systematic search strategies. Not being in my preferred game space and being stuck with Agent Maser made this hand off doubly unpleasant.

Mr. Hampton approaches, eagerly holding out a file and USB for us to grab, looking as if he couldn't be rid of them fast enough but also concerned for us. "I've seen about five minutes. I don't know how you do things over there, but legally I want nothing to do with it. It's all yours. Watch it. I would suggest screening who watches this and giving me a call when you need me to come in for additional questioning. Thank you for coming so quickly." Mr. Hampton's energy speaks louder than his words, giving off a strong your-soul-is-about-to-get-wrecked vibe. He seems damaged enough. Though for Agent Maser and I, I'm sure it's nothing special. Bureau agents see disturbing things all the time.

"I'll be ceasing all contact with him immediately. I'll also send you the office recording of our interaction from yesterday. "

"Thank you, Sir," I say, as Agent Maser finalizes the handoff of the USB. He brandishes it in front of Mr. Hampton with his right hand like it's an Olympic torch.

"We'll be off then. We'll be in touch once it's reviewed," Agent Maser says, nodding to acknowledge our departure.

ON OUR DRIVE BACK, IT'S BLATANTLY CLEAR THAT AGENT MASER isn't familiar with the art of sitting in silence or catching on to the fact that I'd appreciate doing so. He continues talking as I count the narrow planted trees along the sidewalk and the number of homeless people in sleeping bags around the corner passing 26th street. Only three this week. That's good. My heart relaxes a bit.

He gives me a look out of the corner of his eye expecting a response to something he said. Maybe an "Oh yeah" or "mhmm" will do. Was he talking about his weekend plans or did he trail back to the personal "Did you know you wanted to be an agent as a kid?" type of question? I opt for "Oh yeah" blending my tone between a statement and a question, hoping that'll satisfy him.

He raises his arm to the grab handle on the side, exposing the bicep muscle under his fitted polo blocking my view of the blue and white striped, red and yellow Colorado flags hanging across the street poles. He laughs. If it weren't for my irritation at his overly proud nature, I might actually admire the sculpted arm show. He was tall, muscular, and likely intimidating, even without the FBI uniform on, but since I didn't respect his show of arrogance, he had the opposite effect on me. To me he was about as intimidating as soup. If his clean-cut style, parted graham cracker-colored hair, and well-defined jaw swapped bodies with someone else's personality, I might call that person attractive. Still, this was not the case.

"I asked what kind of food you like." His smile is now directed at me. He must be satisfied, catching me fumbling a reply that doesn't make sense.

"Anything but curry," I say, keeping the placid expression. The first and last time I had curry was at Diana's wedding and its effect on me was just as unappetizing as my relationship with Ben was that night.

One minute Ben and I are happily editing each other's best man and maid of honor speeches, sharing funny drafts and meaningful words—lots of compliments for Diana and maybe even a few slipping out for each other—and the next, I'm tasting what I'd call chalky, herb-filled reception gravy with a side of bitter feelings. Feelings brought on by Ben telling me to keep my distance, then later denying me a dance on the checkered floor. I've yet to learn what scared him that day but I've made sure to conceal my feelings for him since. Maybe I was too forward with the compliments.

"You want to stop to eat before heading back? It's past noon," Agent Maser says. And just like that my stomach moans on cue. My Pop-Tart breakfast was long spent. My stomach echoes a hollow void and a rock band starts to sing from within. I can't hide my hunger this time. I agree and ask him to choose the place.

We sit in an industrial cafe close to Broadway street. It's one of those super modernized buildings where exposed pipe and stained wood tabletops are the design theme. We order fancy burgers, the kind that give off a squeaky shine at the peak of the wheat bun. Even the lettuce looks expensive.

After my first bite I exhale a satisfied breath. Whoever concocted this sophisticated spicy blueberry sauce deserves an award. It's the perfect spicy burn.

As I go in for another bite, I can see Agent Maser is ready to start another groundbreaking conversation. I give him minimal attention while I concentrate on the stinging sensation in my mouth.

I've already been briefed on the chemical plant explosion search, heavily aware that it's on pause and under review but nod my head at his reiteration. My mouth starts to burn from the blueberry heat. I need some relief.

Agent Maser must sense I'm in pain or he's spotted the heat and itchiness reddening my eyes. He snatches my glass of coke and places it in front of his stainless steel tray in a playful manner, leaving me without liquid and absolutely speechless. I sigh through pursed lips but it comes out as more of an aggressive exhale.

Then he starts dipping his fries into my drink. The amusement on his face is uncanny.

"Wilber's Heat Burger is hot isn't it?" he says, dipping a second fry into *my* soda—this time flashing a wide smile at me with naughty eyes. If this was his way of getting my attention, it was working. I can't help but let out a soft, unsure laugh.

He begins mumbling something in between bites of fry, engaging his dimple in a way I hadn't seen before.

"My mouth is on fire and you've contaminated my drink with your fries!" I openly squeal. My voice and laughing eyes have given me away. He knows he's succeeded in gaining my attention. He gets up from his chair, continues to sip from my drink, and eyes me again.

"You're seriously going to seize my drink, just like that?" I say.

"Lay off me, I'm starving!" He pulls from a lower pitch imitating an SNL sketch I'm all too familiar with. Butterflies form a kaleidoscope in my stomach and I feel something other than irritation enter my body. Did he really just quote Chris Farley?

I feel a sudden warmth toward Agent Maser, which surprises me.

Chris Farley was a staple in my life, like bread, milk, and eggs. I grew up absorbing his humor, watching all his movies, SNL skits, and even his one music video. Those who'd spent enough time with me quickly figured out I lived for a Chris Farley reference. So this. This was a big deal.

As he heads toward the drinking fountain and fills a glass with coke, I sit in shock, trying to process the idea that Agent Maser might actually have something in common with me.

Maybe I could hear him out in our time away from the office. I'd once been banned by Ben and Diana from suggesting Chris Farley movies, but that didn't stop me from supplying them Chris Farley mugs at the next game night hosted at my apartment. Ben at least understood and entertained my need for the late night sketch comedian. He'd even dressed up as the coffee-table-crashing motivational speaker for my sixteenth Chris Farley-themed birthday. Maybe there was more to Agent Maser than I thought. Maybe he'd let me spout off as many Chris Farley quotes as I'd like, and maybe if I tried a bit harder to let go of his work arrogance his personality would be a better match than I previously thought. He'd just now grabbed my attention with a grand lasso. I could let him rope me in a little.

"You just quoted Chris Farley in the SNL skit with Adam Sandler and David Spade," I say when he arrives back at the table with a new coke and straw and brushes it across the table so that it sits right under my nose.

"I did, didn't I?" He smiles back at me from across the table.

"My dad introduced me to Chris Farley when I was young. My dying wish is to watch *Tommy Boy* just one last time before I go," I say. He nods and scrunches up his chin so that his lips disappear into his face, amused by my response. "I'll forgive you this time, but only because you brought him into it," I say, referring to the man, the myth, the legend.

"Deal." His honey eyes continue to assess me as he puts a napkin to his mouth. How is it that with one quick mention of my favorite comedian I'm able to see past Agent Maser's previously slick behavior?

It's because those who quote Chris Farley on a whim are about as rare as a rainbow eucalyptus and if you've ever seen one it's not something you can ignore.

"I've never tried dipping fries in my coke. Is it any good?" I say. Here we go. I've opened the gates of conversation. I dip the brittle potato into my soda. The bottom breaks off and floats down into the dark abyss, and I taste what's left of the experiment, deciding I don't hate it, but I don't love it either.

We share a laugh and he pushes my chair in before trailing me out the door to the tinted agency SUV.

Agent Maser kept my attention. It wasn't necessary to disappear into my own thoughts when his Chris Farley references dart straight for the bullseye. I begin firing unfiltered answers back at his questions throughout the drive back to the Bureau.

"Doing anything fun this weekend?" he asks.

"I have my ten-year class reunion," I say, coming to accept that it's now that time in my life where my high school mob is supposed to gather for a night and catch up on all the things we could easily look up on Facebook. We'll talk about whether or not we managed to leave our parent's basement, how many kids we reproduced, and gloat about our successful careers or our good-looking spouses—the two were mutually exclusive. I knew from experience.

"Nice. Are you one of those that looks forward to your reunion or are you just going to see how much better you've fared than the rest of them?" His lips curl, matching his earlier expression when he claimed ownership of my drink.

"I get to see my best friend Diana, so it'll be a good time either way. She's in Fort Collins. We see each other now and then, but it's been a while. We had a small group that got along really well back then, so I'm looking forward to catching up with the rest of them." And I was. I only had one real concern. "I still haven't decided which career I'm going to make up for the night," I say.

"Oh yeah. Smart move. Need some ideas?"

"Yes. Something that can compete with cute kid names and hot husbands," I say. We turn onto I-70 from I-25, knitting into uneven rows of a long, stalled traffic scarf. The AC unit finally hits a breath-like state. Agent Maser must have turned down the windstorm aimed at my forearms while I was talking.

"You gotta go with something you know a little bit about. Dental hygienist, accountant, scuba diving instructor?" he says.

"You think I know how to fake being a scuba diving instructor?"

"Probably not." He gives a quick laugh. "I scuba dive for fun… so it came to mind." My brows rise. When does this man have time to scuba dive? "You know, you and I could show up as a married couple who do deep sea dive tours in Hawaii during the summer. I own a scuba diving rental store and you own a thriving cupcakery down-town," he adds. "You'll check all the boxes on the reunion list of success."

"Yeah, cuz that would be believable." I relax at the suggestion. Claiming I own a cupcake shop and have a spouse creates a sense of comfort within me. I consider the possibility.

"You don't think you can fool your high school class into thinking that you've qualified for Food Network's *Bake It or Break It* series and have a final interview set up for next week? If that's not 'successful' I don't know what is." His expression is as thorough as his suggestion.

I muster an eye roll. This is my natural response, but to be truth-ful, I like a little spontaneity every now and then. I'll take him up on this offer. Diana wouldn't mind. She will probably be elated that I brought a man, even if he's a fake.

"I can't bake but enough time has passed they might not question it. It's not like I take my class reunion seriously anyway. For all I care, they can think we're sharing scuba kisses underwater and playing footsie with flippers too," I say, hoping he smells the kittenish sarcasm I just dealt. I was being playful, trying this type of conversation out with Agent Maser, but it didn't mean I was ready to take my playful words and put them into action just yet.

He parks next to the motorcade of tactfully positioned identical black SUVs, next to the second floor elevator of the parking garage, and turns to face me.

"How fun would that be?" he says, warm and animated. "I'd get a kick out of it, as long as you're having fun. I bet you'd have a hell of a lot better time getting creative with it rather than picking a stale job to hide your FBI status." He smiles, quirking that dimple again. "Espe-cially if showing up without a date."

He wasn't wrong. I didn't question his acting skills either. He was good with his words; one of the reasons I found him slick and unlike-able in the first place, but now...

I face him, holding back the words. I don't want to say it but the spontaneity inside me awakens. My expression already says "I'm in."

"Let's make it a date," he says. He's blushing, but confidence never leaves his face.

"It's a date then. You better play up how good my cupcakes taste." I point a finger in his direction.

"Deal"

Chapter Three

Agent Maser and I pass through the double-doored office entrance like a pair of giddy schoolgirls who just got matching tattoos, sociable and slightly clingy. We've solidified our plans for this weekend, and I've got a new energy about me. Enough energy even to clean my desk.

I grab the bottle of Clean Wave spray from the utility cabinet on my way over to my desk and give it a good heavy wipe down with the market's "toughest cleaner." I'd need the good stuff to get rid of the crossword glued to my desk with dried chocolate milk—a mess I'd been meaning to clean for a few weeks now but keep forgetting since my miniature filing cabinet blocks the chocolate crusted powder crime scene from my view.

If it weren't for Ben's reminder last night that my desk looks unsightly even from his desk, I would have likely forgotten about it. I do a little happy dance as I clean, enjoying the new energy and good mood our plans have given me.

When I finish cleaning, I pop into Ben's desk area to see where he's at with the cybercrime case. He's asked for my assistance a few times recently but hasn't involved me much on this one, and I'm curious if he'll need me to analyze anything for it in the future. There's a larger envelope added to the typically 8.5x11-sized stack on his desk, which can only mean a new map or photographs have been added to the evidence. I open the envelope flap, lift the thin paper map out from its casing and take a quick look before deciding I'll need some time to look this over at my own office desk.

"You little thief! Atta Mae Suarez, what are you doing with evidence that belongs on my desk?" Ben says with an ounce of harshness. He has me cornered at the door, and he's used my middle name, so I know he's slightly, possibly more than slightly, aggravated. I drop both arms to my side so that the envelope sways in my fingers around my wide-legged dress pants.

"Put it back on my desk and meet Agent Maser and me in the lab. We're going over the USB now."

❀

THE LAB ROOM IS DARK TODAY; ONLY LIGHT FROM THE LED-framed row of desktop computers highlights Ben deep in conversation with the lab assistant—the most attractive female in our department. They've prepared a few extra chairs around the desk space where one luminescent screen glows brighter than the rest.

Ben finishes off the conversation, eyes lingering on Miss Lab Assistant until she sweeps past the double doors. "You can turn the light on if you'd like," he says, fishing for the middle roller seat.

"Sure thing." Agent Maser acts before I do, slipping past the lab assistant and into the room. He flips on the light switch and the luminescent computer glow disappears from our view. Agent Maser lingers by the lights and when I catch up to him he suggests a time to meet outside of the office so we can quickly plan our fake background for this class reunion hoax.

Ben squints, then widens his gemstone eyes—crystallized brown sugar beads of surprise—at the sight of Agent Maser and I discussing meeting tomorrow to pick out tacky, possibly-matching outfits for my class reunion. With a bewildered stare, Ben gets back up to shut the door, aware that this assignment is for agent personnel only.

Ben and I'd previously had an Agent Kenny Maser conversation. I led him on an in-depth discussion about whether Kenny has ever taken his whey straight or not, if he has any pets at home that get tired of his constant smile, and even hypothesized whether he'd remain unflappable at a pass from another female agent who resembled Ms. Trunchbull, the Roald Dahl character, or not. Ben humored me with short responses like "Straight. His pet will never tire of it. Unflappable but throws up slightly in his mouth."

Ben's been thrown a curveball. He's shocked at my behavior toward Agent Maser and it's written all over his face. I don't blame him. He hasn't heard Agent Maser's "Van Down By The River" Chris Farley reference. If he had, he'd smack his gum like all's right in the world.

"Shall we check this USB out then?" Ben says, washing his face clean of curiosity.

Agent Maser unveils the standard 32 GB USB flash drive and sets it in front of Ben on the desk. Since Ben has claimed the middle seat, I fill in the spot next to him on the right as Agent Maser scoots his chair beneath the desk on Ben's left. While Agent Maser gets comfortable, sliding on a pair of reading glasses and adjusting the monitor, Ben waves the USB in my face to get my attention. When I meet his gaze, he pulls me toward him so that we're both leaning back in our chairs, our faces out of Agent Maser's view.

What uhh…happened to you two? Ben mouths with raised brows. He's referring to my bubbly nature toward Agent Maser of course.

He's a Chris Farley fan! I mouth back.

Ben nods like he's enjoying a slow beat, gradually smiling with understanding. He retreats, popping back up into a seated position.

"So you managed to break Atta's wall today, huh?" Ben says, his hand now resting on Agent Maser's shoulder. The air starts to smell of humiliation. "She usually puts up a defense," he continues, leaving no gap for Agent Maser to respond. He must thrive in my discomfort. If he dares wink at me, I might consider ripping up his Catan cards next time I'm at his apartment.

"Maybe a little short with me at first but not defensive. No need to be defensive when you're having fun, am I right?" Agent Maser says pleasantly. "I never knew she had such a great sense of humor."

Ben purses his lips together into a smile. They twitch to the right, parting slightly. He's amused that I've won over Agent Maser. I've known that expression since my childhood.

Since Ben was just a year older than Diana, I grew to recognize nearly all of his expressions spending weekend after weekend with the Brown family. The same expression showed up whenever he knew I was going to win at something—when I was the first to slice through his mother Robyn's homemade apple pie, skunking Diana at ping-pong, or stuffing my shoes with insoles to reveal I was centimeters taller than his sister. He ended up catching my charade after the results were penciled into the wall. Didn't believe it for one second. Maybe he didn't choose this expression because I had won. Maybe it was because he knew my mischievous nature was behind it all.

Growing up, mischievousness was always his signature move so maybe he sensed a commonality. Ben would walk the halls with us to our lockers after driving Diana and I to school every morning. He also made a perfect fool of me in those same school hallways, reaching around me to make it look like I slapped the nearest male's butt and pushing me into live classrooms so that I'd have to apologize to the teacher for my abrupt interruption. Thank goodness we've matured since then. Our friendship had evolved into what it was today, a professional relationship. One where I formulate a model and quiz Ben on cooperative payoff, against his will, during breaks.

I sometimes considered him Diana's replacement. Four kids and a rancher husband kept my best friend busy and unable to attend game nights. But Ben found mutual benefit in them. A weekly opportunity to network with the ladies, as we'd always had an open door game night policy; invite whoever you want. However, I think he kept up the game night tradition because he secretly enjoys losing to me whenever we play Risk—the game that always takes a few weeks to finish, so we leave it fenced in caution tape on his or my coffee table to pick up where we left off for the next week. I had yet to lose Risk and the regulars were determined to see me fail, this week included.

"So, we ready for this?" Agent Maser asks.

Ben and Agent Maser switch gears, back to work mode. I focus my gaze on the computer screen. A tap dance of clicks sound from Ben's index finger and four folders pop up on the page. Ben chooses the first folder titled "Pics." A few personal photos not meant for our eyes hit the little boxed window. We do a quick scan of the folder, and I take note of what I'm seeing. It's laughable.

The folders get deeper, melting into each other, folder within folder within folder. The lawyer said he found the video within a few minutes and we've run past a few minutes, so we click out of the folders to the main drive and click on the second folder. A film icon file labeled "Marigold" is the first video file in the lineup.

Click.

The room around us fades into a Gaussian blur as I take in the first forty seconds of the video. The contents on the screen are the only clear figures in sight and within seconds I realize I don't have the heart to endure this.

A man lying on the floor of a sunshine-filled conference room, where bright beams of light spill through yellow stained glass windows, yells out in immense pain. As I watch, it becomes all-encompassing. I feel as if I've entered the room and this man's pain is my pain. The bright light ironically highlights the Currant red embroidered jackets circling the man, exposing all the misery in the room. His body spurts blood through his gaping incisions, making what should have been a white shirt, now the most vibrant red color in the room—so vibrant it becomes the only thing I see on the screen. His chest is still visibly pulsating blood, staining the industrial luxury hotel carpet as it lands in a pool around his body.

He's surrounded by jacket-wearing men and women, unable to defend himself and unable to move. Yet, the rise and fall of his chest tells me he's still very much alive and writhing in impossible pain. Wearing embroidered crests with a single marigold flower outline and a few sharp crystal shaped petals—likely meant to be the group's insignia—each group member continues taking turns stabbing the man on various parts of his body. Through it all, I struggle to unlock my gaze from the man's stricken expression.

The knife is handed to the next cult member who drops to a crouch before the dying man to carve out whatever kind of incision he'd like. In the five years at this job, I've seen some disturbing things but never have I witnessed the face of a man in the process of being murdered like this, torn to pieces with this level of slow and calculated cruelty. The torturing techniques that this group possesses are too much for me to handle.

My eyes flit away from the screen as I sink forward into the chair. My stomach now hosts a congregation of scissors doing jumping jacks and all my senses begin trying to comprehend a whole new, unhappy reality of this world I hope is known to very few. I tell myself it could be the probably expired sleeve of Pop-Tarts or the spicy burger Agent Maser and I had for lunch making me feel this ill, but I knew that wasn't the reason. Pop-Tarts had a long shelf life, a couple years past expiration, and I'd proven I could handle the scorpion pepper One Chip Challenge in recent weeks.

The gut scissors motion for a salto backwards tuck dismount prompting everything inside of me to release. I can feel the Pop-Tart and acidic jalapeno juices making their way up my diaphragm as my abs contract from all the pressure.

"Um. Excuse me," I manage to say, leaping from my chair with the goal of reaching the door before something embarrassing happens. I successfully swing the nearest restroom door open before completing my bodily duties until there is nothing left for me to release. I try to steady my breathing as I hover over the loo. I'd really like to black out right now.

My mind feels like a heartbeat in cardiac arrest. Had I known I would see this today, I would've avoided food and this lab altogether.

My body prepares for another launch. Its physical suffering already echoed along the stainless steel bathroom stalls.

"Atta." Ben's soft and low drum of a voice, approaches cautiously. "You okay in there?" He knocks on the stall door.

I can't answer. My throat's somewhere sucked into another dimension. I shrink into the toilet, sprawling my arms against the shiny porcelain seat.

The stall door parts and Ben finds my pathetic self looking like a crumbled cookie on the floor with breakfast and lunch remains decorating my shirt. I might as well have the toilet paper wrapped around me, solidifying my mummification.

He approaches, slowly assessing my state, then grabs a wad of paper towels by the sink. He pops back into my stall and bends down prepping to clean the mess around me. "Agent Maser is going to review the rest of the files. We'll only have you help us with the documentation and strategic planning moving forward," he says, compassion seeping through his words. He's seen my composure collapse in real time.

I raise my head and force my brows to take a more pleasant shape. I need to pull some light from this dark place and show some dignity in front of Ben. I manage a "Thank you," and reach for the paper towels in his hand, adjusting my position so that I'm no longer folded against the toilet.

"You know what this means, right?" I say. Ben seems to carry a new heaviness, as if he's added a few new bricks on his person. His eyes are usually chocolate brown but a fresh silver ring of uncertainty around them now has my gaze.

"I could guess what you're going to say, but I don't know what the full extent of this means," he says.

"This is more than just an issue with the Senator, those people, and what they did. How is it possible that a Senator's even part of this? He stood with them and let it all happen." I rip a section from the paper towel and start patting myself down. "This is going to be a difficult case for everyone in the department. One of those that should be dealt with with as few people as possible and kept away from the public. The details at least."

I accidentally elbow him. He's mid-gulp of air—not going to respond. He begins wiping my shoulder with a crunchy paper towel, keeping the silence while we're both lost in thought. The reality is that we'd seen our share of corruption. Five years of service and I'd encountered plenty of wealthy groups of people with connections to government officials dealing with their money laundering schemes, illegal transactions, and abuse crimes. They were messes and we cleaned them up.

But this wasn't just a mess. This was a psychological trip for the investigators.

"What do you think the department will do with this?" I ask. I've cleaned my white shirt as best as I can and he's cleaned most of the area around me.

"We'll find out soon. Something like this needs to be squashed at the source. Agent Maser and I went over it. We'll talk about reassignments later. We'd best get you out of here and back to the office so you can resume whatever you and him are having at the moment," he says, knowing just how to change the mood and make my cheeks fiery red with embarrassment.

I'm able to feign irritation, hiding my face with my palm until Ben scoops me off the ground, cradling my back and knees while I latch onto his neck in desperation for support as he carries me the length of the hallway.

He grabs the door to the lab, reaches his hand out from under my weight to maintain his balance, and opens it successfully, then spins me like a flag and plops me in front of Agent Maser with a thudded landing. Agent Maser seems to have adopted Ben's positive-in-the-face-of-adversity attitude upon our arrival and I'm now surrounded by two clowns working to make me, the sad child, happy.

Under Agent Maser's optimism is a noticeable energy shift of eagerness. Eagerness brought on by our mutual desire for the man in the USB's justice or eagerness to understand the current and very obvious closeness I share with Ben? I wasn't sure. If he's wondering what kind of relationship we have, he's wasting his energy. If only he knew how uninterested Ben was. This is Ben taking care of his sister. It was his duty after all, being my longtime best friend's brother.

"Since you and Atta hit it off so well today, you should come to game night. Don't you think, Atta?" Ben says to Agent Maser, trying to steer the conversation in a lighter direction, then looks at me for confirmation. Was he trying to play matchmaker now? I can handle my own dating business. I didn't need him meddling, especially when he seems so eager to hand me off to someone.

"Maybe next week. We've already made plans this weekend," I say. Agent Maser's odd, eager expression is gone. He's satisfied and taken Ben's tone as the green light to date me—a nonverbal "Go for it!"

Ben gives me a surprised smile and I hope he reads the laser message my eyes just sent him. I am capable of moving things along by myself, thank you very much. Agent Maser and I got as far as planning a very personal and unconventional date after just one lunch session. How's that for progress?

Ben's goofy smile turns questioning. He still needs an explanation.

"Agent Maser's going to be my plus one this weekend. Class of 2011 Reunion."

Chapter Four

The moon floats like a dim accessory above the colored lantern lights welcoming us to Putter Patter's Mini Golf Center, where the class reunion is being held in the back diner. The smell of nachos and alcohol wafts through the air as Agent Maser opens the door and motions for me to enter in front of him. He reaches down for my hand, then intertwines his rough fingers around mine, as we begin our fake charade and walk into a room full of winking lights and scattered putt-putt golf courses on each side of a carpeted entrance.

The diner mingles with the golf course at the back, making it easy to spot the class members already sipping on drinks and springing into paired-off socializing—raising the noise pollution in the room so that I can barely make out Agent Maser asking if I'm ready.

Our class president sent out the Facebook invite giving us strict instructions that 8:30 would be putt-putt golf time and we would need to gather in groups of six. I was planning to reunite with Diana and her husband, Caleb, which would make four, meaning we'd need to make friends or hijack another couple. If our class president was anything like her high school self, she'd be patrolling the putt-putt holes with a police baton.

I say hello to a few old acquaintances who immediately point out our contrast in clothing. Agent Maser has connections to a t-shirt print company, and with my permission, had a t-shirt made to accommodate our fake storyline. If you're going to lie, why not go all in? If I was going to be a cupcake artist, I might as well be a tacky cupcake artist, who shows up to a class reunion along with her partner wearing their job titles on their chests.

The "Joe's Scuba School" tee fit snug around Agent Maser's chest. Anyone who met him tonight would likely never read his shirt; they'd be too distracted by his build. I, on the other hand, feel like a homemaker trying too hard, with the words "Cakes by Atta" in a bed of flowers branding my purple tee.

I tug on the bottom of my shirt so that it lays flat against my stomach. I should role-play more often. I find an inner delight knowing this look comes off schmaltzy and pretentious. My shirt is already accomplishing what others will spend time tonight boasting about to their peers.

I needed this.

Not taking this reunion too seriously is a good distraction. Messing around and having a little fun at my reunion will easily steer my thoughts in a different direction tonight, away from the disturbing video that wants to replay itself over and over in my head.

"Her cream cheese frosted caramel cupcakes made it to the second round of *Bake It or Break It* a few seasons ago. They're in talks to have her on for a reunion season," Agent Maser touts to the Spanish Club president who's eating up every word of our fiction-based conversation with a genuine smile. I'll be referring to Agent Maser as Kenny for the rest of the night for confidential reasons, of course.

"Kenny's so supportive." I nudge his side playfully. Anyone watching would think we're rotting from the smell of shameless affection. "He helps out every afternoon after finishing up with his scuba classes."

Somehow, Kenny exudes even more confidence wearing his Scuba instructor tee than he does wrapped in a tactical gun belt over his pantsuit. My eyes are drawn to where his gun would be and I slide through Thursday's memory. A reoccurring flash of panic hits when I revisit one of the more disturbing video details and I quickly shut my eyes, trying to block out the short but heavy images. I take a sip of the drink Kenny brought over, hoping its taste will wash away my memories and cue new thoughts. Without such mind tricks, how was I going to make it through the upcoming workweek?

I look up to see Diana B. Brown, my best friend, charging toward me like an excited bull. Just the sight of her makes me want to catch her with a net, rein her in and never let her go. I bend in toward her as she wrangles me up in a hug, causing her big spiral curls to squish up against my neck. She steps on the thick bottom hem of my high-waisted flare jeans.

"I'm so glad you're here!" I say, admiring her cinnamon-painted lips as we release. She catches the light from one of the overhead lanterns. It's official. She is exclusively the most put-together mother of four around; her cable-knit, green sweater and dark blue jeans complement her perfect mocha skin, naturally void of discoloration. This time she's highlighted her natural curls with a honey-blonde mix and I can't help but admire her beauty.

"Love the tee," she says, giving me a pair of knowing, sticker-esque googly-eyes and warmly squeezing my shoulders. The one person my work identity couldn't be kept from was Diana. Her own brother and childhood best friend worked the same hours, required the same amount of secrecy, and spent too much time together to hide how most of our weekday moments revolved around each other.

"How in the world did you find a sitter?" I ask. Caleb stands right behind her surveying the layout of the room. She smiles her soft smile, the one that's appeared more frequently in the last few years. The very same smile that appears when she mentions her brother around me, like he is a shoe that needs its match and I'm the missing shoe.

"Ben's doing me a favor. The little monkeys are probably asking for piggyback trains as we speak," Diana answers. Ben's excitement upon seeing his nephews topped even his excitement for eating his favorite Mama Robyn dish and he always licked that bowl clean. I'm sure he was loving every second of it.

I knew firsthand how easy they were to love, always running around the farm with plastic swords and pool noodles aiming to stab you if you were in their line of sight. Parks, the oldest, stood out from his brothers with hazel eyes, lingering like dusk on his dark skin. He is my little charmer, always throwing compliments my way in an adorable cowboy drawl, while the younger ones greet me by asking for pretzel sticks.

"Long time no see." Caleb greets me with a firm handshake, then pulls me into a hug the way he always does when greeting me. I don't get to see much of him, but I enjoy watching him chase the cows through the gate with his sleeves rolled up, exposing the whitest portion of his farmer's tan when I visit. Luckily, he's opted for a long sleeve tonight, cowboy hat included.

"I see you brought a date," Caleb says, offering his firm farmer's grip to Kenny; the synergy between the two strongest men in the room could break glass. Caleb signals a nod of approval in my direction. He must like that my date could lift a bale of hay over his shoulder at his request—Caleb's only requirement of my future partner.

"You scuba dive?" Diana asks Kenny sweetly, playing along with my career game. She smiles back at him with wide-eyed anticipation.

"I do. Just got back from an escapade at Richelieu Rock. I teach as well," he says.

"That's amazing. Caleb and I will have to try it out sometime. Or better yet, we could all go together, Atta! You two dive together much?" she asks, referring to Kenny and I.

"Oh, all the time." I squeeze a wink in at the end of the sentence. She can't hold back the fuel powering her unruly smile, knowing I've never been scuba diving in my life. She pulls me aside.

"Where'd you pick him up?"

"Work," I whisper back, engulfed in her side hug.

34

"So he knows Ben too?"

"Yeah, we're all in the same department. We hit it off earlier this week. I mentioned needing a fake job title, and he thought reunion role-playing sounded fun."

"I'll have to ask Ben what he thinks of you two together then."

"Oh stop it," I say, pinching her side with my free hand.

We carry on chatting, Kenny and Caleb discussing food, Diana and I catching up on our latest favorite HBO series. The conversation turns to my hypothetical baked masterpieces, thanks to Kenny's imagination. Caleb looks at me in awe as if I'd discovered the moon and this is his first time hearing about it. Baking was not in my resume so I understand his confusion. Diana would have to clue him in on the joke after the party. Lunch lady brownies would be the only item made from these hands he'd ever eat.

Crash, Bang, Clink!

An angry song of shattering glass hits the floor behind us and Diana and I jump at the hit after dodging a whirring sound above. I look up to see a fascinating atmosphere shift in the room as a dark leather pigskin settles among thick glass shards and tiny toothpick umbrellas. Around ten party drinks are now missing from the drink table.

Tyler. Like a gut punch to the air, his presence boosts the energy in the room. Thick Sanuck flip flops and khaki cargo shorts float toward us.

A voice from behind us yells, "Tyler! Way to make an entrance, you scumbag!" We turn to find Evan assessing the damage. He laughs and begins cleaning up the mess on the floor created by his former high school best friend whose spiral throw he failed to catch. Tyler sprints toward Evan and helps him out by picking up the last toothpick umbrella from the floor. Together Tyler and Evan—an awkward pairing of beach-hobo-needs-a-shower and business-casual—stand like two toddlers in the aftermath of a colossal kitchen table water spill.

Diana and I pause our conversation, our attention captured by the sight of our favorite classmates, and my heart warms as I look over to see class president Kaitlyn almost spew her drink in her friend's face at the sight of Evan and Tyler standing in a puddle of water. The mess they created was likely ruining her die-cut letter banner, perfectly lined and organized by color with a mixed cocktail display kind of vibe.

Diana and I break free of our little cluster to approach Tyler and Evan, who'd become good friends with us our senior year. Before that, our encounters had been limited to being used as their volleyball targets in gym class.

Our friendship began with Evan saving Diana from Tyler, after Tyler tried to cut the back of her afro one day in class to see if she'd notice. She kept her hair natural and short even back then. We all beat on Tyler after that, until he apologized and invited us to join him and his family for a week in a boathouse on the lake. She decided to forgive him after we all forged a close friendship on the water that summer.

"Wow! Diana, you're a woman now. How've you been?" Tyler says to Diana, throwing a few shards of glass and the toothpick umbrella into the trash.

"Good, and you?" Diana holds back a laugh, trying not to give in to Tyler's stupid humor. Evan tosses the last few shards of glass from the floor into the trash right after him. We hadn't seen much of these guys over the years, even online. Tyler was off of social media, and Evan kept his limited to LinkedIn.

"I guess you look alright too, Atta."

Tyler nods. This time in my direction.

"Well, you look like you've spent some time with Jack Johnson or Bob Marley and sleep in a tent on the beach. When was the last time you cut your hair?" I say.

"*Mmm.* Yes, that's true. I may have slept on a beach a time or two and haven't cut my hair since college," he says cooly. "What's this cupcake business about? You learned how to use an oven?"

It's as if we never left. Same energy. Same amused smiles slapped on all of our faces.

"Yeah come on, Atta. What do you really do?" Evan slaps his hand on my shoulder. I panic for a split second. I suppose I'm not fooling the people I grew up with.

Kenny jumps in and introduces himself as my partner.

"She can't make a cake if her life depended on it, but give her a muffin tray and cupcake liners and it works somehow."

They all laugh at Kenny's soft blow and make introductions eagerly as if forming bromances was the underlying goal here. No need to worry about our little lie. They were here to goof around and one-up each other with their words; my job was the least of their interests.

The six of us make it through five putt-putt holes before Tyler subjugates us to his "even better idea" plan for the night. With a unanimous vote, we all agree a Tyler and Evan adventure would be much more interesting than the rest of this reunion.

"Thank you for bringing us all back together," I call out to the class president as we shuffle through the exit doors.

"See you ten years from now!" Tyler shouts right after; he holds the heavy door open for Evan and Caleb to walk through. Kaitlyn takes one long gulp from her glass, waving elegantly to the side without looking at us. She couldn't be more relieved Tyler is taking us elsewhere.

WE BREATHE THE FRESH NIGHT AIR. THE OUTLINE OF THE mountains rests underneath the dark sky sprinkled in stars. House lights fill the ground and an empty shadow weaves between homes and the constellations.

In the parking lot, Caleb tosses Diana the three mini golf clubs he'd been concealing behind his back and Kenny pivots toward me, revealing all six golf balls from our incomplete game.

"We're just following your good friend Tyler's orders." Kenny's eyes dance along with his amused smile. He was proving to be quite playful. I kind of liked this off work side of him. He was even hitting it off with my friends.

At this rate, going on a real date with him—one that didn't include lying about my career, baking skills, and relationship—didn't sound so bad. I was beginning to think I might not even mind if this date turned into more than just a fun night of playing white elephant with our careers.

I feel a hand wrap its fingers around mine as the group runs to catch up with Tyler. Kenny's touch gives me the shivers as he leads me to his car.

AFTER A SHORT DRIVE AND A QUICK HIKE UP A TRAIL, WE ALL SIT like ducks waiting for bread to be thrown atop South Table Mountain, a famous spot where all Golden teenagers dream of shooting fireworks and dynamite off the Golden Cliffs that overlook Coors Factory. We wait for Tyler and Evan to set up golf tees among rocks, dirt, and glow sticks. The glow from the city illuminates the edge of the Golden cliff where they plan to tee off into the dark forest opposite the city.

"Thank you President Kaitlyn for providing the fun tonight!" Tyler echoes into the canyon, proudly passing around stolen golf clubs and pulling out a few extra golf balls from the satchel he'd been carrying on his back the entire night. Little did we know he'd prepared this for us ahead of time. The bag holds more than just golf balls. I can't be the only one curious about what else is packed in there.

"So Tyler, we're all curious. What do you do for a living?" I ask. The rest of the group turns their heads, keen for his answer.

"This'll be interesting." Diana pokes me from behind.

"Professional Bird-Watching." He swings his golf club, perfectly rotating his hips. We all laugh.

"Really? You're not actually paid to watch birds are you?" Caleb states the very thing we're all thinking.

"Something like that. It's performance based," he says. A giggle slips through my mouth.

"Are you sure you're not actually just a hitchhiker traveling from beach to beach?" Evan quips. "I picked this guy up in Louisville at Highway 25 and the Westminster exit after stopping for gas. He had his thumb sticking out to the side of the road."

Tyler interjects. "My buddy had an emergency, so I lent him my car this weekend and decided to opt for alternative transportation. It only took three cars and, by some miracle, Evan in the end." Hardly surprising coming from Tyler. The group shares a collective smile, as if the class's pet rabbit had just flipped the carrot with its nose before eating it. The way he decided to live his life was always extra.

My golf club meets the ball and sends it flying through the night sky.

"Good job, Atta. That could have landed on the other side of the highway," Caleb says with a congratulatory voice.

"Didn't all of yours land across the highway? Are you mocking me …wait … they're not close to the highway are they?" I momentarily panic. Images of golf balls shattering car windows float through my mind.

"I'm not that reckless," Tyler says. "We're launching them into the dark hill over there. No cars. No lights. I'm not sure which direction yours went though."

"Oops," I say.

"You're chopping the ground a bit on your swing," Kenny says, coming up behind me. He wraps his arms around me and his hands overlap mine so that we share the responsibility of the golf grip. I notice his smell for the first time. He smells good—fresh and masculine. It's nice, and the warmth of his body around me sends goosebumps down my arms.

He guides me through the swing and I mirror his movements. All I see is darkness in front and faded lights on each side until he whips me around and pulls me in close to his chest using the arm that powers the swing. Then he lowers his head to my forehead. Is he really going to make a move right here on the edge of this mountain with my classmates behind us? I freeze. Here? Now? In front of everyone? I'm not sure I'm ready for it.

He steals a kiss with a soft tug of my lips. It's fast and unsuspecting, but it leaves a smile on my face.

I turn around to see the others oblivious and consumed in their own conversations—Tyler and Evan captivated by each other's presence even more so than the rest of us.

"So you're like a real life Ash Ketchum now. How many birds have you seen so far?" I hear Evan say to Tyler.

"What an honor. No one's ever compared me to a Pokemon trainer before." He smirks, visibly pleased with Evan's reference. "I guess I'm still waiting for the birds to battle each other then. I went for a big year last year and ended up with 705."

"Jeez. How many countries did that take?"

"That was just within the forty-eight contiguous states."

The boys finish off the last of the golf balls with four synchronized swings. Diana and I applaud loudly.

"Come with me," Kenny says, dragging me off to a rock on the decline of the mountain. I lean into him considering whether or not he was planning to continue what we started where we teed off. I wasn't opposed to another kiss. Not only did he acknowledge Chris Farley as the king of comedy, but he fit in well with Caleb and Diana, and was even impressed by Tyler—the parrotfish of the group, a weird fish that poops out digested coral but ultimately creates a nice white sandy beach.

"Thanks for bringing me along tonight. Your friends are pretty great," he says, wrapping his arm around me.

I reach my arm around him, welcoming his side hug. "They've always been up to no good. Thanks for suggesting the idea."

"Of course."

Our faces meet. He tilts his head in closer and I reach up in the heat of the moment, lightly brushing my hands against his curly hair —once again giving in to my curiosity. I pretend to pull a leaf or piece of dirt from his head.

"You're incredibly beautiful. It's very distracting," he says, relaxing into the ice cream scoop shaped cavity of the rock. "It's going to be that much harder working together on cases in the future." The sweet pinch of embarrassment draws color to my cheeks. He lets out a soft laugh.

"I'm sure you'll be fine. Work is distracting enough in itself," I say, finding a seat next to him.

"How've you been since viewing that flash drive?" There's concern in his tone.

I sit without responding for a minute. A minute too long. I'd been distracted most of the night and had successfully repressed the thought. Bringing it up now felt like taking pepper spray to the eyes.

"I know that must've been a lot for you. I worried about you the rest of the day." He fills in my silence with his own reply. It doesn't help. I really want to close the gates on this conversation.

"Yeah, I really don't want to think about it," I say with a shorter tone. Kenny and I had been hitting home runs with the conversation until now. He must've instantly felt my tension because he thinks for a moment without speaking and then opts to lean in for a kiss. Another distraction. I'll take it. I smile when we break. Smart move, Kenny. Bravo.

The group heads down the trail of the mountain with all six cell phones on flashlight mode after we all decide to turn in for the night. Diana and Caleb offer to arrange a dinner for the locals and Kenny and I pair off at the back, slowing our pace behind the others so they're out of earshot. They're just feet away from the cars.

"I handed the assignment off to Biles. It won't see the attention of any other departments," Kenny says as the sound of dirt and gravel crunches beneath our feet. I switch arms to give my hand a break from holding up the phone light.

"From now on I'm requiring you to never speak of Marigold and what you saw on that USB to anyone ever again." He nearly whispers the words and it takes me a minute to register what he said.

He shines his cellphone toward my face to gauge my reaction to his statement. Disbelief is all I feel, but I hold onto a poker face with a life-saving grip. Does he expect me to go along with this just because I let him snuggle up to me all evening?

"What?" I say. "What do you mean exactly?" Needless to say I'm shocked at the bait and switch he seems to be pulling after everything we did tonight.

"What I mean is that this is out of your control and will be dealt with within the proper means. The Bureau will not be looking into this further, so I'm going to need you to stay silent about this video and follow my lead. I won't be able to help you if you don't do as I say. Your job and life will be in jeopardy," Kenny whispers through the cold, night air.

"Is that a threat?" I say.

"I don't want it to be. But it could be if you have any ulterior motive to go against what I'm asking." He stabs an even sharper knife in me with his deceitful tone. It's dark outside, but I don't seem to recognize this expression. This is a different, darker side of Kenny.

"Are you protecting those people?" I ask. How could he be telling me this right now? Is he just going to ignore what we all witnessed? Why? Why would he do that?

His jaw tightens and his curly hair suddenly seems less surfer boy and more like the villain Donquixote Doflamingo from the anime *One Piece*. I grow concerned with the pairing of his current expression and the answer ahead.

"If you utter a word about it to anyone else, you'll have to come home with me tonight. I like you, so it'd put me at ease that you know what's good for you," he says softly. The domineering tone isn't to get me to join him for the night. It's him telling me I'll be forced into silence.

He needn't say more—he's involved in all this somehow. As we approach the bottom of the trail I feel my ankles shake, a physical manifestation of how I feel inside. Uneasy and terrified about what this kind of threat means for my future. My knees may be weak but my blood is boiling and I want so badly to fight him right here and now.

"Message received," I say with a smile, keeping in mind that now is not the time to win a battle. "You can trust me not to say anything."

In this zero-sum game, my non-cooperation will be the equivalent of a negative payoff, since I know full well anyone working with Marigold wouldn't choose to cooperate—not when they were capable of such cruel behavior, and by hiding their crimes Kenny was likely just as dangerous. I know the strategy—cover it up and get rid of any outliers. The only way to establish a dominant strategy with a threat like this is to play their side until I have enough ground to play a dominant card.

"Good. We'll talk more about this on Monday then," he says, guiding me toward the car.

"Kenny do you mind if I head back with my best friend? We didn't get to catch up as much as I'd like to tonight." The air between us smells like treason and disgust and I spot Diana handing some golf balls to Evan as Caleb starts the engine of his Ford F-250.

"You bet, but I'll need your phone first."

"Huh?" I say. He calmly slides the phone out from my palm, and with a few swift twists and turns of his hands, implements a tracking device to the internal drive of my phone. It's an exercise I'm trained in as well.

"If you take it out I'll know, of course. Ben will be warned as well. Discussing this with him will get you both killed. I'm doing this to protect you."

I nod my head. It's dark enough he can't see my eyes running their own escape plan. I guess you could say my first impression of Kenny was the most accurate one. Douchey and arrogant, knows he's good-looking. "Stay far away from him" I'd warned myself during our first encounter. Turns out I really should've stayed far away from him.

I wave down Caleb before they have the chance to put the gear in reverse. My heart hammers as I enter the backseat of their truck. I pull the door shut and say, "I didn't get to see you much tonight. Would you mind taking me to my apartment?"

"YOU THINK KAITLYN WILL GET FINED FOR THE STOLEN GOLF clubs?" I try to keep the conversation even and unsuspecting as we head into downtown Denver. It's possible Kenny's listening in on my conversation.

"Evan said he'll take care of it. How'd your night go with Kenny? You haven't mentioned him before, so he must be a new beau."

"Seemed pretty matchy-matchy to be just a new beau, Di." Caleb cuts me off from Diana's question before I can answer. "You've been hiding him from us haven't you, Atta?"

"No, we just hit it off earlier this week. He seemed to have the same sense of humor as me," I add. Just not the same morals, nor human decency. He might as well be the most detestable human being I know for allowing that group of people to go on without an investigation.

As Caleb pulls into the front lobby parking of my apartment complex I write a note in my planner then tear out the page and hand it to Diana.

I need five minutes to grab something. Wait here. I'm coming home with you.

I exit the car door and run out with my tracked phone before they can question me.

ON THE RIDE BACK TO CALEB AND DIANA'S FARM, I FILL THEM IN with an explanation. I've left my phone at the apartment and switched clothes to shake off Kenny's tracking devices so that our ride to Fort Collins is private. We coordinate a plan to get Ben to change his clothes and drop his phone at a distant relative's place for the weekend in case he was bugged today. I leave out the gruesome video details but let them know Ben and I are being tracked and are now witnesses to information our own department is working hard to squash.

My head lays on the seat belt strap. Time is starting to feel like the last thirty seconds of an escape room. I've found the last piece of the puzzle and secured a key, but I don't know if I'll be able to unlock it in time. Ben is my key. But then again, maybe even he didn't carry the right valleys and cuts for this lock.

I instruct Diana to have Ben meet me in their dojo after ridding himself of any tracking. We need time alone and away from all things digital and trackable to move anywhere but backwards.

He'd been with his nephews all evening. Had he been contacted and notified yet?

I sit up straight, adjusting myself so that I can easily slide the planner out of my camel-colored trench coat jacket pocket.

"Give him this note. Once he reads it he'll know what to do. I just need two traceless days with him to figure out a plan," I say to Diana, leaving another deckled tear trail in the gap of my planner. She agrees and enters the house, while Caleb nods his head in the driver's seat as if his own cows have escaped and he's contemplating a rescue mission.

I TAKE A LOOK AT THE ROOM AROUND ME. I'VE ALWAYS BEEN fond of the farm's dojo. It doubles as a two-star guest house on occasion for family members. Most of the time it's used for movie nights with Diana after her kids go to bed. Every now and then we pop our favorites into the VHS player and microwave popcorn.

Others might argue it'd been lost to the eighties, but I found it incredibly homey. A dozen folded quilts hang along the crooked iron bed frame and the belly of the lumpy couch. An old nineties beige phone with a coiled cord sits on the kitchen counter still connected to a dial-up landline.

Ben slides in through the solid oak door that's beat up from years of neglect with only chipped primer and peeled paint left to show. He's wearing Caleb's old steel gray sweatpants and white college tee that he fills out quite nicely. It's been years since I've seen him in such relaxed clothing, like since high school—waking up from sleeping over with Diana to find Ben with his mom at the table eating breakfast in only baggy sweats and a hat to cover his unstyled coiling curls. Nowadays he's always in slacks, occasionally showing up in jeans for game night.

I sit upright on the couch facing him, analyzing his fallen expression. His chocolate brown eyes lock onto mine with a concerned gaze.

"I left my truck at a friend's house and tossed all my bugged stuff there," he says with an intense thickness to his throat. "What's your plan?"

"Come up with something. Kenny's in on it. The department plans to hide everything. We're basically targets now. Looks like you already sense the gravity of it all," I say, folding my arms over my stomach. I might look relaxed but I'm anything but. Ben sits down at the other end of the couch, his eyes swivel to the door in thought. "We can stay here until Monday, but there's somewhere I want to go first. We'll need the old truck."

Chapter Five

Ben keeps intense concentration on the wheel, though his mind is lost in thought. He had been warned earlier today via a phone call before our class reunion and waited until Kenny and I were separated. There's not much he could've done while the four little monkeys were in his care anyway.

"Do Pops and Marcie know you're coming?" Ben asks, referring to my grandparents. We're heading back to Golden, taking the 287 and 93 backroads to their home, where my Pops' old Windows 95 computer still sits with some sort of internet access. It's likely the closest thing we'll find to a device that won't be traced back to us after our use.

"They don't. We'll sneak in through the back door. It's always unlocked."

We are limited on options. Both apartments are off-limits. Our department knows where we live, what we drive, and pretty much everything about our daily lives, but maybe Pops' old computer could be of use to us tonight. It was the only way I could think to search for that little marigold symbol without the department being able to track the search back to us—the same symbol seen on most of the attendee's coat jackets in the devastating USB video.

We needed more information about that group if we were going to go up against them. Complying with them was a short-term solution, but we needed our own ground to stand on long-term.

We park Caleb's old battered utility truck at the back of my grandparents' house, just outside the fence across from the neighbor's residence. "Follow my lead," I say as I walk past my grandparents' small forest of trees and the old treehouse. We reach the French door at the back and manage to slide in together without a whistle from the door. As we turn the corner to the living room, the fluffy white carpet reminds me to check for midnight snackers and sleepwalkers, in case my grandparents make a surprise appearance on the main floor.

All is clear. We stand eye level with the framed pictures of my high-school-aged mother and her two younger brothers, Steven and Davy, next to the closet door in the hallway. My heart beats with a little childhood magic knowing this door is home to Pops' hidden room—only the two of us are aware of its existence. If Grandma Marcie had discovered it she hadn't said anything in the last forty years since they'd owned the house.

I open the door and unveil a closet full of mixed-color plaid shirts hanging from a thick rod below a built-in bookshelf. To passersby it's just knickknacks and shirtwaists grazing the carpet floor in a small space; little do they know it's all a distraction to conceal the second door and its two knobs behind them. When I spread the curtain of shirts and reach through, my FBI badge tugs against one of Pops' leather jackets. I secure it back into the waistband of my pants and continue feeling for the doorknobs behind the layer of shirts. I feel a slight tingle of betrayal for sharing our secret hideout with another person as I release each lock. There's really no time to dwell on my choices here. Pops would forgive me if he knew the circumstance.

Ben enters Pops' make-shift Narnia before I do. Disneyland levels of excitement enter my body just as he says, "Your grandfather just happens to have a secret passageway to a room in his own home?"

The look on Ben's face is similar to his expression when he's scouting a crime scene location. He inventories the seventies wood panels and pale blue-patterned wallpaper before I guide him to the chair next to the boxy Windows 95 computer where a bottle of Clean Wave cleaner and a few USB and lawyer trinkets lay. Thankfully, it's still connected to the dial-up internet via an updated ethernet connection. Pops must've updated it. He mentioned he'd been doing some light gaming—3D Pinball and Minesweeper—recently.

"This is where Pops keeps all the things he wants no one to touch," I explain. "I've also kept a number of things here as well. It's been a few years since I've been here though."

Ben opens the old metal filing cabinet next to the computer and starts pulling thick stacks of comics out, placing them on the desk in front of me.

"Pull out some newspapers from the shelves below. We can start there," I say, touching the black start-up button on the hard drive and watching as the copyright text loads across the screen. It creates a buzzing noise louder than the old ceiling fan.

I hear hard plastic pieces clicking together like symbols and turn to see that Ben has pulled my old Lenox Sound transparent telephone with rainbow wires from a cardboard box. The box also holds a rusty vintage gumball machine with at least a few dozen gumballs as hard as ball-shaped gunpowder. He sits across from me and begins to dangle the red and yellow spiral cord that attaches the phone to its base in his hands.

"Didn't I give this to you when we were in grade school?" he asks.

"You did! Diana had the same one and you didn't want to have a girly phone like your sister so you gave it to me. I remember being so excited to match with Diana," I reply.

"Those were my grandma's old phone sets. I wonder if it would still work if I connected it into the wall jack?" He holds the phone up close to his face, seriously assessing it.

I dump a stack of newspapers in front of him, ignoring his desire to mess with the cable wire connection underneath the desk and ask him to take a look at the political section.

"The man in the video was a Colorado State Senator for a while before joining the US Senate. We might find something about him in the papers if we read through enough," I say, as he punches buttons to check if there's any life in the phone. I notice the "Important Numbers" sticker with the names and numbers of people I've never met yet still had memorized all these years. Back in the day, those unfamiliar names became targets of our prank calls.

Ben gets up from his seat and places the phone next to me on the desk with a satisfied smirk. He pulls a newspaper from the stack as I load Internet Explorer and wait patiently to type "Marigold Symbol Business Logo" in a very ancient Internet Explorer 4.0 interface version of the search bar.

Surely we take for granted the ease of modern internet. I could have rebooted my Mac, ordered onion rings, and Facebook-stalked every single classmate at the reunion in the amount of time it takes to load the page.

When the page loads I get an error saying "cannot open the internet site," learning that today's Google page works fine in EF4 but all other sites are fatal attempts at any marigold logo information. I play around with some code to try and understand the technical roadblocks but after a few attempts I come to the realization that I'll need a proxy server to get the information I'm wanting. The results page gives me a preview at least. Without clicking on any links, I gather what little bits of information I can from the first page search results.

"Here's something. Look," I say to Ben, who scoots in closer to my chair. He's hovered over me a million times before at work but it's hard to control my urge to smell him when we're in Little Narnia all alone. "The Marigold symbol is the logo for Marigold Company which is a company started by the Sheriden Foundation," I continue, summarizing the information available on screen. "Do you know anything about the Sheriden Foundation?"

"Other than what we saw on the USB video, not much," he says, opening the newspaper and planting himself back in the old wooden chair next to mine.

I read through the rest of the search results trying to make connections to the Marigold logo. I find nothing and click the mouse in frustration. As another error page loads I peer over at a focused Ben. His face is barely visible behind the newspaper but I still have a decent view of his dark and determined eyes. He looks comfortable for a second and the paper lowers.

There it is again. He seizes me for a moment with that boyish expression hidden under the coarse crew cut that highlights his strong facial features. I can't help but find the combination of his looks, character, and determination attractive. No matter what, he had me always wanting and wishing for more. And though I'd wished for it for so long, I knew he'd always only see me as his sister's best friend since childhood.

"So far this sports section's got excellent highlights for 2010, but I'm not finding anything helpful," Ben says. I nod, continuing to scroll the search page for Marigold.

"Let's say we do find more incriminating information on the Sheriden Foundation. How are we gonna tip off a trusted source?" I say to Ben.

"This thing?" He holds the transparent phone up and a smile slips through his lips. It's at this moment that I realize I'm learning something new today about the man I've known for twenty-five years. He's the kind of guy who opts for humor when the world is ending and a solution seems next to impossible.

I notice a bite marked wad of gum stuck to the side of the phone as he dangles it in front of me. Pops must have tried one of those ancient gumballs and disliked it. I wouldn't put it past him to try one, honestly.

I snatch the phone from Ben and give the handset a spray with the Clean Wave bottle cleaner standing on the desk beside me. It works like a charm. The crusty goo slides off instantly and lands on the carpet with a thud. I rub the phone with my shirtsleeve soaking up the shallow puddle of solution.

The wall jack sparks, like a miniature firework display on the wall, causing me to jump a little. I look at Ben to see if he's noticed my overreaction, but he looks just as spooked, still on edge from everything. When we make eye contact we chuckle. The electrical flare is gone just as quickly as it came and I start tapping the blue receiver buttons, dialing the first number on the list with extravagant finger movements. I'm doing this for show. I hope Ben enjoys it.

"1980s called. They want their wallpaper back, Pops!" I say into the clear receiver, making my voice a bit cartoonish. Ben's face melts into a smirk and he shakes his head with closed eyes.

My joke's cut short when the room light begins to flicker, giving us a few seconds of darkness. Did the power really just go out? I can feel all the blood rush down my face and balancing my two feet on the ground becomes an actual task.

A burst of light appears in the form of chaotic sparks—an actual firework show before my eyes.

What is happening?

I can't help but think the room and everything inside it, including us, are going to burn. Before I feel heat from any flame, time speeds up like a collage of memories on a superspeed treadmill.

The collage of memories slows. I'm brought back to reality and an empty room void of sparks. My ears begin ringing as if there's an echoing bell in a conch shell glued to my ear and I feel a sharp pain in my back. Dizziness begins to overwhelm me to the point that I collapse back into the desk chair.

With the worst headache pain imaginable, everything around me goes black again.

Nausea seizes me and my eyes become weighted, heavy as stones. My eyelids feel as if they're trapped under tiny blocks of lead and it's as if I have to will my eyes open, fighting my body for choice.

I begin envisioning myself prying my eyelids open with a crowbar with hopes that they'll open. Come on! Open up! Why did I suddenly black out? After four failed attempts at envisioning crowbars, I feel a lightness wash over me and I pop them open.

Chapter Six

Where is Ben?

The room is eerily empty. I listen for Ben's approaching footsteps as I contemplate the amount of time I would've been passed out unconscious. He wouldn't leave me here. Not without telling me he had to go. He left to search for a cool rag or glass of water, right?

I couldn't have been out for long, yet it felt like hours had blown past.

So where was he?

The silence stretches as I listen for his footsteps outside Little Narnia's walls. Dread curls in my stomach as each minute passes without a squeak of the stair or footstep in the hallway.

Why hadn't he tried to wake me up before leaving?

I glance around the room one more time and notice a small retro alarm clock that reads 6:15 a.m. Something is off. The phone is nowhere in sight and the photos on the desk are gone. Did I knock them over when I passed out or did Ben take them with him?

I walk closer to the desk to see that the newspaper stack has vanished and only a photo of Pops and Grandma Marcie from the early eighties stands next to a vintage lemon glass lamp on the desk. I flip around and notice the bulky box computer is gone too. Why would Ben move the computer and leave me here unconscious?

Lifting the curtain of plaid shirts, I twist the doorknob making my way out of Little Narnia, noticing the shirts dancing behind me aren't the colors I pulled through earlier and the carpet they're nibbling on is shaggy and teal.

I was out for six hours. How could an entire hallway renovation happen in the time I'd lost consciousness? Were carpet installers larks of the renovation industry? My grandparents weren't early risers. And why would they choose such hideous carpet?

The muppet-like fur sprouting from the floor continues down the long hallway, where I also notice a giant embroidered sunflower wall hanging that wasn't there before, more muddy brown than gold, clashing against the off-white wall in between Grandma Marcie's craft room and the storage room on the opposite side. It was dark last night, but not dark enough for me to totally miss out on all these changes.

Who's idea was the burnt orange and brown? Pops or Grandma Marcie?

I hear music start upstairs. The lyrics old, but familiar, ring down the stairwell. A deeper-toned "Turn around" follows and I know Bonnie Tyler's *A Total Eclipse of the Heart* is playing from the bathroom upstairs. Someone's home.

I rush up the stairs skipping steps, then pause midway, as familiar voices carry a conversation in my grandparents' bedroom.

"I won my case yesterday, by the way. I forgot to mention that when I came home. Your taco salad was so good but I couldn't find chips in the cupboard to crunch on top of the Thousand Island and after that all I could think about was chips," says a man that can only be Pops. His voice sounds more vibrant today.

"It's almost 6:30. We've got to get you to the airport. If you miss this flight today, Mt. Kilimanjaro will miss you," Grandma Marcie's familiar voice cuts in.

Pops is going to hike Mt. Kilimanjaro again, just like he did thirty years ago? He is in shape for his age but this worries me. How did he get Grandma Marcie to sign off on this? She's been worrying about his knee since his last surgery, always telling him to be careful when he plays tennis, so why would she let him hike again?

A lean-built man appears at the top of the staircase with an over-sized orange hiking pack strapped to his back. I make out a pair of legs and chunky green hiking boots before he bounces down the stairs.

"Be good for your mother, Atta." Pops bounces past me and turns the corner so that his back now faces me on the switchback staircase. Instead of a head sprouting mostly grays, I see a full head of shiny dark hair. I catch his face for only a second, but my heart races in shock.

That can't be him. This man is too young. Is Grandma Marcie sending my uncle off to hike? He wouldn't even attempt a 14er with me last time I offered and why did he mention my mother? I could've sworn that was Pops' voice.

I walk into my grandmother's room to find a beautiful lady with shoulder-length hair as dark as mud on a rainy day staring back at me.

"Your sister's been looking for you all morning. Where've you been?" she says, pulling a heavy pink sweater over her cream-colored turtleneck and stuffing it into the waistband of some overly acid-washed, high-waisted jeans.

I don't have a sister or any siblings. What is this woman, who looks like my mother, or more accurately, a younger version of my grand-mother, talking about?

"I've got to take your dad to the airport. Make sure the boys behave themselves while we're out. Davy's been walking around the house naked lately. Make sure he puts some shorts on at least," she says, closing in on me. The lady who looks eerily like my grandmother, without peppered hair or wrinkles, wraps her arms around me and plants a loud kiss on my cheek with puckered lips. I squeal from embarrassment. Who is this person? She walks toward the stairs, resting her arm on her leather skinny-strapped purse and smiles back at me. I must be deep in some dream. Those are definitely my grand-ma's lips; they dip when she smiles.

I run toward the bathroom door, directly across from the stairs, and start pinching and flicking my cheeks aggressively. Time to wake up! I need to get back to Ben and look at the Sheriden company's Wikipedia page. I could've bought a proxy server and cracked the search results on the Windows 95 by now if I hadn't taken a full nap in Pops' hidden room.

Pinching my cheeks isn't working. I look in the bathroom mirror and appreciate my soft camel trench coat and its massive pockets. It's draped around my shoulders like a sturdy yet wearable blanket giving me that relaxed yet professional look. In fact, I look so relaxed the crow's feet around my eyes seem to have disappeared. I scan the mirror and the rest of my face. How do my under eyes look so smooth? It's as if someone's photoshopped my face to look younger. I lean in closer to the mirror to make sure I'm seeing things clearly.

I've got it! Every time I empty my bladder in my dreams I always wake up. It never fails. It's like a disconnect in my REM sleep that has to be dealt with in real life.

I finish the bodily task with ease. No waking occurs.

My stomach flips. This can't be real, can it? I was only making a dumb comment into the phone before I passed out. It's not like I'd actually be able to land myself in an alternate universe or something.

"Atta! You up there? Come out here and help me find my cassette tape." The sound of my mother's voice comes from the floor below.

I run down the stairs following her voice.

"Cassette tape?" I say, landing at the bottom of the stairs just a few feet from the closet door that hides Pops' secret room. The wall where my mother and uncles' photos hang in age-descending order looks the same, but with one exception, a photo I've never seen before hangs between them. A photo of me with bangs, so high that they drop like Niagara Falls.

"Where's my Depeche Mode tape? You had it last."

"I did?" I turn around and see Erica, my mother, all dolled up with thick blue eyeliner tracing her lower eyelids. Her lips are shiny, roseberry pink, and her skin is flawless. She looks like a—no, she is—a teenager who's just let the curlers out of her hair.

"Is it in your room?" she asks, then walks into the old storage room. I follow her and take a deep breath at the site of the room. My younger-looking mom is throwing things onto the bed of what is clearly a 1980s teenage room. I can't help but wonder if I've actually transported myself to a different dimension because this feels all too real.

"Greg will be here any minute, and he never has any good music in his truck. "

"Who's Greg?"

"Haha funny." She laughs and starts rummaging through the white shelves behind the bed.

"It's not in your room. Did you move it to my car?"

"I don't know. I've got to be dreaming," I say, with a defeated breath.

"Aw, he's here! Gotta go! I'm taking your 38 Special cassette tape instead. Don't be mad." She runs out of the room with enough pep to rally a student section, and I follow her to the door.

I need answers now. I need to get back to Ben and we really need to figure out a way to exploit Marigold before the weekend runs out. I pinch my cheeks again, standing by the front window.

Nothing. I can't wake from this dream. I watch Mom—young Erica—hop into a truck parked against the curb and kiss the young man in the driver's seat. Must be Greg? They drive away as I head outside for some fresh air.

Grandma Marcie's house behind me isn't blue anymore. It's a muted seventies tan with brandy-colored window trim and all the cars in the neighboring driveways are '85 and older. I've never seen so many wood-paneled Volkswagens on one block.

I need to verify today's date. This doesn't feel like a dream. The world is too clear and there's no haziness behind my thoughts. No. I just need to go to my apartment. Once I'm there I can take care of this schizophrenic episode. A nap on my couch should do the trick.

An engine purrs across the street where the neighbor cop adjusts a strap over his ears, creating a ripple down his curly shoulder-length mullet. He runs his hand over his sandy mustache and adjusts his glasses while straddling his bike.

With no cars left at the house, this is my opportunity.

"Officer, Officer!" I yell, waving my FBI badge in the air to get his attention.

"How may I help you?" He grins, sliding off his shades to take a closer look at the thick leather symbol of authority.

"My partner had to leave with our vehicle. I have an emergency case that will require you to give me a lift," I say, as he studies my face and FBI badge about as quickly as most people do when they're pressured by law enforcement.

"Don't really have a choice do I?" he says with a deep chuckle as if teasing a female agent is a form of flattery. "I won't mind a pretty thing like you on the back of my bike."

"Please take me downtown to Walnut Street in Denver. River North Apartments," I say unfazed. I fling my leg over his bike seat and place my feet next to his shiny black boots.

The engine purr turns into a roar as we peel out of the neighborhood onto the main road. The officer turns on his siren lights and rushes past the 55 mph sign as if it's a base requirement rather than a speed limit. I don't mind. The sooner I get there the better.

He begins weaving through a myriad of angled and boxy cars causing me to grab onto him with a tighter hold. I watch his mullet flap against the side of his helmet. He's rather young for an officer, and dare I say, maybe a bit too careless and free for someone holding such a position. I feel more like I'm on a date with a man trying to impress me using daredevil riding tactics than a respected man of the law. But it's exactly what I'd expect from an officer wearing a sitcom-worthy, khaki-colored uniform that seems to highlight his holster and laced-up boots.

We pass 36th Street and arrive at Walnut where my apartment should be standing, but there's no sign of the building. I check the street signs again. This is the right spot. I can see the long brick building with the painted lightning bolt logo that sits around the corner from my apartment complex. But we're in the middle of a houseboat sales lot. My apartment is nonexistent. There's nowhere for me to nap off this dream and I'm starting to feel like I've actually gone nuts.

"You doing operations in a houseboat or something?" he asks.

"Something like that," I respond.

Are details even necessary at this point? I am stuck and can't explain that the building I'm looking for doesn't seem to exist. I'll have to find another way back to Golden.

"Thanks for the ride. Officer Berrett, is it?" I find his name badge clipped to his chest.

"Anything to help out law enforcement," he says, giving me a silly salute wave and the golden quality of his cheeks tint with his blush. It makes me reassess his appeal. His mullet and stash are quite attractive.

"I enjoyed the ride. Have a nice day." My smile is wide and cocky and I'm trying really hard to act as if everything is going according to plan. Officer Berrett takes off on his bike, likely heading back to his post in Golden.

I decide to tear a page from Tyler's notebook on life and hitchhike back to my grandparents' home. Hitchhiking was a common method of transportation in the eighties, right? So it shouldn't be that hard.

I walk a few blocks to the edge of the road where cars are loading onto the highway. My gun and holster were left back at my apartment —which doesn't seem to exist now—so I feel a bit uneasy. I'll have to rely on my close-quarters combat skills if anything sketchy comes up trying to get a ride back to the mountains. A little gutter fighting should do the trick.

The wind whips my hair across my face as cars fly by without a glance in my direction, but I stay committed to holding the thumbs-up sign.

Thirty minutes pass and a white-haired couple pull over to my side with a friendly wave. I chuckle when they come to a full stop; the man and woman, who are likely in their seventies, are accompanied by three dogs with the same white hair color. The fluffy marshmallow pups pant with wide open slobbery mouths in the backseat of the couple's old, blue Mercedes. They welcome me with a warm, wet hello as I slide in and one of the pups lunges for me, making me feel as if I'm being pelted by a pompom.

"Don't mind them. They like to play when they're excited," the cute old lady, who introduces herself as Gladys, says. She asks where I'm from and what I'm doing on the side of the road. I opt for a simple 'I don't have a ride today' explanation and avoid telling them the truth about losing my apartment to a thirty-year time gap.

"That's a unique hairstyle you have. All the young ladies are wearing their hair curly nowadays. Are you the tomboy type?" the old man says, referring to my flat, side-parted hairstyle.

"It's nice and sleek," his wife adds to make it sound more like a compliment.

"Thank you," I say, peeking at the newspaper underneath the largest marshmallow's nubby paws.

I reach over and slide it out from underneath the pup. My eyes find the date at the top underneath the headline, *Denver Post, February 2, 1987.*

"Is this today's newspaper?" I ask, casually holding it up for Gladys to see through the rearview mirror. If her answer is yes, I'm positive my hand gripping the newspaper will start to shake.

"Just picked it up this morning, hun," she says. The day and the month seem correct but the year…1987? I nod confirming the fact that I seem to be the only one who doesn't acknowledge 2023 as the current year. Logically I can't acknowledge it, but deep down my intuition tells me this is reality—alternate reality—but reality nonetheless, and whether or not I understand how I got here I'm not dreaming. Everything around me is too clear, too vivid and all my senses are telling me it's real.

The thought that I might not wake up from what I thought was a dream brings an uneasy feeling to my stomach. I feel like I might hurl again but I do everything I can to push the uneasiness somewhere else and remain collected in my seat.

I skim through the pages for some noteworthy news. I'd be scanning old newspapers if I were back with Ben anyway. It somehow feels like I should still continue so I skim through the sports and comics sections, moving on to the business section as we pass Coors Brewery. The front page article is dominated by a wavy "W" logo—the kind of squiggly wave you would expect on a paper cup at the food court mall. It's stamped next to one of the top headlines that reads:

Sheriden Foundation Adds New Company to Their Roster.

A new division has been added to the relatively new Sheriden Foundation company.

"We're at Holiday Rd. Which house number is it?" Gladys' voice interrupts the words I'm reading.

"2929. Have you read this paper yet?" I ask.

The newspaper mentioned the Sheriden Foundation, which I learned not even twenty-four hours before, via Google's search results, is the foundation that started the Marigold Company. If I can take this article with me it might actually tell me more about Marigold than my Pops Windows 95 computer could.

"Not yet but plan to when we get home. Any interesting articles?" the old man says.

"If you like comics, *For Better Or For Worse* is pretty good," I say.

These people are too sweet. I'd feel awkward stealing the newspaper from them after they so kindly plucked me off the street. I'll have to get the *Denver Post* elsewhere. I set it on the seat next to me between the dogs before crawling out of the back door.

They ride off like two snails on warm cement, extending the sendoff wave by an embarrassing amount of time and I make a mental note to find today's newspaper mentioning Sheriden as soon as possible.

"You happy, Universe!? I'm in 1987." I yell into the cool noon air, hoping it will give up on its sick joke and send me back to my own time if only I say it out loud.

Chapter Seven

If I'd thought a full night's sleep would wake me from this reality, even after yesterday's failed attempt at a twenty minute nap, the sound of an old plastic digital clock and the site of my grandma's youthful face when I hit the snooze button a few too many times, told me otherwise. I wasn't getting out of this alternate universe with sleep.

"Hey Erica, do you believe in time travel? Do you think it's possible?" I'll wait for her answer and then try explaining. "Would you believe me if I told you I've time traveled and I need to find one of those clear phones, with color wires inside? At least I think that's how I got here."

I lay up in bed against the back of the white metal bed frame under a baby blue tie quilt, practicing the words out loud. It sounds so ridiculous. I feel like a fool saying it to myself. I might as well say something like "If I plan to stab someone today should I wear a pink tutu or something more clean-cut like a pencil skirt? Oh, and I think I'll enjoy it, do you think I'll enjoy it?" Either sentence is going to get me committed to a mental hospital.

I mean is there a good way to tell someone you don't belong in their century? That wasn't a hypothetical I ever practiced growing up.

We always stuck to things like "If I won the lottery..." or "If you had to choose between eating only rats for the rest of your life or peeing through your nose, which would you choose?"

I wished I would've asked better hypotheticals or had it at least come up in my shower thoughts. Even more so, I wished I had an explanation. There's no way I could just bring this up casually. I get nervous just thinking about the other person's reaction. I wouldn't take anyone seriously who came at me with a question like that.

I rub my tired eyes and swallow the strange sight around me. If sleeping near band posters, teddy bear wall art, and the three-foot stack of magazines on top of a checkered blue record carrying case wasn't odd enough, my mom calling me "sis" all night last night is the culmination of odd things.

My young uncles wrestle each other in the wood-paneled living room as I walk past the buffalo and carrot-orange-colored couch. Erica —it's so hard not to think of her as *Mom*—extends her legs outwards in a split stretch a few feet away while she watches a morning show I don't recognize on a vintage TV cabinet. The cabinet has an accordion door curtain and at least nine potted plants on top of it.

"Are you riding with me or Diana today? If you're riding with Diana you better get your butt moving. She'll be here any minute," Erica says, with the look of judgment as she scans me from head to toe. She holds her gaze on my dark ink-splattered eyes that currently suffer from an old makeup and crusty eye sauce combination and I can't tell what she finds worse, that or the baggy blue sweats and smelly oversized tee that I picked up off the floor.

Diana's coming to get me? Diana, born in 1993 Diana? She's here? In 1987? The once Jamba-Juice-loving, Harry-Potter-obsessed, purple-Air-Force-One-sporting, now cowboy-kissing, floral-dress-wearing woman I know, is here with me in 1987?

I run back to the room 1987 had assigned me, my socks slipping off against the carpet on the way, the way my life is currently slipping out of my hands. I stare at a poster of piggies-doing-jazzercise above the dresser drawer as the horn buzzes outside. I don't bother changing my clothes and shove the FBI badge into the waistband of my baggy blue sweats, then catch myself staring at a familiar white-faced geisha figurine sitting on the dresser when I should be running outside to find out what Diana's doing here in the 1980s. So much in this room reminds me of my mom's things, but here in this time they're mine? "Who knows…" I mumble and rush out of the room.

"I'm going with Diana," I shout when I reach the front door. If Diana is in the eighties with me maybe she'll have some answers.

Diana bobs her head up and down in the front seat of a little cherry-red sports car, to a powerful beat I can hear from the middle of the lawn. Her passenger window is rolled down and she greets me with "Morning! Hop in."

I lean against her car window, admiring her short rounded afro—a look I haven't seen her wear since high school. She's wearing an acid-wash denim dress with a pink waist belt and I wonder if all women in this era have a hard time staying away from denim that has to be rubbed away with stones for hours on end.

She continues messing with the volume dial without looking in my direction as if this is routine for her.

"Did you bring your sister's Depeche Mode tape?"

"I don't know where that is. She was asking for it yesterday," I say, recalling yesterday's moment when I first set eyes on my eighteen-year-old mother as she questioned me about the cassette tape I had suppos-edly borrowed from her.

"Don't you usually shove her tapes in your Tootsie Roll can? It's probably there," she says, then looks up at me. Thick, white hoop earrings dangle beneath her earlobes. She's ready to shoo me away with her hand, so that I retreat back into the house to search for a Tootsie Roll can.

"Do you remember where I put that last?" I say, not knowing if I can meet the expectation and find such a novel item. Eighties me owns a Tootsie Roll can that holds pilfered goods?

"I mean the only place I know of is the bottom drawer of your dresser where you stash the real Tootsie Rolls. Is it not there?"

"Be right back," I say heading toward the sidewalk path framed with trimmed bushes and planted flowers that curve up to the front screen door.

I grab for the bottom dresser drawer handle and open it wide once I'm back in the room. There it is. A six-inch long tube wide enough to hold a cassette tape inside, floating amongst a sea of pinky-sized Tootsie Rolls. The drawer is three-quarters full of them.

Back at the car I hand the cassette tape over to Diana. She slides it into the player and whisks me out of the cul-de-sac, massacring her way through the Depeche Mode lyrics as we drive.

"You look a little haggard today. Is everything okay?" Diana says, turning the volume down so that I can hear her over the music as we pull into the school parking lot.

I want so badly to confide in her. She's always been easygoing and I can't help but wonder how she would react if I told her what I'd just experienced. Maybe she's having the same experience as me? Is it possible that she is also a guest to this time period and unsure of how to bring it up?

If that's the case I'd rather bring it up to her now than wait for time to tell me. But what if she isn't and she doesn't believe me? She'd never commit me to a mental hospital. That's against the best friend code right? The most I'd get from her was a soft scolding about saying stupid things. And if she did take it the wrong way, creating trouble in her sweet, only rainbow-and-butterfly-filled mind, she'd scrunch up her pretty button nose like The Hulk's fist, and whisper threats in my direction like a passive aggressive debater.

In her defense, this tactic worked quite well when she was frustrated. It was hard to counter. Sarcasm was the only way to match it.

My first encounter with Diana's quiet frustration came long ago when she'd discovered I was storing love notes to her brother under a baseball cap in the back of my closet. She'd threatened that she'd tell Ben my little secret if I didnt get rid of my shameless shrine—the baseball cap was his. I'd stolen it from his room. The moment she learned of my crush, she made sure to confront me with the expected serious question. "You really like that disgusting snob? Well then, who would you choose if we were in danger and you could only save one of us?"

"I'd drag you by a rope tied to the back of the horse Ben and I are riding. It might be painful but it would be an exotic way to go," I'd said, mirroring her soft tone with obvious sarcasm.

Even back then I could throw a punch with words in the face of mockery. It worked. She laughed it off and has only threatened that embarrassing story a few more times since, including a few years ago when she used it as a cute attempt to set Ben and me up. Obviously, it didn't work, and I laughed his unenthusiastic response off with a shrug, while remarking how silly young crushes are.

The memory makes me even more concerned about our separation. We'd been separated not even forty-eight hours. What was he doing? Was he searching for me? Had I disappeared from him the same way he'd disappeared from me? Kenny would threaten him at work if they hadn't already gotten to him during the weekend. What if my departure had made things harder for him? If he involved anyone else in a search for me, that would surely complicate things. I hoped he was staying silent.

"I'm not feeling myself today. It seems like things are turned upside down lately," I say, explaining my grisly appearance as we find an open parking spot close to the school entrance.

"Yesterday was all sorts of weird and I'm just trying to figure out why," I continue. Diana listens intently. "Have you ever had something so strange happen to you that you wonder if time travel or mixed dimensions exist?" Diana's empty eyes and genuine smile tell me she hasn't, but she tries to empathize anyway.

"Whatever you need, I'm here. I suppose life can feel so out of sorts that it doesn't feel real anymore." This time her face shows more concern. She's clearly not experiencing the same thing I am. I don't see how diving into an explanation any further will get me anywhere, so I leave it at that and close the car door behind me.

"My sister's good with that kind of stuff. She's into reading philosophy and finding inner peace lately when she's not working the night shift at the hospital. Maybe she could help," Diana says. My mouth hangs to the floor. What does she mean by that? Diana doesn't have a sister. It's always been just her and Ben.

"Your sister?"

"Yeah. Come over after school. I'm sure she'll be there. Maybe she'll lend you a book."

If Diana has a sister that exists in this world, does Ben Brown exist here?

Ben was with me before I disappeared in front of his eyes. Did he join me? If I could find him here, maybe I had a chance at figuring this out. I could get him to tell me what happened with the flickering lights and my old transparent phone. Maybe he'd know how to send us back.

Diana swings her car door shut and I follow behind. When we walk through the school together, I take in the teal, color-blocked halls around me. It's hard to describe the feeling of walking through this high school thirty years before it was actually "mine" to claim. The feeling's indescribable, but the smell and sounds are distinct. If this hallway were a scent, it would be a sheet of Scratch 'n Sniff stickers. I can't help but notice the edge of my mouth turn up at the stale smell.

A group of rough-looking junior or senior boys that could pass for working-class adults trudge by in Levi's, knocking their thick boots across the floor with a masculine swagger. The sound echoes off the poster-filled walls amongst spirited group chatter and the scent shifts to locker-room Drakkar Noir, a citrusy cologne that almost masks the BO seeping from a few open muscle tees.

"Is Ben around?" I ask Diana.

"Since when are you wanting to know where he's at first thing in the morning?" Diana says.

Good. He is here! The sense of urgency to find him is unbearable. Waiting isn't an option. I will scour the building for my best friend's brother if I have to.

"I need to see him. Now!" I say, marching a few steps to the right to peek over the group of fluffy-haired teens deep in conversation.

Could he be down one of these stuffed yellow hallways? Classes hadn't started yet.

"Easy, Atta." Diana pulls a smile and concerned eyes. "I thought you weren't talking to him? Isn't he avoiding you right now?"

"What do you mean avoiding me?" I ask.

"I'm not sure. Didn't you say he was angry with you the last couple of weeks and pretending you're just empty air in front of him?"

"I doubt that's the case." Ben's been severely annoyed with me many times but never angry with me to the point of not talking. He's not the type to use the silent treatment.

Why did nothing make sense in this eighties alternate universe? Yesterday's me, the one that these eighties people seem to know, isn't the me I know. I have no recollection of Depeche Mode tapes and now Ben's silent treatment.

"Well, I must find him regardless," I say fidgeting with the locker next to Diana's assuming it's mine. I don't have the code. I know I'm not going to get it open and she's not questioning my actions, so it must be mine. Click. Click. Click. I roll random numbers, faking my actions so as not to cause suspicion in front of her.

"Hey, Di! Hey, Atta!" A familiar Philly accent says, walking up behind us. I turn, thankful for an excuse to quit this bad locker-opening acting. Evan, who I'd seen just two days ago at the reunion, stands right in front of me. His floppy surfer bangs that normally hang like curtains around his long rounded face are fluffier. Must be a perm.

His young face is the face I'm most familiar with, since I'd only seen him slightly aged earlier this week. One night of seeing adult Evan isn't washing away how I saw him most of my early life. Here he is. The same teenager I grew up with but here in this eighties atmosphere.

It's as if my generation was transposed in with our parents' genera-tion, restarting life at seventeen to wear cherry-red letterman jackets with teal trim and tie bandanas across our foreheads for fun. So far these notable differences stood out the most along with everyone greeting each other with headlocks instead of hugs. Every other

70

student in this generation seemed to do this as I passed by this morning.

A sly look crawls up his face, and he slides a folded piece of paper into my hand as if we're Vada and Thomas from *My Girl* exchanging spit handshakes. I smile back awkwardly and feel my eyes sheepishly fall to the brown speckled floor. He doesn't seem to notice the heat of confusion emanating from my cheeks and saunters off, turning his baseball cap backward on his mountain of hair. A bendy square of thick paper with strudel-like layers now floats in my hand and Diana is oblivious to the whole transaction.

"You can always count on Evan to keep up relationships. I feel like he's always trying to be the peacemaker between Tyler and I," Diana says with an arm full of books.

They must be in the in-between stages of their high school love-hate relationship. I recall that being a rocky road for them for a while, before it eventually turned into a mushy-kisses-in-the-park and shar-ing-cheezits-through-each-others-car-windows kind of relationship.

I'M PRETTY SURE I LOOK LIKE A GERENUK—THE ANTELOPE WITH a giraffe-like neck and an unusually small head standing on its hind legs whistling amongst the shrubbery, waiting for the hallway to empty. Diana's in class and I don't plan on filling my time in eighties Golden High with anything but searching for her absent brother.

The last hallway straggler exits to the right and I'm left with the hallway to myself. I peel open the little lined paper that's been tucked in between my fingers, carefully unwrapping the creased corners, to discover an ongoing pen-and-pencil conversation with remarkably familiar writing—I recognize it as my own—and responding sloppy, slanted writing on the right. *Ms. Clark, 2nd Period* is written at the top left.

I'm really sorry about Ty. He shouldn't have gone that far with Diana.

I would've pulled it out of the car before she saw it if I knew he was going to do that.

> *She really hates snakes and it was dead and bloody, so I don't think she'll forgive him anytime soon, but you're forgiven. We all know Ty can't be supervised, even by you.*

I realize I'm reading a conversation between Evan, and what I presume is myself. A slight grin escapes me. Diana does hate snakes. Snakes are her worst fear next to being asked to clog at the county fair. I still remember the time she was asked to join a clogging group in middle school and was so upset. She could barely articulate a few sloppy sentences through her tears. "Do I look like I'd be a good clogger? Atta, seriously, please tell me the truth. This is almost as humiliating as failing a four-foot pole vault at a track meet." Pole vaulting was her pride and joy. Middle school Diana had a melodramatic side.

He can't be managed. Say a prayer for me. I run with a dangerous crowd. BTW your white dress looks cute today.

> *Thank you. I like it too! If only he'd chosen to "rattlesnake" my car. Then we could avoid these two interacting with each other and I could audition for a Carrie sequel.*

She got blood on her clothes? Shoot! You don't even have a car, so wishful thinking. Do you like horror films?

> *Not really? Do you like the worst movie genre in the history of mankind?*

Love it! Give me anything with an adrenaline rush.

> *Ah, now I get why you chose Tyler as your best friend.*

You may be on to something… I could take a short break from the addiction though. How about the theater this weekend?
You and me + popcorn.

Can I pick?

Your pick. 7pm, Saturday. I'll pick you up?

The rest of the page is empty waiting for an answer from me.

No, I will not go to the movies with seventeen-year-old Evan. I slide the note into my sweatpants pockets and head down the hall.

Another bell rings and thirty classroom windows later, I realize I'm conducting this operation all wrong. I'm treating this like an ordinary day at work—though I'm missing a sense of purpose, washed hair, and decent attire—and it's clear, peeking through the tiny doggy-door-sized windows to see nothing but front-row desk seats and a teacher writing on the classroom chalkboard isn't getting me anywhere.

I gather my thoughts, chewing on my nail next to five full-length lockers and an uplifting wall of school-color-themed posters, before I make my way to the office to request Ben's schedule. Easy enough. I don't know why that wasn't my first thought.

The hallway is so peaceful while second period is in session, a complete contrast to the boisterous festival noise made by countless small groups and cliques prior to the morning bell. The office is just a hallway over, past the group of girls in baggy sweaters and Reebok hightops studying together with notecards. I continue my walk to the office as two kids light up cigarettes in the boy's bathroom entryway.

The silence becomes disrupted by two pairs of sneakers running down the hallway in my direction. A boy carrying a large bird diorama with a bit of difficulty is being chased by another classmate in desperation. The closer he gets, the more my senses tell me that I know this person.

It turns out that those are Tyler's beady blue eyes behind that greater yellowlegs beak. Professional birdwatcher Tyler. Had we really missed all the signs growing up? Here he stands with a bird diorama in hand, and I feel the soft punch of two worlds colliding.

"Tyler, get back here! How could you claim that as yours and leave me with nothing to present?" the kid behind him yells.

Tyler stops a few feet away from me and turns back around to face the person he's wronged, dropping his head, raising the dramatics as if he's a general at war accepting defeat and his last effort for peace is to hold out the diorama as a surrendering gift. The kid takes the cardboard theater-shaped box and smacks the side of Tyler's shoulder.

"You didn't get any of the bird's names right. Good luck even getting a passing grade on this after I present today. Your paper doesn't even match your presentation," the boy says, almost too comfortable with the situation. It's as if he expects this from Tyler and therefore is less outraged. He's not wrong. That was how I felt toward Tyler most days.

"Why were you running away with that?" I ask my sandy-blonde friend whose curls are currently sculpted into a short mullet. It's a new look for him that he actually pulls off quite well.

As soon as I think it, I question my taste in style. First, I'm appreciating the neighbor cop's mullet—to be fair he was riding a motorcycle which always boosts the appeal—and now I'm even subconsciously complimenting Tyler's styled mullet.

"The dude stood up after I finished my speech and chased after me. I had to bring the fight out into the hallway or the teacher would know it wasn't mine."

"I think the teacher's going to know regardless," I say, letting my smile wind through my words. He sends a smarmy smirk back and then studies my face, glancing all the way down to my toes.

"You lose your hairbrush, Atta?" I know he's referring to my hair with one side noticeably straighter than the other.

"Don't avoid the topic. I know what I look like today."

"Like you should've just stayed in bed?"

"Actually, have you seen Ben around? Do you know what class he has?" I whip the conversation in a different direction.

"Ben, Diana's brother Ben? The one who's told you multiple times he's not speaking to you. That Ben?" I nod to confirm. That's two people now telling me Ben is avoiding me. "I think he's in the gym. Hey, if you find him tell him I need to talk to him too." He casts a look around the hall, as if making sure something doesn't pop out of the corner, and then springs his hands up toward my hair.

"Let me smooth those rat tails out for ya," he says, patting down the side of my head with closed-fingered hands, the way an older brother would successfully torture a sibling. I fend him off with a couple of swats until he's discouraged from touching my head anymore.

I pass by the school office, completely ignoring it, as I head toward the gym. The gym doors are closed and I presume physical education class is in session, but this is urgent.

The doors take a good gust of strength from both of my arms to open and I look up to see the gymnasium is wide and high, just as it was in 2010, which would be twenty-some years in the future, except the plastic-coated bleachers are now solid wood bleachers seated ten rows high and claiming half of the room.

A group of students, in various colored sweats with elastic cuffs and oversized tees, jog toward the bleachers where a skinny man with a whistle and towel tucked into the waistband of his shorts points to the next exercise written in blue expo marker on a small whiteboard. *50 Pushups.*

There he is, standing the furthest away from the PE teacher and closest to the wood-paneled wall I have my back to. There's my partner, the man I've laughed, studied, and theorized with almost every day for the past five years. The man that's had my back in the most terrifying of conditions. The man that tries picking a fight to distract me right before I'm about to win the entire game of Risk. The one I've loved for as long as I can remember and whose face is the last thing I saw before waking up in this unknown world.

Ben Brown.

Chapter Eight

He's noticed me. His form becomes noticeably worse with the last five push-ups, likely because he keeps looking over in my direction after each bicep extension rather than keeping his eyes on the floor. He can't get through each set without pulling a face of disgust, so I give a friendly wave the next time he looks in my direction.

I wait until the class ends and run over to him before he can escape to the men's locker room.

"Ben! I need to speak with you," I say with a hopeful smile. Please let him be disturbed about something other than my presence. I'm holding out my last hope for him to be the Ben that knows Agent Suarez, not this eighties version everyone claims is avoiding me.

"Come with me." The tone of Ben's voice is short.

He walks through the bulky gym doors and leads me to the vending machines by the rounded lounge chairs just outside the gym. I follow behind, observing his quick pace and familiar build—same wide shoulders and defined muscle, noticeably younger though and not quite as filled out as the last time I'd seen him in uniform. He stops and pulls his college tee out from its untucked position as if it's uncomfortable and wants to take revenge on its placement, then puts a few spare coins from his pocket into one of the soda machines and hands me the second soda that drops from the vending machine.

"Here, this is for you. You can take it as a parting gift and continue to stay away from me." He shoves the can into my palm.

"Wait. I...," I start, unsure of how to proceed. I was betting everything on him ever since Diana showed up, thinking he might be the answer to finding my way back to the future. Now the sounding alarm in my head is telling me I've got to shoot my shot before Eighties Ben actually avoids me forever. I tell myself there's a chance his current bad mood is due to confusion. Maybe he feels out of place in this weird world too.

"Do you remember my Pops' closet, Marigold, the video?" I say. He stares blankly at me as if I'm speaking Korean and he's never heard a word of the language in his life. He turns away, shaking his head in the process, and walks off toward the gym.

"What about the phone and the fireworks?" I run after him in desperation. An uncomfortable laugh emerges from him and he looks outright surprised.

"Seriously Atta, what are you playing at?" He looks like he wants to plead with me. "You said you wouldn't bring up the phone incident again with me." His beautiful brown eyes fill with apprehension.

"You say 'phone incident' like it was a bad thing for you and not the both of us. I don't understand. We can talk about it and figure out a way back together. If it's just you and me no one here would even know," I push.

"You sound crazy, you know. I've got to go." I drag my hand over my forehead in frustration as he proceeds down the hallway, gaining an even greater distance from me. It's inevitable, his strides laugh at mine—full-on tongue-out-taunting from his soles looking back at mine.

He didn't smile once during our interaction, and I realize I miss his dimple that pokes through his smooth cheek whenever he's mildly entertained.

"There he is! Looks like you found him." Tyler appears before us. He catches up to me as Ben stops a few feet ahead at the sound of Tyler's voice. Ben's back remains turned away from Ty and I and he looks like he might bolt.

"Ben, I need a favor. Let's race after school. K?"

"That's gunna be a no from me. Not today Tyler. I kicked your trash last time anyway, remember?"

Ben, who resembles a defeated boxer, sweaty from gym class and clearly worn from the toll both Tyler and I are putting on him at this moment, turns around to face Tyler.

"That's why we've got to do a rematch."

"No, Ty. Really."

"You know you owe me right? I've already spread it around school. Harper St. behind the school again. That or we can fight. Put on a show for everyone, you know since I've already put the word out." Tyler's prancing around Ben like a kid begging for candy. "Come on, it'll be fun. Plus, if I lose I won't ask Bennette to the movies." Ben perks up in defense a little and then resolves to let his comment slide a few seconds later, knowing all too well Tyler's just trying to be provoking.

"She's already with me you punk."

"Ain't nothing wrong with some healthy competition." Tyler laughs. "Or she could find out what you did with Corky." Ben looks from me to Tyler and back this time. By the look in his eyes, it looks like this threat worked.

"No fight. Just a race. Let's make it quick. I have to be somewhere at five. Oh and prepare to get your trash kicked," Ben says, his eyes are harsh and piercing.

DIANA AND I FIND OURSELVES MIGRATING WITH THE CROWD toward the track and field. The afternoon sun burns bright in the sky and I feel quite warm even without a jacket. Colorado weather remains unpredictable but I have a feeling it's going to be another warm February.

Diana leads me with the pull of her arm. She's curious about the ant hill of people marching together like a bunch of camp followers, and I know she doesn't have a clue that they are going to watch the race between Tyler and her brother, just like she had no clue I spent the rest of the class periods in the lounge next to the soda machines, doodling on the back of Evan's note.

"Where is everyone heading?" she asks, dragging me with her as she picks up her pace.

"Tyler challenged your brother to a race," I say as we head out the doors following the trail of students.

"They're doing it behind the baseball fields this time? Tyler must be worried about what that new officer said to them the other day."

"What did he say?" I ask as we reach the long dirt road that runs a direct line behind the school baseball field. A closed road barrier marks the end of the road a quarter mile down, next to a run-down gas station. Traffic hardly touches the road, making it the adopted school event parking and the perfect spot for Tyler to force Ben into racing their dirt bikes between two fields of dry countryside.

"Last weekend a police officer on a motorcycle, who we've never seen before, stopped Tyler and Ben at the foot of the mountain. He told them to stay out of the mountains, without an explanation. Rumor has it he's taken a few girls up there and is cheating on his wife and it's like he wants the mountain all to himself. I guess Ben and Ty are going to race at the usual fight spot instead."

"Yikes," I say, wondering how many Golden police officers ride around on motorcycles in this town. I've been here for a day and I've already managed to ask one of them for a ride. "Did they get the police officer's name?"

"Officer Berrett, I believe," she says.

I almost stumble over my feet when the attractive officer with the shaggy mullet's name badge comes to mind. When I thanked him for the ride I said his name out loud and he blushed before giving me a weird salute wave. That guy's the cop preventing them from racing their dirt bikes in the mountains? My grandparents' neighbor?

I become weary of the thought that he may have subtly hit on me when I approached him. But I was law enforcement. As long as he knew that he wouldn't be creepy toward me, right?

"I can't believe they're doing this again. Tyler's even upgraded his bike," Diana says as we wiggle our way to the front of the small crowd watching Ben straddling an old red dirt bike.

Tyler's next to him, shirtless and proud, straddling a yellow bike, noticeably cleaner than Ben's. Diana folds her arms in annoyance. She's dangerously contemplating Tyler's tactics and I witness her eye twitch with vehemence at him.

Tyler rushes over to Diana and me with the white tee he's abandoned for the cause. One look at Diana and he knows to ask me and not her to wave them off.

I unenthusiastically accept and Ben starts his engine over the loud herd of students while Tyler drums his chest like a bongo walking back to his bike. Tacky, but the swarm of mostly feathery-haired girls in more acid-wash denim seem to love it.

"This is the last time we race. You know, if we get caught out here riding and your dad finds out, I'm going to be more screwed than you." I overhear Ben say to Tyler as I walk between the two bikes.

Ben meets my gaze and his eyes harden. He's not happy I'm here to wield the makeshift t-shirt flag bestowed upon us by an inevitable birdwatcher. Someone else should be handling this assignment.

"I know. He won't find out. Lighten up. They love it when we compete." Tyler points his head to the mass of graphic tees and various-sized striped-shirt-wearing students surrounding them, which now includes Erica, more cheerleaders, and a group of what I presume are senior boys.

"Atta, we're ready," Tyler shouts. I'm not sure what fashion of wave he's wanting, but I stand a few feet in front of them and brandish his shirt around like it's one of those checkered race car flags.

They're off with the flick of my wrist and I feel my adrenaline spike as they whiz past me on both sides. My neck receives a cold whip as my hair's swept up into my face.

As far as anyone can tell, they seem to be matching speed. The people around me are half-engaged, mostly occupied with their friends around them and my thoughts drift to Tyler and Ben's earlier conversation where Tyler blackmailed Ben with his secret to get here.

That secret, whatever it is, is critical enough to get him to agree to race with about the same swiftness as his dirt bike had taking off from the yellowing grass marker. He made it sound like Ben did something with Corky without his girlfriend knowing. Ben had many girlfriends in the years I'd known him, but I guess this time it was a girl named Bennette?

"Hey Diana, is Corky or Bennette around here?" I ask, curious to know what these two people look like.

"Yeah, didn't you see them? Over there by Erica. Corky's wearing the same slouchy boots as me today." She points to a tall girl dressed in pastel with choppy layered blonde waves, symmetrical eyes, and a cute button nose. A girl standing a few inches shorter with jet black waves, beautiful smooth eyes that lift like the brush movement of Chinese calligraphy, wearing three bangles on each wrist, holds the blonde's arm as they stand amongst a group of guys. She must be Bennette, Ben's girlfriend, and the subject of his secret must be her best friend, Corky.

Hollers from the basketball boys erupt as Ben shows off, lifting his front tire into the air so that he's riding on one wheel. This Ben clearly has no recollection of the future. His biggest concern is landing his wheelie, not time travel, not Marigold, and not his friendship with me. Instead, he has the race in the bag and he knows it.

Diana and I call out as he crosses the end-of-road barrier ahead of Tyler. It's obvious, Diana's cheering for Tyler's grand loss more than she is about her brother's win.

His win is a good thing for me. Ben's cold mood is temporarily erased by his victory over Tyler and the missing dimple finally makes an appearance with his full-lipped smile. A small reminder of his warm and high-spirited nature comes back.

Ben's even found his laugh making his way off the bike, giving Tyler a shoulder squeeze before performing celebratory dance moves in front of the crowd. He takes a step to each side and leans back to an inaudible beat, then rolls his hands like he's tossing dough and mixes in some kneading motions here and there, flashing a slinky smile.

Tyler looks grateful for the race, and if he's disappointed at the loss he's hiding it well.

"Well, looks like even your new bike is no match for old red," Evan says, wrapping his sweatshirt sleeve around the stray curls poking out from Tyler's neck. I scoot behind Diana, hoping he doesn't spot me. We're far enough away that I might have a chance, but if he finds me he's going to expect me to hand over the folded piece of paper with an answer about our date.

Instead, I'd be handing over a game theory graph filled with Marigold doodles—the symbol on the cult-like members' jackets from the USB video that I couldn't get out of my head.

With Diana blocking me from Evan's sight, my view is limited to the right-side crowd, a view constrained to dry grass and boys in mesh basketball jerseys. I spot Corky and Bennette again and almost choke on my spit when I catch Erica giving vertical mouth to mouth to a man with a dust broom coffee-colored mustache. This must be her boyfriend Greg—the one that pulled up at the house in his truck the other day. My mom decided not to date after my Spanish father passed when I was young so watching her kiss someone was just so strange, something I'd never seen before.

"Diana, I've been looking for you and Ben everywhere around the school. I need you to help me pick out a present for Mom's birthday."

Diana and I turn at the sound of her mother, Robyn, approaching. She steps between Diana and I, blocking Evan completely from my lane. I let out a sigh of relief, but it's cut short when I realize Mama Robyn looks years younger. She's wearing a CNA tag with her name clipped to the v-neckline of her unflattering scrubs and her character is much more apprehensive than I remember. She looks like an innocent young nurse-trainee who might take four pokes to stick your IV.

But she also looks lighter, not just skinnier, like she's Diana's sister, not her mother. Non-80s-Land Robyn, the Mama Robyn I grew up with, lost her husband in 2010 to an untreated illness after he played ten seasons with the Denver Nuggets. It was a weight she shouldered bravely, always trying to make her kid's lives as normal as possible. It's clear this 1987 Robyn isn't carrying the weight of losing a husband.

Ben's grandma in Non-80s-Land, Harriet, the one who gifted Ben and Diana the old transparent phones, had once told me Mama Robyn's whole demeanor had changed since their father passed. That was Grandma Harriet's response when I had asked her how long she planned to stay with her grandkids.

Grandma Harriet ended up moving in with Mama Robyn, Ben, and Diana our junior year of high school. She'd said she wouldn't have her daughter raise her kids alone, especially not when her daughter seemed to be dipping further and further into depression. So she stayed with Mama Robyn to support her and comfort her while I spent that year comforting Diana. Even up until a week ago, in Non-80s-Land, if I needed to get a hold of Mama Robyn, all I needed to do was call Grandma Harriet.

The picture of a young, bright Mama Robyn in front of me is so baffling that I only gulp in response when she gives me a small wave.

"What are you doing here, sis?" Ben says behind her. Mama Robyn turns to face him, leaving me exposed to the crowd that's left in the road.

Diana mentioned something about a "sister" and now it's adding up as both of our mothers stand within feet of us, in an arched line of students not appearing or acting a day older than the rest of them.

I think I understand the dynamic of this alternate universe now. The freaky gathering before me holds no generational gap between my childhood friends and our parents.

Ben and Diana's grandma, Harriet—the mom Robyn was referring to—is Ben and Diana's mom in this alternate universe and Mama

Robyn is their sister, the same way Erica, my mother, has become my sister. It's just that. We've been mushed in with them as if time wanted to hold on to us but chose to drop us off where time was reversed. Everything about it makes my head hurt.

"Atta, you should come too. You're usually over at our place anyway after school," Robyn says. I smile and tell her I will after getting a confirmation nod from Diana, when I hear another voice calling my name.

"Hey, Atta!" Evan meets my gaze. He's spotted me and he's headed this way, expecting my answer.

Chapter Nine

I ready my fingers on our back-and-forth paper conversation. I can hand the paper over as is and leave without saying anything to Evan. That's what I decide to do when Robyn begins leading Diana and I out to the fields.

Evan spots the note in my hand and playfully pulls it from my grasp as he follows behind me. I lift my hand trying to fabricate a natural response. A courtly wave is enough for him to leave content, without a word. Awkward encounter avoided. Thankfully.

I can't help but feel bothered by what Tyler said to Ben before the race. Ben is keeping some sort of secret.

Internally, I've already decided. I need to know more about Bennette, the girl Ben is supposedly dating. But more than that, I need to know what Tyler meant when he said "Bennette could find out what Ben did with Corky." Ben has always stood on the highest of pedestals in my mind, so allowing my perception of his character to be shattered just by something Tyler said in passing won't do. I needed real evidence. Ben had dated a lot, but he'd never dated multiple girls at a time. Not while in a relationship. Simply hearing Tyler allude to such a thing makes anger bubble inside of me.

With so many unknowns, this shouldn't be my main concern right now, but I was finding it hard to separate Ben in the eighties with my partner at the Bureau. Alternate reality or not, shouldn't they be the same person?

THE NEXT MORNING I WAKE TO THE PLASTIC ALARM BOX vibrating on the dresser next to my bed. I made sure to set it the night before so that I have time to tame both sides of my hair before Diana arrives, unlike yesterday.

Today is the day I go along with it all, request a class schedule, navigate eighties high school, and hopefully find some answers, as I see no other option at this point.

I pull out the dresser drawers like a mad woman looking for something decent to wear. My options prove to be disappointing until I pull out the bottom drawer and unwrap a handful of Tootsie Rolls from my mass collection. I'm as giddy as a capricious child popping them into my dry mouth.

I find a jean skirt, boots, and a warm white sweater before heading to the bathroom to brush out my hair knowing full well I'm not going to find a straightener in this era.

"Erica, are you down here?" I call out from the bathroom door after hearing someone walk down the hallway. I brighten at the sight of my mother looking like a fresh-faced teen as she peeps into the bathroom. The brunette shine of her hair is incredible and each set of curls is its own defined slide as if she's mastered Hollywood waves. She adjusts her teal cheerleading skirt in the mirror next to me and begins brushing her eyelashes with mascara.

"You don't need a ride today do you?"

"Diana comes every day, right?" I ask.

She pauses the brush movement looking up through her eyelids in confusion and opts for a nod.

"Cool. Yeah, I'll ride with her."

"You want some help with your hair?" she offers. I accept and she smiles an evil smile, the way a mother does when a child agrees to their master plan. Hardly surprising, considering her usual mother role seems to be translating quite well to this sister character.

She begins flipping and teasing the front section of my hair where eighties bangs should be. It hurts and part of me wants to tower over her small 5'1" frame and threaten her with my fists.

"Now it's fixed." She's proud and glowing and the spark in her young eyes is something I haven't seen in many years, so I hold back my hairstyle-based anger. She's the older sister trying to pull me in with vacuum-like suction to get me to spend more time with her.

I've felt it since the first night here.

"I saw you at the parking lot yesterday. Were you there for Ben or Tyler?"

"I guess both."

"So Ben then," she says with a knowing wink. She teases my hair some more and hands me a tube of pink lipstick. "Try this. I think it will look cute with your outfit."

Afterwards, I make my way to the kitchen to shuffle through the newspaper stack on the counter, eager to find the *Denver Post* I wasn't able to finish a couple of days ago.

Grandma Marcie walks in and adjusts the crooked powder blue framed goose clock on the wall. She fumbles around the kitchen until she finds a jar of brown sugar and I can't help but stare. I can't wrap my mind around thinking of Grandma Marcie as "Mom." She's too young to resemble any sort of grandma but I still couldn't deny my own reality.

Erica's shift from mother to sister was easier to accept. Our relationship was already closer to a big sister type of relationship, but Grandma Marcie was always going to be Grandma Marcie, no matter how fresh her skin glowed or how dark and vibrant her hair was.

I would just have to be careful not to call her Grandma in this universe. I wouldn't be able to call her Mom, but Marcie would do.

The room begins to smell of hot porridge. I spot February 2nd's

Denver Post in the stack of papers at the island counter, then make my way back to the table to do some research and drool over the bowl Marcie just placed in front of me. A huge cloud of steam releases in waves, causing me to spend most of my time cooling off the food instead of reading.

I try to get some reading in during the commute with Diana as she floats Depeche Mode's song lyrics in my ear, scanning through unimportant articles like the song of the week, "Amanda" by Boston, and a full-page article about PepsiCo negotiating with Moscow to open up a hundred new Pizza Hut restaurants in the Soviet Union all while I search for the Sheriden article with the new "W" logo from the other day. It was here somewhere.

"Reading the paper today?" Diana says, interrupting her own song lyrics. "That's new." She's wearing a denim acid-washed skirt today too and she's lively, more chipper even than the day before. Could it be because her brother crushed her enemy in a dirt bike race not even twenty-four hours ago?

BARTERING WITH THE OFFICE RECEPTIONIST IS THE ONLY WAY TO get a copy of my schedule this morning before class. A lone wolf in the office, the receptionist insists on making a Valentine's themed bulletin board, having no interest in sparing any of that time to help me with my request to look through the schedule files. So I offer my height in exchange, insisting she search through the filing cabinet as I hang the string of Valentine's Day hearts across the top of the board.

The red painted eagle on the wall stares back at me through the large set of windows as I walk out of the office with my class list in hand. Most of the students I pass on the way to first period Chemistry look like they've lived through some stuff, be it the clothing, cigarettes, or too much sunlight. I'm having a hard time accepting their high school status. The same goes for the students sitting at barstool chairs along a half-moon desk surrounding the teacher's experiment station in my first period of the day.

I find an empty seat near half-filled beakers that tempt me a few feet away and I can't help but feel a lurking sense of confinement. This part of my life has been completed; so why is it that I'm forcing myself back into a classroom?

"Cuz it's filled with perms and mullets this time. Obviously worth a do-over." I mock my own doubts, knowing this is where the people I know are and there's nothing outside of this town for me right now, until I figure out how to get back to the future, anyway.

The boy next to me has to nudge me in the side when the teacher calls "Atta Atkinson" during roll call. It takes his nudge for me to realize they have me listed under my mother's maiden name rather than Suarez—another fringe benefit that comes along with this parallel universe time travel package.

The newspaper fits well enough under the table, stretched out across my legs, so I read through the entire business section to confirm that I really can't find the "W" article. The date on the front page is the 2nd. That's the right date, so where's the page? I must've dropped it on the way out or maybe it was taken from the stack?

With no luck, I turn to the main headline of the sports section. The section highlights thirty-two-year-old, Pro-Golfer, Robert Schills' career and an announcement that he'll be retiring early from golf at the end of the year, with the article quoting him saying, "I've had a good run throughout the years. Now it's time for me to transition golf back to the hobby it started as, using it for personal and business relation-ships, rather than competition. I'm looking forward to relaxing on the course from now on."

How interesting. A man retiring early from a career that pays him extremely well for swinging a tiny ball with a club. I continue reading, curious as to why he's retiring so early, and hear the faint sound of the teacher instructing the class.

Pop. BANG!

My knees knock the underside of the desk in shock as the rest of the class claps for the chemical explosion. The shock surges when I spot Ben at the end of the table clapping along with the rest of the students as Mr. Davis continues pouring new liquids into beakers and mixing them for a new reaction. This means yesterday's search for Ben was a complete waste. All I had to do was make it to my first period class and I would've found him.

My attention shifts to the chemical show and Ben's animated reactions to the teacher mixing solutions. He sits in all black, hiding under a white ball cap as his serious expression fades into a smile with each chemical reaction.

I'm sure my face is doing the same. These chemical combinations react like small bombs and turn into rolling sheets of foam. A few bangs and blasts have already brought me a few inches off my seat. But the real entertainment comes from the chemistry teacher who is experiencing the most excitement. He knows he's captivated even the most indifferent students, Ben included, and he'll need to wipe the pride off of his face soon before he transforms into a mad scientist.

"Alright, everyone, that's it for today. Assembly's in ten minutes. Feel free to leave early and get good seats," Mr. Davis says, cleaning the last two beakers off the table. He waves us out the door.

A few students stake out spots in the hallway and the rest head toward the gym. I follow, shoving my newspaper on top of the lockers, since I still haven't figured out the lock code and I'm not sure if I ever will. I've tried all my passwords, even childhood ones, with no luck.

Ben continues to keep his distance from me, as if he knows I want to walk right up next to him and chat. He's not wrong. I always caught up to him around the office back in Non-80s-Land, bringing up work-related stuff, his game night losing streak, or requesting he teach me a dance move—he was always coming up with new moves that I would foolishly try to replicate and fail at. My failed dance moves made him laugh though, so I continued asking.

Diana shows up not long after I take a seat by myself in the empty space on the right side of the massive wooden gym bleachers. We listen as a brawl breaks out in the corner locker room between two boys.

Diana just shrugs and Erica spots us a few seconds later, bringing half the cheerleading team with her, including the two cheerleaders Diana pointed out yesterday, Bennette and Corky, who plop themselves in the seats right in front of us next to Erica.

"Hi, Diana!" Tyler calls out as he makes his way up the bleacher steps. He's cleaned up his look today with a white collared button-up underneath a dark leather jacket. Diana sends him a strong middle finger message back as he forges a space between a group of basketball boys, seemingly unfazed by her response.

I watch as Ben seats himself next to Bennette. Naturally, it makes sense he sits next to her. She is his girlfriend after all. As he does so, he looks uncomfortably up at me, as if sitting this close to me is a problem for him. He puts his arm around her and squeezes her closer into his side. It's not what I'd expect of someone who's trying to find their way back to the modern world but thanks to Bennette, Ben and I will be within chatting distance. The seating situation might give me another chance to verify whether or not he's experienced time travel and Diana can act as a buffer in case I try something fatal.

Evan and a group of basketball boys choose the cozy open spot next to me, making me curse myself for not employing a neighbor to occupy that seat. I try my best to hold a smile and subside the bug eyes begging to pop out in frustration beneath my cool, calm potato. The man wearing Bottle-Caps-candy grape, who speaks primarily Philly jargon, continues to wedge his way in closer, which wouldn't be a problem and all, if he wasn't trying to date me. What if he brings up the note I didn't respond to? It's all impromptu from there.

"You should be out there with us, Ben." Evan leans into Ben and Bennette's space below.

At this moment, I realize how their couple name would simply be Bennette. Ben and Bennette. She's just a Ben with a fancy female -ette added. Does that complicate things for them? Do they both look in the same direction when someone starts saying one of their names? I knew two Taylors who dated. They seemed to make it work. The back of her letterman's jacket says Chen. Maybe she even goes by that when they're together. Bennette Chen.

Ben's display doesn't look like an act. Bennette's beautiful. Of course he looks like he enjoys sitting next to her. But why is Ben ignoring me? Could he be acting? Could it be because he knows something I don't know—like that there is a threat brought on by time travel and he's worried that if I mention it I'll run into more trouble? So he's choosing to avoid me until it's safe to talk about it? It was a stretch, but anything was possible.

"But Ben, I still don't get why you won't just show up to practice. Coach would let you start if you came back today and played the last month," Evan continues.

"That's what I told him," Tyler butts in from across the stair rail. "We need you, man."

"I'm not playing. You're doing fine without me," Ben manages.

"Fine isn't a State Championship."

"I already had this conversation with your dad, Tyler. Don't push it."

Tyler's face becomes contemplative. He nods instead of answering back.

Another mullet-haired boy, who looks like he's at least twenty-five, with hair as light as dough and skin leathery from the sun, starts riling up the entire student body with erratic-style host behavior.

In my world, in Non-80s-Land, Tyler and Ben were acquaintances through basketball and Ben spent a reasonable amount of time with him since Diana dated Tyler back in 2010. Ben quit basketball his senior year, but I never thought anything of it back then. He never said much about it, and I often tried to keep my distance during high school, so Diana wouldn't accuse me of choosing him over her.

I lean into Diana, taking up whisper mode while covering my mouth with my hand.

"What's Tyler and Ben's relationship like?" I ask.

"Tyler's dad has a shop so he spends most of his time working on his bike at Tyler's house. The last few months he's been hanging out there after school even though Tyler's at practice. I haven't seen him at home much, especially since he flipped out on you. But you know that. I think he's avoiding you."

"So he spends time at Tyler's house while Tyler's at practice?" I whisper. "That doesn't make sense and why is he avoiding me? If he's avoiding me, he must have a good reason, right?"

"I can't think of any other reason. You told me not to be surprised if he pretends you don't exist," Diana says.

"I said that? When? What happened between us?"

"You're asking me? A few weeks ago you said you'd pissed him off and got all tight-lipped when I asked questions. You got all surreptitious and said you'd promised him you wouldn't say anything. Why would you ask me? Are you now willing to tell me what's going on between you two?"

"I still don't know," I say, acting as if I understand why I would have said that.

"Still don't know? You know what...as long as the secret's not you two getting together, I don't care. And I know it's not that since he hasn't talked to you in weeks," she says.

Nothing makes sense. This eighties past and the weeks prior to my arrival collide heavily with the status of my relationships in Non-80s-Land. I grip the bleacher seat tighter. There's something I'm missing.

Our whispers become inaudible over the ramped-up bustle from the crowd. Evan abandons the seat next to me to join his team, and Tyler literally lassos freshmen out of the stands with a lariat rope from the gym floor, managing to capture one student with difficulty and the crowd soaks it up with laughter.

"Tyler sure looks like he's missing you," Diana says to Ben, who's now one of the only guys left in our section. I look over to see Tyler playing up the dramatics, gazing longingly in Ben's direction with doe eyes.

"He's just trying to make a point. He wants me out there," Ben says. My laugh gets an eye roll from Ben.

Why is my existence such a threat to him right now? The built up emotion of his distance hits me like a nighttime cold. I feel the train of emotion about to derail but this time in the form of anger. Not even a bottle of NyQuil could ease the agitation. I'm already feeling dizzy and drowsy from the confusion as is.

I've spent too many years by his side, experiencing the hardest of days on the job with him and yet this person in front of me is giving me nothing. If he's doing this on purpose it must be for a reason. A reason that he thinks is for my benefit? I calm myself thinking these things in quiet contemplation. That's what Ben would do. He's calculative. Surely it's for my benefit and there's something I'm missing. Maybe he senses a time travel threat and this is his way of protecting me. The bubbling undercurrent of confusion makes me want to have a confrontation right here and now, but I hesitate and contemplate a little longer.

Erica, Bennette and the other seven matching cheerleaders in white skirts and teal-striped vests stand upright with tightly closed fists on the gym floor in front of us. Like dominoes falling, Erica spears her teal pom-pom into Bennette's back with her fist and the chain reaction continues until they've made a collective pom-pom fence with their arms. A wave of teal and cherry red isosceles triangles fan out from underneath white pleats across the gym floor as they pivot and purl.

"I can see Bennette's undershorts." Diana leans into me this time. We've become those girls who nearly sit on each other's laps to have a conversation.

"It looks like her skirt got stuck up in her waistband. Yikes," I reply, silently thanking Bennette for a distraction.

They forge a three-layer pyramid stack and then disband into three sets stacked on each other's shoulders as if they're about to play pool chicken. Bennette lands the stunt with her skirt caught in her underwear lining and Erica runs over like The Flash, to help her. Luckily, only those with eyes glued to Bennette's mini-skirt are the only ones to notice, and Erica's able to end the performance with a front-back handspring as she flashes her large doe eyes to the crowd, as perfect as polished malachite, upon landing.

The basketball boys take their seats just before the cheerleaders make their way up the bleachers. "Bennette's all good now. She's been fixed." Tyler turns Ben's ball cap backward as he says it.

"Thanks, Tyler. She can pull anything off though, even that," Ben says, defending Bennette as she walks up to join him.

She hears him and by the way she plants her lips on his after, I'd say she's pleased. He kisses her back with passion, nothing but frankness in his mannerism and it's at this point when I know. He's definitely not acting. There's no time travel threat. I think she really is his girlfriend in the eighties and his actions have nothing to do with protecting me.

I turn to catch Corky's reaction, knowing she's the subject of Ben's secret according to Tyler. Corky sweetly smiles to herself at the pair's public affection. She either really enjoys being the third wheel, or is one of those people who receives joy from other people's joy. How can I suspect something's up with Ben and Corky when Corky and Bennette act so amicable?

Evan finds his seat next to me, bringing Tyler and the basketball boys, who've reached a new level of volume, as if the gym is their jungle and they plan to shake coconuts from trees with their hooting and hollering. It only worsens as students are being recruited from the stands to throw tin pies filled with whipped cream at other students' faces. Corky makes her way to the gym floor to complete her volunteer service and ends up with a face full of whipped cream. She shows all signs of the extrovert type and even pulls off a few toe touches and a side hurdler for the crowd to show she's unfazed by the mess.

The gym is a circus, but my focus is narrowly zoned-in on Ben. The way he turns his head toward Bennette to whisper something soft in her ear, the way he interacts with Tyler as if he's a friend but also in some ways a mentor, and the way he drums his fingers on his knee as if he truly wishes to throw a ball through the hoop yet firm in his decision to not wear a team jersey and take the basketball team to state. I take it all in, focusing on the way he processes the room around him. The more I watch the more I can see it.

This Ben isn't the Ben I left that night. Is it possible he's just Ben in an alternate universe, younger, unknowing and living life the way anyone would if they were born in the eighties? The same way my mother doesn't understand I'm from the future, sandwiched into a past decade because of some unexplainable reason, Ben also doesn't understand. He's unaware just like the rest of them.

Eighties Ben is angry at me for some other reason and that reason is most likely because of his secret about his relationship with Corky and Bennette. The two girls who seem so opposite, yet tight as a knotted rope. And then it hits me. I know just what my next move will be. I lean back into Diana and speak with a whisper.

"I have an idea."

Chapter Ten

"No. Atta. You can't!" Diana's response to my plan is interwoven in laughter. "I won't let you. This is your dumbest idea yet. Their season's halfway over and you're the least flexible person I know." She continues laughing, likely envisioning me alongside Corky and Bennette lifting my leg in the air with little success.

"Oh, come on. I can't be that bad at it."

"Yes, yes, you can. Cheerleading is not for your kind." Diana looks like she wants to give me even more reasons why I shouldn't go through with my idea and join the cheer squad to get closer to Bennette and Corky and her tone tells me she's just quoting reasons I've previously given, like I've listed them off more than a few times. "What happened to you? You always give Erica a hard time every year when she asks you to join," she continues. "Joining the team just to have an in with Corky isn't like you at all. Why would you need an in with Corky in the first place?"

"What if I am good at it?"

"But you're not good at it. I've seen you dance. Erica will have an aneurysm if you tell her. You're the last person she would expect to join. In fact, you're the last person I'd expect! Are you sure this isn't a weird way of getting revenge on her? Are you going to join and then mess up her routine? Did she mess with your cassette tapes again?"

I bite my lip knowing cheerleading is out of character for me in any alternate dimension. I wouldn't have been caught dead cheerleading back in high school nor had any interest in it as an adult, but circumstances are different here. How else am I supposed to get close enough to Bennette and Corky to figure out what's going on with Ben? And I was flexible enough. Special agent training required serious physical strength. I'd been in the best shape of my life for the last five years. I would catch on quickly. Cheerleading shouldn't be a problem for someone who takes jiu-jitsu classes on the side to keep fit for the job, right?

"It's not revenge. I promise. I just need to figure out what's going on between Ben, Corky, and Bennette."

"Wait, what?" she whispers. "Something's going on between them? Is that why Ben's not talking to you because you suspect something between Corky and Ben?"

"I don't know. That's what I need to figure out. You could join me," I whisper back, offering to include her in my scheme.

"I could just ask Ben, you know. I doubt Corky will divulge all of her secrets to you just because you joined the team. And no thanks, if the cheers were done to Def Leppard and AC/DC I might consider it, but until then I'll pass," she says with a satisfied smile on her face.

"You could ask Ben. But if he's avoiding me, do you really think he'll tell you what his deal is when he knows you'll just turn around and tell me?" I look over at Ben to make sure he's still distracted by Bennette, which he is. "I can at least try to weasel my way into a conversation and see if one of them will spill, plus Erica's cheer captain and I'm almost positive she'll let me join."

Diana keeps her voice at a low whisper. "Yeah, you're right. He never tells me anything anyway. You know I'm going to make fun of you from the sidelines, right?"

"I don't doubt it," I say, laying my hands to the side in an attempt to once again grip the wood bleacher's edge bruised from years of bums encroaching on it.

The assembly skits continue and as I stare into the open gym filled with scattered students, a thick block of a hand lands over my knuckles and then curls its fingers between mine. My insides choke all at once.

These hands aren't Diana's. Her hands are thin and delicate, not massive and bony, and sending a flare-like distress signal up my veins to my heart. I'm frozen, unable to look to my side to see whose hand is currently dominating mine. I have a heightened urge to slap it with my other hand, but I'm not here to make a scene, so I rub my free hand back and forth against the wood grain seat full of pencil markings to contain myself.

My lower lip clings to my teeth with intense indecision, as I debate fight or flight mode. I manage the courage to roll my eyes to the side until I find a familiar chalky soda pop colored tee. It's Evan. Evan has hijacked my hand.

If only I was well versed in quietly escaping awkward situations. That would come in more handy at this moment than what the FBI in-service trainings had taught me. I stretch my fingers in his palm until he lets them free, then smile as I stretch my arms wide behind both his and Diana's backs, exaggerating my yawn to really sell it. Thankfully, the assembly is dismissed before I need to explain and I cling on to Diana with a life-saving grip as students trickle down the steps like we're all leaving the grounds of a mosh pit.

"Atta!" Evan inadvertently brushes up against my back, allowing him to conveniently slap the shared note back into my hand from behind. "Your doodles were pretty, but you forgot to answer me and give me a time," he says, sliding through a few bodies to try and face me. I turn my head to find him and my lips unintentionally squish up against his back, staining his shirt with the tinted lip stain Erica gifted me this morning.

"Oh yeah," I manage, staring at the pink smudge on his shirt with a weak gaze, unsure of how to let him down with all these people sandwiched up against us. He's going to be upset enough about the coming rejection, whenever I get to it—no need to tip the cow with news of a stained shirt too.

He's sucked back into the crowd and I swallow embarrassment for not breaking whatever he thinks we have off and for the stain he'll find later.

BURR OAK AND KENTUCKY COFFEE TREES GREET US AT THE TURN before Diana pulls up to Marcie's freshly cut lawn outside of their two-story home. Since Pops is currently living on a trail on the tallest mountain in Africa, she must have mowed today or had one of the boys do it.

Diana's car tires screech against the curb.

"Good luck with your cheerleading manipulation speech. Call me after you get your sister's reaction. I want all the details. Oh, and ask your mom if you can spend the night this weekend." Diana pulls out a pick from her glove box and starts combing her short curls.

"You going somewhere after this?" I ask as she checks herself out in the sun visor mirror.

"Taking my sis to see Mom at Miner's Diner. We get free apple pie and ice cream on her break today. You'll come over after school tomorrow, right?"

"Sure," I say, waving her off with a carefree motion before she speeds off like a comet disappearing in a noisy blink.

"Excuse me, miss."

I turn around to see who's calling me.

"Special Agent Suarez, was it?" The neighbor cop who lent me a ride just a couple of days ago approaches me in uniform.

"How have you been?" I say holding both elbows with my hands, arms crossed in a comfort position. Diana's comment about Officer Berrett and his escapades with girls in the mountains creeps into my mind and I mentally slap myself for finding him even slightly attractive upon our first meeting.

"I've been well. Tell me, are you on assignment here? You looked like two teenagers riding up in that car just now."

"Oh yes, I am. That's my friend. She's a bit reckless." I let out a nervous laugh. It was going to be hard to maintain a double life here without curious neighbors finding out I actually attend high school and that my FBI badge won't show up on the Bureau registry if anyone tries looking.

"Have you lived here long? My wife and I moved in a few weeks ago."

"I hope you like it here," I say, not answering his question.

If this cop was interested in me, I needed to keep my distance. Now didn't seem like the time to be involved with the neighbor who was actively looking to cheat on his wife.

"Did you get to where you needed to be the other day? I heard there was an incident with Colorado's infamous crime family in addition to the Hee murder that day. The details aren't yet out, but the Hee murder report says it was multiple stab wounds," he says. He must be interested in more information related to the case, otherwise, he wouldn't be continuing this conversation right when I felt like it'd hit a dead end.

"Multiple stab wounds," I mutter under my breath in anger. Death is death, but slower forms of death are the crueler kind. Watching that Pop-Tart-vomit-inducing video of this very form of torture made me come up with this conclusion. "Just like Marigold," I let slip from my mouth, quiet enough I doubt the neighbor cop even heard.

Despite the many unpleasant things I've witnessed in the last few years, I catch myself in a zoned out daze recalling the facial expression of a man with the greatest possible amount of fear in his eyes, still alive and unable to speed up the inhumane process being forced upon him as each person took turns stabbing and removing parts of him one at a time. My head shakes back and forth in opposition in front of Officer Berrett.

"Yes, thanks for the ride. It seems I owe you one." I spit the words out quickly and matter-of-factly after realizing my commenting on a case is better left inside my head while standing in front of this cop. Even though his kindness was greatly appreciated the other day, I needed him to stay out of my business, so I leave it at that.

"By any chance have you been introduced to Deanna?" Officer Berrett asks, boosting his chin so that he stands in front of me with a new elevated posture. His reversal of an expression, now mirroring Rolf from *The Sound of Music* after he greets the Captain and offers a Nazi salute, concerns me.

"I have not. Is she your wife?" I wait for an explanation.

"No. She's just an acquaintance who's familiar with a few people over at the Bureau. Have you been following the Hee case? Our Golden department was involved the other day and I wondered if you've touched it since it was moved from local police to the Denver Bureau," he says.

This time I shoot him a wide smile—the complete opposite of what I would typically do in this situation—encouraging him to provide more details, as many details as possible in fact. The idea that I could use this opportunity to learn more about the Denver Bureau—my workplace—before my time sounds too good to pass up.

"I'm not at liberty to discuss," I say, trying to speak instead with my eyes. I want them to say "speak freely though."

His lips squirm in place and then rev back up as if he understands.

"Bill Hee, the director of the EPA was killed yesterday after his visit to Coors Brewery. According to the report, a suspect has not been named so far. They're interviewing anyone on site that day since it happened as he was leaving the factory. It's going to be an extensive investigation I bet, so if you're involved, I wish you the best of luck," he says, swapping his motorcycle helmet for the police hat.

"Are any of your officers still involved," I reply, trying to get as much out of him as possible.

"Some of them are. Yeah. They've met in Denver for the last two days now. I know you can't say much, but since you're my neighbor and all, I couldn't help but wonder about your involvement." I look over at our muted-sand-colored house to find a purple Buick sliding into our driveway, eggy fumes emoting from its muffler and I get the urge to end this conversation before it turns into some flirtation plot to get me to ride with him into the mountains.

"I can't say much about the brewery, but I'll be in the area on assignment for a while," I respond. I can feel my FBI badge carving a cavity into my stomach the way it's tucked into my denim skirt waistband, reminding me that my badge carries no authority in this alternate universe. I give my side a little wiggle so that it rests into a more comfortable position. I'm sure it looks unprofessional, but was professionalism even regarded in this decade? His tan pants are clinging to his thighs with magnetic hold, so I don't know who's more unprincipled here, me or him? Anyone willing to wear those shouldn't be able to call themselves a respectable government official.

"Since I'm obligated to keep my status a secret, I must request that you don't mention what I'm doing here to anyone." I add. He didn't owe me anything; on the contrary, I owed him, and also forfeited secrecy in exchange for a motorcycle ride, but I need him to stay out of my business.

"Of course," he says, sliding an unbuttoned shirt sleeve up his arm so that it exposes his forearm as he turns to the sound of crunching grass.

I spot a familiar inked outline just below his elbow as he scratches the area. Officer Berrett has a tattoo. And it's not just any tattoo. I know this symbol well. I confirmed it from Google's search results and copied the design multiple times on the back of the note Evan passed me. The Marigold Company insignia—crystal shaped petals, same emblem border and all—is inked on his skin.

Officer Berrett belongs to Marigold!

If Officer Berrett is involved, Marigold must have had its foot in the Golden Police Department all these years. And Officer Berrett mentioned he has connections at the Bureau. Has Marigold had a tight hold on my department since the eighties?

The heavy realization that Marigold has been dropped on me like a nuclear bomb not once but twice now disturbs me. This time it's with blaring warning sirens in the form of body ink, alerting me that I must do everything I can to stay away from the neighbor cop.

I suppose as long as Officer Berrett doesn't suspect me of anything, I might have a chance at surviving the rest of the week in this alternate universe.

Chapter Eleven

When I enter the house—after Officer Berrett's wife swooped in and saved me from having any further conversation with her husband—I find all of my family members huddled in the living room around a young woman who looks to be in her forties with the largest hair circumference on this side of Denver. They surround the buffalo plaid couch where she stands.

Everything about the mystery visitor is concealed by my family's lack of care for personal space and only the couch and two butterscotch butterfly wall hangings on the wood-paneled wall stare back at me. Davy moves aside and reveals her feathery champaign curls and steeply arched eyebrows. I know this woman.

Great Aunt Jevie, whose citrusy scent has taken over the living room, paves her way through Erica's younger brothers and rushes at me with open arms.

It's really her, as if she'd experienced rapid-fire de-aging since the last time I'd visited her in Florida for Grandma Marcie's seventieth beach birthday party in Non-80s-Land. Vacationing with three old ladies in oversized sun hats, spending hours attempting to catch sight of crocodiles, was more exhausting than you'd think. Jevie had run off to Florida with her third husband sometime in the late eighties and in my mother's words "wouldn't come back until we fly her back in a casket."

"Atta girl! So glad you're here." Her bowl-shaped hair grazes my chin. "I missed you!" As quickly as I fall into her embrace, she dashes off to her significantly more pale sister to catch up on whatever sisters catch up on in their forties.

I watch Erica flee the living room after leaping over a series of takedown attempts from Steven. My young uncles resume wrestling each other in the hallway. Davy manages a reversal, gaining control over Steven and I hop over the action, using the wall for support in pursuit of Erica. I need to catch her before she makes her nightly call to Greg.

Erica's wall is sprinkled with printed photos and polaroids, a pig calendar, and three cubby holes filled with vinyl records. To no surprise, her room's much girlier than mine, and the twenty-some pastel stuffed bears sitting atop the dresser—fit for a Brach's conversation heart color pallet—attest to that fact. Erica changes out of her cheerleading uniform into an oversized red *Ghostbusters* tee and baggy flannel pajama bottoms. Her white phone attached to a landline wall outlet rests on her duvet waiting for the nightly call with her boyfriend. I step into her space.

"Erica, I have a question for you, and before you say no I just need you to hear me out," I blurt out, realizing I'm using the same language that I would when trying to persuade her to do something for me as her daughter. Her face looks freshly rinsed and her berry lips smile back at me in surprise.

"Atta," she sighs while maintaining a smirk. "I'm not going to prank call Ben, so you can deliver a coded message and get him to spill whether or not he's with Bennette or Corky. I'm not trying that again."

"I asked you to prank call Ben? Does that mean you know what happened between Bennette, Ben, and Corky?" Why hadn't I thought to ask her in the first place? She's close enough with both girls that it's no surprise she would know something.

"Yeah, you asked me to do that. It's not like you don't know that. Did you already forget that it blew up in your face?

"I guess. Ben won't speak to me."

"Aren't you not speaking to him either after he sent Tyler to our house with a homemade ashtray and a cigar, claiming you made it in ceramics class when Dad opened the door? Ben knew it was guaranteed to get you grounded."

"So you know what's going on between Corky and Ben then?

"I already told you Bennette and Corky are acting normal as always. Nothing's going on between them. You act like you don't know anything tonight."

"You sure nothing's going on?" I ask.

"Don't you think you're misunderstanding? He's probably just mad because you prank called. You might have also struck a nerve pretending to be a college basketball media rep and prodding him with questions right after he quit the basketball team. Or it could have been that you had the gall to say 'these tickets are yours only after you answer the age-old question, Brunettes or Blondes?' I could hear him yelling your name before you hung up without his answer."

"I don't think so. I think I knew something about his relationship with Bennette and Corky?" I say as Erica finishes off tying a low French braid that sprouts a fluffy fountain-like curl where the elastic is tied.

"So you've said. You've been suspecting them of something since you overheard him on the line at Diana's house. You wouldn't tell me what you heard the first time and now you're not even sure what you heard." She stares longingly at the phone block on her bed before dragging it by the cord down to the floor where her socks dig into the cinnamon carpet.

"Okay, well..." I need to hold the conversation a little longer before she dials Greg's number. "I actually came to ask you if I could join the cheer team," I say with an ounce of reluctance.

Is this really a good idea? I don't plan to stay here much longer if I can help it and "perky cheerleader" wasn't exactly listed in my federal resume.

"Did someone slip you something? Why are you asking me all these weird questions?" She's chewing on the inside of her cheek, more satisfied with my request than she is worried if I'm intoxicated or not.

"No one slipped me anything and I'm much stronger and more flexible than you think. I know it might be too late in the season, but you're the cheer captain so you can make it happen, right?"

Erica leaves me hanging. Her devilish smile tells me she already knows the answer. She's just holding out to enjoy my anticipation, whether it be because I've finally succumbed to her master plan and she wants to savor the moment envisioning me jumping, kicking, and cheering.

"We need a base. You can be a base."

Although my cheer terminology knowledge isn't great, I grasp this. She's saying yes. No request has come this easy between me and my mother before in my life. I'm capable of standing with a bunch of other girls while holding someone's leg.

"I'll have to run it by our coach and the girls. I'll give her a call tonight. But I swear if you wake up sober and take this all back, I will unwind all of the tape from your 38 Special cassette. If you join, you're stuck with us for the rest of the season."

I'll be gone in a week, I tell myself.

"I won't back out. I promise."

"Oh, and one other requirement."

"What's that?" I say flipping through all the possible requests she might have for me in my mind.

"You've got to get a perm."

⁂

I eye the sock basket in the corner where a partially filled out crossword puzzle sits at the top of the large mound of socks. It's been two and a half days since I've had access to my planner and my hand misses jotting down important notes and keeping track of my daily schedule; though my schedule isn't nearly as booked as it was in Non-80s-Land and my new daily activities seem silly in comparison. Still, I would feel more myself if I could at least jot down my eighties class schedule and keep track of the things happening in this alternate universe, including where I stand with Ben on any given day and keep track of any potential Marigold findings on top of what Officer Berrett's revealed.

I grab the partially filled out crossword puzzle from the sock pile while Erica gives the cheer coach a ring.

When I pop back into Erica's room she gives me the good news. Her coach is out for two weeks on vacation but doesn't mind if I join the team as long as Erica's confident I won't ruin the routines. Erica's confident. I, however, am not.

Together, Erica and I find Aunt Jevie in the kitchen, deep in conversation with Marcie discussing the game plan for tomorrow's move. Marcie will help Jevie pack, so that by the time her third husband Gary flies in, they can load the trailer together and drive both cars with the rest of her belongings back to their new place in Florida.

"Hello, Sweethearts." Jevie turns around and pulls us both into a warm hug.

"How long are you here for Aunt Jevie?" I can tell the hairstylist manipulation tactic is about to be actualized. Erica's going to have my hair in tightly wound plastic perm rods before the end of the night.

"So Auntie, could you spare some time before you leave?" Erica folds her fingers into a prayer-style beg then asks Aunt Jevie if she'll be able to perm my hair before she leaves. I can hear Marcie's jaw clank against the floor on the other side of the kitchen.

"I should have some time tonight. I just need to stop by my house to get some supplies. Marcie, would you mind if I permed Atta's hair while we watch MTV?" Jevie asks her while fumbling around in her purse for her car keys.

Marcie rolls her eyes and walks to the fridge. She pulls out the green grapes and tosses them into two ceramic bowls with a yellow floral pattern ring.

"Does it have to be MTV? *MacGyver* has a new episode tonight. How about that?"

"You promised me we'd watch MTV, so I can show you the sexy Huey Lewis I keep telling you about. His song from *Back to the Future* was number one a couple of years ago and it played all the time. You've seen *Back to the Future*, right?"

"No Jevie. I haven't seen *Back to the Future*, but since you're my guest we can watch whatever you want," Marcie says, upping the sass while admitting defeat.

Erica nudges her elbow into my side, confirming I've caught their sportive sisterly squabble too.

"I'm heading out now. If I can rent *Back to the Future* on my way out we'll watch that, Marcie," Jevie says. Marcie shoos her off with a wave and Jevie exits the kitchen, passing the brick firewood stove platform on the far side of the living room.

"Atta's getting a perm?" Marcie says reaching for the *Gilligan's Island* ceramic cookie jar and pulling out a Twix bar. She places it between her teeth, unopened, and moves a glass dish of mushroom-colored goo into the oven, as if she's preparing to let loose a little tonight with Jevie.

"She's joining the cheer team," Erica says. This time the Twix shoots from her mouth as her jaw falls back to the floor.

Erica wastes no time before putting me through her nightly TV stretching routine while Jevie's out to get hair supplies. I feel cracked. The stretching position Erica has me in sends daggers of pain up my leg and my dogs are seriously barking. She maneuvers me into multiple split stretches and one, specifically focused on stretching the groin area, makes me question this plan in the first place. If this is how it's going to be from now on, I'm going to have to harness the powers of Gumby and somehow suffer through these muscle-snapping splits.

Jevie tiptoes through the door with a paper bag full of curlers and chemicals, prompting an end to Erica's stretching session. Erica then follows Jevie into the kitchen where my insanely young-looking grandmother uses her oven mitts to slide the kitchen towel over and pull her casserole out of the oven, before walking over to the table to drop it off on a crochet pot holder. She surveys the table setting and combs through her short dark curls after tossing the oven mittens next to the kitchen sink.

"Mom, is the food ready yet?" Davy yells for the third time now down the stairwell.

"It's out already. Can't you smell it?" Jevie yells back, walking into the family room so that Davy can hear. She sets her bags down next to the mid-century dark cherry hutch by the side wall. She's right. The steamy smell of a crispy grilled onion and creamy mushroom had traveled all throughout the first floor. If anything said "Dinner's ready" it was the new scent of the house.

The rest of the family trickles down the stairs while I still sit in a deep-seated split—a really horrible spot actually. Stuck and knowing what sensation is about to occur when I lift myself from the position, I almost wish to continue splitting here. I must get it over with quickly. I tell my legs to move, but I'm physically unable to until Marcie runs over and pulls me up in a swift snap motion. My legs meet each other and I bend over in quiet rage, feeling a lingering tearing sensation.

I'm the last to gather in the newly renovated kitchen, with a fancy popcorn ceiling and grand honey oak cabinet focal point. It feels like a completely separate entity in an entirely seventies-dressed home. The whites and creams and ivory rosebud drapes—fatter than my childhood pet pig—with silky bottom ruffles, don't qualify for newly renovated in my mind, but the eighties design is a decade upgrade in this household.

Marcie takes a seat next to Jevie, untying her apron in the process, and sets down a plate of warm butter rolls onto the floral tablecloth to go along with the casserole. I don't hesitate and grab a bubbly glazed roll before the others.

"Steven, how was wrestling today?" Marcie begins the dinner discussion ritual.

"I pinned Jeffrey and I'm working on a single leg takedown."

"That's a load of bull. Steven got pinned twice after pinning Jeff," Davy cuts in, shoving his older brother off the high tower of high-handedness.

"Thank you for that, Davy." Marcie sits on an endless plain of irritation as far as the eye can see with them. She turns to face me to disregard the conversation entirely. "How's Diana? I haven't seen her in a while. Tell her to come here more. You girls are always over at her place."

I shove another glorious roll into my mouth. I did spend quite a bit more time at her house, rather than my own, growing up. Most likely because she had an older brother who I found just as captivating. Mama Robyn and Grandma Harriet also wanted her home since Ben was always at practice, and Mama Robyn liked to have Diana around for company.

"I will, but she asked if I could stay over at her house this weekend." I clench my teeth waiting for an answer.

"I don't see why not. Just tell her to show her face over here more often. We miss you when you're not here."

"Don't forget you have a basketball game to cheer at this Saturday," Erica chimes in. This time with a satisfied grin.

Steven's the first one to look up from his plate as if he's heard me say milk now comes from cats. Davy joins him in disbelief.

"Did I hear that right? Steven, check my ear. Is it clogged with earwax? Did Erica just say that Atta is going to be cheering?"

"I heard it too."

"She's joining the team. You heard it right." Erica's words sound like a cheer wants to burst through them.

"What did you do with our sister?" Steven makes a shocked-Yoda-like sound.

"There's got to be something in it for her if she agreed to this. Is it a bet? Did they somehow incorporate chess into cheering, or do they play Rummikub during cheer breaks?" He knows me well. His jokes are on par. These things were more my level, but there was something in it for me, and in the same nerdy sense he was referring to—a mystery to be solved.

"Hey!" Erica slaps the raspberry red ball cap off of Davy's twiggy little head. "Atta wouldn't do that. You aren't doing this because of a bet, are you?" Erica turns to me with real signs of oncoming disappointment. Everyone's awaiting my answer.

I hold up my hands, surrendering.

"There is no bet."

AUNT JEVIE SEATS ME IN A FOLDING CHAIR IN FRONT OF THE vintage TV cabinet, whose antennas are longer than the TV itself, leaving me nine potted plants scattered on top to stare at, as she pulls back the accordion door curtain and tunes the cable dial. She picks out a strand of my naturally, mostly straight hair and begins rolling it up in a thick roller as she sings along to Loverboy playing on the television.

This feels like a historical moment. I'm watching, for the first time ever, music that played on MTV when MTV actually played music videos. Neon-colored cartoons transition each segment, and Marcie and Erica sit curled up together on the couch sharing a disgustingly vibrant brown, yellow, and orange knitted afghan that only the seventies could've produced. I feel unexpectedly warm, as if the coziest blanket has me wrapped up in a hug of comfort with all the women in my family gathered in this dim-lit living room.

"I mean they aren't The Rolling Stones but it's just so wonderful, isn't it?" Aunt Jevie says, looking for a positive response from her sister, Marcie.

"This Huey Lewis better have a really nice butt," Marcie says as Jevie inhales a long deep breath.

"Eww, Mom," Erica smacks her with the lace crochet pillow, and

Marcie gives her smoochy kisses as she leaves for her room to make her nightly call with Greg.

It takes Jevie rolling my entire head in rollers until Huey Lewis finally appears on screen. And when he does, Jevie does jumping jacks in celebration before pulling Marcie and I into a cha-cha train while his song "If This Is It" plays on the fuzzy and slightly pixilated TV screen.

"Atta, some rollers fell out!" Marcie says, breaking the train to fetch the small finger-trap-shaped rollers.

"I'll re-roll them. We got all evening, sis," Jevie says as we sit back down to re-roll the liberated hairs.

She pulls out a bottle of chemical treatment and hairspray from the paper bag on the floor. A bright red "Keep away from copper" warning shines against the steel bottle just below the "W" squiggle wave branding. The symbol stares back at me with a knowing look from its stamped position and I recognize it as the same symbol from the newspaper I'd read the other day, seated in the back of the older couple's car with their fluffy dogs. This symbol is the branding for the new company that the Sheriden Foundation had just acquired, according to the article.

Another Marigold reminder. The eighties seem to carry a few of them. A newspaper snippet, Officer Berrett and his tattoo, and even Aunt Jevie's hairspray can seem to have a relation. The Marigold symbol isn't the only logo associated with the Sheriden Foundation. How many other companies did they own and why hair chemicals? Did "W" make other products as well? The questions fire hard inside of me.

How was I going to fully understand Sheriden, Marigold, and now W's relationship, with only symbols and newspaper articles to go off of?

"Aunt Jevie, what brand is this?"

"Clean Wave," she says. "They're big in household and hair products. I have their dish soap and laundry detergent as well. I use everything. They just came out with a new instantaneous clean technology, so most of the hair products hold like steel until water's applied."

"Have you tried this before?" I ask, holding up the hairspray can.

"I tried it last week and my curls didn't move for hours. From a hairstylist's perspective it's a game changer."

So Marigold was connected to Clean Wave through the Sheriden Foundation. I would need to add this to my partially filled crossword book which now dubs as my planner and I would do so the second these heavy rollers left my head.

Finally, I could make a connection to a name I was familiar with. Sheriden had acquired Clean Wave. I recall the brand from the future. In fact, I'd used a Clean Wave product to spray the wad of gum off of the corded telephone in Pops' hidden room before coming here.

I wouldn't have recognized the branding though. It had been updated in the last decade at least. I don't know what the hairspray looked like in the future but I knew the cleaning product. It had a neon yellow-orange colored wrap and simple text. No squiggly "W" logo in sight.

"I read recently that they were acquired by the Sheriden Foundation in the paper. Do you know anything about the Sheriden Foundation?" I ask.

"The Sheriden Foundation? I've heard them talked about on the news, but I don't know much about them. Sorry," she says as Marcie walks back into the room with three whipped jello desserts on small plates with excessive cool whip.

"I thought we could use some orange fluff. Looks like you're finishing up." She hands me a plate and lays Jevie's down on the small square brick platform next to the wall.

"I know Erica's got a boyfriend. How's your dating life, Atta?" Jevie's finished applying the chemicals. So this is what she wants to do with me sitting here trapped in a heat cap. She wants the dirty details.

"There's not a lot of men in my life. Not much to tell," I say. And it was true. Most recently I took a leap with a guy who seemed promising due to his interest in Chris Farley and well, look how that one turned out.

That was the last date I had been on since Diana tried to set me up with Ben officially two years ago. He'd set the date and time according to his sister's wishes, then stood me up after forgetting it entirely and spending the evening looking for the best hamburger in Denver with three of our Ju Jitsu buddies.

Ben met me at work the very next day, so excited to tell me about the "Atomic Cowboy" they found at Fat Sully's after trying four other places. He was overflowing with joy from their discovery, and I didn't dare say anything to shake the perfect ground of friendship we'd stood on for all these years. So, when Diana called to reprimand him the next day, I let him off the hook and laughed a bro-we're-good-mates-no-need-for-this kind of laugh, as if it wasn't a big deal.

I knew what this meant for us; I wasn't a dating option for him. If I was, he would've been looking forward to it enough to remember it. That fact still didn't stop me from secretly loving him the way I had most of my early life, even if I knew I had to move on and realize he might give me his coat jacket when I offer to get drinks for game night, but he'll request it back so he can give it to another woman later that night.

"You must not be paying attention then. I'm sure there are many men interested in that pretty face of yours. Keep an eye out for the cute ones, okay?" Jevie says.

"I'm sure that's the case. It's probably not that I'd rather solve crossword puzzles and hang out with Ben and Diana more," I say. Really it was because all my time was spent at the Bureau and what little free time I had was spent with colleagues and family. I'd been through all the prospects at work, so Aunt Jevie was wrong about that. There are not many men in my circle interested in this "pretty" face of mine. Just me, interested in my best friend and partner agent who's somehow decades—maybe even universes—away yet also living across town, absolutely not interested in me.

Still, I needed to find a way to get back to him. And soon. I'd give myself till the end of the week to figure out the Ben and Corky mystery before trying to find my way back home. I just needed to somehow get my hands on a transparent phone.

Chapter Twelve

Nothing about life at the moment feels normal—the spaces and rapid de-aging of family members, not to mention the new addition of wavy curls framing my face like thick ribbons as I walk the school hallways—but the crossword puzzle tucked between my clenched fingers brings a sense of familiarity thanks to the chicken scratch schedule and a few recent notes about Marigold I've added to the right side of the page.

Carrying around a crossword puzzle and planner was a sign of normalcy for me; I often left one at my desk at the Bureau in case a word came to me in the middle of the day. Having one with me now feels like a piece of home I can hold in my hands while in this foreign world, even if I can't recall filling in the first thirty crosswords that share my handwriting, nor am I confident I'll be able to fill out the seventy other ones since they're likely inspired by eighties references and clues.

I pass by four cheerleaders who will become my teammates this afternoon, giggling as they pass through the large wooden doors to the gym. Each has their brushed-out curls tied half up with giant scrunchies and they are wearing the same matching teal windbreaker-style drawstring bags over their shoulders. I continue past them absorbing the cherry-postered walls around me where teal painted eagles claim most of the wood panels.

"Hey, you! You new here?" A voice hollers from across the hallway like a catcalling tourist. "Your hair is looking fine."

Whoever's heckling me from behind has a posse of snickering heathens echoing his words with light cackles. I take it that my perm looks good from the back. Erica already confirmed that last night when she kept shouting at me in the midst of helping finish the blow-dry and tease, "See I told you. You should've permed your hair when I first suggested it. It looks so good. Look at those perfect waves."

I didn't hate it, so at least there was that, and though I plan to leave in the coming days, at least I'll be fashionable according to eighties' standards for the time remaining. Even so, I still feel like a matchstick in a line of cotton swabs.

A generous, lemony sheen of sunlight peaks through the frosted glass bathroom window as I peek around to find the syrupy sweet talker trying to garner my attention.

I see Ben, who tenses up, like sandals shrinking from too much heat, at the sight of me. He's perched in front of the boy's bathroom entry with Tyler and Evan, leaning up against the wall and the color of his face confirms it was him. The catcaller. His words now creep into my memory, and I can see the embarrassment set in on his face.

"Woah Ben, you know that's Atta right?" Tyler laughs awkwardly. It's clear he didn't recognize my backside with new exaggerated hair and all. "You better say something to her or dig your grave now," Evan adds. Frustrated emotion scars Evan's throat. He's concerned with the direction this is going.

Ben flirting with me—well, my backside more accurately—so blatantly, makes my heart hum with hope. Before I let the hope inflate and then float away so far I can't catch up to it, I remind myself that he hates me for doing something I'm still unaware of and has never once been interested in me that way in his life. It's false hope for my heart to hum here, just as false as it was in Non-80s-Land.

"Would you guys give us a second?" Ben slips over to my side of the wall trying to save face as Evan and Tyler walk in the opposite direction. Evan makes sure to hold his gaze on us until he clears the corner.

"I swear I had no idea it was you. You changed your hair, huh?" Ben says as diplomatically as possible, making sure to leave all signs of emotion out of his response. "If I would have known it was you, I wouldn't have done that."

"Thanks, I guess," I say, feeling quite uncomfortable with this side of Ben. "So if you knew it was me, you wouldn't have tried hitting on me from behind while you have a beautiful girlfriend waiting for you a few hallways down? " His face reads annoyance at my response. It's as troublesome as the untied shoelace spilling from his gray converse high-tops. "Is that what you're trying to say?"

"I know you know things, and I really need you to keep quiet and stay out of my business, Atta." Did bringing up the issue of him catcalling remind him of our confrontation at the vending machines? Erica confirmed I had suspected something about Ben's relationship with Bennette and Corky. Was this the "thing" he was referring to?

"Ben, what do I know?" I let out a laugh of frustration. The Ben I knew wasn't the unfaithful type. The kind who dates a lot? Yes. A player? No. But that Ben would never show interest in someone else while in a serious relationship. So seeing his chocolate eyes melt from the heat of our conversation, I'm unsure if this version of Ben is anything like the present-day, Non-80s-Land Ben I grew up with. Even so, I don't want to believe what all these assumptions seem to be leading to. He's better than that.

"Ugh, Atta. Don't play with me like that. Don't push it when you already know enough. I told you to stay out of it." He tugs on his ball cap and runs off without a glance to catch up with Tweedledee and Tweedledum.

At this rate, I was going to need a time machine to get Ben to find his cool—to take him to a time before I angered him to the point of not speaking to me. I was planning the attempt soon, but I was also committed to discovering Ben's secret before the end of the week. If anything, it would help put my curiosity at ease. Curiosity that would stick with me even if I was to leave this alternate universe.

CHEER PRACTICE BEGINS WITH ERICA INTRODUCING ME AS THE new recruit in a circle of feathery-haired girls with faces glued to me as I stand next to my mother, "my sister", the cheer captain. As she reminds everyone of our sibling status, she has the squad run and stretch, and makes sure to point out the distance I have from accomplishing a perfect split.

Erica instructs a few of the girls to demonstrate a touch-up, spread eagle, and a toe touch. I follow along with intense concentration, as if this is jiu-jitsu class and the consequence will be harsh judgment from my colleagues if I somehow fail the fundamentals. After running through the stunt in my head a few times I kick both legs out wide using the jump technique I'd learned from vertical jump training—I'd even managed to add an extra block to the stackable weights at the last session with some fellow agents, so I was confident I'd gain some height with my attempt. But this time I make sure to hold my posture upright with the maneuver, my arms level with my shoulders, just like the dishwater blonde-haired girl does in front of me. I land with an audible thud.

"Not half bad!" Dishwater blonde applauds.

"You got higher than all of us," Bennette encourages me. "What type of hidden magic is in your Converse? Erica, I don't think these Reeboks are doing their job."

"Your shoes are fine, Bennette," Erica says, then looks at me. "Atta, you'll just want to land a little softer. Think *Flashdance,* not Sylvester Stallone in *Rambo First Blood.*"

I haven't seen the movies she's referring to, but I can assume she means more delicate and less federal-agent-using-self-defense style. "Will do."

While observing practice stunts from the sideline, I spot Bennette airborne above a thick yellow tumbling mat. She lands a front-back handspring. Corky walks onto the mat and high-fives her with a shot of best friend energy and I watch as they giggle in conversation.

Unfortunately, I'm too far away to hear any of it and I briefly consider whether I can tumble well enough to join them. I cut that thought short though when I think of the tuck and roll maneuver I was trained to use whenever ducking out of a live fire situation. That's as much rolling as I'm comfortable with. I'll have to consider another time to start up a conversation with those two. If I attempted to tumble with the big girls I'd look like Chris Farley endlessly rolling down the mountain in the movie *Black Sheep*. The image puts a smile on my face. If only that movie existed at this time. I'd kill to go home after this and relax in front of Grandma Marcie's TV and watch it, even if it was mostly just fuzzy video.

Erica gifts me a familiar teal drawstring bag made from eighties windbreaker material—material I've only ever seen on old, ugly joggers —that sounds like wind tunnels when the pant legs get rubbed together. I sling it over my shoulders and consider myself an official part of the pack, ready to mingle with the others in the locker room.

My chance to chat up Bennette or Corky is hijacked when the overall conversation turns to the topic of an earlier speedo sighting.

"It was neon green! I didn't get to see it for long. Just a split second," one girl, a small brunette, says. "He invited all the girls in the locker room to a party at his house this weekend."

"How did I miss it?" Dishwater blonde says. "I changed early and ran to the director's office to get the mats."

"Tyler probably came in while you were in there. Sorry, you missed it." Her words trail off in a giggle.

So I heard it right. It was Tyler they were talking about. He's still up to his old antics, never missing a beat.

"Tyler's raiding the girl's locker room again?" I chime in.

"He's done this before?" the giggling girl asks.

"What hasn't he done? His life's work is to disrupt and make his presence known."

"At least he's cute," the brunette pops in. "Do you know him well?"

"I guess you could say that. I've known him longer. Fifteen-plus years and he managed to get into the girl's locker room twice growing up." I realize what I said and expect some sort of look or reaction from the girls, but I guess they are too distracted by the topic of Tyler to notice.

"Could you introduce me?" the brunette asks with a hopeful grin on her face. I was never a fan of matchmaking, and I didn't come here to be the matchmaker for my tactless friend who would end up having a future as a birdwatcher, but I needed to befriend my cheer team-mates to get as much information as possible about Bennette and Corky's relationship before the end of the week. I make plans with the girls to formally introduce them to Tyler when the time's right.

SINCE DIANA REJECTED MY SUGGESTION TO JOIN THE CHEER team and isn't here to give me a ride home, I jump in the car with Erica, who couldn't be happier that I'm riding home with her. It's my first time riding in her red Volvo 480 model with *Back-to-the-Future*-style pop-up lights. We cruise along the hillside with a throng of seven-ties and eighties model cars around us on our way back home. I stare at the people in the cars passing by, hardly a tinted window in sight, and begin to wonder if the paint on the road is thicker, then briefly consider if I'd ever get used to driving a road void of newer model cars —ones that I'm used to. Every vehicle looks like a tin can on wheels with shiny metal bumpers and the newer 1985 models noticeably stand out from the others. It's as if the designers were aiming to please the Jetsons.

"I saw you staring at Bennette and Corky most of practice. I know what you're up to, Atta. Don't be so obvious next time," Erica says, looking over at me with both of her hands at the top of the wheel.

"I'm not trying to be obvious. Just curious and hoping I'll catch a conversation that'll help me connect some dots."

"Sure you are. So that's why you joined the team. It makes sense now. You're stuck with us now that you've joined though. So don't think of quitting even if you don't get what you want within the week."

"I won't. I told you I'm committed," I assure her.

"I'm staying out of it. So don't involve me in your scheming." Her tone is motherly and familiar while she holds onto the steering wheel with a tight grip and forced smile.

"You think I'm scheming?" I say, unable to contain my smile. This dynamic is somewhat satisfying.

"I know you're scheming," she suppresses a laugh trying to resist my cheekiness.

Chapter Thirteen

D iana and I wander into the computer room the next day. She needs to pick up a book she left in a desk cubby while playing *The Oregon Trail*. I have to tag along to see these advanced computers. I was fairly certain Google wasn't available until the late nineties, but I still felt the need to test these machine's capabilities. Maybe I could find local company and organization information here, like a hard drive version of the phone book on one of these computers. The fact that I hadn't even thought to look for this information in the physical phone book laying on Marcie's kitchen island makes me shake my head. I make a mental note to go through it at home. There's a good possibility Sheriden or Marigold could be listed locally.

As we enter the room I spot Evan coming out of the classroom two doors behind us. He meets my gaze and picks up his pace toward me, likely wanting an answer to his earlier date request. Diana reaches the computer desk before me and I look around for possible places to hide just as she begins a performance of outstretched cheer arms in an attempt to mimic my first day of cheer practice.

"Will she trip or will she fall? Hoo-rah, hoo-hoo-rah! Will she be okay at all? Hoo-rah, hoo-hoo-rah!" she chants as her arms move back and forth in a tight-fisted satirical motion.

I manage a light punch to her armpit while her arms are lifted and instantly pull back to a defensive position in case she tries to get me back.

"Ouch! Jeez! Where did you learn to hit like that, Atta?" Diana rubs her pit as if I'd actually done some damage. "It feels like you left a bruise, and why are you standing like a bodyguard open carrying? It's like James Bond stole your personality this week or something," she muses. I suppose I can use a little less finesse in everyday life, I remind myself. I'm so used to carrying my body a certain way, especially after pulling a quick pass at something.

"Maybe you won't be half bad this weekend if you keep everything so stiff like that. You know, to be honest, I've never seen you do anything remotely cheery. You're more the runner type, but like running to a chessboard," she continues.

"That describes me really well. Thanks," I say with sarcasm.

Diana jumps at the sound of movement behind us as Evan pops in from behind and extends his hand out to me. I'm temporarily shaken, unsure if he wants me to grab his fingers and walk hand in hand with him down the hall or not. Thankfully, I notice a slip of paper poking out from between his middle and index finger. I grab for the folded note. He smiles at me, leaving our conversation solely to paper, and takes off, his dark permed hair parted down the middle lifting like two bird wings flapping in the sky on his way out.

This time I open the note in front of Diana. It's a fresh piece of paper with only his handwriting and she doesn't seem to find it odd that I'm reading what is very obviously a love note clearly passed to me from Evan.

Hey, let's try for next weekend. I was going to pick you up at 7 tomorrow night but Tyler's having a house party and I can't miss that. You're invited, by the way. You should come. I'll meet you there. :)

"Hasn't anyone noticed that Evan seems to have a thing for me?" I ask Diana.

"Well, it's not like it's a secret. He's been pursuing you for weeks. We're all just waiting to see how long you're going to hold out on him. At this rate, it won't be long before you cave, right?" Diana says nonchalantly.

I shake my head in thought trying to understand why Eighties Atta was leading him on.

I follow Diana's lead and insert the disk into the Apple Macintosh and begin playing *The Oregon Trail* next to her, following the same sequence of clicks. The computer instructs me to "Input names and press enter" and for a few seconds I marvel at the wonder of a simple eighties life before diving into the relaxing world of retrogaming. We both select our character's profession, decide between options like banker, carpenter, or farmer, and are given a salary based on our choice. I give the party members ridiculous names like "Snoop Lion", "T-Pain", "Tommy Boy", and "El Niño"—the last two, a reference to a couple of my favorite Chris Farley characters. The irony of unfamiliar modern-day names found by someone in this era brings a smile to my face. Like a perfect inside joke. We begin purchasing supplies and start our wagon journey West.

"T-Pain just died of dysentery," I snicker. The slight disappointment I feel turns quickly to amusement.

"Character simulated experiences where you suddenly fall ill. You won't know your fate until you starve, lose your cart, or lose your cattle on the way. Isn't it exciting?" Diana says, almost giddy, from a higher octave.

A two-inch rubber eraser slaps Diana's cheek right in front of me. Our heads turn murderously toward the door.

"Diana, are you available this weekend?" Tyler struts toward us.

"First off," Diana says, barely louder than a whisper, "what makes you think throwing an eraser at me is remotely okay?" She rubs her cheeks as if it's in pain. "Second, why would you ever think I would want to spend my weekend around you?"

"Woah!" Tyler acts as if he's taken aback. "I was only trying to invite you both to a party at my house this weekend." He feigns an innocent smile between the ratty mullet curls that poke out at his neck. Diana scrapes the chair against the floor, standing in a quiet fit of anger. Her short slouchy boots look just as angry and I fear Tyler's toes have it coming for them.

"Tyler. You're a piece of work. I don't know how my brother even stands to be around you. You're mean and reckless, and frankly, I'd love it if you'd never throw an eraser at me again."

I sit, watching history repeat itself in another dimension. Diana had made a similar statement back in 2009 after he'd cut her hair, pushed her into a pool, and made one too many mistakes over the course of a year. Her lecture back then became more of a lesson on the politics of black hair and how insulting and offensive it was for him to even touch her hair without her permission, rightly so. I wondered where this eraser lecture was headed.

Tyler melts into a sad puppy right before our eyes, experiencing the emotion of shame for what was likely the first time in his life. From what I knew of his younger self, Diana was the only one who could evoke that feeling from him.

"I'm sorry," Tyler says stiffly. "But you won't even look in my direction, so I have to resort to other means to get your attention. I didn't mean to hurt you. I shouldn't have done that." Diana shifts her weight to the other side, absorbing his words.

"We will consider going." Diana turns her back to Tyler. "Atta, you're staying at my house Saturday anyway, right?"

I nod.

"Hope to see you there," Tyler says. He seems satisfied with Diana's answer and Diana seems to be lost in her own thoughts as we head in opposite directions.

AT HOME, AUNT JEVIE MUSES OVER THE COOKBOOK RACK IN THE kitchen. Alphabetic tabs spill out of the attached recipe card drawers as she sifts through each stained index card. It's Saturday morning and she's still here. Too many boxes that didn't fit and a few days of negotiations with her new husband, Gary, about what they can and can't keep made it impossible for them to leave earlier this week and since the original plan fell apart, they decided to stay a few more days. I guess they want to rendezvous a few more days amongst the dewy rainwashed foothills and sun-kissed red rocks or drive by the Golden City historic archway—that happens to remind me of a bowed Oh Henry! candy bar dangling from the sky.

Marcie enters the room and growls at the maritime blue "Today's Mood" chart—A hand-painted wood wall hanging with six pegs strewn under two carved hearts and dangly circular honey wood pieces with various emotions drawn in fine-tip permanent marker. I remember adjusting Grandma's mood chart for fun as a child. I'd choose "Feeling Flossy" because I thought it was funny she had an emotion about tooth care. Little did I know, it meant she'd be feeling bright and ostentatious that day if she chose it.

I watch to see what emotion she'll assign after giving it a stubborn morning growl. "Feeling Squirrely" is today's pick. She must have done something dumb this morning. I really could use one of these at my desk. That way the fellow agents around me could read "Feeling motivated!", "Feeling curious enough to solve this case" or "When is lunch?" moods when passing my desk and maybe enjoy a quick laugh.

My young uncles enter the living room in stringy wrestling singlets under pea-green sweats with sweaty ear guards dangling from their necks like gold chains. It's a sight of my uncles I never needed to see.

"Are you ready to cheer today? Did you get enough practice in with Erica yesterday? Do you think you'll remember all of the cheers?" Marcie asks, clearly concerned with my abilities in regards to today's game.

"If I forget, I'll just smile, Marcie," I say with a derisive grin. I practiced the four cheer routines until late into the night last night and even drew out the steps in my crossword book-turned-planner. I'm confident I won't ruin their performance.

"Marcie? You little toot! You're my daughter. You're not allowed to call me that, Atta."

"Mmhmm," I laugh inside. I can't call her Mom. That would be betraying my conscience.

"THIS ISN'T THE WAY TO THE MALL IS IT?" I ASK ERICA ON THE highway. Things have changed drastically for me since time traveling to the past but not enough for me to forget the way into Denver. Erica's driving in the opposite direction, toward the abandoned mine-filled mountains instead of the highway.

"Greg called this morning asking if I'd pick up five fishing nets at the mall for him. We've got to stop by and grab his money before we go."

"He's going fishing instead of watching the game today?" I ask. I still hadn't quite grasped what kind of guy Greg was. He walked around like a twenty-five-year-old that didn't belong in young Erica's world, sporting a handlebar mustache and cowboy boots tucked under tight jeans, but his wave amidst the car filled with boys during my first encounter was youthful.

"He'll be there. He didn't say he was heading anywhere, just that his friends needed the nets today." Five fishing nets. How odd. What in the world do they need five fishing nets for? It's not like they needed that many to fish. I'd been fishing enough times to know one was enough for a small group. I can't help but dwell on his absurd request.

Erica pulls up to a golden brown home with a large angular rooftop where sunroom windows collect gold and orange hues underneath green tree leaf shadows from the morning sunlight. For a house built in the seventies, the atrium design is spectacular. I admire the sky between the rooftop and the trees above, which looks more like stained glass watercolor art perched behind a thousand tree branches rather than a piece of sky.

The dark brown garage door to our side begins to rise, exposing two tight acid-wash jean covered legs as it reaches the halfway point. I take in the second pair of acid-wash jeans—so intensely acid-washed they appear more white than blue—realizing this pair belongs to Ben who's hovering over a ping-pong table holding a cardboard box with large red markings. I watch from my window as Erica's boyfriend Greg greets Erica at her door and hands her a fifty-dollar bill.

"Just get two or three nets at Sports Castle. We don't need five anymore," he says, smiling back at her for a lengthy period of time before brushing his short chestnut mullet back with his hand and holding it there. The continued stare toward her lips tells me that he's thinking of something other than fishing nets and we're all brought back to reality when his hand lets go of its hold and a spring of bangs fling back into place.

Erica leans forward and their mushy embrace prompts me to turn back to the garage where I find Ben biting his cheek and glaring in my direction. At least this expression makes his dimple pop more than usual, but I feel his annoyance. It's as if he thinks my whole purpose in life is to blackmail him for something he thinks I know, that I actually don't. I stare back at him with a gaze that only a clear conscience could muster. I wasn't guilty of anything, yet.

"What's in the box?" I say, hoping to coax something other than a glare out of him.

"Dynamite," he responds.

"Haha funny." My eyes roll up toward my lashes with that response. He pushes the box further into the table. "K, but really, what is it?

"I told you. Dynamite."

"Oh, you're serious? What in the world do you need dynamite for?" At this point intense curiosity has me leaning against the window crank, arms dangling out the car door window to get a better glimpse at the box in his hands.

Against his will toward hating me, his face lights up and a smile sneaks through. Whatever sanguine thoughts he's thinking must be greater than his angry facade. What could Erica's boyfriend and Ben be up to with a box of dynamite and a few fishing nets that makes him unable to resist smirking when he's so keen on keeping a stony face in front of me?

He chooses not to answer and I can't help but imagine Ben and Greg out on a boat lighting sticks of dynamite with tiny matches and dropping them into a nearby lake to blow up some fish, then scooping out the remains using fishing nets with the hopes of "catching fish." It's not logically sound, but it's what I can come up with given the details provided. I try not to be too disappointed when we take off and Ben doesn't even look back after refusing to answer my question.

"Greg's house is nice. What's the atrium like up there? It looks amazing from the outside," I ask Erica as we head toward the mall this time.

"Oh, that's actually Tyler's house. Greg and Ben were just organizing stuff for the party tonight since they don't play anymore and the rest of the guys are having a shooting practice before the game."

So this is where Tyler's family lived in this alternate universe. The subdivision where he lived in Non-80s-Land hadn't even been built yet. I'd learned this on that first drive to the school with Diana.

"They have dynamite and fishing nets. Aren't you the least bit curious about what they're going to do?"

"They're always doing random things like that. I can't keep up with those boys, so I don't pay it much attention."

"Dynamite, Erica. Dynamite."

"Ben's just messing with you, Atta. Don't put too much thought into it."

❦

WHILE ERICA CHECKS OUT AT THE SPORTS CASTLE REGISTER with three wood fishing nets in hand, I find myself being watched by her large skeptical eyes as I scout out the neighboring shops for a sign of an electronics store. My actions incite confusion within her, but I'm already gone in terms of concocting a somewhat insane escape plan, so I don't care.

The mall's my chance to find a transparent phone. Erica's eagerly on the lookout for shoes and I find myself deeply contemplating how I'm going to execute the plan. It's just a simple mission of theft, but Erica's watching me and my conscience feels for the eighties business owner I'm going to wrong, thanks to the lack of funds my eighties self possesses. The pathetic pickle jar of mostly pennies on my dresser drawer is testament to that.

The lavish and somewhat obnoxious tile path turns into a red brick cobblestone mall floor as we pass by store names I don't recognize: Brookstone, Waldenbooks, Babbages, Contempo Casuals, and Gadzooks. My eyes scan each chunky bold neon sign floating above every store entrance for the eighties equivalent of a Best Buy.

We pass by Wall Music, where the entire store is a bright shade of candy apple red and a thousand silver trays line the wall along with stands holding cassettes and vinyls of various sizes. My heart flutters at the thought of spending an hour digging through popular albums from the seventies and eighties and I can't help but hesitate a few steps until Erica pulls me forward with the tug of her hand.

An overwhelming smell hits my nose as we ascend up the cream-puff-colored escalator. I catch a draft of popcorn air and look over the moving railing to see a display of floating mini air balloons on an up-and-down rotating set of wires. On the other side of the forest green water fountain, another display holds giant-sized Venus flytraps and welded lily pads spouting water into drains in the floor below. It's clear the circular bench around the water fountain is this mall's designated public make-out destination, and I find it hard to tell from this distance which of each pair of mullet-styled heads smashed together was the girl or the boy in the relationship.

As we take the leap of faith off the escalator exit, I hear the jostling of plastic straws. Orange Julius and the red and yellow-tiled ribbon that wraps around the food court greets us first. It's the first store I recognize from my world, Non-80s-Land, and I curse myself for thinking poorly of that jar of pennies. That money could have bought me one of those frothy foam-filled orange paper cups.

A Tandy Electronics sign as bright and as red as a hanging stoplight jumps out at me as we head for the Kinney Shoes store tucked in between a Wicks 'N' Sticks and a Waldenbooks. Erica's already got the attention of the sales associate and I'm formulating my plan to sneak over to the Tandy store without her.

"You're size 7.5 right?"

Erica crams a shoe over my dangling foot. The white Reebok Classics are a half an inch too small but the real concern fumbling through my mind is whether Erica has enough money in her purse to buy me a phone from Tandy's next door, a more preferred route of theft. I rustle through Erica's purse the second she leaves to request the next size up. My fingers feel for a plastic card, but all I find is two twenty-dollar bills, barely enough to pay for the Reeboks. Original plan it is.

"Let's stop at Waldenbooks before we head out. I need a new crossword puzzle," I say as we walk out of the store with a new box of cheer shoes in hand.

She agrees, so I direct her to the magazine display next door where I have a hunch she'll remain for at least ten minutes. With three magazines tucked in her underarm and an open magazine in hand, I've set my trap. I just hope the weight will hold while I make an escape.

"Be right back," I say, pointing to the other side of the store.

I make a u-turn at the newspaper stand and bolt to Tandy's. With a slightly increased pulse rate and heavier breaths I peruse the coiled phone aisle in search of a transparent phone. There was a chance the everyday run-of-the-mill corded phone would work, but I was looking for exactness and it was the transparent phone with colored wire that could only replicate the trans-dimensional time travel I'd done in Pops' hidden room. If I was going to attempt time travel I'd need a chewed wad of gum, a bottle of Clean Wave spray, and a phone, preferably transparent, in case its uniquely placed color-coated copper wires altered the makeup of the phone enough to make a difference.

At the very end of the aisle, upon a flat table, sits the rainbow wired phone, all of its colors exposed and snagging my attention with its boldness, but I'm unable to snatch it because a coke-bottle-glasses-wearing male store associate is lurking nearby. My time is limited. Erica can only flip through a magazine without sensing my disappearance for so long. I approach the man, doing my best to play the part of an innocent, not-going-to-steal-a-phone teenager.

"Um, I think she's asking about the calculators," I say, looking at a girl at the front of the store. I give him an encouraging nod toward her and carefully watch as he makes his way over to get into the nitty-gritty details of the electronic calculator. I'm slightly disappointed I won't be able to stay for the awkward interaction, but I only have a few seconds to slip this phone inside my teal drawstring cheerleading bag.

It's in. The phone is in. I straighten and add a confident, almost provocative swagger to my steps walking down the aisle and out the store opening as if I'm George Clooney in *Out Of Sight*, which actually isn't too far off. I am robbing someone after all.

Chapter Fourteen

My first official store heists go a little too well. Call me a professional pilferer. I made my way out of the mall with a few extra newspapers, a magazine, and their most flamboyant store item without Erica or the mall security noticing.

I should be concerned about the lack of adequate security. Instead, a sense of accomplishment fills my mind as I check out my cheerleading uniform in the girls locker-room mirror. I stick out like a sore thumb in red but at least my white shoes now match the rest of the squad. I bend down, reaching for my ankles to make sure that the slouchy socks are bunched two inches high above my ankles just the way everyone else has them.

Corky joins me, stepping into the mirror space next to mine, adjusting her skirt and fiddling with a pair of headphones with bright orange foam ear cushions, ensuring the cord is connected to her Walkman cassette tape player. Now is the perfect time to approach her.

It shouldn't be difficult at all. I'd been approaching strangers under unusual circumstances as an agent for the last five years. It was finding a topic of conversation that was the difficult part of this situation. It wasn't work related, but it was my opportunity to learn more about her relationship with Ben.

"What are you listening to?" I ask, pointing to her hand-sized cassette player. Looking up through the feathery curls framing her face, she reaches for the earpiece and smiles.

"Genesis." She adds a bit of a bounce to her sway as she says it and I know she's smiling about the question I asked, not the fact that I approached her.

"Phil Collins, Genesis?" I try to match the excitement in my voice.

"You're familiar?"

"I'm familiar," I say. I've heard of Genesis and I'm aware the band was Phil Collins' before he went solo, but I can't say that I've been a huge fan or anything. I probably know one song, and I can't think of the title right now. Her countenance is entirely bubbly at this point. She appears to be a die-hard Genesis fan, and her eyes are dilating the same way a person does when they can't hide their adoration in front of a crush.

"I've listened to it with Diana on the way to school," I say, recalling where I've seen Genesis recently. One of Diana's mixtapes had a Genesis song scribbled in her handwriting on the cassette tape case.

"'That's All.' I really like 'That's All'," I say, able to revive the Genesis song title written in Sharpie, after picturing the cassette case being tossed into the space underneath the car player.

Corky even blushes at the song's mention.

"Have you heard their new album? I went to their concert a few weeks ago. It was seriously the best night of my life."

"I haven't," I say with a shake of my head. She looks as if she's going to start cheering for the new album, with toe-lifting footwork and all.

"You have to listen to 'Land of Confusion' and 'Invisible Touch.'" She hands me her skinny foam ear headset and I adjust the placement on my ears until I hear the music play through the speakers. I bop along to the melody enjoying the synth sounds and Phil Collins' voice.

It was actually a good song, worthy of getting me pumped up for the cheering that was about to take place.

"This one might be my favorite, actually," I say with confidence.

"Isn't it so good? 'Land of Confusion' is my favorite from the album. It's so weird and catchy."

"Corky, right?"

"Yep, and you're Erica's sister, Atta. Nice to meet you."

"It's nice to meet you too. I like your taste in music."

"And I love you!" she says. We both know she means she loves that I love her taste in music.

"Talk music with me anytime." She looks over my shoulder, toward the locker-room exit. "It looks like everyone's heading out for the warm-up. Shall we?"

I need to ask her about Ben. I'll be kicking myself if I don't ask. Though whatever business she has with Ben, I can't imagine it being negative. She's possibly one of the sweetest, most cheery types of people around. Her sunny disposition is blinding, like looking directly at the sun. She is a giant sun.

"Uh yeah. Wait one sec. I have something to ask you." I stop her with my arm.

"Yeah?" She looks surprised.

"I overheard Tyler a few days ago and he threatened Ben. He said you did something with Ben. Something that Bennette wouldn't want to find out. I wanted to hear from you what that could mean, since Ben seems to be acting strange lately." I try to say it pleasantly and leave out any tone of accusation. She's too sweet to be the problem here, anyway. There's some key information I'm missing and Corky should be able to lead me in the right direction.

"Oh, you know Tyler," Corky says. "You can't trust any words that come out of his mouth. He was probably just saying crap to embarrass Ben in front of you. I don't know what he meant by that." Her response is absolutely no help.

"Has he said anything about me? Like the reason that he doesn't want to talk with me?" I ask.

"Sorry, Atta. Ben doesn't talk to me much, except about music. I only overhear his and Bennette's conversations and I've never heard them talk about you. Maybe he's annoyed with his sister and you're his sister's best friend so it feels like he's taking it out on you too."

She manages a smile, as vacuous as could be, as if she's turned on a switch that only has interest in getting out to the cheer sideline as quickly as possible. Much to my chagrin, I still don't have an answer. Have I exhausted every avenue? It's not like Bennette would know. Am I really going to have this stupid question haunting me every day of my existence? Should I look into counseling for unmanageable curiosity? I laugh at the thought.

On the sideline, I mimic Bennette, Erica, and Corky's footwork and begin punching the air in front of me with giant tinsel pom-poms to the melodic shouts of a low-pressure cheer.

The more difficult cheers come. I stand at the back during the timeout routines and make myself invisible while four flyers find their way to the top of the base's shoulders, standing with one leg held high until they glide toward the floor like a set of dominoes or a heavy rolling sea tide.

I find Ben and Diana sitting amongst a pocket of parents in the bleachers. Diana notices me and gives an exaggerated wave my direction as I hum along to the high school pep band playing The Beatles' "Eleanor Rigby" via brass instruments.

Ben never looks in my direction. From the sideline, I keep my eyes glued to him as he follows the game intently. He makes inaudible calls and pulls at his shirt sleeves in frustration. Erica leads us in shouting "Fire on...up! Fire on...up! Shake-ah! Shake-ah! Shake-ah! Shake-ah! FIRE ON...UP!" With two seconds remaining in the half, Ben gets up and I lose sight of him as our cheer team shuffles out to the middle of the court and lines up in formation along the honey hardwood gym floor for the halftime performance.

I wave the pom-pom in my free hand with enthusiasm, having survived the first routine. With one last stunt to nail, we get in pyramid formation just like we practiced. My job is relatively unnecessary, but I still stand with bent knees grounded and feet slightly apart, making sure I'm ready to help the left spotter in the unlikely chance she disappears into thin air.

The flyer in the middle, holding the center balance, counts to three. I brace myself and lightly touch the back of the flyer's ankle. With the signal for release, the center flyer spins into the air with a basket toss, like a delicate bird ascending, extends her arms in a V-shape, and then lands perfectly in a pike position in the middle of the base's man made nest. It looks even better than practiced from my view behind, but I lose sight of my flyer, Kelly, when a loud military sound echoes an audible "Reveille" in my eardrum followed by the sound of one or two rubber bands snapping, interrupting any concentration I previously had.

A few translucent red plastic tubes and shoelace-like strings sail high toward the gym ceiling, showering some feathery heads close to the stands and I no longer see her ankle or the two bases in front of me. I question whether it's just me experiencing this dizzying confusion or if the team is collectively losing its balance from the shock of the blowing horn. A long, extended leg dives toward my face at what feels like a snail's pace. Before I know it, Kelly's rubber-soled shoe strikes my forehead. I'm knocked to the polished gym floor instantaneously, reacting like a soda can shot back a few feet after being struck by a bullet.

When I come to my senses, I feel Kelly's butt stamped against my ribcage. We're now a wacky two-person pile-up sprawled on the hard gym floor. I groan and Kelly rolls onto the floor after realizing she's carving into my stomach with her weight.

Her ankle looks like it might have been injured catching the fall with my forehead, so I jump up, landing swiftly on my feet and reach down to her with an extended hand, asking if she's okay. A collective gasp followed by a roar of nervous laughter erupts from the crowd.

"I'm okay!" she says with shock still plastered to her face. "Your face!" she cries. "You don't look alright."

A few drops of blood hit my hand, causing me to reach up and wipe my forehead. When I do, I feel the swelling skin that has ruptured at Kelly's point of contact.

The sound of rubber bands snapping continues and Kelly and I turn our attention toward Ben who's launching plastic semi-transparent red tubes into the crowd from a large wooden slingshot. One of Ben's friends slings red tubes next to him as Greg and another boy in a cherry red letterman's jacket stand in the crowd attempting to catch them with fishing nets, as they drop like dead pigeons into the bleachers.

I look from the red stick loaded on Ben's wooden device back to the fishing nets in the crowd and it all comes together. The supplies from earlier today at Tyler's house. Ben's launching "Dynamite" labeled tubes into the crowd. I just don't know why or what's in them. It's clearly not dynamite.

Laughter echoes against the home bleachers as a few students catch some "Dynamite" stragglers, popping off the plastic lids and pulling out silky underwear in patterns and colors you'd only find on seventies' wallpaper. One student dangles a tangerine patterned pair with squirrel red polka dots, and another waves a peacock patterned brief with dirt brown stripes around like a prize.

The basketball team enters the gym as Ben launches another round into the crowd sparking profanity from Tyler when he realizes what's happening. Tyler tries stopping him but Ben yells, "We've all had our fair share of pranks Tyler, it's time for a little payback." Then he announces to the crowd, "These are captain Tyler's precious Dynamite underwear. Don't worry, most aren't used." He winks at the teachers and administration who look amused from the sideline, then aims and shoots at Tyler this time.

Tyler's face is hot from embarrassment, but he decides to go along with the satire—it's him versus an entire gym after all. He grabs the tube he dodged and the paper advertisement from the cardboard box.

"This isn't underwear. It's Dynamite!" he sings as if it's some sort of brand jingle, at the same time he pops the plastic lid off of the tube in his hand. The parent section laughs, confirming it must be some sort of well-known catchphrase from the previous generation and Tyler waves a pair of underwear at the crowd before spending the last thirty seconds of the halftime countdown running around trying to retrieve Greg and the other guy's fishing nets filled with his butt-covering property.

"Don't be too mad. We made sure to catch most of them so you won't lose your collection," Greg says, handing the wood fishing net over to Tyler.

"You better not lose any of them. They're a collection. I'm lucky to even have them thanks to my dad and they are nothing to be embarrassed about," Tyler says. He approaches Ben at the sideline while I manage to transport Kelly off the court with a few other cheerleaders.

"Aww Ty, your collection may be impressive, but your face still turned three different shades of red," Ben says, then slaps Tyler's backside. "Go get 'em!" he shouts, watching Tyler walk out onto the court with a huffy expression.

Diana offers to take me home to clean up after the halftime injury. My mouth sours into a frown at the suggestion. I still haven't been able to solve the Ben mystery and it's not like having my forehead split by Kelly's shoe is anything serious. I'd maybe need an ice pack later for the galaxy-like bruise that had started to form in various purple hues. But Erica joins Diana in pressuring me to leave, enough that I find myself riding shotgun back to my grandparents' home with Diana, carrying the weight of not knowing Ben's secret.

I DITCH DIANA IN THE KITCHEN AND GRAB THE CLEAN WAVE branded spray from the closet while she thinks I've left to the bathroom to freshen up and clean my wound. She plans for us to go to Tyler's house party after the game but I had never planned to finish this day out here in this universe. I turn the corner with gentle rabbit-like steps and walk through the curtain of Pops' hanging shirts, holding my breath as I reach for both doorknobs behind, only exhaling as the door clicks open.

I'm in. It's been a day or so since my last visit to Pops' hidden room, where I made sure to check the site for all the items that could've caused the wall jack to spark. I'd found Pops' vintage gumball machine—surprised he'd already collected it at this point—located the Clean Wave spray that's now tucked under my left arm and secured the phone this morning. Who knows where my original transparent phone would be at this time, if it has even been made into existence. And though I realize there's no way for me to replicate exactly what happened, I'm as close as I can get. I have to hold out on hope.

Hope; being that a mix of these items, all containing chemicals and elements made up of molecules that have the capability to cause reactions—possibly even time traveling reactions—will bring me back. I didn't expect to understand which of these molecules created such an unfathomable experience, but I could try to replicate everything I had done seconds before the spark turned to a time and universe swap.

I idle before Pops' old gumball collectible, swinging the drawstring bag from my shoulder onto the desk and bravely consider chewing an ancient gumball from the glass globe. Pulling the stolen colored-wire phone from the bag, I filter my thoughts with positives. Instead of wondering how old the gum is, I become thankful that the gum is twenty to thirty years newer than the piece that was stuck to my old transparent phone in Non-80s-Land.

The process is quick. In the first few seconds I replay my last moment in the future with Ben—Non-80s-Land Ben—Agent Brown Ben. My memory comes alive with detail, as if it's fully revived at the faintest glimmer of encouragement and I act according to the memory, each motion guided by every little detail that comes to mind, as if exactness is of the essence in achieving the test of time travel.

The memory ends with my last words echoed back to me, "1980s called. They want their wallpaper back, Pops." But instead of repeating what was initially a joke, I try something different, "Calling February 2nd, 2023."

Chapter Fifteen

The only sound in the room comes from my racing heart—expecting, anticipating. But there's no spark. No fireworks. No lights turning on and off.

Perhaps the most disappointing is the lack of dizziness I feel. I take a look at the phone in my hands, following the coiled wire trail down to the phone jack, assessing every last detail, wondering why my motions hadn't sparked a reaction and I find myself wishing for that groggy feeling, the headache, and the back pain. The feeling of being consumed by illness right before passing out. The feeling I knew to be time travel experienced.

The shaggy, teal carpet, yellow tinted vases—very obvious signs that we're still in the eighties—burn in my vision, like a haunted picture, a reminder that no matter how cool and nostalgic vintage items are, they are emblems of the past. The very past I'm trying to escape. I curse at them and this situation for not working as I'd planned it to and test the phone a few more times, spitting out phrases like "2023 called. They want their wallpaper back, Ben!" and "Take me to 2023, in the future." But the room remains silent. Time remains unaffected.

It must be one of the variables. Not all of these things have remained constant. It's not the same gum chewed thirty years in the future nor the same bottle of spray that I cleaned the phone with in front of Ben. I'd have to wait until thirty years had passed to replicate the age of the gum or the exact recipe of the spray and what if the wall jack sparked spontaneously? If traveling through time was the result of a spontaneous spark in the wall, I wasn't getting out.

"Atta, you finished yet? I grabbed graham crackers from the kitchen. Do you think your mom will freak if I eat a couple?" Diana bellows from the hallway.

I set the phone back down on Pops' desk, giving up my mission and accepting defeat. My attempt to go home clearly isn't working.

I wait until Diana's voice carries upstairs, then sneak out of the hidden room with my drawstring bag. After shutting the door to time travel, I whirl around to find Diana a fist bump away from my chest.

"Must eat. Now," she says, nearly ready to shake me.

We hurry over to Diana's house where I sit in front of a plate of her grandma's homemade spicy buffalo wings and forget my time traveling woes to thick orange-glazed heat and the smell of ranch next to me.

I spent the evening up 'til now accepting the fact that I have no choice but to continue living in this world, making the best of it, and accepting that that includes going to Tyler's party tonight. Still, I can't help thinking about what's happening in Non-80s-Land. Is time progressing there while I am stuck here? Is Ben, the Ben that actually cares about me, even if only as a sister, is that Ben okay?

"The bruise is just getting worse," Diana says.

"What?" My attention comes back to the present that isn't the present I want to be in.

Diana points at my forehead with a chicken wing. "I can see the tread patterns where the sneaker kissed your head."

"Oh. Yeah. That." I reach up and touch the bump above my brows —it's not huge, but it's not small either.

Diana contemplates my forehead situation as we finish off our orange glaze-stained plates.

"You really don't care that a good chunk of your forehead is discolored? I thought you would've added some foundation to it back at your house."

I shrug. "I guess I didn't think it would be an issue." It wouldn't have been an issue if time travel would have worked. Or would it? I realize I don't know what changes go with a person as they time travel. I picture Non-80s-Land Ben reacting to my permed hair.

"Why are you grinning? It's not funny. Maybe we can cover it with my shimmery powder," Diana suggests. "My foundation is too dark. You don't have a coverup stick in your bag somewhere, do you? We don't have time to go to the drugstore."

"Just shoes and newspapers in here," I say.

In her room, I let her sprinkle something shimmery on my face as I take inventory of the butter-colored walls. Each door in this house has thin brown-stained wood trim. Trim that hadn't made a comeback in my lifetime and I secretly hoped never would.

Diana helps me to her closet and I play along, as if I really had planned to attend the party and spend the weekend at her house. She realizes her hunger emergency prevented us from allowing me to change out of my cheer uniform back at my grandparents' house.

I'm given free rein to her closet and told to find an outfit that's "deadly." I snort at my best friend's use of the very eighties word and begin sifting through her hangers, ignoring all of her denim jeans and dresses, since there's no way I'm going to slide my hips into something that fits Diana's much bonier frame.

The belted dresses in her closet made entirely of denim would entrap me like dough bulging from a popped can of Pillsbury Biscuits, but might look nice if completely covered up by a giant cardigan. I slide the hangers back to the right side of the closet, giving up, and brush my toes against Diana's shaggy carafe brown carpet on my way to her bed.

I lean into the plush burgundy duvet cover, admiring her poster of Whitney Houston in a pink leotard, mid-handclap wearing long, tight, honey curls. I pull Diana's gold throw pillow into my chest. As Diana begins searching her closet, I pop my face into the pillow, discouraged about where to go from here. It seems I'm trapped. In the eighties.

After a few relaxing breathing exercises, I lift my head from the pillow and say, "I think I'm going to need you to pick out something deadly."

Diana reaches into a stack of folded sweatshirts and lifts out a pair of white stirrup leggings—the kind of leggings mothers wore in the early nineties with oversized denim jackets and Birkenstocks. An odd strap sits under the foot, making me question the need for legging security. Oh no. What would happen without the strap to secure the pants down? Maybe the point is to hide any evidence of ankles? I laugh at my own inner monologue. They look like they'll fit and they seem to fit Diana's definition of deadly so I toss the pillow and try them on.

"And I have the perfect top for this," she says, handing me an olive green military cuffed-sleeve shirt with heavy front pockets that include flaps on both sides of the chest. I'm confident I can pass the army's dress code regulations and jump into training immediately.

I try on the outfit and walk around the room testing the strap under my foot.

"You surprised me today. You did pretty well out there," Diana says, picking out a pair of earrings to go with her blue sweater and heavily applied matching eyeshadow. The sparkly dust is on its way to her eyebrows.

"Thanks! If you say I didn't suck, that means I really didn't suck."

"But I'm not sure it's your calling ya know. I think the fact that you got lacerated by a kick at the very end might be a sign to never do it again."

"The kick was *your* brother's doing. Did you know Ben was going to prank Tyler like that?" I ask. I feel a bit disappointed she might have known and not shared it with me.

"Unfortunately, Ben doesn't tip me off to things like that, but I can't say I didn't enjoy the show. Minus your injury of course." Her smile splits so her teeth show through and she rolls her eyes back so that she looks somewhat haunted. It's Diana's classic funny face. The one she makes when she's being facetious. I come across it a lot.

"You are such a good friend," I say sarcastically. I mean it sincerely though.

"Tyler deserves all the underwear pranks in the world."

"But you've accepted his invitation to the party. I mean, that's where we're going instead of spending the evening here," I say, trying to fish for her current stance on their ongoing childhood love-hate relationship.

"I guess I did, didn't I?" she says softer than usual, almost embarrassed. I can feel it.

"Have your feelings changed now that you know he has a *Saturday Night Fever* style underwear collection?" I say. She tries swatting me with her hand. I dodge.

"Do you think he puts them back in the plastic tubing after washing, so that he can pop the plastic lid again like dynamite?" She tries to ask it seriously but a giggle slides out of both of us.

I walk over to her music bin that sits in the corner. It holds at least a hundred cassette tapes.

"Metallica and Styx?" I ask, pulling them out from the stack.

"Metallica is probably Ben's, and Styx, well Styx is the gag gift Ben got me for Christmas last year. I don't hate it as much as he wanted me to." The Browns have given each other gag gifts every year since they were really young. I remember Ben giving Diana an old apple chewed down to the core for Christmas in like 2005, and I was there for last year's gift exchange when Ben gifted Diana a hippo lawn sculpture, which now happily rests by the farm's chicken coop.

"Do you happen to have the new Genesis album?" I ask, remembering my conversation with Corky earlier today.

"I think Ben bought the cassette tape when it came out. Feel free to snatch it from his room. I wouldn't mind listening to something new while we finish getting ready." A little adrenaline rush hits me as I think of sneaking into Ben's bedroom. He hates me right now and I mostly kept to Diana's bedroom growing up—back in Non-80s-Land where his grandmother wasn't his mother and his mother wasn't his sister. It wasn't a big deal to Diana if I ran into her brother's room, but nosying around his space still felt risky.

I'd been over to his midnight-blue-painted apartment in the city every week for many years. We'd sink into his couch and theorize before our guests arrived for game night. I've stolen a crossword puzzle book from his room, but other than that, I stayed clear of it and it's not like I'd been invited in either. That was set aside for other guests, like the cute girl a few game nights ago, who came with some of Ben's buddies from his basketball league. She and I kept it cordial during Catan; I managed to complete an entire crossword puzzle throughout the game while she maintained the lead and then I swept in at the very end to win it. But she ended up scoring Ben after anyway, so my win felt essentially useless that night.

I WALK INTO BEN'S ROOM COVERED IN WOOD PANELS, SIMILAR TO my grandmother's living room. If one thing was to be said about the eighties, there was a heck of a lot more brown than ever depicted in movie remakes and Halloween costumes. School textbooks litter his white comforter and fuzzy Denver Broncos blankets. His cream-colored dressers are covered in all kinds of band decals. I could examine every inch of his room, but I'm here for Genesis. I spot a tilted stack of vinyls next to a scattered pile of white socks on his floor. The new album must be with a stack of cassette tapes somewhere in this room.

I find them on the bookshelf next to his closet. His tapes fill three of the bottom shelves under a dozen sports trophies tucked between two giant speakers—the kind of speakers you would see at your local goodwill by the early 2000s.

I kneel in front of the shelves to get a better look at the plastic case spines and spot a shiny Kansas City keychain. The metal keychain shines brightly against the bookshelf, drawing attention to the blue and gold shapes—Kansas City's basketball team colors. I pick it up. I didn't know Ben was a Kansas City fan.

He was always so loyal to professional sports teams in Colorado that he didn't really have any interest in other teams. At least that's what I knew. But Eighties Ben wasn't exactly the same as the Ben I'd spent all my time with for the last five years; this alternate universe version of him had grown up in a different era. But why Kansas City? Because it's the next closest professional sports team—maybe that's it. He's expanded his sports interests to neighboring cities.

I set the keychain back down and find the Genesis tape at the end of the stack right behind a bottle of brandy-colored cologne. I take one last delicious whiff of the room and victoriously hold the Genesis tape in my hand as I walk out from Ben's doorframe without getting caught.

Diana taps the cassette casing with her fingernails before opening her cassette tape player. A "click" and "shuffle" later we're listening to the A-side of the cassette.

I sink back into her duvet cover and pull the stolen mall magazine and rubber band-bound newspapers out from my stuffed drawstring bag. *The New York Times* lays out in front of me and I read a few articles looking for a Marigold connection until I come across a quarter-page *Genesis Invisible Touch Tour!* advertisement next to a few other national ads. What a coincidence. I roll through the tour dates. There aren't any listed in Denver, but the nearest concert is in Kansas City dated three weeks ago. The tour goes into July and will be in Hartford next week at the Civic Center.

Kansas City tokens seem to be popping up everywhere today. The Kansas City tour held in January triggers familiarity in my brain, and I can't quite pinpoint exactly what. I sit on this thought until Corky's face from earlier this morning pops into my mind and I make the connection. Corky went to a Genesis concert three weeks ago, which means she was in Kansas City. There is no Denver listing, so the nearest concert would've been Kansas City.

Erica mentioned I had said something vague a few weeks ago, suspecting Ben and Corky of doing something.

"Hey Di, has your brother been to a Kansas City basketball game ever?" I ask Diana.

"I don't think so. He just watches them on TV. Why?" she says.

"Just asking."

I understand now. Ben picked that Kansas City keychain up in Kansas City at the Kemper Arena where the Genesis concert was held. There's no reason to hide a Kansas City basketball game from his sister, but there is a reason to hide a concert held in Kansas City if he went without his girlfriend and with someone he wasn't supposed to.

"Was he absent from school a few weeks ago?" I ask. The advertisement lists the Kansas City concert for January 21st which would have been a Wednesday.

"He was sick one of the days. Why do you care?"

"I think I figured something out."

"Ooh. Give me more," she says and I tell her I will once I think it through some more.

What were the odds that Ben was absent a few weeks ago, around the same time as this concert, and that Ben and Corky—two of the three main characters in my unsolved puzzle—had connections to Kansas City recently, and also possessed the new *The Invisible Touch* Genesis album? The odds are high that Ben and Corky are concert-going delinquents with a reason to leave Ben's girlfriend out of the equation. A Ben-and-Corky-concert-filled picture becomes crystal clear before my eyes.

Is that what Ben thought I already knew? Is this what Erica was alluding to when she said I'd overheard a phone conversation between Corky and Ben? That they went to a concert together without Ben's girlfriend?

Whatever it is, Kansas City seems to hold a few secrets from Bennette.

THE UNEXPECTED DISCOVERY OF SUCH A SIGNIFICANT PIECE OF the puzzle hinders my ability to enjoy *Calvin and Hobbs* in the comic section. I'm processing my discovery while I'm supposed to be looking for keywords like Marigold, Sheriden, Clean Wave or any mention of cleaning and hair products to find more information, but there are too many distractions running through my mind as I scan the paper.

I run across an article on a newly approved chemical by the EPA. The title piques my interest despite my lack of concentration. *New EPA Director Approves a MaG Compound for Chemical Product Use.*

I continue reading the small snippet.

This MaG Compound (MUM2259) is a cold, yellow-orange powdered finite resource. Producers of MaG have sought pre-approval multiple times in the past due to its instantaneous cleaning property and ability to latch onto other compounds with incredible strength. It has been denied approval three times historically due to a lack of testing, but after conducting multiple tests and meeting sample size requirements to achieve statistical confidence for approval, they've successfully achieved it after a long road. This is a great day for the MaG market.

I'd never heard of the MaG compound. Yellow-orange powder isn't at all what I imagined a chemical compound would be colored, but then again I am no scientist. I'd imagined all compounds to be bland; the color of dark rocks. At least that's what comes to mind when I picture a periodical element in physical form. It's an interesting thought and I should probably look it up, but I'm unable to concentrate on the paper for any longer. I put the newspaper aside and shove the magazine back into my overstuffed cheer bag.

My brain produces a halo of soapy thoughts, floating above, giving me ammunition to overthink everything going on in my life at the moment. But I choose to pop all the thought bubbles with the exception of Ben and Corky's concert issue sans Bennette.

A plan develops from the one thought bubble I've yet to pop and I know what my next move needs to be.

Chapter Sixteen

Diana and I sit in comfortable silence listening to Genesis and reading until she sets her magazine down, pops the cassette tape out from the player, grabs a purse from her chair and says, "Well we'd better get going." She holds the Genesis tape extended in her hand. "Take this back will ya?"

I'm to place the tape back where I found it. Her connotation reads *you know the drill—same place, so he never suspects.*

I make a left for Ben's room with the tape in hand. When I approach the basketball trophies on his shelf, I look for the inch of emptiness below where I first pulled the cassette from.

The Kansas City basketball keychain, that initially sparked a few answers to my suspicions, raises another question. I stare at its bold colors—bright and shining against the plain white shelf—deep in thought. Why did he quit basketball a few weeks ago, mid-season and around the same time as the concert? If he quit because he doesn't enjoy it anymore, why did he pick up a Kansas City basketball keychain?

I hesitate with the tape in hand, closing my fingers tightly around the casing as I get an idea that may speed up my plan.

I shove the tape into the waistband of my stretchy pants, deciding to take the risk and hold onto Genesis just a little bit longer.

"Atta!"

The male voice behind me gives me the greatest spook of my life. When I turn to face him, I can see the heat emanating from his shoulders. His voice, low and stern, speaks for itself. Irritability seeps through with just the call of my name. I can't look him in the face. I feel my body trying to sink inside itself. Ben is giving me the look my father used to give me when he was disappointed in me. I haven't experienced it since I was five, the same year he passed, but it was chilling enough for me to remember. I'd rather summon a black pit to fall into at this moment than have the conversation Ben and I are about to have.

I've been caught red-handed—literally. The cover of Genesis' *Invisible Touch* cassette case is a literal red-orange hand in front of a green box and its square shape is creating a lump in the elastic band at my waist.

I lift my head. He's farther away than I thought, standing in the open doorway. Whether he knows I've taken his tape or not, I'm still in the doghouse for loitering in his room. I do a humble walk of shame and meet him at the door.

"It's not…" I begin, then quickly change my tone. "It's not what you think or maybe it is," I say with a nervous laugh. I'm trying my best to fake the upbeat tone I've had to use with Ben since landing in this eighties universe, in hopes that he'll reconsider his beef with me. His eyes burst into embers, like dancing ashes of irritation.

"You stole one of my tapes, didn't you? It's there. Let me see that," he says pointing at my waist.

"See this?" I point to the bulge, hoping he'll give up if I question his request.

"What else? It's my tape, isn't it? Why else would you be in my room?"

I have nothing to say to that, so I pull out the tape and place it in his open hand.

"Genesis? You grabbed Genesis, huh?" He doesn't wait for me to answer before saying "You're taking this too far, Atta!"

"Diana simply asked me to get Genesis out of your room," I say. It's partially the truth—"feel free to get it" was her way of saying she wouldn't mind listening to it too.

"Why do you insist on making my personal life your business? What do you plan on doing with that tape, when you know perfectly well I don't want you to bring up Genesis? It's not like you're interested in Genesis. We both know you're doing this to get back at me for some reason."

He stands looking more vulnerable than I've ever seen him. The crease in his brow folds as if it's given up on expressing peace, joy, and happiness for good.

"Why'd you do it?" I say calmly. "Why'd you sneak off to a concert with Corky and not tell your girlfriend?" I lock my eyes on his. "Bennette. Your girlfriend. Why would you go to a concert with her best friend without her knowing?" I'm shooting from the hip here, hoping my accusations are correct. There's always the chance I'm off, but all the evidence has led me to this.

"Listen, I'll say it again, just like I did the night you hopped on the line while we were on the phone. Corky and I are just friends. We just went to a concert together. That's all." He tries to keep his tone calm this time.

"Then why keep it a secret? Why has it been such a big deal that I don't mention anything around you? You've been mad at me all week and why? Because you innocently went to a concert, not because there's something you're trying to hide?"

He wipes the sweat off his forehead with the sleeve of his black Motley Crew tee. The worried expression on his face softens my view of him. It brings me back to our younger selves, the Non-80s-Land ones, when he approached me with worried eyes. Like the time my dog had decimated two of my chickens, leaving me absolutely devastated. I'd become friends with Lady and Bessy and the incident was traumatizing for my eight-year-old self, so when Ben Brown walked out of his house to find me at my mailbox with tears streaming down my cheeks, to my delight he looked back at me with worried eyes, walked me to my front porch, and wrapped me in a hug while I cried on his shoulder.

He did the same thing when I came home from college and learned that my mother had accidentally thrown out my late father's Tió de Nadal, the Christmas log our parents used to place small candies and toys under while we warmed our sticks in the kitchen Christmas morning. Once they were warm we would beat the Tió with sticks and pull a gift out from the blanket and sing "Caga Tió" to honor my father's Spanish heritage and fantastic humor. She had thrown it out while doing some spring cleaning and was just as devastated as I was.

When I broke my wrist while on assignment a few years ago, he'd shown the same worried expression. I almost enjoyed it as he held me trying to keep my bones in position—his long arms supporting me as we navigated the twists and turns of the road on the way to the hospital.

He's wearing the same worried face.

But this time he isn't worried about me, he's worried about getting caught having to respond truthfully to my questions.

Diana appears in the hallway. "What are you doing at home, Ben? I thought you were at Tyler's," she says, biting her lip as if concealing a portion of it will conceal the fact that I've wrongfully trespassed into Ben's space and been caught. "I had Atta grab the Genesis tape from your room," she says trying to save me and snatches the tape from his fingers.

"Sure, Diana." Ben walks past her rolling his eyes in the process.

"Let's get out of here. You ready, Atta?" Diana waves the tape like a snack in front of me.

WHEN WE WALK OUT TO THE DRIVEWAY, WE FIND BEN LOOKING defeated leaning against Diana's Honda Civic with a very eighties triangular roof, but a forced smile hits his face when we appear.

"Di, give me a ride." Ben looks over at his dirt bike in the garage. "My bike won't start and I don't have time to fix it."

Diana arches an eyebrow as if to say *Why's that my problem?*

"C'mon, Di," Ben says. "Tyler's been alone for less than twenty minutes. I can only imagine what he's been able to scheme up for my payback in that amount of time."

"Backseat," Diana commands. "Atta, you're in shotgun."

Ben and I keep our silence the majority of the drive, that is until Diana starts questioning Ben.

"How's Bennette? I haven't seen her in a while," Diana says. She's either genuinely curious about Bennette or trying to agitate him after she caught us arguing in his doorway and wants to start round two.

"She's good, Diana," Ben says with a short tone.

I turn around in my seat to gauge just how irritated he is. His hands are tucked into his leather jacket pockets and his brown eyes, dusted with caramel-colored flakes, are peeled upwards in my direction. His chin is tilted into his chest and it's as if he's giving me a glare of death.

"Are you going with me and Robyn on Tuesday? She wants us to go to the concert at the mall," Diana asks Ben.

"Yeah, Greg's coming with me," he responds.

"Did you invite Bennette or are you keeping this concert a secret from her too?" I interrupt. It was a ruthless move, and part of me felt bad for bringing it up again, but the other part wanted us to finish the conversation we started earlier.

"Atta, come on. You're my sister's best friend, not my girlfriend. Holding this information over me is stupid," Ben says, with some ice in his tone.

Diana lets out a thick sigh.

"I just want to know why you didn't tell her," I say, turning around in my seat to look at Ben in the back.

"You already know why. So why sneak into my room with the Genesis tape? It looks like you're trying to threaten me with it. You can see that, right?" His full lips are pursed together, waiting. Ben scoots over to the middle seat and grabs the steel bars under our headrests, his upper half leaning in toward the front of the car, ready for a full-fledged debate.

"Diana and I really wanted to listen to Genesis. Corky suggested I listen to Genesis and Diana agreed we should grab it from your room. That's it," I say with an uneasy smile. He wasn't making this easy on me.

"Bull, Atta. That is such bull."

"I'm telling you the full truth." I hold up my fingers with the ol' scout's honor sign, somewhat put off with his angry tone.

My memory flips back to our sibling-like squabble last month.

"Try the homemade dip, Atta," he pressured me for the third time that night in Non-80s-Land. We sat on his couch watching *New Girl* after his latest female interest left us for a family function earlier that night—too early in a feeling-things-out kind of courtship for Ben to accompany her. He'd poured his heart into a fancy artichoke dip made from scratch and I wouldn't touch artichokes or mayonnaise. Especially not the yellow kind made from scratch.

"Your girl already tried it. Rely on her feedback. Not mine."

"There's nothing I've made that you haven't tried and disliked. You'll like it. Come on. A tiny taste." He'd held the bowl out as if he intended to force spoon feed me.

"Nothing you say will convince me to put that near my mouth."

"Nothing?"

"Nothing."

"Would you be this stubborn if your boyfriend asked you to try something he slaved all afternoon over?" he'd asked.

"I don't have a boyfriend."

"You really should get one," he'd said with sternness before grabbing hold of me and forcing the spoon at my mouth. He'd left me with a long streak of appetizer smeared across my face when I refused to taste it and I'd left him disappointed.

Irritated that I wouldn't taste his food he'd said, "That's your punishment, little sis."

In the Civic, I lower my hand, pressing it against the dashboard. Diana looks annoyed taking the sharp turn. I recall Erica making the same turn this morning. Thankfully we're close, just a minute or two out from Tyler's grandparents' house.

"And since when have you ever wanted to be a cheerleader?" Ben says. "You joined the cheer team to mess with me. To be near Bennette and Corky, and to what? Blackmail me? Make me nervous that you'll expose what you know to Bennette?"

He brings his head into the nook between our headrests.

"Paranoid much?" I say, rolling my eyes back into my head. He wouldn't answer my question and now he's accusing me of blackmail.

"Fine, don't take me seriously. You've done nothing but irritate me all week with your not-so-subtle moves. You're either jealous or extremely bored. Bennette and I are happy. Things are great between us. I don't need you judging what I do." He spits out that last bit under his breath, but he's so physically close I have no problem hearing.

"Oh great. We're having this conversation so you can tell me all about how great of a boyfriend you are," I say with derision. Ben looks uncomfortable. He sits up straight then leans back into his seat.

"Yes, that was my master plan. I walked into my bedroom earlier so that I could find you and tell you just how great of a boyfriend I am," he says.

"I knew it!" I say. My mood has reached the answers-only-in-sarcasm level. I can feel the steam-powered fumes force their way out of my nostrils like an angry bull cartoon.

"I can't do this right now," he says, shoving the back door open as Diana rolls into Tyler's driveway. Ben's out before Diana actually stops the car and the garage walls tremble from the blaring music inside. It's muffled, but I can almost make out song lyrics from the grass until we reach the professionally landscaped shrubs at the front door.

"What was all of that about in the car? You two were arguing like a married couple. Are you sure you aren't jealous of him dating Bennette? I get the frustration, but that was heavy, even for you two," Diana says as we linger at the door. Neither of us has decided to knock.

"I'm not jealous."

"Oh, Atta. Please don't fall for my brother. He's not worth it. Like not worth it all. Look what he's doing to Bennette. If you somehow ended up together, I'd be your third wheel. Please. No."

Young Diana was a stark contrast to older Diana who was practically begging me to date her brother. But I couldn't blame her for this reaction. At this age we were inseparable and both of us hated the thought of someone getting in the way of our friendship.

"It's not like that. He's dating her and I'm not jealous."

"So you've never liked him, right?" she says, her eyes pleading for me to deny, deny, deny as we stall in front of Tyler's home. I stare at her with an awkward cheeky smile, sucking my lips in instead of answering. We both know I can't honestly answer this question. My face has already given it away. Diana's eyes widen. "Well?" she says.

"You don't have to worry. Trust me, I know for a fact he'd never date me."

Chapter Seventeen

D iana and I enter the wooden steps to the concrete garage floor, to find Ben, Tyler, Evan, and a handful of basketball boys hovering around a ping-pong table in the garage amidst a small sea of people. Evan's in a frog-legged squat, bouncing up and down shouting "I wanna rock!...ROCK!" with the rest of the boys to the Twisted Sister song shaking the stereo on the garage shelf. Diana still has the Genesis tape and due to the already-provided garage music I'm not sure if I'll get to execute my plan. At least not anytime soon.

The room has a display of large black posters tacked to the wall—a Disneyland map, an ad for Nike Air Force shoes with a pair of lone tanned eighties legs flying amidst a cloudy sky with a black border; and a poster that says "Cocaine. It can cost you your brain."

Erica, Bennette, and three men whose skinny bellies and face are etched in red war paint walk past us through the doorway to the kitchen. Greg's one of them, wearing minimal clothing and face paint, but instead of leaving with them he heads toward the ping-pong table. He may have a promising future as a rodeo clown. He's the only one with accessories—a cropped top and cowboy hat.

Diana shuffles through the mass of bodies surrounding the ping-pong table, dragging me with her to a less crowded area. We migrate toward a colonial couch next to a hanging inflatable orange crayon in the corner. Her master plan is obvious—get the good couch and leave the boys playing ping-pong with the frumpy bean bag in the corner.

"Atta, got a foot to the face today, didn't you?" Evan turns, setting his paddle down on the table making his way to our couch.

"Yeah, I heard Kelly plowed through you." Greg approaches our couch first, smiles at me and raises his eyebrows in mockery. Greg can claim this bruise as his doing. It wouldn't be painted on without him and Ben.

"That's all thanks to you, Greg." Kelly bursts through the growing circle and points her finger like a dagger, poking him in the forehead. Someone behind a camera makes their way around the room, adding clicks and flashes to the chaos as more people crowd around.

"No pictures!" Bennette and Corky yell in unison a few feet away at the cameraman. I study Bennette and Corky. Linked arm in arm, with puckered red solo cups in their hands, they seem as close as ever. Diana appears at my side and gives the camera a full-toothed smile and then sticks her tongue out. I raise my red solo cup as it passes by.

A neglected photo of Tyler's family rests on the garage shelf to my right. Tyler's father stands next to Tyler in what must be a recent picture, appearing no older than twenty-five, yet he's with Tyler who's seventeen. Not quite the grown adult in his forties serving meals for us on the houseboat our senior year of high school, he must be considered Tyler's brother here, standing next to what I assume are Tyler's parents in this alternate universe—the same way Diana and I had somehow become imbedded into our mother's young adult existence, experiencing something of a generational time-squish.

Tyler makes a bold move squeezing his cheeks in between mine and Diana's. He gently pushes me aside so that Evan can burrow in next to me. I send Diana siren signals with my eyes from across the couch, but apparently it's not enough to motivate her to blow Tyler off and save me. She gets up off the couch and leaves me to endure the impending conversation alone sandwiched in between Tyler and Evan.

"How are you?" Evan starts the conversation and lowers his sunglasses to look at my forehead.

"A little purple thanks to Ben," I say with a hint of cynicism. The fact that I'm still brewing about our earlier conversation doesn't help. I give my best answers to Evan's following small talk as my eyes search for Diana amongst the crowd. Luckily enough, he doesn't mention the fact that he'd planned this night for our first date.

A flood of familiar feathery-haired teens enter the garage and storm each other with hugs—true eighties headlock style. Diana makes her way through as if she has the powers to part a red sea full of jean jackets, bleached hair and patchy, zit covered faces. She taps me on the shoulder and gifts me a handful of peanuts, then hands out cups of ice cream drizzled in chocolate syrup to the three of us on the couch. She's giving me the honors of showering everyone's Peanut Buster Parfait with peanuts.

Diana's ice cream offering comes at a perfect time. Throughout the evening my time travel failure and where I went wrong has weighed upon me, but the more impending issue—having to let Evan down makes me feel like I'm at the bottom of a pile of toppled cheerleaders, each passing minute adding another body to the wreck. I welcome the sugary distraction as Diana slides back in next to Tyler on the couch and we all dig into the parfaits, scooping chocolatey goo against the glass with silver spoons. My tastebuds experience a sweet and salty explosion, taking my mind to a whole other level of a flavor-filled bliss as I look across the room and spot Ben eating ice cream in the other corner with Bennette.

My dessert-fueled escape is interrupted when I catch Tyler jogging past the ping-pong table with both palms dipped in black paint. I watch as each of his movements become calculated like a striking tiger. Those with an unblocked view of the door to the kitchen can see that Greg is the target prey and before Greg has the chance to see his attacker, Tyler takes a double-handed swat to Greg's Levi-covered butt cheeks, resulting in two victimized back pockets that are now success-fully and permanently branded in Tyler's handprint revenge. The space around me fills with laughter, and I join in the fun with a few congrat-ulatory claps.

"It's only a matter of time before he gets Ben," Diana whispers. I scrape the last of the parfait from my glass as Tyler reemerges through the kitchen door with a newly re-dipped pair of hands. This is it. Tyler's going to strike again. The anticipation builds as I watch Ben and Bennette wipe ice cream off of the top of each other's lips. I can't help but feel a surge of jealousy and then delight, knowing Ben's the next target.

Tyler's party now consists of box cake and purely chaotic teenage discord. Yet here I am a ball of anxiety in between bobbing heads and bodies, ready to bounce out the door as I run lines through my head about how best to turn Evan down. I plan to tell him as soon as he ends his conversation with the basketball player who lingers at the end of the couch.

Most of the room is so consumed with devouring what's left of Erica's sun-shaped box cake that they don't follow Tyler's windup and release. The result reverberates through the carpeted room like a muffled snap of a whip. Only Diana, Bennette, and I catch the smack in action. Tyler slaps Ben's behind with much greater force than he did with Greg. There's no laughing or clapping this time, just a startled Ben who spontaneously reacts by hopping over the stubby couch arm to get away from Tyler's swing. He turns back to give Tyler a brotherly shove, but chooses not to follow as Tyler sprints off in the other direction.

Twenty minutes later Evan's still talking basketball and Tyler, with his magnet-like properties toward Diana, reappears and accompanies us back to the garage, where we fall into the lumpy sofa cushions with the enthusiasm of the *Friends* characters in the opening credits. Then Ben pays us a visit for the first time tonight without Bennette.

"I need your car keys, Diana." Ben slips me a callous glance while Diana reaches for her keys in her back pocket. Ben looks to Tyler who sits at the edge of the couch. "That was your weakest attempt at payback. I thought you'd put a little more effort into it. You might as well have whipped me with a flower." Ben turns around and makes a strongman pose. "These buns of steel felt nothing."

At Ben's remark the three of us look at each other with surprised expressions, and then all of our heads turn to once again assess Ty's black handprints on the butt of Ben's pants. "A slap in the butt in front of my girlfriend hardly competes with airing your Dynamite thongs for everyone to see."

"Hey now," Tyler says. "We all saw. They were boxers and briefs. Not thongs, and I'll admit it wasn't my best effort, but it was funny."

Ben turns back around and shakes his head as if Tyler's spewing complete nonsense.

"I don't know. I was a bit disappointed that you ran away thinking touching my butt was an actual prank," Ben says. He holds his palm cupped and arm stretched out for Diana to set the keys into. He stands in front of us waiting for a response from Diana, and Tyler's eyes light up as if he's been told the last present under the Christmas tree is his. He turns toward Diana to lean in and whisper in her ear. At the same moment, I realize what Tyler already knows. Ben has absolutely no idea his butt is inked.

"Who'd have thought your brother would be so oblivious?" I over-hear Tyler whisper. They both squeal with soft laughter. It seems Diana's completely forgiven Tyler as her eyes form thin slits of joy as she laughs next to him. She's giving Ben a range of silly looks to poke fun at him as he cluelessly stares at the two of them behaving so chummy.

"You really think I'd just go for a slap on the butt to get back at you for displaying my Dynamite collection in public. You're right, that wasn't the prank. You were too busy licking Bennette's lips to notice," Tyler says, changing the subject, then pauses, enjoying Ben's uncom-fortable anticipation.

Ben looks around the room for something out of place, something unusual or marked by Tyler's deviant misbehavior. He turns to study

Tyler and slides his hands into his back pockets leaving his thumbs hanging. He's angled so that I see him rubbing his thumb back and forth like a windshield wiper feeling the thickness of wet paint against his backside. Realizing the slimy texture is an unusual addition to the tough thread of his jeans, his lips pinch together in defeat.

"Paint? Really? Ty, you know these are my good jeans. Not every pair of jeans can handle this fine of an apple." I snort at his reference to his tush before he turns away to do something about his jeans.

"The bathroom sink should give you a better view," Tyler adds, then turns his head to whisper something clever into Diana's ear but catches her lips in between his words instead.

Chapter Eighteen

I silently gasp.

The brush of their lips leaves them both frozen and pressed together. Neither of them turns away, instead letting their lips explore, slowly at first, and then they just continue kissing.

Diana is actually kissing him back. Here it is, the high school romance between Diana and Ty. I'm back for round two, eighties universe edition.

I can't tell who breaks away first, but the wave of lips part as Diana's hands glide down from Tyler's shoulders to his elbows. They both look surprised, but Diana's trying to hide a smile that's eager to reveal itself.

"That was unexpected," I say, shooting up out of my seat. "I'm going to get a drink. You two enjoy yourselves." I reach for Diana's purse while her concentration is elsewhere, digging into its contents in search of the Genesis tape. My hands grasp nothing but straw wrappers, lipsticks, and credit cards, so I leave them to continue whatever's supposed to come after accidental kissing—more kissing, talking, possibly sitting in silence. And find that my plan will likely be unsuccessful in the end.

I head to the living room. As soon as I get there I glance at the clock shaped like a sunflower on the wall. It's a quarter to seven and a slice of sun still warms the carpet through the stained-glass door windows. After exploring a little, I find myself admiring the steep wood-paneled stairwell on the far side of the living room that leads to the stargazing atrium window of my dreams. I hear the leaves of the aspen tree tapping a dull song onto the ceiling's french sun window. I've wanted to take a look at the sky from their second story atrium since the moment we pulled up to Tyler's dark and angled wood home.

I'm not sure how long I've been wandering when Diana finds me on the stairs. "Can you believe it? Tyler and I kissed. For, like, twenty minutes until he said he had to leave and left with Evan."

"What? He just left after kissing you?" I ask, mildly surprised.

"He said he needed a break and just kind of ran off."

"What an idiot." I shake my head, unsure of what Tyler's trying to pull by acting like this.

"Yeah. I don't want to think this way, but what if kissing me was just one of his stupid pranks?" Diana says. The wheels must be turning at supersonic speeds inside that head of hers.

I watch as she paces the length of the living room. She spots the idle stereo where Ben and others stand mingling about and by the determination in her steps I can tell she's fabricating some sort of angry plan.

"Diana? Doing the dirty work for me?" I mutter to myself, grabbing the wood rail and pressing my back against the fourth stair up to comfortably watch the show from afar. There's no way she knew what I had planned to do with that Genesis tape, but watching her approach the stereo with multiple cassette player slots, it seems she's about to do exactly as I had planned.

Ben stands near the speakers with Greg and Erica, completely oblivious to his sister's presence, while Bennette and Corky cuddle on a couch in the corner. I see right through Diana, she's planning to bait them with Genesis to see how our earlier car conversation questions will play out in real life. We both want to know, how will Ben and Corky react?

I'm thankful that Diana has chosen this path instead of me. I'm about to relax—comfortably watch Diana confront her brother in a room full of unglued people—when I realize I would have been the one to do this very thing.

An uneasy feeling creeps through me—my quest for answers didn't take other people's feelings or lives into consideration. I look over at Bennette snuggled up against Corky. What kind of outburst will this produce? If my enemy was cuddled up against me as I learn of her betrayal it wouldn't be a small storm, but a full-on blitzkrieg.

Diana opens the cassette slot, clicks the tape into place, and presses play. Genesis rings delicately through the speakers before Diana rolls the volume dial all the way up. The sound of drums and boppy synthe-sizer hits, punching some energy into the room as the first line of Side A Track 1 begins. A few couples wrap their arms around each other and begin to sway to the music.

Diana turns around, pivoting her slouchy boots to face the couch where Corky slowly lets lyrics fall from her lips. I watch as Diana approaches and asks, "Good song, right?"

Corky adjusts herself so she's no longer pressed against Bennette's side and perks up at Diana's remark.

"I didn't know you were a Genesis fan," Corky eagerly replies.

"Yeah, I went to their concert a few weeks ago," Diana lies.

"You went? Who'd you go with? Why didn't you go with Ben and I? We..." Corky's words halt as soon as she realizes she's said some-thing that might confuse Bennette. Uneasiness pours from her eyes.

I've never seen Corky so uncertain. She stays still sitting in an upright position on the couch, careful not to turn her head toward Bennette until she's able to conceal her worry with a disguised smile—faking peace of mind and innocence.

Bennette's eyes bounce from Corky to Diana as she comprehends Corky's words. She sits up promptly from her slouched position, matching Corky's upright stance then turns her head sideways to face Corky. Corky takes a second too long to face Bennette.

"You went to the Genesis concert with Ben?" she says, a few inches away from Corky's face, in an accusatory voice. She's upset and Corky bites her lower lip as it trembles. "Ben said he went with a friend…and you were out of town that week," Bennette continues, seemingly connecting the dots.

Ben seems to have heard the entire interaction and meets my gaze from across the room looking resentful and huffy. He waits for Corky to respond before stepping in and from the look of his gaze I know his thoughts are targeted toward my betrayal—Diana's too. But he must think I shared the information with her, and thus it's my betrayal. I could hide—head upstairs for a while.

"We um…It's not what you think," I hear Corky say as I grip the rail harder and turn to face the top stair that leads to the narrow atrium hallway above.

"Why would you keep that from me if there's nothing going on between you two? She's my best friend, Ben!" Bennette shouts.

Ben walks toward them and responds with a calm hushed tone and I'm unable to hear what's said from the stairwell. It looks as if he's calming the situation with a quiet explanation. I continue watching with my head turned back to see how that tactic plays out, ready to run if I get brought into it. But Ben remains calm amongst a shaky Corky and watery-eyed Bennette.

That is until he turns his head to the stairwell and his sugary brown eyes land on me. He has the face of a man wanting to chase another man and tackle him into a pool. I fly up the steps like a cheetah feeling the threat of a lion. My sprint is light, feeling my arms pump perfectly at ninety degrees at my sides—it's good to know my training hasn't been lost on me as I skip every other stair in the process just to evade the coming wrath of Ben.

Chapter Nineteen

As soon as I make it up the narrow wood-paneled stairwell, I enter the second-story atrium I've been wanting to visit since this morning, just not under this current set of circumstances. The atrium is just as charming as I imagined with a built-in hardwood desk underneath the paneled window and dark jasper green walls. The opposite wall holds an antique apothecary cabinet, custom built between dark floral wallpaper.

I pause. Suspended with a choice of which route to take—the closed door with an old knob or back down the stairs. I test the door, feeling the heat of the situation, and yank the knob with no luck. Locked. So I listen for the sound of Ben's steps coming up the stairs and when they don't appear, I make myself comfortable.

The apothecary unit is impressive, claiming nearly half of the wall and begging me to dig through its contents. I use the gaudy bronze knobs to pull out each tiny drawer, my curiosity overflowing with what these little cubbies contain. Ben hasn't chased after me and Evan ran off with Tyler, so I take it that I have time to explore them.

There's an entire row dedicated to small constellation books and constellation guides. I pull a royal blue book titled *Sir Patrick Moore -*

Science Book Night Sky Constellations from the fourth drawer and flip through the tiny navy blocks within its pages that map out constellations. I pause on Puppis and try to find it in the night sky above me as I sit at the wall desk.

The outskirts of Golden, at the base of the mountain, give a much better view of the stars than Denver ever could with all its city lights. They must have built this house knowing the atrium would be the perfect spot for stargazing.

The sky between the trees wears a thousand tiny snowflakes. The stars dusted across the sky pulse above me as I save the Puppis constellation page with my index finger and bring the book over to the telescope which sits at the corner of the wall desk.

My lack of experience in astronomy is obvious and I find myself struggling to focus. Instead, my thoughts go from the perplexity of connecting dots in the night sky to thinking about how the tiniest percentage of stars actually shine bright enough for us to make them out. Stars bright enough to see from the earth are quite scarce, percentage-wise, so does that make the stars that shine for us special in some way?

Just like the mystery of me being here at this time. Time travel is just as scarce as the percentage of stars that shine, right? That had to be why no one deemed it possible, since most people have likely never known someone who's experienced it. Since it was rare, did that make it special or more meaningful? Was my experience here by chance or was it fate—did it have any meaning? Was I plucked from the jar of destiny to be sent here to find something that would help me out with this unusual predicament—being threatened by a corrupt FBI department for knowledge that could get me killed was a rare occurrence, right?

I didn't know if I believed in that sort of thing, but I believed in making the most of my circumstances. Part of me had wanted a vacation from the everyday routine of pleated dress pants, sliding my FBI badge into my camel-colored coat, and hopping into my orange Volkswagen bug with a protein bar in my mouth, to spend the day tagging along with partner agents.

And if I was honest, I didn't mind the change of pace. At this point I hope being here is destiny and maybe I can solve the Marigold issue from this past. Maybe, then, I could do something about it all, back in Non-80s-Land.

If I ever got back.

The thought of Ben, Agent Brown—Ben, suffering alone without me, breaks me. But what if it's my destiny to save our future selves using information from the eighties. Energy stirs within me at the possibility.

Shuffling through a few more tiny drawers in the wall I come across knickknacks that don't have a home—buttons, coins, nails— and then, newspaper clippings. I flip through a few headlines to find that everything's dated late 1986 and 1987, and pull a clipped set from the bunch. I drop the set on the desk and begin running my fingers through the thinness of the papers, the crunch of my fingers against paper becoming louder than the muffled chatter from the main room downstairs.

I hit a gap in between pages, where a small but thick manila envelope breaks the flow of papers. When I bust open the unsealed envelope, I find a picture of three men. All three wear identical red jackets with a symbol that draws my attention like an accident on the side of the road. The Marigold symbol with pointed crystal petals. The same symbol that was embroidered on the pockets of those same red jackets worn by every member passing around a knife in that horrifying USB video. The same symbol coincidentally tattooed on Officer Berrett's kettlebell sculpted arm.

Back in Non-80s-Land, I had left the Marigold symbol glowing on Pops' pixelated Windows 95 search screen, but it is ever so present in this timeline. It's as if my life is a game of Clue and I'm being slapped in the face with cards that only lead me to one room, the Marigold room. Its persistent presence gives me concern but I'm also encouraged. I feel like I've been given a golden opportunity. I've seen enough Marigold clues that I should be able to start proving and disproving theories. As long as the cards keep coming I should be able to correctly guess the three cards in the enclosed envelope that represent the solution at the end of the game. Maybe the eighties has all the cards I need and someone within Tyler's household is already showing me their hand through this set of newspaper clippings.

The first newspaper clipping is from this week.

I feel a little uneasy knowing I'm going through Tyler's family's drawers especially with such recent and relevant articles. I turn around and check once more to make sure I'm still the only one up here.

The headline reads "Sheriden Foundation Purchases Household Brand, Clean Wave, Under Pro Golfer Robert Schills' New Management." The name Robert Schills sounds familiar. I vaguely remember reading an article about his early retirement from golfing just a few days ago.

I plow through the article, which discusses Robert and his team's direction and their hopes for the new company. My heart races as I read on, knowing this article confirms Sheriden's connection to Clean Wave. And now I have a name. Robert Schills.

I get an even greater chill realizing someone in Tyler's household has made the same connection I have. How would they know about this? What concern tipped them off in the first place? We're thirty-some years before I would have any idea something was wrong in Non-80s-Land with this group. Taking a deep sigh to contain my excitement, I flip through a few more clippings that I can't quite make connections with.

The stairs creak from the weight of someone's feet making noisy progress up the stairs; each step's squeak becomes a little bit noisier than the last. A soft yet creepy timbre of footsteps, like something from a scary movie cinematic soundtrack leaks into my mind as I turn my head toward the dim lit stairwell and I shove the newspapers in my drawstring bag with a sense of panic.

Chapter Twenty

I turn to see a familiar shadow standing at the top of the stairs.

"I see you found the Jacobson's atrium."

Ben Brown's voice echoes from the stairwell. He must be ready to tell me off for what went down downstairs.

"Yeah, I did," I say, turning to face Ben gingerly. I know he's a ticking time bomb ready to blast me with shrapnel and radioactive dust now that we're alone together.

"Why are you up here and not down there watching my relationship crumble?" He scoffs and walks over to the apothecary wall a few feet from where I stand.

"I didn't want to see your relationship crumble," I say. And I mean it. I wanted to get to the bottom of why he wasn't speaking with me though.

"No, but you thought you'd torture me by hinting blackmail all week and then have my sister do the dirty work for you. Why'd you leave? The drama wasn't good enough for you?" The mysterious sneer underneath his dark tone matches the mystery of the night sky above the atrium's glass ceiling.

"I left because I felt like I was in danger," I say as if I'm about to let a frightened laugh Heimlich out of me.

"Well, you did plan this," he says, clearly unsure of what to think of me. He's angry but he's glazing everything over with a sneer as if he knows it's punishment enough.

"There were too many people in that room. I couldn't have done what Diana did. And I couldn't have gotten as much out of Corky as she did. It seems like Diana was going to do it regardless."

"Seriously, Atta?" He folds his arms over in amused annoyance. "All the interfering, investigating, and bumping into me at school every day and now involving my sister to crash my relationship. What's with the newfound obsession? Don't tell me it's because you're actually jealous of Bennette."

I'm instantly taken aback. So much so that I knock the astronomy book over with a frantic swipe. What obsession?

He was my best friend. I was in no way obsessed with him. My ongoing childhood infatuation with him may still be a flame that ceases to be blown out, but calling it an obsession is a bit much. I'd given up on him long ago. I suppose I'd been a bit more aggressive seeking him out under these circumstances, when alternate reality called for it and he didn't have any recollection of our history. So to him perhaps it looked like I was acting out of jealousy.

"Obsessed? You think pretty highly of yourself to make that kind of claim," I say collecting the astronomy book from the floor.

"Are you not? Since when have you made it your business to care who I date and what I do when I date?" he says as he pulls open the nearest apothecary drawer.

"Never," I say, feeling unqualified to have this conversation.

"Don't tell me you think that because I went to a concert with Corky that gave everyone, including you, an open door to claim me while I'm still dating Bennette."

"Wow, your head is so inflated I'm afraid you might float through the glass." I motion a finger to the atrium above. Ben just chuckles.

"You think you know my motive but I promise you, you don't," I continue.

"Try me." His eyes are daring. "You like me and you're too afraid to admit it, unless you have a better explanation for your weird behavior all week," he says, baiting me.

Unwilling to get into time travel, I opt for a partial truth. "Like I've said a million times before, I'm just trying to understand why you would choose the concert with Corky and not tell Bennette. It's not like you to be so uncaring, and yes, I've always liked you Ben. I hardly see how this is the first time you've noticed, but that's not why I cornered you." It was the first time I'd admitted it like that, and it felt good to express the truth to him. Even if I couldn't share the full truth, some truth felt comfortable. Like our normal friendship, we'd share almost everything with each other.

"That wasn't so hard, was it?" he says looking as if he might pat my head like he would a younger sibling who's done a good deed. Not exactly the response I'd hoped for, but it's what I'd come to expect. "Then I guess you deserve to hear why I did it, again. Since you seem to have forgotten our phone conversation last month when you hopped on the line and interrupted the connection." He squats down against the wall of small apothecary drawers and begins digging through a side of drawers I haven't touched yet and pulls out a random cassette tape.

"Ahh," he sighs. "This makes everything better." He holds the tape out as if to show me its importance. His hold on it feels familiar, like the way I stroke my crossword when crap hits the fan.

I suppose solving puzzles was a comforting distraction—board games, puzzles, solving cases with game theory. Who needed a therapist when scribbling letters in tiny boxes made me feel better—at least that's how I saw it. My world made sense when I became the investigator, as if I could solve my own internal pain by solving someone else's puzzle.

"I know the feeling," I assure him. I guess we're both going to ignore the fact that I confessed my feelings for him.

"Corky offered me a ride to the concert when she found out we'd both bought tickets to Genesis. I went with her and didn't tell Bennette but I didn't mean anything else by it."

"You didn't think to tell Bennette you planned to go to the concert with her best friend or at least offer an invite to her?" I say. He didn't think this through very well it seems.

"Before the concert, Corky bought the new Genesis album. She wanted to show me in her car after basketball practice because we're both obsessed with Genesis. Bennette flipped out on both of us before I could even get out of the car to greet her," he says shuffling through the wall drawers. "I wasn't going to miss the concert and neither was Corky. Bennette would never approve of us going together so we thought it would be best to just keep it from her."

"So you chose a band over your girlfriend," I say, chuckling like he's some stupid teen making amateur choices.

"Bennette's just upset because Corky and I like the same music. It's not like we'd ever end up together."

"Or it could be that you lied to her," I say in a mocking tone once again.

"I guess. It doesn't matter now anyway," he says, holding three tapes fanned out in his long fingers. I take it that he and Bennette are no longer an item.

"But who invites her best friend's boyfriend to a concert and hides it? Are you sure Corky doesn't have an ulterior motive?" I ask.

"Says the woman who also tried to use a cassette tape to break up my relationship." He's now mocking me. I'll be considering him the fifth Golden Girl if he keeps up the sassiness.

"I shouldn't have grabbed your Genesis tape in the first place and shouldn't have had Diana confront you with it, but do you really care so little for Bennette? You act like you aren't even phased about her breaking up with you." His look turns a bit more menacing, as if I had exposed his true feelings that he'd rather keep hidden.

"I've had all week to prepare for the loss." He nods at me. "I knew this would happen the moment you broke your word and got involved." He lowers into a seated position with his knees up and feet flat against the hardwood floor. "It doesn't matter anyway," he says as if his goal is to move on entirely.

He becomes lost in thought and I find the silence deafening. It's our first successful conversation since I was sucked into this weird world and I don't want it to end here.

"So music?" I say, shattering his moment of solitude.

"I grab a tape from the Jacobson family collection every time I'm here." He reaches into his front pockets and pulls out an ocean blue tape with five men at a bar on the plastic cover. The *Sports* album from Huey Lewis and The News. He opens the drawer that the first tape came from and replaces Huey Lewis in its spot.

"And you called me a thief!" I say, fabricating surprise.

"Tyler knows. His dad OK'd me to sample anything I like here."

"And you like…" I pause reading the title of the tape in his hand. "Aerosmith."

"Yes. This is their newest album *Classics Live*. I've got four of their nine albums." He hands me the tape this time to look at. The only song I'm familiar with is "Dream On", but I can't help but think of "Dude (Looks Like a Lady)"—to me that song encompasses Aerosmith.

"I've always wondered what the story is behind some of these song titles," I say, deeply zoned into the words on the plastic casing. "Like here 'Lord of the Thighs' and 'Three Mile Smile.'" A lighthearted laugh splashes out from my mouth. Ben furrows his brows at my song picks and then appears casually delighted.

"You've always wondered things like that? What do you think the story behind it is?" His smugness keeps emerging within the brief moments he seems to forget his deep-seated breakup sorrows.

"Well in 'Dude Looks Like a Lady,' I always imagined a jazzercise instructor with long lion-like hair pulled back in a yellow headband and matching leotard, who looks like a sexy stewardess from the back but then when he turns around it's really Tarzan but with a Guy Fieri goatee." I describe the song just as I envision it every single time I hear the chorus.

"I have no idea what you're saying right now." Ben smiles. He looks charmed and confused all at the same time. "What's 'Dude Looks Like a Lady?'"

I realize I must have a date issue since this Ben knows his music and has four out of nine albums. Is that crazy song not out yet?

"Don't worry about it," I say, hoping that gets me out of an explanation for my nonsensical description. At least it was nonsensical for someone who isn't familiar with the unreleased song and Guy Fieri. Those came later.

"Do you do this often—wonder why people name their songs the way they do?" he asks, observing me as if I'm a foreign object—a new Atta. It's possible he's mistaking me for a music lover, when really it's just a matter of my constant, unmanageable curiosity.

The drawer next to him is jammed with more tapes. I pull a handful out thinking this will be a good way to waste some time with my best friend. I sit down beside him and he doesn't flinch or seem to mind my close proximity.

"Aw, here we go. 'You're The Reason Our Kids Are Ugly,'" I say, flipping the cassette tape over to show him the Loretta Lynn and Conway Twitty album cover.

"She's dissing her ex-husband. There's no other possible explanation for that name title," he says and we both snicker.

He shoots me a half smile and uses a kneeling maneuver to pull out another handful of tapes from the wall, before scattering them on the floor in front of me. We shuffle through until—Little Richard. He holds the tape close to my face pointing to a song.

I read the song title out loud, "'Cats Iron Arm.' Not a metaphor. He must be singing about a prosthetic bionic arm attachment for his fuzzy friend."

Ben shakes his head. "Are you sure it's not 'Cast Iron Arm?'" he says, trying to suppress a smile.

I look down at the cassette and realize it is in fact cast and not cat.

I look over at him and laugh. He lets a crooked smile escape. We've actually managed to entertain each other up here despite the contention we were both feeling just a half an hour ago.

"Oh oh, this one's a good one! Johnny Cash," I say excitedly. "'I've Been Flushed From The Bathroom Of Your Heart.'" A flash of a smile hits his face.

"You made that up," he objects.

"No, it's right here." I hold the tape up close to him so he can read the small text.

"That's one way to write a breakup song. Comparing the relationship to the shitter." His words leave his mouth with pleasure.

He clicks open a gray tape.

"Joe Walsh. You have to listen to 'Inner Tube - Theme from Boat Weirdos.' It's all instrumental but such a good track. You should take that one home and give it a listen. Trust me, it's beautiful," he says and it's at this point I feel I've done it. I've crossed the barrier that was put in front of me since entering this alternate universe. Ben and I. I think we are friends again.

"Okay. I will." I take the tape he's handed to me.

"Does it hurt?" He points to the bruise on my forehead that I was unable to cover with Diana's shimmery makeup.

"Only if I press on it," I say. He leans in a little toward me, a devilish gaze in his eyes. "No, you can't touch it!" I form an arm barricade around my face so he's unable to press a finger to my forehead.

"Hey, Ben," I begin, confident he won't try to touch my bruise. He's too buried in cassette tapes to move close enough to me.

"Yeah?" He looks up from the hill of tapes lounging against his strong thighs.

"I really wasn't trying to get between you and Bennette." His face remains neutral at my confession.

"Then what were you planning to do?" His mouth finally pulls up into a smirk.

"Not that. I missed talking to you and..." I look up toward the atrium to see if the stars look as vulnerable up in the vast island universe as I feel right now.

"You two are up here?" Diana says from the top step. Her footsteps are much softer than Ben's. That or she crept up on tiptoe to surprise us. It worked since we both feel our dark, remote, and somewhat cozy environment fade away. From the look on Diana's face, she's been looking for us for a while now and she's ready to leave.

"You both go ahead without me. I've got a late night ahead of me," Ben says, heading toward the locked door on the opposite side of the stairwell where the rest of the house and likely Tyler's bedroom nest away.

Chapter Twenty-One

"So he's really not into Corky?" Diana says. We sit outside of her home in her little red sports car while I give a retelling of my time with her brother, specifically his explanation of why he kept the concert with Corky a secret from Bennette.

"Based on his reaction, I don't think he's into either of them. He seems apathetic to all of it." I lay my arms out across the dashboard as if I were in a deliberation room, letting my arms emphasize the reasons for Ben's actions. "He even admitted to choosing music over his girlfriend and said Bennette hates Genesis but would have wanted to join them if she knew they were going. Sounds like she's already gotten upset with Ben for listening to music with Corky in her car." I give a final shrug. "He basically said she'd ruin the whole night for them if she came," I explain.

A group of kids playing night games kick a ball back and forth over the next door neighbor's roof, like a game of ping-pong. The little runners and squealers look like they're in middle school, about Davy and Steven's age and before we know it, large scale ping-pong turns into a game of redrover. I ask Diana how late they'll be out. It's nearing midnight and there's at least a gang of twenty preteens running around in the dark.

"They'll turn in around twelve." She tells me about the neighbor lady who comes out with a ladle and whips it around with a warning if they stay out past that time.

"Did Tyler ever come back?" I ask.

"No, I haven't heard from him, that hoser," she says, fanning her long painted fingers across the wheel. "Evan came back for a second to grab something. He said to tell you he had to leave for a family emergency."

"Oh. I hope everything's okay," I say.

"You missed all the good action though. Right after I confronted Ben, some guy named Tony came over and asked Ben and Corky how they liked the concert. He'd made the trip to Kansas City and saw them there as well. They both looked so exposed. He would've exposed them even if I hadn't." She yanks the keys out of the car letting the engine exhale one last growl. "Bennette let Corky have it. She's such a small, tiny thing but it looked like she could've done some damage to Corky the way she was standing. I felt like we were at a boxing weigh-in watching an intense staredown."

"And she didn't freak out on Ben? He acted like they were over," I say.

"Oh no. She did. She wasn't able to say anything for a while but then she pulled Ben into the corner and kept repeating something like 'Why would you keep a secret like that from me?'"

"And what did he say?"

"He didn't have much of an answer. I think he tried saying Corky and him are just friends and have nothing in common except for liking Genesis. She kept asking questions about the ride to Kansas City and saying they must have quite a lot in common to enjoy a car ride together. He was calm until he told her she'd ruin the whole experience, and I think she dumped him right after that. It was kind of painful to watch."

Car headlights beam across the house as the outline of a car appears behind us. Diana and I watch the light around us go dark and the door slam shut at the front of the house.

"Ben must be home," Diana says as we throw our bags over our shoulders and head on into the house.

IT'S LATE, NEARLY THREE O'CLOCK IN THE MORNING, BUT WE'RE still wiry and flipping through magazines while giggling about a time Diana helped me attempt pole vault—her all-time favorite sport. It was my first time hearing this rendition of me clinging to the pole, like a koala clinging onto a bamboo branch as it breaks off and falls to the ground. Apparently, I made it into the air but instead of pushing past the bar, I held on as it fell back the way it came. Non-80s-Land-Atta would never actually attempt pole vault, but Diana's alternate universe memory made me laugh.

At the sound of knocking on Diana's door we pop straight up in her bed. I close the magazine pages that hold the stolen manila folder of newspaper clippings that I'm trying to secretly sort through under the covers.

"Come in," Diana says, frustrated at the late night interruption.

Ben bursts through the door, his late night sweat catching the dim light of the room. His dark eyes burn with intensity as he lands at the foot of Diana's bed, leaning forward, unknowingly exposing his wide shoulders and bare chest, without warning. It had been years since I'd seen him in just pajama bottoms. He takes a quick glance in my direction, acknowledging my presence and then averts his gaze quickly, turning back to face his sister.

"I heard you kissed Tyler tonight. What were you thinking?" he says with a gust of interrogation-style energy. Intensity flares inside of him so thick it causes me to have temporary confusion between this universe and the next. It's as if my partner Agent Brown is back and Diana is his next suspect in the interrogation room. They become quiet for a moment but I can sense the frustration bubbling inside of

Ben. He lets out a few breaths to calm himself but his disapproving eyes give away the fact that he's still steadily troubled.

"I kissed him?" Diana rakes her long fingers through her hair, tying a night scarf around it so it isn't disfigured in her sleep. "We…it was an accident, Ben. Why do you even care? Isn't he one of your good friends anyway?" she asks, securing the scarf into place.

"So you didn't kiss him? Then why did Evan tell me you did?"

"We accidentally touched lips when your dumb self couldn't figure out that he'd left his fingerprints on your back pockets."

"So that's all it was? An accident? Just promise me you won't go with him." He grips his hands around the bed frame.

"I can't promise you a thing," Diana sprays dismissal in his face.

"I know him pretty well, Di. He's not good for you."

"Says the one who lost his girlfriend and ruined her relationship with her best friend tonight." Ben leans backward, his hands still gripping the metal frame.

"You're the one who ruined that tonight. The rest of us were keeping things hush-hush to avoid all this." He flings his hands up, like they can encompass the entire debacle. He lowers his hands and takes a slow breath. "Don't be surprised if he isn't the committed type," he adds, craning his neck in a casual stretch. He obviously intends to drop the topic and pick back up the one he barged in about.

"Just like you?" she says, pressing him hard. Anger seeps through her tone. I hadn't realized how disappointed Diana was in her brother for keeping this little secret from his girlfriend and from her. Ben holds back his response and by the look on his face I can tell it's because of my presence.

"Think what you want, Diana," he says, swallowing Diana's jab. "Oh and I'd like my Genesis tape back, little sis." He motions for her to cough it up, lingering by the doorway in his pajama bottoms—a few inches too short for him.

Diana leans over the side of the bed and retrieves the plastic cassette tape from her purse that's lying on the carpet next to her nightstand. Before she has a chance to sit back up, Ben swoops in and snatches it from her and then paces back to the door.

"Oh and Atta, if you ever need to take any of my things from my room, make sure to be more discreet. Your infatuation is sweet, but I don't want to have to hunt you down to collect my things anymore than you want me finding out that you took them," he says in a playfully dark tone.

The smoothness. He managed to get the last word in and own it well. But the exchange causes my fighting spirit to kick in. I shake off what's left of the blankets covering me and stand on the bed just as he shuts the door to leave the room.

"What are you doing?" Diana prods. I might've looked guilty had I not been so determined to follow after him and take back my dignity. "He teases you all the time. Don't tell me you're going after him," Diana says, flailing her arms in protest as I hop off the bed and grab the doorknob.

"We just cleared the air at the party, and he's still accusing me of quote, unquote, 'obsessing over him,'" I say before twisting the knob.

"Are you really surprised? He's always talking down to us," Diana says. "Do you really care enough to chase after him?"

I shrug in defeat and open the door. She looks frozen in thought, rolled up in the bedding like an uneven cinnamon roll.

I tiptoe after him, my cold feet—half covered with Diana's baggy Fruit of the Loom sweatpants—gently grinding against the hallway floor. I'm as comfortable as it gets in the oversized tee Diana lent me for the night. It says "To Cause Trouble" with some cat friends holding a match, a jug of gasoline, and an overall group identity that bleeds pure mischief. And at this moment I carry the same energy as the characters on the rebel tee cascading off my shoulders.

I try to keep my steps soft to avoid waking Mama Robyn and Grandma Harriet. Even so, Ben hears me coming and abruptly stops and turns, right in front of the open doorframe to his room.

"What are you doing, Atta?" he asks softly, his voice deep and low as if exhaustion has taken over.

"I'm not letting you leave like that," I say. I hear the late night fatigue talking for me. Do I do things late at night that I would easily rationalize myself out of during the day time? Yes. Yes, I do. But he can't leave accusing me of obsessing over him like that. It'll eat at me, sleeping in the same house as him tonight.

"Like what?" His fake show of teasing has worn off and I can see his genuine confusion and beaten temperament sag through. Our relationship was composed of that brotherly annoyance and I knew I shouldn't be calling him out like this. I'm making too big of a deal about it, but it feels good, so I continue.

"You know I'm not obsessed with you, right?" I hurl the words at him. "And if I hadn't carried out that strategy, I would be absolutely clueless right now, so what looks like obsession to you is actually just determination to get my questions answered."

"Really? You got all your questions answered? That's great, Atta. Really great. All it took was some determination?" He looks tired. The night is fanning the flames for unfiltered thoughts and expressions.

"Yeah I guess," I say. I'm not sure where he's trying to go with this. I just need him to know it wasn't out of obsession.

"And you found out everything you ever wanted to know?" he asks. The smug lip bite is back again. This time with a fraction of the energy.

"Well no," I say.

"And I bet you have a million other questions and that's why you're following me back to my room?"

"Just take me seriously for two seconds, would you?" I just want to continue with our honest conversation earlier, minus the lip.

"Why do you need to know everything?" he asks, as if he's looking for a deeper meaning behind my actions.

I don't know how to respond, so I leave him hanging.

"Not all of us need to know everything, Atta. Some of us let things work themselves out on their own," he says, leaning against the door-frame. His abs are ever so present. It's hard to keep my eyes on just his face. "You want a mystery to solve, I'll give you one. Why my sister would want anything to do with my psycho friend is a huge mystery to me. Keep an eye on Tyler and my sister for me, would you?"

I understand his concern, but unlike him I've seen this play out before and know it's harmless. That was the great thing about knowing the future.

"I can do that if you honestly answer me one more question. Will you?" I say hoping he'll be upfront with me. "Why'd you quit basketball around the same time you and Corky went to the concert? You're obviously still friends with the players and I've heard you're good enough to play college ball."

I remember him playing basketball all through high school. He quit his senior year after his dad passed away. He didn't even start the season. But that wasn't the situation in this universe. His grandfather —father in this universe—wasn't an NBA player and had been gone for over a year now, so that wouldn't be the reason. Plus the rumors were that Ben quit in the middle of the season this time. So what was it?

Ben just looks at me, staring into the depths of my being, as if trying to assess whether he truly trusts me or not.

"There's only one other person in my life who asks as many questions as you do," he says, slighting my offer but his response surprises me, shifting my thought process entirely.

"And who's that?" I press him.

"Again with the questions," he scoffs.

"You leave everything open-ended. They're questions begging to be asked," I say as he stands there quietly contemplating his next words.

"Someone I look up to. He's someone who's done the biggest favor for me in my life. He's been pestering me with questions and only recently have I realized I need him," he says and it's clear that's all he's willing to give me. He's entrusted me with a line of vulnerability and he's hesitant to say more.

"We all need a person like that in our lives," I say. It seems like an appropriate response.

Instead of responding, he steps a foot closer to me so that we're standing just inches apart. I can feel his body heat rise against me. I see the rise and fall of his chest. I have the urge to flee the scene as I become nervous about his close proximity.

It seems purposeful.

His hand reaches for my face and to my surprise he tucks a loose feathery strand of hair behind my ear, then brushes his hands around the back of my neck in one steady motion, making butterflies erupt in my stomach.

What is this? He looks as if he's going to kiss me while I stand frozen, wide-eyed in anticipation.

I watch his movements closely, unable to decipher what he's going to do next. Will his warmness turn cold at the drop of a hat? He nearly brushes his lips against my cheek, on the same side he'd tucked my hair behind my ear and whispers, "You're right. Goodnight, detective."

He pulls back and shuts his door, leaving me ineffective and unable to say anything. He's just played me and I find myself wanting more than I ever have from him.

I remember. This is how it felt to have Ben Brown mess with your heart a little. He's left me mystified, alone in the hallway, and I feel disoriented hashing out whether he meant anything by that as I dust my feet slowly against the floor on the carpeted trail back to Diana's room.

Diana lays peacefully asleep with both arms raised above her head. If it weren't for her bold moves tonight I might not have gotten this far with Ben. Somehow, someway, he let me in just a little, but it felt like we'd made massive waves of progress. It was a huge step forward even if it was dipped in a thin layer of resentment. I feel lucky to have her in my life as I climb over her sleeping body and burrow into my little cove of blankets next to her.

Chapter Twenty-Two

T he sight in front of me makes me shift uncomfortably in my seat as Diana pulls into the curb next to my grandparents' thick grassy lawn. Our neighbor, Officer Berrett, wearing a greasy smile, is chatting with Aunt Jevie in front of the house near our wrinkled sidewalk.

This can't be good. My eyes flit directly to Officer Berrett's Marigold tattoo and I stall in the process of opening the car door as a flutter of nerves skips through my ribs. What are they doing out here with the sun positioned directly above, midday on a Saturday afternoon? And why is he in uniform, talking to my great-aunt?

I slip past them on the side of the yellowing front window blinds wearing oversized sweats and Diana's cat tee from last night, nearly crushing the flowers mixed in between the soil and the thin concrete barrier as I try not to involve myself in their seemingly friendly conversation.

Officer Berrett says hello from over Aunt Jevie's shoulder and I watch as calculations begin circulating behind his eyes. He must notice just how juvenile I look right now. Hopefully, my rugged attire and lackadaisical exit from Diana's car—as she blasts "Your Love" by The

Outfield while shouting "Bring my sweater to school. K? Love ya!" over the car stereo with bushy-tailed enthusiasm—isn't raising questions about my dual status here in this universe.

Officer Berrett knew I was on assignment from our conversations in passing and I was banking on the hope that he'd believed me and wasn't going to question me further about the Bureau.

Truthfully, I hadn't expected to have another encounter with him, not after I thought I could get back to the future. Since that failed, I'd almost forgotten the neighbor officer could be just as much of a threat to me as Marigold was in the future.

Was there a way for me to figure out exactly what Officer Berrett's involvement with Marigold was without sparking suspicion? For now all I could do is maintain the role he thought I was playing—FBI agent working undercover as a spunky teenager. I was already doing that with some success. I think.

My worries escalate as I shut the door behind me. I feel as if I've stepped on a dull nail, unsure of how to assess the risk. Should I be feeling a tetanus-shot-worthy level of concern or are Officer Berrett's neighborly conversations dull nails that present no danger.

Maybe he's eager to chat with anyone and everyone. Totally exempt from ulterior motives. His reputation and questionable choice of body ink make me think otherwise. He could be questioning Jevie about me right now.

I take in the savory smell of brown gravy from the living room as I enter the house and peek into the kitchen where Marcie's setting the table with forks and sharp knives. The sun peeks through the back door producing a prismatic light pattern onto the kitchen table thanks to a few cracks in the small forest of backyard trees.

My tongue prickles with delight as the shadow casts a spotlight on the heavy steam rising from the hot plates. Yum. Country-fried chicken. The prickling intensifies and I find my mouth watering, as if I can't dig into Marcie's home-cooked meal fast enough.

I drop my drawstring bag underneath Marcie's mood sign and sit down at the table where Davy and Steven wait impatiently. Davy's tapping his fork aggressively and Steven looks like he's having an internal battle over whether or not to dig in before everyone's seated.

I rub my thumbs together in anticipation and occupy my mind with Marcie's mood sign which has a new setting, "Feeling Frisky." Like a knee-jerk reaction, I cower in embarrassment. Pops is on Mt. Kilimanjaro right now, living out of his backpack, which would make him unable to help her with anything "frisky," right? I stop that train of thought before it even leaves the station.

When she sees me eyeing the food again, Marcie welcomes me back. Jevie's new husband, Gary, joins us just shortly before Jevie saunters in from outside. She sits down and Erica floats into the kitchen a few minutes later to complete the lunch circle.

Davy's already stabbed at his chicken, shoved a piece into his mouth and moaned with pleasure before everyone's seated, but somehow Marcie's focus lands on me and the fact that I've failed to change out of Diana's cat pajamas for our family lunch.

"You look *purrrty* relaxed in Diana's cat tee," Marcie teases, placing the dinner rolls at the center of the table before sitting down to eat with us. "How is Diana by the way? I haven't seen her in a few weeks," she says as Davy licks the gravy from his fingers next to her. Marcie actually notices this time and slaps his wrist with a bread roll.

"She's good," I reply, brushing the wrinkles out of my shirt with both hands under the table, wondering why my outfit trumps Davy's table manners.

"You should have her come over here next time instead of going over to her place."

"Yeah, maybe we'll spend next weekend over here," I say, attempting to fulfill her request.

"No. Eww. This house doesn't need any more girls in it," Davy says, shoving a roll into his brace-filled mouth. I can't help but chuckle at his snide remark. The further he pushes the limits at the dinner table the wider his smile becomes.

"No, no please do." Steven makes a winky face at me. "She's hot!" he says. I make it a point to ignore his comment.

"I just met your neighbor." Jevie cuts in as we fall silent, our mouths full of gravy. "The cop with the motorcycle, outside. Nice guy." She leans over her new husband to hand me a business card. "He asked me to give this to you."

I stare at the tiny paper in my hand. Why would a cop have a business card? The name Robert Schills rests on the front of the card under a bubbly Schills and Sons logo. When I flip it over I find a handwritten message addressed to me. My heart races as I read.

You mentioned Marigold the last time we met. If you need a ride to chase the flowers I'll take you there. Leave a note in my mailbox.

The card feels like a scorching flame in my hands.

"Officer Berrett asked to have dinner with you all and his family soon," Jevie says to the rest of the family. My heart sinks a little at this announcement.

"That would be lovely," Marcie says.

I sit in silence waiting for my heart to steady. What appetite I had has left me and I'm unable to finish off the last few bites of country-fried chicken after the interruption of Officer Berrett's cryptic note.

Davy leads the table in a discussion about whether or not Ewoks are furry and cute, or vicious and predatory, but it's not enough of a distraction for me to occupy my thoughts elsewhere. Officer Berrett is up to something and it doesn't take much to decipher what he meant by writing that note. He suspects I have something to do with Marigold and he's baiting me.

"He asked how long you were going to be around and mentioned something about giving you an emergency ride," Jevie adds as Steven proposes a theory in favor of Ewoks being vicious and predatory. Jevie winks at me, keeping her words at a low whisper behind her husband's back. "I would've told my aunt instantly if I'd received a ride on a cop's motorcycle."

Officer Berrett was definitely baiting me—inserting himself into my life through family members and asking questions. Was he baiting me to get me to go with him to the mountains? Or did he somehow think I had an interest in Marigold?

"Yeah. He helped me out this week when I was in a bind," I say, hoping my short explanation won't encourage more questions.

"Maybe I should find myself in a bind," Jevie quips with ease.

I would laugh at her joke were it not so concerning that he took the time to corner a family member in order to personally deliver a cryptic message.

What was he doing bringing up our initial encounter with my family when I explicitly told him not to? My family couldn't find out about my FBI badge and status. It would raise too many questions. He must be trying to give me a signal in the form of blackmail. As if he plans to disclose my FBI status to my family if I don't "ride to chase the flowers" with him. That or he somehow knows of my Marigold connection and intends to introduce me to his cult.

Sickening. I become heated just thinking about it.

LATER AT NIGHT, I'M STILL DISGRUNTLED OVER OFFICER BERRETT approaching a family member, when I remember the manila envelope of newspaper clippings shoved in my cheerleading drawstring bag. I'd already decided not to respond to Officer Berrett's note but I had plans to do more Marigold research.

I make my way through the rod of flannel shirts into Little Narnia after waiting for all the family members downstairs to relocate themselves back upstairs. I plan to review the stolen envelope of clippings within the privacy of Little Narnia's walls. That and Pops has hundreds of newspaper clippings stored within two large metal filing cabinets. I might find valuable historical information there as well.

In Little Narnia, I walk toward the metal cabinets and run my fingers over Pops' pea green and mustard accessories scattered throughout his hideout. I open the first metal drawer and pull out a small collection of newspapers.

I set the newspaper stack next to my stolen manila folder on Pops' desk, sit down and begin taking notes in my crossword about what I'd found yesterday in Tyler's atrium. I jot down concerns about Officer Berrett and brainstorm our last two encounters trying to discern when he would've suspected me of having a Marigold connection. I mumbled Marigold under my breath during our second encounter after he mentioned the stabbing at the brewery. Did he hear me? Or is he aware of more than I thought possible. Could he have some sort of connection with the future and time travel? He mentioned he has connections to the Bureau. Were they capable of tracing me through time? As I write this down I realize I'm becoming a bit paranoid. The Bureau knew nothing of time travel.

When I'm finished, my fingers spread across the folded creases of the atrium sourced newspaper clippings and I read a few of the cutout headlines.

One headline from the stack flashes in front of me with familiarity. It reads "Bill Hee, EPA Director's Death Shocks Local Community" and the date at the top, *Denver Post, February 5, 1987.* The article is recent, as in cut from *The Denver Post* just a few days ago. The name is familiar so I sit for a minute thinking about where I've heard the name Bill Hee and then it hits me. Officer Berrett. The very man responsible for my bad mood this evening, mentioned that name to me last Tuesday before I'd discovered his Marigold tattoo.

He was prodding me to see if I was involved in Hee's case while I was trying to get as much information as possible without confirming or denying involvement. How could I have not known it at the time?

Officer Berrett's connected to Marigold and so must be Bill Hee's death. The person who clipped these newspaper articles and paper-clipped them together knows that much. Why else would they have shoved them in the same manila folder?

Whoever these clippings belonged to thought the EPA director's death had something to do with Marigold, the Sheriden Foundation, and Clean Wave. My last conversation with Officer Berrett confirms the same.

Could that be why Sheriden recently acquired the brand Clean Wave, so that they can sell household and hair products? Products that need to be approved by the EPA. So why the death of the EPA director? Did Marigold need an EPA death to get their product approved?

If the newspaper clippings were grouped together for a reason, then I trusted someone in the Jacobson household had made this connection too. Tyler's parents were his grandparents in Non-80s-Land thanks to this alternate universe's generational time-squish.

Truthfully the alternate timeline made my head hurt. I try hard to think of what his grandparents' professions were in Non-80s-Land. A retired school teacher and lawyer, I think? Whoever compiled these newspaper clippings, they were further along in their investigation than I was.

Why they had made the connection between Marigold and the EPA, I hadn't a clue, but I know I have to find one.

Chapter Twenty-three

By the time Thursday rolls around, I've gone through the motions of school and cheer practice. I spend the late afternoons with Diana. She listens to music and reads magazines, gathering as much information as she can on track and field across the country in preparation for the upcoming season. I obsess over the pile of newspaper clippings stolen from Tyler's atrium.

I should've returned the clippings by now. I worry one of the Jacobsons will be looking for them, but Tyler threw the party because they were out of town looking for a specialist or something and I'd heard through the grapevine that their trip would last longer than just the weekend. The EPA and Marigold connections were all I could think about the last few days, and I was now determined to figure out why Tyler's household held these crucial bits of information.

Midway through history class the thought occurs to ask Tyler—who sits two rows in front of me—whether or not his parents have come home from their trip. Diana has made a point to ignore him, unless of course, he approaches her first. He made a sorry exit after kissing her at the party and hasn't offered her a word since. Despite all of that drama, I plan to approach him after class.

Moments later, as I'm reading newspapers from Pops' Little Narnia under the school desk, I feel a pair of eyes land on me. When I look up, I discover Tyler attempting to make eye contact with me by doing a caterpillar dance with his eyebrows.

As soon as I catch his glance, he sends a nervous smile my way—a look I'd never seen forged on his face before. He holds a lined piece of paper, folded like sad origami with a triangular-looking point, and bumps the shoulder of the guy in front of me, motioning for him to hand the note to me while mouthing the words "Hand to Atta."

The guy in front of me slides the note across his desk with two long fingers before curving his arm back behind his shoulder like the beak of a crane so that my only option is to pick the note from his hand like a kid picking apples. I snatch it from him before the teacher sees, then carefully unravel the open edges from the creased folds so the paper lays flat across my stack of newspapers under the table. Tyler's handwriting is too tilted for me to read at this angle, so I flip the paper over to find another message which reads *Please give to Diana*. I snag Tyler's attention, nodding to assure him I understand the assignment.

Throughout the remainder of class Tyler's leg shakes nervously and it seems I'm not the only one to notice. The entire class pays more attention to Tyler acting like a nervous wreck than the Axis powers diagram etched on the chalkboard. As the primary witness to Diana and Tyler's 2010 love escapade, I particularly enjoy watching the part where Tyler sweats bullets trying to make this relationship happen. The only thing that might push it to the brink—to avante-garde potential —would be if Caleb, Diana's current Non-80s-Land husband, were able to watch it with me.

Caleb was the king of romance. The first time he expressed interest in Diana he'd laid a trail of flowers along their college's pole vault track leading up to a miniature toy tractor that held a note requesting she meet him after practice in the parking lot. And that's how it all started. She met him in the school parking lot and they drove five miles an hour in Caleb's tractor to catch a movie somewhere in Fort Collins.

In comparison, up to this point, Tyler's attempts at communicating with Diana had been akin to Chris Farley masterfully breaking a table and falling flat on his face as Matt Foley, motivational speaker—reckless, overbearing—a total crash and burn.

After class lets out, I take a quick look at Tyler's note while stepping over a group of girls in pointed flats and black and white sweaters. They're sitting with their legs sprawled out, making various squealing and snorting sounds as I dodge a bunch of objects being thrown from a rowdy bunch of boys in the lounge area. The level of disarray only increases as I walk past the congested tide of students on my way to deliver Tyler's message.

The cafeteria booms with loud chatter. I search the open layout for Diana as students pull out yellow chairs to accommodate new people at the cafeteria tables. One kid delivers a mockery of an opera performance for a table of cackling band students. A hair-metal-loving jock plays guitar with his friend's leg to Metallica at a table that blasts music from a boombox. His friends watch intently with their girlfriends perched on their laps.

Eventually, I brush by Tyler and his group. I move quick enough that I manage to avoid Evan, but I feel Tyler's anxious eyes on my back as I weave my way through the melting pot of nerds, burners, and jocks.

I find Diana at the far side of the cafeteria. To my surprise, Ben is eating next to her.

"Atta," Ben says, acknowledging my presence, which causes Diana to look up from peeling her orange. I slide in next to her and meet Tyler's stare from across the room. He quickly looks away, knowing what I'm about to do.

"I have something for you," I say, handing her the note with a closed fist so that Ben doesn't grab it before she does. "I might have peeped," I say, beaming with excited anticipation.

"Of course you did," Ben cuts in.

"Thanks, Ben," I say dryly.

Diana unfolds the finely creased paper so that it lays in front of both of us and leans forward making it difficult for Ben to peep. It reads,

> Diana,
>
> I'm kicking myself for accidentally kissing you the other night.
>
> I didn't expect that to happen. It was an accident and I'm sorry I haven't said a word to you for the past few days. Accidentally kissing you has made it difficult for me to do anything but think about you.
>
> I know you've hated me for a while and I don't deserve your attention, so I waited three days just thinking about whether or not I should even write this letter.
>
> I got my hopes up when you kissed me back and I'd really like to date you, so here I am taking my shot even if it means you might reject me.
>
> Circle yes if you'll go with me to the roller rink on Saturday.
>
> Yes
>
> No
>
> Ty

Diana reaches into her purse and pulls out a pen, unknowingly giving Ben a visual of the crinkled love note long enough that he's able to get the gist of the letter. Diana lifts her pen with the intent to circle Tyler's handwritten "Yes" at the bottom of the note but before her pen lands on paper Ben throws his hands on top of hers.

"Diana, no!" Ben says.

Diana brazenly whips her hands, and the note, away from Ben with dramatic flare, pressing her full lips together to form a taunting grin. She lays the paper flat on the table and against her brother's wishes, circles "Yes."

"Sorry," she says, rather pleased with herself. I try to remain neutral-faced, as Ben sends her a hard glare.

"I find it sweet that he wasn't sure how to approach me. And he put in some effort with the note. It was cute."

"Yeah, if you call 'writing a love note' effort." Ben scoffs at his own friend's handwritten gesture. Diana doesn't give him any reaction as she stands up from the table.

We both watch the back of Diana's denim jacket weave in and out of tables as she heads toward Tyler and a group of cheerleaders. Ben shoots out of his seat and quickly closes the gap between them, reaching for her rolled up sleeve.

Tyler meets Diana's gaze with a hopeful look. He stands up, nervously fumbling into his chair in the process and as if forgetting everyone else's presence around him, he approaches Diana. I stop a few feet short of them, weary that a fight might break out between Tyler and Ben.

"Here." Diana smiles handing him the note. She waits patiently as he unfolds the note in front of her and finds his "Yes" circled in blue ink.

***

BEN PULLS ME ASIDE JUST OUTSIDE THE DOOR NEXT TO A WALL of lockers after fifth period.

"Glad your head's all healed up." He pokes my forehead where my yellowing bruise would be if I hadn't covered it up with Erica's heavy foundation this morning.

"Why would you do that? Jeez! It still hurts," I say, eager to swat his hand if he tries poking me again.

"Oh sorry," he says, withdrawing his hand from my face. "You have to help me out." He pleads in as casual a way as he can muster.

"Help you out with what, Ben? If this is about Tyler and Diana, I like them together and I don't plan on interfering. She can make her own decisions, ya know."

"So you're really going to let her date the most obnoxious man in this school?" he says.

"Isn't he one of your best friends?" I didn't expect him to be so against this relationship.

"Yeah, which is why I know it's not a good fit," he says. I stand arms folded, waiting for him to elaborate.

"He relies on rebellion to function. He craves attention like caffeine and my sister is a softie who will tag along with anything if she believes that person has an ounce of goodness in them. Imagine her tagging along with him!"

Ben wasn't wrong. Diana was a total softie when it came to people she liked. She'd buzz around them like a loyal bee, happy to harvest the entire hive for them as long as it made them happy. I give Ben an understanding smile before contradicting it by saying, "Maybe he'll boost her creativity."

"Go to the roller rink with me on Saturday." There's an unrelenting force to his interjection. "I need to make sure nothing happens between those two. Especially because Tyler's parents are out of town until Monday."

I'm relieved and shocked at the same time. Relieved to hear his parents are still out of town—that means they haven't been looking for the newspaper clippings in the time I've had them—and shocked at his request, or was it an invitation?

"You?…what?" I say, replaying his request back again in my head wondering if I heard him correctly.

"Go to the roller rink with me. We can make this a double."

"You're only doing this to keep tabs on your sister. What if they want to go by themselves?"

"I can make it a double," Ben says with confidence.

Chapter Twenty-Four

A cat patrols the neighbor cop's home, hissing and swatting at the air as if warning me another look in its direction will land me a fully-scratched face. I watch it from across the street while waiting for Tyler to pick me up. Somehow, Ben got Tyler to agree to the double date and conned him into letting us ride with him and Diana to the roller rink.

I sit on the square cement step in front of my grandparents' house with my back pressed against the screen door, weary that Officer Berrett's motorcycle will pop in at any moment—a routine I'd adopted since the day he'd written asking me to "ride with him to chase the flowers," whatever that meant.

Thankfully it's still just me and the cat outside on a late winter Saturday afternoon as Colorado's unpredictable weather continues to dominate the sky. Two days of scorching temperatures and it seemed the sun was begging for attention in early February. In this rolling heat wave, lightweight loose-fitting capri pants, a matching cotton tank and pink converse from my eighties closet seemed like an appropriate option for waiting outside for Tyler. And cute enough for my date with Ben. Though calling it a date is a bit of an exaggeration—more like Ben's plan to keep an eye on his sister.

Tyler pulls up in his family's wood-paneled station wagon, with Diana waving at me through the passenger window. He blasts the horn as I approach the car door, causing me to jump in surprise. Ben laughs through the back window, kicking the door open for me with his dirty Reeboks.

"Hop in," Diana calls from the front. I scooch in next to Ben who actually dressed up for the occasion; the midnight blue sweater and light jeans make him look like he actually took the double date memo seriously. I remind myself once again that this date is merely a guise for him to keep tabs on his sister and nothing more.

AT THE SKATE RINK, DIANA'S ARMS HANG FROM TYLER'S NECK with interlocked fingers in a show of shameless affection that seems to have magnified since Thursday. Ben and I wait in line behind them, irritation skimming the shadows of Ben's face. He's looking up, down, to the side—anywhere but them.

"Are you any good at skating, Diana?" Tyler says, adjusting his position so that he stands behind her, comfortable enough to simultaneously hug and talk into her ear. I don't hear Diana's response over the roller rink speakers playing "Sail On" by the Commodores, but I know she can skate. At the public rink in Non-80s-Land, as children, she used to roll circles around me while I stood frozen in place, refusing to move in my skates. I never improved as I got older and that should have me worried, but I let Lionel Richie's singing distract me. The song has me swaying back and forth and singing along on my own. I stop when I'm asked my shoe size at the counter.

"Have you skated much?" Ben finds a conversation piece almost identical to Tyler's. I hold my hands out for the guy behind the counter to hand me a pair of quad skates. They're dreamy—with perfect white laces and a cream-colored body.

"No, not really," I answer truthfully. Just holding the skates in my hands makes my stomach twist in terrible ways. I didn't fear much. I'd learned to suppress fear habitually thanks to working at the Bureau, but the thought of standing in that skating rink with only tiny wheels on my feet is terrifying—I might as well have yo-yos taped to my shoes. The only thing motivating me to put the shoes on is the chance to spend time with Ben.

We lose Ty and Diana to a group of shufflers. Packed in tight, a wave of older men in office shirts and plump, older ladies wearing embroidered blouses whoosh past.

"You ready? Let's go," Ben says, ushering me to stand up. The area smells like sugared oranges and carbonated drinks.

I slowly inch my way into a standing position. When I'm upright I begin to pray that my balancing instincts will take the reins on their own. My legs wobble against the carpet, but I stride fast enough to make it to the skate barrier without falling.

"You'll be fine. It's easy. You'll catch on real quick," Ben says as he watches me calculate each step off of the rink barrier. He enters the rink, moving from a pattern of confident steps to a perfectly even glide.

He glides nobly around, showing off his skating skills in just a few circles, as I make a few choppy steps back to the rail where I feel comfortable enough to stand and catch my shaky, jittery breath. He finds my gaze and surprisingly shoots a pleasant smile my way for encouragement, likely because he realizes just how much I am struggling.

He holds out his hands, ready for me to take them. An evil couple guns through the space between us, forcing Ben to put his hands back at his side. With perfectly even breaths, I stay suctioned to the wall like a starfish, absorbing its support as if my life depends on it.

A flock of shufflers lap us about twenty times with their precise—almost mechanical—funky movements, each rotation so synchronized they'd give swimmers and soldiers a run for their money. Another set of skaters pace the rink like a school of fish and all I can think about is how half of this room has the potential to become an organized cult. But, like a really fun one.

Ben decides to take a full lap around the rink with the hopes of encouraging me to leave the wall. It doesn't work. I lean back comfortably against the barrier, watching as Ben gives up and starts actively looking for his sister.

Diana's holding hands with Tyler doing a shuffle skate. All of Tyler's energy is put toward making sure Diana's having a good time. It might be the first time in a while that I've seen his face full of concentration rather than mischief.

Ben catches my gaze and skates back toward me. I feed my gaze back to the soda counter, where I currently wish I was. I stay put, knowing the trek there is too dangerous in skates.

"Plan on letting go of the barrier anytime soon?" Ben says now a few feet away, reaching out both of his hands again for me to hold.

"I…uh. I don't know. I'm pretty comfortable here," I say, wholeheartedly meaning it.

"Come on. I can teach you," he offers. "Just hold my hands and I'll help you glide."

"You'll be supporting all of this." I point at the length of my body and almost fall over for the effort.

"Don't you want to at least learn how to do this?" He performs a shuffle pushback and then spins around in front of me.

"If that's what you want me to start with," I say, "I'd rather army crawl back to the carpet."

Ben lets out a quick snort. "Now that would be a sight to see."

As if the shuffling cult wasn't already?

"Do you trust me?" Ben says. His tone is borderline gentle, a far cry from his usual harassment.

He motions for my hands, but this time with determination. For a second I spot interest in his eyes and forget about my aversion to skating. I clasp my hands with his before he pulls me in, my skates gliding freely toward him.

"See? Already making progress. It isn't so bad, is it?" he says.

I gain a fraction of confidence, even though he's doing all the work, and let go to see if I can glide on my own. With just one step I scramble to gain my balance, switching slowly from left to right, chopping the slippery floor as momentum keeps me leaning forward.

"You sure you don't want my hands? Skating backward is my specialty," he says as I try taking longer strides on my own, moving from a chop to a short graze. With the next graze of my skate, I become a Mario Kart vehicle spinning out over a banana peel and receive a panoramic view of the disco ball and neon light-covered ceiling on my way down, smacking my hip and arms in the process. I giggle in pain on the hardwood floor as Ben comes to my rescue.

"That's it!" His ribbing words of encouragement break with a chuckle. I hold my hands out for him to pull me back up to my feet and meet his gaze to find that his face is now a permanent smirk—like a portrait painted exclusively to gloat in my humiliation—which makes me feel the need to rip the expression off his face.

I shift my momentum back to the floor with purposeful deadweight and drag him down using a self defense arm grab so that he loses his balance and lands on the floor next to me. He pops back up quickly as I experience the best laugh of my life, inhaling chokes of laughter like a round of bullets from a metal storm.

He playfully shakes his head in disapproval and instead of getting up, I sit on the rink floor attacking my skate laces, trying to set my feet free while skaters whip past.

On my march back to the table in socks I spot Diana alone. Ben follows and we both stop at the barrier wall to watch Tyler in a leather jacket getting ready to jump a human barricade of young men kneeling on their hands and knees in a straight line. They're like an expanse of cars ready for Evel Knievel—or in this case Tyler—to clear, or not clear them.

Tyler comes flying around the corner looking to gain speed in his loose parachute pants. Determination floods his eyes and it looks like he's going to make the four-man jump with about eight feet to clear as long as he pulls off an impressive vertical. Teenagers outside the rink hoot and howl, raising their sodas as Tyler lands the stunt with bent knees. I mentally slap myself for thinking Tyler could go a night without seeking the room's attention.

Diana's eyes light up with amusement. Their night seems to be a lot more successful than ours. I can thank my deep-seated fear of walking on wheels for that.

I'm sitting at the table, feet free of quad skates, when a Southern rock beat with heavy electric guitar claps from the speakers. Ben appears at my side with a corndog. Although this wasn't a real date, I always felt a little special when he handed me food—his horrible artichoke dip made from homemade mayonnaise back in Non-80s-Land being the exception.

Non-80s-Land Ben excelled when it came to cooking and often made me taste his weekly game night appetizers, having me sample everything from sakura strawberry cream puffs to mozzarella caprese skewers before guests arrived. How could I not find him attractive handing me a plate of five-star food for testing, let alone a simple yet delicious corndog?

"You're doing good, you know," he says, giving me a sympathetic smile. "You tried skating on your own which is a huge improvement from clinging to the wall." He must sense that I feel as if I've been defeated by my pretty quad skates.

"Here, trade me." He hands me the cornmeal-upgraded hotdog in exchange for my skates.

"You only got one?" I ask. He nods his head. "You want some?" I offer up the corndog and he leans in, taking a bite. My heart flutters again at his close proximity.

"You can have the rest if you go out there one more time." He grabs the stick from my hand and signals toward the rink with the tip of his chin. "I promise to do all the legwork," he says with some warmth. His lips part to say something and then he looks into my yielding eyes. Instead of speaking, he sings to the song "Caught Up In

You" blasting from speakers above as if this were karaoke and I'm his entire audience. Even if his soft voice is drowned out by the rink's booming speakers.

As soon as I sit, he bends down and begins lacing up my skates, carefully tugging and tying the laces until they're secured, and I almost choke from the shock. He grasps my wrist and leads me onto the roller floor, where he pulls me into his chest. He wraps his arms around me, supporting all my weight so I can glide with him. With our bodies so close, an uncontrollable smile spasms across my face from the excitement.

The chord progression of "Caught Up In You" picks up as we finish a lap together around the rink, pushing my excitement to another level—a level only certain songs with certain settings can achieve. It's so overpowering that a brief romantically thrilling commercial of the two of us floats through my mind.

"This has got to be one of my favorite songs right now," I say loud enough with my head twisted back so that he can hear me.

"Oh, I know. Your love for 38 Special isn't a secret. 'Hold On Loosely' would be fun to skate to too. You know that the lead singer's brother is the main vocalist for Lynyrd Skynyrd?" he says as we continue gliding together behind a few pairs of girlfriends. I must be missing something. Was it common knowledge that I liked this band from the eighties?

He smiles and then pulls me in a little tighter so that it feels like we're sharing a meaningful hug more so than having him act as my guide.

Ben holds me for another two laps and I find myself wishing "Caught Up In You" would play on repeat for the rest of the night. The way Ben sang along—like he was singing to me—had my heart racing.

I'd be okay if we just stayed like this forever, forgetting everything else, the day-to-day, time travel, our FBI department in charge of whether or not Non-80s-Land Ben and I make it out alive with what we know. For the first time since landing in the eighties, staying sounded quite nice actually.

Although we'd spent more time together over the years than with our own family members, Non-80s-Land Ben had never been so physically close to me. He hadn't offered to tie my shoelaces or hold me close to him. He'd kept a brotherly kind of distance, even when we sat on the sofa together for game nights. He just acted as if I was his little sister's best friend, whom he teased just as much as he teased his own sister.

That's what this is, I tell myself. He's doing nothing more than he would do for his sister if she were in this position. When I decided to forfeit my skates and leave him alone out on the roller rink, he would've become the third wheel to Diana and Tyler's date. Of course, he would do everything possible to get me back out there, especially after I'd made such a show of quitting. But what was he doing locking eyes with me and singing to me? That was more than a little friendly.

Trumpets snap me out of my thoughts and the moment as "Y.M.C.A." terminates the couple's skate. The song is met with an explosion of hand gestures from the crowd. Ben looks at me, his raised eyebrows inquiring if I want to stay out. I shake my head and laugh.

"No roller choreography for me, thanks!" I yell over the loud music.

Ben smiles and guides me to the exit so that I can stand on my own next to the barrier. He turns to face the rink looking through the dancing crowd for Tyler and Diana.

"Have you seen them anywhere?" he asks.

I hadn't. I was so absorbed in the music and his closeness that I hadn't thought about Ty and Diana at all. We both scan the room but find no sign of them. I suggest checking the restrooms, so we stash our skates and part ways. With no luck, we meet back up to search outside where we find a parking lot full of mostly old, seventies-model station wagons and no sign of life.

"Where's Ty's car?" I ask, roaming around in the poorly lit lot. "They could be in there."

He looks unhappy about that prospect.

Ben searches the entire parking lot, shaking his head with disappointment. "I knew he would do something like this."

"Something like what exactly?" I ask.

"Tyler's always got to make every situation exciting. He probably went for a spin with Diana or something. He better be back soon or I'm going to shove his face in."

Chapter Twenty-Five

"They left us without a ride?" I say, shamelessly considering my own feelings over this predicament.

My cheek muscles hurt from all the grinning I've been doing and I feel like I'll never come down from this skate high. I massage the lingering cheek ache as we go back inside the building and Ben returns our skates.

I'm hanging on to the fresh memory of us together on the rink floor. Those actions—his actions felt real, almost purposeful. Like he knew exactly what he was doing. And even though it was likely a tease, meant only to keep things light and playful, I can't get it out of my head. The buzzing aftereffect of what it must feel like to walk on clouds fills me despite the new need to draw up some best friend and her boyfriend 'wanted' posters.

I trail after Ben who leads me to a booth instead of a table this time. We sit at the back wall where only the food court separates us from the arcade games. Thanks to the disappearance of Diana and Tyler, the night has gone from unexpectedly perfect to, dare I say, awkward.

At this point, we've nonverbally decided to sit and wait until Tyler and Diana come back with the car or until the rink closes—whichever comes first. The music sounds muffled outside of the main rink as we sit in silence and I'm able to hear my own thoughts a little too well. Is Tyler and Diana's departure the reason he wanted to quit skating, or was he over having to carry me around the rink?

Ben gets up, heaving a strong sigh, leaving me to wait by myself. He must be so over this double date when his whole objective's been rattled. He was here for "them," not "us." I'd known that from the start.

He's not gone long and returns with two sodas, looking as if he'd given himself a little pep talk to pull himself out of his own mood on the walk back over.

Slurping into my wide straw, I cast a look at Ben who's like a watchdog guarding the front entrance with his eyes. It's a chance for me to admire his facial features and dewy skin that shines like clay. His chocolate brown eyes look deep and sincere as he switches his expression to an anxious one. Concern may be hovering over his disposition like an angry storm cloud but he still manages to look square and strong despite the fact that he's troubled—not to mention ten years younger than I am used to.

Ben catches me staring a few seconds too long, triggering him to lift his eyebrows with a knowing look and a heckling smile. I fold my arms across my chest feeling a flush in my cheeks and look to my side where the neon-lit arcade games stand. He can play this game of catch and release all he wants. I really didn't need him to fall for me. I had years of experience as his non-romantic partner. *He* was the confusing one, pulling me against his chest and acting all warm and gooey intermittently throughout the night, not expecting me to adore that. He can think and do as he pleases, and though I don't want to play this game, I can play it. I had more to attain here than a love interest. I just needed him to be friends with me.

"I still can't believe Diana would leave with Ty. I mean it's been three days." Ben cuts the silence. He must want my attention though it's lost on the desk manager overfilling a soda cup and spraying clear carbonated liquid all over his hand. I turn back to face Ben in the booth seat across from me.

"Why would she go along with something like that? What if she goes off and does something stupid?" he says. "Something she'll regret."

"What makes you think she'll do something stupid?" I ask.

"Because Tyler's stupid," he says, very matter-of-factly.

"You're not wrong." I smile, thinking of all the stupid things Tyler has done over the last week and in all the years I've known him. "Your sister's smart though. She's capable of handling herself. I'm sure she'll make the right decisions." I lay both hands flat on the table in front of me, signaling some heavy "trust me" body language.

"How can you be so sure?" he says. We sit in silence for a few short seconds. "She only has me to protect her. I'm with her on her date and I can't even do that. How is she going to know who'll stay and who won't?"

The way he says it makes me sense there's more to this than I can comprehend. Though his father in this universe passed away in '85 and Ben has taken care of the family ever since, it's not like his father left them.

We had a similar experience growing up with both of our father's passing. Though I was much younger when my father passed and I recall spending a lot of time comforting Diana after her father passed. He declined quickly after his last season in the NBA, but that wasn't the case here in Non-80s-Land. Ben's grandfather—who would be his father in this universe—would have passed within the last couple of years. But Ben shouldn't be concerned or feel the need to take on the overprotective father position when it comes to Tyler. I'd known Tyler long enough to know that his irresponsible behavior wouldn't end up hurting Diana. If only I could convey that to him and help him over-come the trust issue he seems to have with Tyler. Ben knew Tyler better than any of us which gave him the right not to trust him but I knew the future. Tyler and Diana would date for a short year and then amicably part ways. There really wasn't much to worry about.

I don't know how to respond, so I reach for his arm across the table.

"Diana's full of hope and potential and she knows it. Tyler's just a short-term fling. I promise. You can relax."

"That's what scares me."

"A short-term fling? Why?" I ask.

"It might ruin our friendship," he says, letting my hand rest on his arm without a care.

"It will all work out."

"What makes you so confident?" He looks down at my arm holding onto his, with a serious face that says he's confiding in me.

"I've seen the future," I say with a smirk, knowing the truth might make for a nice sarcastic sounding remark that will hopefully put a smile on his face, even if it's just for a quick second.

"Atta, seriously," he says, with a heated half-smile. He wants an honest response, not a sarcastic sounding one.

"We used to talk about our future spouses growing up, you know as all girls do. If I remember correctly, Diana wanted someone that makes good banana bread—like *really* good banana bread," I say, raising evil eyebrows so that they're super high-arching. "Our interests back then were based on what kind of food could be provided," I finish.

I was never good at serious conversations. I always needed a little humor to get me through them. I wait for Ben to slip a smile but he doesn't, so I continue. "Tyler can't make banana bread can he?" I ask. This gets a smile.

"No, Tyler can barely get his Fruit Roll-Ups unraveled."

"Well, good. She'll never accept a proposal then. Plus, she wanted someone hardworking, that wants a lot of kids. That isn't Tyler. She's just having some fun right now. Even though Tyler looks like he could ruin her, he won't. She won't let him," I say.

Ben nods, as if working through some deep thoughts.

"So what did you want?" he asks, catching me off guard with a question like that.

"Want what?" Is he asking what I think he's asking? For my preferences in a man?

"What kind of guy do you want to end up with?" he answers.

I didn't expect those words to ever come out of him.

"Someone who I see as more than a friend," I say with impertinence.

My glib remark is met with an eyeroll.

"Well, obviously," he interjects.

"I think I would've said something like he must be handsome and super into me. Someone who'd do anything for me and I'd do anything for him," I say, feeling more comfortable answering the question as if I was recollecting childhood memories. Though my answer still applies. I'd felt that way for as long as I can remember. "I'm sure I also said something like he'll give me Tootsie Rolls every day since I was young and most of the interest came from what kind of food a boy could offer."

"A man with Tootsie Rolls," he says as neon spotlights once again sprinkle over the maroon and blue paint-splattered table. Those same lights travel back to the rink, highlighting the mix of young and old skaters continuing their cult-like behavior. Diana and Tyler are still nowhere to be seen.

"Have you found a good Tootsie Roll-supplying prospect?" he says looking up through his dark lashes, rubbing his knuckle with his other hand.

"I think you and I both know the answer to that," I say, taking a long sip of the cream soda in front of me. I suddenly feel incredibly thirsty. "I wouldn't be monitoring Diana and Ty with you on this quote, unquote 'double date' if I had someone else to be with." I cringe at my use of "quote, unquote." After it came out, I realized that might give away my feelings about how seriously I want this to be a date.

My thoughts go back to my last date prospect, Kenny, who turned out to be a real sociopath. I suppose if I did have another prospect, I'd still spend my evening with Ben.

"I'm glad you're here," is his response. "The look on your face makes me think you've got someone on your mind. Who would you rather be on this date with, Atta?"

I don't have an answer for him. No one else, if I'm being honest. I shake my head instead of choosing to answer.

"You're not going to answer?" He looks as if he's ready to pester me for the next two hours.

"Are you ever going to answer my question? Why did you quit basketball your senior year?" I make it a point to turn the tables and switch the subject.

He presses both hands into the table's flat surface and pushes off the table to stand up. His eyes, dark chocolate in the dim light, emit defeat. He reaches out for my hand. I take it and walk with him and, to my surprise, he doesn't let go of my hand.

"The other night, when you asked me that question, I answered it. I just left out all the details." He pulls me toward the arcade.

"That much I figured," I say shyly, aware that he still has my hand and I don't quite know what message he's trying to send. False hope? Standard of friendship in the eighties? Or maybe Good Samaritan trying to lead the blind? It was definitely the latter—he continues to pull me by the arm, his long strides hard to keep up with. "You said you confided in someone the other night. Who was it?"

He pauses in front of the car simulator in the middle of the arcade then hesitates, but his hand continues to hold mine. I take inventory of the arcade. There's no one else in the area.

"Tyler's dad," he says. I turn, giving him my full attention. He seems conflicted.

"Tyler's dad is the guy you were talking about the other night?" I ask. "The person who asks too many questions?"

He nods.

I repeat this information a few times in my head. Why?

"Tyler had raced bikes with me a few times over the years and his dad asked me to be more present in Tyler's life recently. He thought Tyler could use a positive influence or something. Heaven knows why," he says sarcastically. "When I'd come over, Tyler's dad kept asking me questions. The man is intimidating, so eventually I opened up."

"What kind of questions?"

"Homelife, my motivations, why I wanted to quit basketball. I was surprised when he understood. It made it easy to trust him," he says. "He has been there for me over the last few months." He lets go of my hand and sits down at the wheel of a racing game. I mirror his actions and sit in the car seat next to him.

"I've thought about it and I figure, since confiding in him's been a good thing for me, I can share my thoughts when it feels like the right time. You're asking just as many questions and it's been nagging at me. Why are you doing it?"

"Because I have many of them," I say, grabbing the racing wheel and watching as the very two-dimensional car graphic runs red and orange cars past my screen.

"You want to know why I quit basketball?"

"Yes," I say softly, patiently.

"When my father passed last year it became a strain on my family financially." We both pause at the wheel. I wait intently for him to continue. "After the concert with Corky, Mom scolded me for using money we didn't have to drive to Kansas City and I ultimately decided to just quit so I could focus on working." He tilts his head back looking toward the ceiling as if he's reflecting on his decision.

"I love to play, but there comes a point when trying to support your family becomes more important. Seeing my grandma and mom so desperate for my help and disappointed that I wasn't taking their situation seriously made me rethink what I should be doing."

He looks at me, almost as if to assess my reaction. I remain quiet, contemplating whether or not his reasoning for quitting basketball was the same as it was back in Non-80s-Land. Shortly after his father passed he quit basketball. But his family wasn't short on money at the time, being that his father's NBA career was successful enough to keep his mom and grandmother stable for years to come. The circumstances he was facing here in this universe were as unexpected as his explanation.

"It's a pretty lame excuse, isn't it?" He looks over at me. At this revelation, I'm more comfortable staring at the race on the screen while processing his words.

"You're left to support your family on your own?" I ask, a bit stunned at his confession.

"Not on my own. Robyn works as many night shifts as she can, but I'm expected to help. It's not that unreasonable of a request really, especially after skipping school and having my mom discover the amount Corky and I had spent at the concert."

"I'm sorry, Ben. Diana's never told me any of this," I say.

"She doesn't know."

"But you said Tyler's dad encouraged you to quit?" I ask.

"He didn't encourage me to quit but he did give me a job opportunity. He has friends who need their cars and bikes detailed and fixed. He's got a lot of work set up for me that can easily be done after school." He spins the racing wheel with both hands like he wishes to race the game but needs to finish telling his story.

"It won't take away from school and trying to graduate."

"I'm glad he's able to support you. Do you still talk to Ty's dad?" I smile and look up at him.

"Yeah." He perks up a bit at my question. "He's actually helping me prepare for college as well. When he offered me the job I told him what I had planned for my future. He's got me mapping out the next few years so that it'll work out for me. The man's a rigid planner and has his crap together. I study at his house every day after working a few hours in his garage."

"I wish you would have told me sooner. I can't imagine how hard that was for you to come back from Kansas City and be told that you're the man of the house now and responsible for the whole family. You're barely eighteen." I say it keeping my eyes locked on his, so that he can feel the sincerity of my words. "But I'm proud of you. You've had to give up a lot in just the last few weeks. If there was a way I could lighten your load for you I would." My eyes stay locked on his a few seconds too long. My words "I'm proud of you" strike feelings that spread all over his face.

He leans in closer, until I feel a zing of awareness as he enters my seat space. The car on the game screen zooms past background scenery with a whining rocket-powered VROOM as Ben's eyes catch on my lips, falling the way I'd fallen for him, like snowflakes that meet a bed of snow, slow and purposeful with a perfect landing. His eyes have found the perfect landing.

"I'm going to kiss you," he says, as a rebellious grin spreads over his face.

I lean in as his hand slides around my neck. My stomach flips and everything inside takes a free fall as he coasts closer toward me, pulling me in toward his face for a second that feels like forever—until his lips brush up against mine. His kiss is soft and his lips are much bigger than mine, like firm juicy rosebuds curved into a smile. They beg me to kiss him back.

I feel reckless and my whole heart beats with profound power. He doesn't stop, so I continue kissing him back, matching his movements with my hands still at the wheel. My grip on the race car wheel tightens. He kisses me so sweetly and deeply, as if we're only capable of sharing the type of meaningful kiss that only deep-rooted lifelong friends could have.

Chapter Twenty-Six

Reality is sometimes hard to discern. But just like I know the difference between the hazy frustration that is not being able to move your feet while running in a dream or feeling cold wind slap me in waves as tangible sweat runs down my back during an actual run—I know with certainty that the very thing I've dreamed about for more than half of my life is happening to me. I'm kissing Ben and I feel like I should break into song or a dance.

That is, until the nerves come and I fear the knots in my stomach will never be undone. When our lips part and everything is slowly brought back into focus, I feel the alternate universe choke on its own cruel and twisted laugh. I'd somehow managed to appeal to Eighties Ben without trying.

The shock of it all leaves me silent and introspective, unable to see anything outside of the arcade room blur. The alternate universe must be playing an inside joke on me since all of my attempts to get closer to Ben while attempting to reverse my situation and find my way back home have led me into romance with him. My already muddy situation just became much more complex. I might as well be a pig drowning in the mud.

"Gag me with a spoon!" Diana emerges from behind the arcade chairs making the two of us jump in our seats. "That's my best friend, Ben! How long have you two been sharing saliva?" Her eyes gape at Ben and then turn back to scrutinize me.

She made it sound so gross. Just as she hinted earlier this week, she doesn't seem to be okay with our pairing. I give her an apologetic look, though I don't feel apologetic one bit. Thirty-year-old, Non-80s-Land Diana encouraged this.

"We just kissed," Ben says. His words are icy. His annoyance seems to loom over the passion I felt from him just moments ago. *This is going to be fun.*

"Where's Tyler?" he asks, his tone slips into a more serious one.

"Getting drinks over there." Diana points to Tyler who's walking back from the food counter with two sodas in hand. She beams when he waves.

Ben stands. He looks large and puffed out like an animal ready to fight. He swoops in with an arm grab and cuffs Tyler's forearm before Tyler is able to hand the drink off to Diana.

"You and me. After this, we've got to talk," he says as friendly as a roaring bear can. Tyler's carbonated attitude breaks and he walks over to Diana, then calmly and carefully hands her the drink, not because he's afraid of spilling, but because he's afraid handing the drink to Diana will be too close a touch for Brother Bear Ben to handle right now.

***

Diana insisted on spending Sunday with me. Tyler had asked her to spend Sunday with him, but in an attempt to show me her loyalty and send me an underlying message, she'd said no. In her own words, she'd spent the last half of the week "moseying around with Ty" and she needed girl time.

Though I see right through her words. Her underlying message to me is: *I'm turning down date night for you, thus you should do the same. If you're going to date my brother, he will come second to our friendship and we will have uninterrupted time together just like before, which the boys are exempt from.*

I was learning that in 80s-Landia if you kissed someone it was assumed by the general public that you were now going with them. My mess with Ben was a lot more complicated now that Diana assumed her brother and I were together. Though the only way I'd know for sure that we were "together" is if he sat me down and told me just that. I wanted more than anything to be in a relationship with him, but at the same time I hadn't yet admitted time travel defeat. Was I planning to stay?

Diana passes me a plate to set on my side of the table as I lay knives and forks along Marcie's muted floral patterned tablecloth. I position each utensil with exactness to meet her table setting expectations. We'd been assigned kitchen table duty before dinner with Officer Berrett's family this evening at five. As soon as I heard the news that he'd been invited over I'd spiraled into a bit of a panic. I'd promised Marcie that we'd spend the rest of the weekend at home and despite painstaking efforts, pleading to redirect our dinner elsewhere, Marcie wasn't having any of it.

The stabbing sensation dancing around in my body worsens as the blue goose clock on the wall draws nearer to Officer Berrett's arrival. The feeling becomes more and more unsettling with each minute that passes. Time is pulling pranks on my mind. I don't want five to arrive, but I also can't stand playing the waiting game either. So after Marcie gives us her table setting approval, Diana and I sit on my bed, legs sprawled out next to each other with our backs smushed against pillows and the wall, listening to a 38 Special cassette tape.

My nerves rapidly escalate with each glance at the digital clock and I am leaning on 38 Special to get me through—its musical dissociating powers are strong enough to preoccupy my mind with thoughts of Ben and skating rather than the impending doom that is eating dinner with Officer Berrett. I'd come to find that after twenty-four hours of replaying "Caught Up In You," rewind after rewind, I could experience the same butterfly-inducing sensation with each listen. Turns out the feelings didn't stop.

Diana had yet to mention my lip-locking incident with her brother. I was okay with that for the time being. I needed less complicated things to occupy my mind to keep the pre-Berrett family dinner nerves at bay.

Diana rolls gracefully off the bed and begins looking under it for something as if she's done this very same maneuver multiple times before.

"So I'm thinking of growing my hair out a bit like Rosie Perez from *Soul Train*. It looked so good last night," she says. We'd come home and turned on the *Soul Train* line for half an hour before bed.

"You'd rock that. You do kind of look like her," I say. "But not the eyes. She has really intense eyes. You have innocent eyes," I say with exaggeration to provoke her, and she thanks me for the compliment, never minding the innocent tag I'd just given her. She had enough mature garnishment that she could be confident in the bits of innocence that came with her looks.

She pulls out a can of Coca-Cola from under my bed and tosses it at me. That's new. I didn't know I had those stashed under the bed. I could've popped a can open all these nights instead of sneaking into the kitchen looking for snacks, hyperaware that if Marcie caught me I'd be punished severely. She was a three-meal-a-day, no-snacking kind of helmsman.

"Where'd you and Tyler go last night?" I ask. "You ditched us for a good two hours." Diana's cheeks turn the color of raspberry truffles.

"We drove around. Tyler wasn't feeling well," she says.

"You're kidding? He jumped over like eight people."

"I guess even Tyler has limits. You can't bring up my date without me asking about yours. I almost peed my pants last night seeing you kiss my brother." She chews on the Coke can tab nervously, obviously meaning to change the subject. "Who kissed who first?"

The door flings open and hits the wall with force, revealing casual, ponytail-wearing Erica who looks as if she's been reading in her room all day. Her reading glasses sit crooked on the brim of her nose.

"You kissed Ben? How? I thought he hated you." Erica nearly shouts.

Erica snaps her fingers together and then points under the bed. "Hand me a Coke from under there, would ya?"

"Yes, somehow those two kissed," Diana says and tosses her a can.

"He's the one that kissed me!" I defend myself so Diana doesn't think I made advances on him. I'm just as shocked as they are about the kiss.

"It's only been a few days since he and Bennette broke up," Erica says, looking confused. "Anyway, Mom told me to tell you dinner's ready. We'll talk later."

I grab the crossword puzzle planner on my dresser, knowing I'll need something comforting to hold in my hands for this nerve-racking dinner, and follow her into the kitchen.

The doorbell rings as Marcie uses her ladle to scoop something she calls "hamburger casserole cabbage patch stew" into the remaining bowls at the table setting. I look down at my bowl. The rich smell sparks a peppery, piquant something in my senses. Spring-colored, crunchy cabbage pokes out of the juicy brown liquid that shares space with a few purple beans, chopped up tomatoes, and coarse ground meat in the bowl in front of me.

My stomach grumbles and I can't tell if it's because the food smells good or if it's because Officer Berrett and his family are walking into the living room. The Berrett family surrounds our table as I reach into the harvest gold painted dish and sprinkle shredded cheddar at the peak of my purple bean mound. Officer Berrett smiles at me from across the table leaf as I bring my head up to taste my first peppery, sweet bite. He's brought his wife and son, who are about to claim a seat on each side of him.

"Kenneth sure loves stew. Good choice for dinner, Mrs. Atkinson," Officer Berrett says. The table of eyes peer over in little Kenneth's direction as they settle in around us. The boy lives up to the allegations and begins slurping without hesitation. Across from him, Diana matches his energy, shoving in spoonfuls as if eating cabbage patch stew was a timed event. Her case was likely due to hunger more than taste. She'd overslept, missing Marcie's scheduled Saturday morning breakfast, and with no snacking allowed, had only enjoyed lunch. Her fast metabolism needed sustenance.

The conversation rears toward Pops' two week hike up Mount Kilimanjaro where a lot of sipping, nodding, and questions about how long he'll be on the mountain and potential dangers he might face in the wilderness occur.

After I've finished my soup, I realize my nerves have settled a bit. Officer Berrett remains relatively uninterested in my presence. I wonder if he's given up on suspecting my involvement with Marigold and questioning me about FBI related topics, as I stir my spoon around my empty bowl.

The conversation has died down and I catch Erica discretely reading *The Two Towers* underneath the tablecloth while Diana sits like a proper 1950s private school student charmingly focused on the teacher with a pleasant smile. She's always been good with adults.

The adults become lost in conversation as Kenneth runs his fifth lap around the table. I consider this the right atmosphere to glance at an already half-finished crossword under the table, scanning the numbers hoping to find a clue that stands out, playing it by mood.

The first to catch my eye is *#14. Boob Tube.* I struggle with my hand stretched underneath the table trying to scratch the word *TELEVISION* into the ten boxes. As I write the letters, I notice the word next to it has been filled in but it's not my handwriting.

I recognize the handwriting as Ben's, having read his notes every day for the last five years. The word says *BEATS* across *#27*'s blocks, but the prompt is *One Crying "Uncle!,"* which is clearly not the right word.

"So how are your kids liking school this year?" Officer Berrett asks.

My chin dips down to my neck to take a closer look at the writing and this time the words *38 SPECIAL* pop out at me like a whale amongst a thousand tiny sea creatures. I gulp wondering how I hadn't noticed this block of letters until now. The phrase *GENESIS BEATS 38 SPECIAL* has been manipulated into puzzle squares near the bottom with random letters filled in around it. This puzzle's totally compromised with Ben's doodles.

"Davy likes his teacher," Marcie says, "Steven not so much, but I remind Stevie every week that sucking up to his teacher goes a long way. He's brought a few apples to school." Marcie laughs as if her comment is some sort of inside joke.

"She doesn't know I ate them." I hear Steven whisper to Davy next to me.

"Atta joined the cheer team that Erica's captain of," Marcie continues. I softly shut the pages of my spoiled crossword underneath the table, largely aware that the attention is now focused on me. I'm right. A flock of furrowed eyebrows shoots my way.

"It must be nice having Atta back at the house," Officer Berrett says, referring to the absence that would have been if I really were an FBI agent on assignment in the eighties. But I'm not. My badge is from the future and the family had never experienced my absence.

Curiosity over Ben spoiling my crossword lasts mere seconds before alarm bells of concern ring in my ears about where Officer Berrett plans to take this conversation.

If Officer Berrett wants to play games and confuse my family around me, he can try. I'll handle the consequences. But what if he's looked into my connections with the Bureau over the last few weeks? Has he been curious enough to ask his Marigold friends about my status at the FBI? Berrett had more power than me in this dynamic, and I couldn't help but think he was still chewing on my mention of Marigold.

"Yes, she does get lost a lot at Diana's. It's nice to see her here this weekend," Marcie says. She might as well purchase a billboard with my picture on it that says "Atta Atkinson, Not a bona fide FBI agent. Using false aliases to con officers into motorcycle rides. Wanted for arrest" so that Officer Berrett can ride by on his motorcycle and see it on his way to work. This conversation is starting to gear toward the feeling of walking on feet-pinching Legos and it will soon feel more like walking on fractured shards of glass if we don't rein it in. I stare at Diana with pleading eyes asking her to help me out—I don't want this conversation to linger on me.

"Atta and I spend almost every weekend together," Diana says, being the good sidekick that she is. She shrugs apologetically at me, knowing she has no control over whether or not the dinner table continues to talk about me.

"How long have you been back exactly?" Officer Berrett challenges. He raises his clear yellow-tinted glass to his face and shows an oversized smile. At this, I know this cunning fox is trying to play me, confirming my suspicions. He wants more details.

"Back from the dead, you mean?" Davy can't resist the traitorous comment. I'm grateful for his immaturity at this moment.

"About two weeks," I snap. Under the table I'm crossing my fingers, and toes, and tempted to cross my crossword puzzle with some expletive words, that he will stop the questions there.

The befuddled look on everyone's faces certifies a smirk on Officer Berrett's.

"Sounds like Atta's living a fun double life," he says and then smiles at me. "Atta, I never heard back about the marigolds. If you're still interested in seeing them, the offer's still there."

"Oh, I'm sure Atta would love to see your flowers," Marcie says. "Did you catch her trying to glimpse at them through your fence? She's always been a curious one, that one."

This is interesting territory. How am I going to ward off Officer Berrett? The urge to formulate an emergency exit plan from the table hits me hard but I manage an answer instead.

"Yes, I'll have to stop by sometime."

Officer Berrett ends the questioning there, but to my dismay looks thoroughly satisfied for the rest of dinner. I spend the last bit of conversation stealing glances at my crossword under the table, attempting to appear clueless about his flower comment. I end up finding a tiny asterisk an ant step above Ben's *GENESIS BEATS 38 SPECIAL*. The pairing footnote to the asterisk contains Ben's microscopic graffiti. *My mom even thinks so.* is written in tiny, hardly legible writing.

My head nearly hits the table trying to read the text. Then a small reminder hits me at the mention of Ben's mom—who is actually his grandmother in Non-80s-Land. She was the one who gifted Ben and Diana the plastic color-wired phone before it had been given to me.

"Atta has her face shoved in the butt crack of a book, Mom! And you said I had to leave Stretch Armstrong in my room during dinnertime," Davy fusses, then flashes a cagey smile in my direction. I let the book fall into my lap.

"Atta, come on. Now's not the time to bury your face in a puzzle. Not with our guests at the dinner table," Marcie's voice cracks. She grabs the book out of my lap and sets it on the kitchen island.

Chapter Twenty-Seven

I'm about to head out the door to catch my morning ride with Diana when I remember my crossword book is lying on the counter. I grab it from off the island, thankful I won't be left without a few eighties references to ruminate over after I plot out my day on the way to school under another unfinished puzzle line.

Ben has made notes at random within the incomplete crosswords and from what I can tell this was some sort of ruse to mess with me. I'm finding *GENESIS* planted in between blocks with blank spaces untouched past a few tabbed pages. It seemed one thing would remain constant between my two worlds: Ben's track record of messing with my crosswords. It wouldn't be my first time scratching out his markings and filling in everything around it, ignoring his graffiti. He's also supplied me with a few blocks of profanity and rated a few of the clues.

*This one will take you days to find
*This one's beyond your comprehension
*Better chance of finding a leprechaun than getting this one
*Good luck. You're going to need it.

Gee, thanks for the encouragement, Ben.

❀

ON MY WAY TO SECOND PERIOD THE ANSWER FOR CLUE #16, *Section with time travel stories,* haunts me as I walk the hallways surrounded by teenagers in oversized everything. I think I know the answer.

"Science Fiction," I say underneath my breath as a pack of unfledged boys wearing Kentucky Waterfall hairstyles slide their arms around their girlfriends passing by me. Every now and then one boosts their girlfriend up for a piggyback ride—a most romantic form of transportation. I've gotten used to dodging flying objects as I pass through—Rubik's Cube-like toys, and my personal favorite, hostess cupcakes still in the wrapper. It was like wading through a pool of fearless teenagers who look like full-grown adults and I knew one thing for sure. It wasn't science fiction. I was living it.

I stare across from me at a girl's Huarache shoes that I'd seen on half of the cheerleaders last week. It's a bit chilly today so I opted for black slouchy boots and black tights to go under a denim miniskirt—I'd learned the significance of a miniskirt in the eighties. It was as if it were a tacitly implied rule to wear one a couple of times a week.

"Cute outfit," the girl with the Huarache shoes says. I thank her, saying the same about her shoes as a familiar set of legs pass by with a flock of cheerleaders. Legs that tall and lean belong to only one person, Corky—whom I hadn't had another conversation with since Diana popped Genesis into the tape player at the party. I didn't expect to talk to her after I became partially to blame for her and Bennette's drama.

I catch Diana's name floating by in the air of their conversation and perk up to make out what's being said as they step around the corner.

"Yeah, can you believe it? On their first date." Tiffany, the petite flyer, says. "They've only been with each other for like a week and their first kiss was an accident."

"So, Annie heard this?" Corky looks to verify.

"No, she saw them parked behind the milkshake shack next to the lookout. When they drove by a second time their car was all fogged up. Supposedly they were at the skate rink and ditched Ben and Atta."

A third girl I don't know chimes in. "Ben and Atta were together?"

"Yeah, and caught kissing too," Tiffany confirms. I feel a sense of imminent danger at that and leap into the nearest classroom before anyone can see me react to their conversation.

Thoughts begin to swivel through my head like a spinning top, as if bullying forces are coming at me from all directions. First, I think of what's being said about Diana. They were probably parked because Tyler was tired. Though I'd never seen Tyler act or say he was tired in my life, it's still a plausible explanation.

But I can't help but think if this rumor gets around to Ben he's not going to like it. I'm afraid he'll do something about it, just like Bennette might when she hears Ben and I kissed less than a week after their breakup.

Teenage life is stressful when the gossip rolls around. I can't help but feel out of place as an adult—at least in mind and spirit—hiding behind the classroom doorframe in a world where other girls find fault in my relationship with the man I'd spent more than half of my life with.

Feeling even an ounce of guilt in this situation wasn't worth it. Ben's open confession that night was groundbreaking stuff, warranting passionate behavior. After such a vulnerable, emotional conversation it was bound to happen, but just because he got caught up in the moment of intense feelings doesn't mean he wants to be with me. I had yet to get his thoughts about *us*.

I had planned to gauge his response after our kiss but that was becoming increasingly difficult since he had decided not to show up to class. We hadn't exactly left on satisfying terms that night either. Ben seemed more focused on the fact that Tyler had wronged him by ditching us, breathing fire down Tyler's neck behind the headrest as the four of us rode back home together. They dropped me off first, Ben hardly acknowledging my departure, and I spent the rest of the weekend wondering what he thought of the other night.

Typically someone who planned to pursue a relationship after kissing them would make a lot of effort to see that person, right?

Was he avoiding me?

AFTER LUNCH I OFFICIALLY CALL IT QUITS ON READING newspapers in class while the teacher scratches the chalkboard. Six hours a day, for weeks on end, staring at headlines, ignoring what's being taught in eighties high school, and hoping for Marigold answers is tiring. So I decide to gawk over a few crossword boxes instead, occasionally admiring Ben's graffiti scattered throughout the pages.

I take inventory of the uneventful schedule I've written for today and notice the pages are stuck together. With both hands, I separate today's crossword from the page behind it, noticing the newly freed page is not only another target of graffiti but it occupies someone else's handwriting. Someone other than Ben. My eyes look fixedly at the lines of handwriting I don't recognize.

Agent Suarez. I've been in touch with all of my contacts at the Bureau. No one seems to know who you are. After our dinner tonight I can't help but think you're avoiding me. We need to chat about Marigold. I'll be in touch.

  -Officer Berrett

I shake my pen between my fingers, startling myself when I accidentally hit it against the desk. How did he manage to leave a message in my crossword?

The island counter. After dinner.

Officer Berrett is digging more than I thought. Why does he think we need to chat about Marigold? There's no way he'd know about the future or even time travel.

Should I be more concerned? They were pretty relaxed in the eighties, right? No one wore seatbelts and half of the jocks rode to school in the back bed of someone's truck. And in the few weeks he'd been here, Officer Berrett had gained the reputation of taking girls up into the mountains on his police motorcycle. So it was safe to say I likely wouldn't be prosecuted for requesting a ride from an officer using an FBI badge from the future. If anything it's Officer Berrett's connection with Marigold and his desire to question me that should scare me. And it does.

As long as I could convince him I know nothing of Marigold or, better yet, if I avoided him entirely, I was safe.

A fuzzy, distinctive telephone sound chirps through the classroom's intercom speaker, an early signal that the main office has taken the phone off the hook to project an announcement. The room collectively pops their heads up from a sluggish my-desk-might-as-well-be-a-bean-bag position.

"Atta Atkinson, Jamie Williams, and Brad Jones you're needed in the front office." I look up from the crossword under my desk to stare at the teacher in confusion.

Who needs me in the office enough to make me stand up and turn my back to a bunch of students who'll stare at my backside en masse right now?

I walk down the hall, taking a right turn at the corner. When I reach the hallway to the front office area, I only make it halfway before stopping in my tracks. The office looks empty through its large rectangular windows, except for a man standing and facing the front desk lady.

Two boys, who must be Jamie and Brad, walk out the office door with what looks like the wrestling coach, leaving me to conclude that the man is here for me. I need to get closer to see who he is. Does he have something to do with why Ben wasn't in class today?

I approach the middle of the hallway carefully, ready to drop low to the ground if he turns around and spots me before I'm able to identify him. As I walk down the hall, with slow, accessing steps, my eyes sweep over his face. From this distance his outline is uncanny. Curls that shape only take on one form. A mullet. A familiar mullet and an eerily familiar uniform.

I hit the ground fast.

Chapter Twenty-Eight

Why is Officer Berrett waiting for me? My internal alarm bell rings.

Commence army crawl.

My elbows scrape the floor. My goal is the women's bathroom a dozen yards down the hall. The scenario takes me away into my own farce-like thoughts, imagining I'm in the trenches while machine guns are firing live rounds in this hallway jungle. The more rapid my execution of bent arms and a perfect plank, the better chance I have at survival.

A few teenagers walk past looking at me as if I'm some wild animal, completely flummoxed, just as a boy approaches the hallway corner choking on a laugh before he asks his friend what in the world I am doing. I smile back at them and then look over my shoulder to find Officer Berrett in the front office turning his head so that he has a clear window view of the school hallway. If he turns any more, he will have a clear view of me.

Any humorous thoughts that had entered my mind in response to my actions are instantly wiped as I process Officer Berrett's searching expression. Fear pounds inside my chest and I exert all my physical effort into the last ten feet of my crawl.

Why is he here! Did he spot me? The nerves I felt at dinner the night before are back in full force, this time strangling my intestines so that my stomach feels like it's a ball of knots about to turn into stone from the internal pressure.

He meant it when he wrote in my crossword book that he'd be in touch. He must've sensed my crumbling foundation at dinner and now he wants to send a final jackhammer through it with more clarifying questions. I can't let him approach me.

I spring up off the floor in a single operative motion. The humid bathroom air greets me with a needless amount of air freshener and I find the nearest stall, claiming it as my hiding spot.

The minutes pass slowly, inhaling stuffy bathroom fumes until my patience wavers enough that I lean my head out past the stall door in order to glance at the clock on the wall. There's still ten minutes until the wave of students spill out of the classrooms like reservoir water being released from the spillway. It'll be much harder for a cop to find me in a river of students.

A thud at the door brings in a group of squealing girls.

"His last note was so romantic though. I always leave him a lipstick kiss at the bottom when I write back. You should try it sometime. It really heats up the conversation if ya know what I mean." A familiar voice boasts to the giggling girls. I recognize it as Erica's—she must be checking her hair in the mirror with some friends. I gracefully slide out from the stall and greet her friends, before pulling her aside.

"Was a police officer out in the hallways?" I ask her.

"No, we walked here from the mechanics building outside but I didn't see a cop anywhere," she answers.

"Was there a cop car in the parking lot?" I ask. She shakes her head. "A motorcycle? A police motorcycle?" I clarify.

"No. Nothing like that. Why?"

"It's our neighbor cop. He's giving me the creeps. I saw him in the office earlier. He had them call me over the intercom, and I've been hiding in the bathroom ever since."

"Weird," she says, contemplating why I'd be hiding from our neighbor cop. She looks concerned but moves on.

"You brought the shorts to practice, right? We're doing pictures today. I laid the uniform on your bed."

"Yeah, the red and white striped shorts? I did," I assure her. The thought of receiving developed photos of myself in red and white striped cotton mini shorts, matching the rest of the team in split poses makes me want to shudder and snort at the same time.

It was only an hour until school was out.

If Officer Berrett decided to look for me after school I'd need Diana to act as my sidekick for the afternoon. Enlisting her for lookout duty was one way I'd be able to endure posing for cheerleading team pictures with a genuine smile and not a distracted gaze.

"We're going to be taking them outside the gym in the courtyard behind the school where the four large trees are," she says. Good. That wasn't where we usually held practice, so if Officer Berrett asked, he wouldn't easily find me.

WHEN I FIND DIANA, SHE'S AT HER LOCKER DEEP IN THOUGHT. Her back rests against the tall locker with her feet stretched out wide. She looks dazed but in a happy sort of way, as if she's love drunk on Tyler, the future bird-watcher.

"Di, you think you can come with me to cheer practice today? We're doing pictures for half an hour or so," I say, working to convince her.

Just like always, it doesn't take long for her to say yes.

"You need a ride or something?"

"Actually, Officer Berrett, the one at dinner last night, stopped by the school today and requested that I meet him in the office. I need you if he decides to show up again."

"Are you serious?" The daze has fully passed and her cheeks grow hot from my statement. "What is he doing? He was looking for you?"

"Yes." I stare at the locker I have yet to unlock.

"What a pervert. He already tried getting you on his bike," she starts. While that's not technically true, I'm fine with her thinking that to help my case.

"Is he obsessed with you or something?" she asks.

"Possibly. I just need to avoid him. That way I won't have any more creepy encounters."

"Ugh, but he's your neighbor. How are you going to avoid him?"

"I don't know," I say. Another problem I don't have a solution to.

DIANA MEETS ME AT MY LOCKER AFTER SCHOOL TO ACCOMPANY me on my walk to the photoshoot in the school's courtyard. She's not what I'd call a qualified lookout, carrying her bag stuffed with textbooks and spinning her keychain around her fingers, but she'll give me fair warning via a thwack to my side if Officer Berrett shows up.

"Have you seen Ben around today?" I ask, trying to get to the bottom of his disappearance since he should have been in the two classes we have together.

"Once or twice," she says without much care.

"Has he said anything about me?"

"Not particularly." The way she says it tells me he hasn't said a thing about me to her.

"So Tyler. You really like him, don't you?" I say. "You sure he was tired and it wasn't just an excuse to spend two hours alone kissing?

Diana bumps me with her hip. "It wasn't like *that*. He really wore himself out. He almost threw up that night. He wasn't feeling well." She lets out a smile and we both laugh.

THE PHOTOSHOOT IS JUST AS SYRUPY AS I THOUGHT IT WOULD be. Thin red stripes run down the legs of our white cotton shorts and matching red bungee cord bracelets dangle along our wrists. Erica walks around checking to make sure our white shirts are crisply tucked into our shorts and that our red wool socks bubble over our white Keds.

Diana sits in the grass watching us with a pleasant smile as the photographer guides the team into various acrobatic positions. Corky and Bennette are on opposite sides of the picture, but I catch them both sending Diana a few glares in between posed smiles, during the game of "avoiding eye contact" that they both seem to be playing. It seems they have yet to make up.

We finish team photos with a trickle of rain dotting our clothes, just a minute's worth. The sun peeks through, promising a blue sky of warmth but I still feel the goosebumps skate down my legs. By the time we get to individual photos, most of the team has lost all seriousness. The photographer will face a roll of funny faces and fuzzy photos when he goes to print, due to all the shimmering and laughing that's happening at this point in the session. I watch as a photo contest to see who can create the best shoulder shake emerges from all the chaos.

At Erica's request, we sneak in a sister photo, one that includes a mini stuffed bear posed in our begging hands—the kind of pose you'd only see in an eighties photo studio. If I were to ever have the chance to tell my mother—Non-80s-Land Erica—about time traveling to her past, I'd give her such a hard time about this.

"This means a lot to me," she says, as we break the corny pose together. "Regardless of your reasons for joining, I love that you're here with me." Her eyes scrunch when she smiles and when I take a closer look I can see they are glossy with watery emotion as if the experience is playing back in her eyes. I feel a ping-pong ball try to make its way down my throat at the realization that sitting in the split position in front of the accordion TV with Erica every night before bed makes her happy.

Taking a time travel vacation may have given me a lens to look at my life from an outside perspective. A perspective where I see an opportunity for improvement—to spend more quality time with my mom whether it be in this life or the other one.

With the amount of time I hadn't spent with her over the last few years anyone would think I'd signed my time over to the Bureau.

As long as I was here I'd make it a point to give her my time, as her sister.

"I'm glad I joined the team," I say, hoping she takes it as a heartfelt comment and not as the sarcasm that typically splits out of my mouth.

Corky finishes off a group photo with Kelly and another cheerleader, then starts walking toward Erica and me.

"Atta, I need to talk to you for a sec," she says, pulling me aside, smiling at Erica as she does so. The other cheerleaders' eyes follow our movement as we agree to plant our conversation a few feet away next to a large tree in the courtyard.

"It's about you and Ben. You've really hurt Bennette you know. I've hurt her too, so I'm not qualified to say this, but I was trying to keep the secret for the best interest of their relationship. I had good intentions, despite acting stupidly, but couldn't you wait to kiss Ben?" she says with righteous indignation. "It hasn't even been a week. You didn't think how she would feel for one second or give it some time!"

Diana appears at my side and cuts in with the defense. "I get it, Corky. I really do, but that's between Ben and Atta who've had a friendship since they were five."

"You shouldn't have done that you know," Corky says to Diana. She's now referring to Diana's Genesis concert confrontation.

"I'm sorry, but if anything, you should blame my brother. If he'd answered our questions in the first place, I wouldn't have had to do that."

"You thought about your situation, but you didn't think for one second about Bennette." Corky stands in front of us with her arms folded across her chest.

"True, but this all started because you and Ben kept a secret from Bennette."

Corky looks down knowing they're both in the wrong. She must feel Bennette's eyes on her because she turns to look at her with an unsure smile.

"Are you and Bennette still doing track this year?" Diana asks, trying to ease the conversation.

"I am. I hope she is too." She looks over at Bennette again.

"It starts soon," Diana says. "I hope she does. I was thinking about joining the 4x400 meter relay on top of pole vaulting, but I'll have to make things work with Bennette first."

"Good luck to the both of us I guess," Corky says before walking away. Her temperament seems to have softened after Diana tried to tie some strings together with track and field small talk. For me, the turn of conversation is just another reminder that Diana starts pole vaulting in just a week.

I scan the courtyard and surrounding trees for Officer Berrett as Diana carries our current conversation, feeling grateful she was able to steer me clear of high school drama in the previous one. Officer Berrett still hasn't shown himself around these parts, thankfully. Maybe it was a bit of an overreaction having Diana act as my after-school intelligence officer.

A faint thumping of rubber steps beats against the cold sidewalk, distant and out of eyesight. As the sound grows closer the members of the team turn around to the fluttering sound of a man sprinting around the corner wall. I freeze as his pulsing steps draw nearer.

How did the cop find me here? Was he going to make a scene in front of all these people? My hip begins to tremble as I brace myself for a running start. My emergency senses flare, imploring me to grab Diana's bare arm and drag her away with me. She was at the dinner, too. She's potential bait.

Diana looks confused, but she's firm in her position, not giving in when I try dragging her away with me. She knows what I don't know—that the pair of black All-Star high-tops and gray sweats running toward the gym doors don't belong to Officer Berrett but to Ben.

He looks a bit ruffled with his grubby tee and messy hair. What could've possibly happened to make him look so disheveled? He jogs past me and Diana, just as the doors burst open like pressurized water, letting the basketball team flood out from the gym, with Tyler at the lead.

Everyone stops to watch as the intensity in the air becomes as thick as the evening fog. The sun is hardly a promising sign, tucked behind clouds and a bruised sky.

Ben looks as if he's about to initiate something with Tyler who's just ten feet away. He has clenched fists and I notice his forearm veins are bulging out of his skin as he walks toward the basketball team with an intensity I hardly recognize. I can't tell if he's trying to look intimidating or if that's just how a former basketball player greets his past teammates, and then I remember Corky's little package of gossip from earlier today. That must be it. We are about to witness Ben's wrath in the form of killing Tyler. He must believe the rumors. The one about Diana, Tyler, and the foggy parked car. This is it. The end of Tyler's funny business. The end of Tyler.

Ben closes in on Tyler, who lets out a yelp like a frightened dog before a case of hiccups erupts from his throat. He holds a basketball from the gym in one hand and a water bottle in the other, unable to defend himself if Ben's next move is to throw a punch. They exchange a few words and I'm unable to hear anything until someone begins to shout. But it's not Tyler who's shouting.

The bird-like chatter dissipates as we all try to tune in to the conversation and make out what's being said—so loudly across the courtyard—from a visibly distressed Evan.

I'm not able to make out much of it, but the look on Evan's face becomes unpleasant with aggression. With Ben's back turned to me I can only imagine the face he's giving Evan. Likely anger—he's possibly even taunting Evan now. But as Ben backs away from both Tyler and

Evan coolly, as if belligerent steps will rock a boat that's about to sink them all, it's clear to me Ben's facial expression is no longer anger but confusion.

Evan lunges forward, sending a full swing at Ben. His knuckles scrape against Ben's jaw with more force than Ben's ready for, rocking Ben's face back with the blow.

Chapter Twenty-Nine

An audible gasp breaks out from the small crowd. I'm not the only one surprised the hit came from Evan and not Tyler.

Evan was Tyler's closest friend and Tyler's rational other half so it was normal for Evan to support Tyler, even if he was the one apologizing on behalf of Tyler everytime they fled a scene—even the cases when Tyler had gone too far.

Ben gains his footing and faces Evan, looking more angered than injured, though from the sound of the contact it looked like the hit might've done some damage.

Ben and I weren't the subject of the rumor I'd heard, so why would Evan throw Ben so much heat?

The mature Ben I know—Agent Ben Brown—would think for a moment, assess what course of action would produce the best outcome, then calmly approach a loose cannon with the goal of diffusing it. Not this Ben. This Ben doesn't hesitate before swinging a clenched fist back at Evan, matching the same jawline target and leaving Evan with a bloody scrape across his lip.

The crowd grows around them. The basketball boys, hoping for some more action, rile up Ben and Evan with coarse encouragement.

As anticipation builds for who will throw the next swing, the sun escapes the gate of clouds, allowing its rays to stretch across the base of the Rocky Mountains before it falls behind them for the night. The sun's brief appearance warms the courtyard while Ben and Evan forgo throwing punches, deciding instead to sear through each other's skulls with dangerous gazes.

Diana leans into my side as the intensity grows between the boys. Tyler stands to the right of them looking relatively calm despite the context of the fight. And to my surprise Diana looks just as calm. In fact, she has the temperament of a person standing outside the ring of a boxing match, rooting for whoever puts up the best fight.

"Why would you?…I told you that morning we were going with Tyler to the rink," Ben says to Evan.

One of the cheerleaders shouts right behind me. "What's going on over here?" I flinch at her yelling, missing the part of the verbal exchange in front of me.

"—as friends? Sounds like she was easy," Evan snaps.

"At least not with me!" Ben replies.

"That's not what I heard." Evan smiles with satisfaction as if he knows this will hit a nerve.

The confusing accusations being thrown around make me think this conversation isn't about Diana anymore.

Ben scoffs and without warning slams his fist into Evan's smooth face, making another ugly sound and likely altering his scratch to an open cut. A thick stream of blood trickles down Evan's lip.

"Ben, let him go," Tyler steps between the two of them.

"Got anything else to say?" Ben directs his words back to Evan. Instead of answering, Evan lunges at Ben, throwing five or six punches anywhere he's able. A few of them make the connection, injuring Ben's left ribs. He hunches over clenching his side.

"You kissed your sister's best friend even though you spent the last three weeks wishing she'd leave the country? She was with me. I thought we were…" Evan trails off, glancing at me for a second before quickly looking away.

"What you heard today wasn't meant for you, Evan," Tyler says, pulling Evan away from Ben, who's raging and unable to take a deep calming breath. Tyler seems to struggle, defeated by his two best friends arguing. It shows as he weakly pulls at Evan.

The whole cheer team has caught on to Evan's allegations. Everyone stares at me as Ben walks away steaming like a pressure cooker ready to blow. Did they think I was just a rebound or a two-timer? They might be right about the rebound.

Whether Ben's avoiding me because of a rumor or because he made a mistake kissing me, it all feels the same. What progress I've made with Ben is faltering; it's chugging down a broken-down railway heading for the edge of a cliff.

I run after him, managing to grab onto his loose tee and drag him to a tree, away from the others. He whips me around with competing force and leads me to the cafeteria's back entrance underneath the doorframe where a sibling-like struggle ensues.

The whole entanglement appears more like a dance due to our battle of strengths. He wins, but only because of the height he has over me, then lays his hands on my shoulders as if one of us has something to explain. Though I'm not sure who he thinks should do the explaining. It's certainly not me. I hadn't done anything that warranted explaining. The most I'd done wrong here is kiss him too soon after he broke up with Bennette. That's hardly an offense. Ben didn't seem to care either at the time since he was the one who initiated it.

"Where've you been all day?" I say pinned to the door. He loosens his hold on me.

"I was in the mechanic shop."

"So you've been avoiding me all day," I say as if it's a statement, yet we both know I mean to lure him in and fish for more detail. I might as well have phrased it as a question.

"If that's how you want to put it, sure," he says and I can tell he's becoming increasingly cold.

"So kissing me the other night? You think it's fine to just ignore that it happened? It must've meant nothing to you if you're just going to leave me hanging like this."

"From what I heard, it sounds like it meant nothing to you either."

"What are you talking about?" I say with more confusion than I felt in the moment Evan swung at Ben instead of Tyler.

"Why bother having this conversation? Do me a favor and pretend nothing happened," he's quick to say.

At that, I feel my years-long pent-up feelings bubble inside of me. He's crushing me the same way he did after Diana's wedding. He'd rather leave me to come up with the conclusion myself, with no courtesy to tell me the truth. After flirting with me on one occasion, he'd come to the conclusion that he doesn't want to be with his sister's best friend—both in this universe and the last.

Just because Ben and I have been lifelong friends doesn't mean I don't deserve an open and honest explanation now or in the past—future—whatever. I've had enough.

I shove his hand away. Mild volcanic activity rises up in my chest, and I shove all of him away from me with clenched fists. He stumbles back against the cafeteria door before regaining his balance and watches me as I debate my next move.

I've held on to my disappointment before with no qualms, so why can't I do the same this time? Is it because we actually kissed this time? He actually physically initiated something with me and set all the hope I'd ever had on fire just to take it back without words.

I come back at him with an FBI defensive tactic, a shot to his shoulder, throwing my fist strategically into the crease between his chest and armpit with more strength than I should've.

"Ugh," he grunts.

And just as I land it, I know I've done the wrong thing. This isn't right in a romantic relationship. Not even if I'd felt like I'd been winding in and out of a brotherly relationship with him for most of my life. And then it hits me, as if my own actions have proven the kind of brother-sister relationship this really is.

I secretly shed a few tears. Three angry tears. Tears I wipe away quickly before walking away. He's done it again. Given me hope just to crush it.

Chapter Thirty

I f I didn't have these teenage hormones coursing through my body I would've been able to maintain dry eyes, not to mention keep my crap together in this situation, like I did the first time Ben rejected me without explanation. How irritating that it happened this way. I keep my back to him as I march off, embarrassment trailing me like a taunting ghost. I turn the corner to find Diana eavesdropping on us, swinging her keys back and forth as if she's bugged by our behavior.

"Let's go," I say, dragging Diana toward the car and away from Ben.

Gasps and startled cries from the group of cheerleaders in the parking lot pauses my retreat. Diana and I look back to see Tyler collapsed in Evan's arms, his eyelids fluttering as if he's trying his hardest to keep them open. That or he is just waking up after losing consciousness. His basketball teammates question him and a cheerleader hollers from across the nearest parking spot, "Tyler, are you okay?"

Diana yanks my arm as if she plans to burn through the small gathered crowd and rescue Tyler with the determination of a heroic firefighter facing down a burning building. Before she has the chance to strap on boots, slide down a pole, and shatter a window with an ax, Ben stops her halfway.

"He's probably dehydrated from practice. Stay here. I'll check on him." Ben holds Diana back before running over to Tyler and Evan.

"Is he okay?" Diana asks when Ben reappears. Evan dragged Tyler off somewhere at the conclusion of their discourse, Tyler looking like a feverish rag doll hanging off of Evan's shoulder as the rest of the basketball team dispersed into the parking lot like ants being released from an ant farm.

"Evan's taking him to the hospital. He'll be alright. He doesn't want a bunch of people tagging along and Tyler doesn't want to worry anyone."

"Shouldn't I go with them?" Diana asks.

Ben shakes his head. "He'll catch up with you later." His tone aims to provide comfort until he looks at me and then back at Diana and says, "My bike's not working. I need a ride too, Di."

Ben reaches the passenger seat before I can, claiming his stake as I sheepishly open the back door. Diana gives him a disapproving look.

Diana turns down the radio dial for a lecture as soon as she starts the car. "Okay you two. I did not spend three years of my life worrying Atta would choose you over me just to have you both kiss and not even two days later ruin your friendship."

Using one hand to steer, Diana shoves at Ben with the other. He's been looking out the passenger window since his sister started talking.

"You've been avoiding Atta for weeks now and then you kiss her?" Diana says, staring into Ben's soul, breaking the sentence long enough for us to know it's emphasized. "Start talking."

"I don't see the point in talking," I say from the backseat. "Ben won't explain himself, anyway."

My verbal jab must have struck true. Ben flips around to stare daggers at me.

"If you want an explanation that bad…" His bluster deflates a bit as he regains a bit of his composure. "I wasn't avoiding you. I just needed time to think. In the mechanic shop. While I fix my bike."

"Think about what?" Diana pries.

"None of you are making this easy on me. Especially you." He looks at Diana. "I told you how I felt about you dating Tyler."

"And I told you how I felt about you dating Atta," Diana counters.

"Yeah, when you were ten and both socially awkward. Your request was safe when Atta had a bowl cut." I can't help but smile a little at this statement.

"And Atta's involved with other people. I'm not going to start something with her when Evan's willing to fight me for it. I didn't realize her relationships were so messy."

"What? You think I have something with Evan?" I say.

"Yeah. So just forget about the other night," he says with so much ease it's irritating.

"Just take me home, Diana," I say defeated, bringing my attention out the angular car window where a majority of red and brown cars pass by us on the main road.

"Stop here!" Ben jolts forward in his seat, pointing to a bush in a field a few yards away from a gas station. "Hold on a second."

Diana stops the car and Ben leaps out to pull a red motorbike out of a clump of velvety bushes, wheeling it over before directing me to take his spot at the front. He folds the seat down and pops the bike into the trunk of the car, crawling in next to it.

"We're not going home until you two resolve this," Diana pushes, using a motherly tone, as if we're two kids acting up and it's worthy of a scolding.

"What did Evan say to you before he threw a punch?" I ask.

"He said you kissed him the day of our date," Ben says and I immediately shoot a look at Diana.

"No way," Diana says, confused. "I thought the rumor was about me and Tyler."

"It was. I heard Tiffany and Corky spreading it like fleas in the hallway," I add.

"Diana if that's true you…no…Tyler's in deep trouble." Ben says in frustration. He adjusts his position so that he has a clear view of both of us. He looks at Diana through the rearview mirror.

"It's not true. Neither is the rumor about Atta!" Diana barks at Ben. I didn't think Diana's innocent eyes could turn so severe.

"It's not? Then why did Evan say that?" Ben stares out the car window, visibly frustrated.

I can't believe what I'm hearing. "He obviously lied!"

"Why would he make that up? He said you guys have been writing notes in class for months and even meeting up for dates."

I take in a deep breath, trying not to yell. "He has been writing me notes and tried to get me to go on a date with him, but I was never interested."

"You sure? He was pretty angry when he heard I'd kissed you, and even more angry when I told him that you even went joyriding with that cop. The one who's looking for you."

For a moment I feel like I can't feel my legs. Is this what it feels like to go past shock? How did that information find its way to Ben?

"What are you talking about? Who said anything about a cop?" I say with absolute panic in my brain. This is one giant misunderstanding in a merry-go-round of gossip.

"Jamie and Brad. The cop asked them about you. He said you were really friendly, and when they asked what you had done, he said something about riding into the city with him and that he wants to talk with you. You know what the best part is? It's the same cop who banned Tyler and I from dirt biking in the mountains so he could take girls up there on his motorcycle. I can't believe it, Atta. You were one of *those* girls."

Those girls? The full weight of what he thinks I was doing with Officer Berrett, what he probably thinks I did with Evan, hits me. Hot tears brim in my eyes. "Are you kidding me?" I say.

"Jamie's in mechanics. I heard it from him in the shop today, and then I heard another guy say that the cop was looking for you in the hallways, asking people if they'd seen you. Why would a cop be saying this stuff if it wasn't true, Atta?" Ben says. He looks hurt.

"That psycho!" I fume in my seat.

"Diana thought something was up at dinner with you two the other night. She said he was asking about you a lot. He's a thirty-some-year-old married man, Atta!" Ben scolds me the way I would scold him if he had been with a married woman, his voice loud and exasperated.

Diana starts to defend me. "That's not what I meant though. He was being creepy, Ben, but Atta didn't do anything."

"Diana, it's a cop. He wouldn't just say things that don't mean anything, especially in public," Ben says. I understand his eagerness to trust law enforcement. After all, the Non-80s-Land version of him becomes an agent, but it hurts to think my best friend and partner thinks so little of me and won't even wait to hear my account.

"I can't believe he walked the halls searching for me."

Diana's face matches mine with concern flooding from her brows.

"Let's get the record straight," I say. "I got a ride from him, but I never hit on him." I may have thought Officer Berrett was attractive initially, but that quickly faded with each frustrating encounter. I pause to breathe in the untrusting air behind me.

"Why would you need to get a ride from him? Why would both Evan and a cop lie about you?" He tries fumbling with his bike, so that he can yell at me directly without the bike wheel or headrest blocking his sore expression. The conflict I see in Ben's face tears at me. I can see he's struggling to not believe the rumors, but it's a fight that he's losing. "He's a thirty-year-old, married man looking for you at school. You can't deny you got a ride from him! You can't deny that you and Evan wrote letters. So how am I supposed to believe you aren't involved with two other guys?"

I look straight into his eyes. "Because you know me."

I needed Ben to like me, to be friends with me, even if he did not want to be with me. Even if this alternate universe wasn't the same, it still mattered. It was still Ben. I needed his approval and it hurt to not have his trust. Every rational brain cell in my body wants to go on strike and adopt the meltdown strategy of a toddler.

He sits for a moment contemplating my words.

Diana tries to disappear, leaning as far as she can into the car window, as if she's subconsciously trying to escape the conversation. Ben opens his mouth to say more before I can form a response.

"Atta!" Diana shouts. She jolts the car to a complete stop in front of a tall clearing of bushes at the entrance of her neighborhood. We're a quarter mile down the road from Ben and Diana's house, but able to make out a police motorcycle and a man in uniform, straddling the dipped bike seat waiting on the Browns' sidewalk.

"He can't see us can he?" she asks.

"Who?" Ben says from the backseat.

"Officer Berrett is sitting on his motorcycle outside our house," Diana says.

"How did he find your house?" I say under my breath. I can't believe how persistent he is. I'm surprised he hasn't barged into my house at this rate. A stable person would have boundaries and maintain neighborly distance. He'd need something official to physically make me meet him, right?

Diana manages to put the car in reverse, step on the gas and dart from the neighborhood before Officer Berrett notices. I keep my eyes peeled on the back window in case he actually saw us.

"Looks like he found where we hang out after practice," Diana says.

This whole cop chase was starting to feel like a thriller. One that I might not make it through. I tried watching a thriller once. I couldn't make it through the first five minutes of *A Quiet Place* in Non-80s-Land before handing my bucket of popcorn to Ben's date and spending the rest of the night in the theater hallway as a distant third wheel.

"Why is the cop waiting for you at our house?" Ben says. He's obviously as surprised by this turn of events as I am, but it's not helping my case at all.

"Isn't it weird that supposedly I'm the one hitting on him, but he shows up to my school and your house just to find me? Is that how that kind of relationship works? I hit on him but he does all the stalking?" I taunt Ben as we drive. "When I asked him for a ride into Denver it was a serious emergency. I think he's trying to get back at me because I've been ignoring him."

"So you, on his bike, in the mountains. It's not true. He's the one trying to go after you?" Ben says, realization settling in on his face. Then his face twists in anger, the way it did when he was preparing to pound Evan's face in.

"Something like that, so I think it's best if I avoid him at all costs."

"Yeah, this is too weird," Diana agrees. She purposely avoids my driveway and pulls into the neighborhood behind my grandparents' home, parking next to the chain-link fence where five large leafy sky pencils separate our backyard from the dead-end street loop. The car idles as I stare at my grandparents' sliding glass door beyond their dark grassy lawn. Officer Berrett would come home at some point. If I was going to avoid him I'd need to use the back door from now on.

"I'm coming with you," Ben says as I exit the car. He opens the back door, getting out with me.

"How will you get home?" Diana asks.

"I'll find a way." He shuts the door and waves her off.

Chapter Thirty-One

Ben hops the fence in one swift motion, thrusting both of his legs over with a pommel-horse-like action. I'd seen this particular move countless times on the job, in Ben's slacks, not the dirty sweats he wore working all day today in the mechanic's shop.

I attempt the same motion, stalling at the top of the wobbly chain-link fence. Ben helps me down and I'm reminded of our partner agent relationship—often operating like a synchronized pair.

We cross the open grass to the treehouse built over a thick round stump that sits ten feet from the sliding screen door. I'd spent much of my childhood making mud pies to sell to my grandparents out of the open treehouse window, but it had been years since I'd stepped foot in here.

"This'll be better," he says. I follow him through the small tree-house back door.

It's getting dark, but there's a strong strip of light shining along the floorboards from the open window. We sit, maintaining a few feet of distance on two old pea green and sunflower yellow cushions, positioned on each side of an ice cream toy machine filled with dirt. I throw the orange crochet blanket bunched next to me over to Ben. The least I can do is offer more cushion.

"I'm sorry," Ben says, turning his head to the side to face me. "I shouldn't have assumed the rumors were true." He remains calm and apologetic as he tries to make amends. "Lately you keep surprising me. Your meddling in the whole Corky and Bennette situation was unexpected, as if you wanted Bennette and I to break up so we could be together or something. I thought for a moment that riding into the mountains with that cop was just another one of your surprises. I was wrong."

I nod, accepting his apology. Relief washes over me.

"But I have to ask. What about Evan?" Ben's muscular arms fold across his knees.

"There's no Evan. I bet he was mad when he heard that you and I kissed," I say.

"You weren't out with him that day?"

"I wasn't out with Evan. Ever." The words come out firm. Honest.

He nods. "This is a mess you know." He gives me a comforting smile that pushes the shadows on his face upward. His brown skin is glowing in the dim light and his dimple takes on a deeper shadow.

"I know," I say, trying to keep it lighthearted.

The night darkens quickly and the dark blue fade in the sky sets a mysterious tone that only the moonlight can create. It's probably the hope I feel from this cold-toned romantic setting, but Ben's eyes seem to sparkle like sunlight reflecting off a muddy lake and I can't help but show a sheepish smile when I notice. I consider him the most stable thing in my life both here and in the future. How could I not be in love with those eyes when they keep me from losing my balance?

He stares at me with a soft, forgiving gaze, scooting in closer to me so we're only a foot away from each other, and I want this second kiss more than I wanted the first.

"Now about us," he says. My head remains turned toward him as he lowers his nose to meet mine.

"Hmm?" I squeak like a mouse with pent-up anticipation. He had to sense my infatuation with him. I was not very cool in this moment, and he was the face of control and confidence.

"So you aren't interested in cops with mullets?" A hint of seriousness peeks through his sarcasm.

"I. Am. Not."

"So then maybe you could be into your best friend's brother?"

"I could be," I tease.

"Do you want to be with me?" he asks. Any thought processing about the future that should have happened in this moment doesn't. I only know one thing. My answer.

"Yes."

I say it so softly it rolls off my tongue like summer pudding. In this moment, the buzz of uneasiness and crashing alternate universes should have hit me like a truck slamming into the median of a freeway, so that I'd consider the choice I was making. A choice that impacted more than just me and Ben. It impacted time—the alternate universe I would be choosing over the present. Instead, I feel calm, immersed in utter contentment and joy. I choose what I've always wanted. Ben.

Chapter Thirty-Two

I leave through the sliding glass door in the backyard the next morning walking through thick grass, hoping Diana remembered to pick me up at the back. I assumed she would, but what if she was out front, vulnerable to Officer Berrett's questioning.

I hear wet grass crunching behind me. Expecting to hear one of the siblings ask me why I'm going out the back I turn and see a very disheveled Ben, looking as if he'd collected all the dirt from the tree-house floor with his sweats and shirt in his sleep. Was he unable to get a hold of Diana last night? I guess I didn't really offer him a phone, did I? And it's not like he had a cell phone—a detail of the eighties I may have overlooked last night.

"How'd you sleep?" I say, embarrassed that I let him stay there. That I assumed he'd work it out rather than sleep in my grandparents' treehouse.

"Not half-bad, I grabbed the wool blanket from the piano room. I figured your parents wouldn't approve if I snuck into your bed with you," he says with a smile.

"I thought you went home," I say in disbelief. I smirk thinking

261

about how he survived an, albeit unseasonably warm, winter night in that tiny treehouse.

Ben dusts the dirt off his clothes like he's Indiana Jones recovering from having found more than a few dead bones in a cave as we wait for Diana to pick us up. I run back into the house and peek through the living room blinds to see if she's parked out front. She isn't but Officer Berrett's motorcycle stands next to his wife's car in their driveway. I run back to Ben in the backyard without delay.

"What are we going to do if she doesn't show up?"

"Make out all day," is Ben's response. I snort just as the sound of Diana's engine rumbles as she peels around the corner and slows to a stop in front of us.

"There you are." She looks at Ben, taking in his disheveled state. "I've been looking for you for an hour. I'm not even going to ask why you didn't show up at the house last night and why you look like that," Diana says so sweetly it's scary. "You two made up I assume?" she asks.

I'm a bit scared to answer. I know she's had a rough morning wondering where her brother spent the night when she forces a blanket of sweetness over what should be audible aggression.

A FEW PEOPLE CONFRONT DIANA AND ME ABOUT THE FIGHT IN the first few hours of school before lunch. I'm too focused on figuring out crossword line #50 across to care much about the drama. I simply laugh their questions off and answer with a simple "It's all a big misunderstanding."

The crossword clue reads *Hero Worshipper* which has seven open spaces and starts with an "L." I'm going to need a dictionary at this point to complete the crossword, so I decide to make my way to the library, knowing at some point today the one to confront me is going to be Bennette, and it's not going to go well for me, especially after the theatrical fight display of Evan and Ben fighting over me. I'd pour all my focus into completing as many crossword puzzles as possible until the rumors dissipate and then somehow try to survive cheerleading practice.

In history class I notice Tyler's up to no good again, running his own classroom sweatshop in the form of student mail carriers with the amount of folded notes he's sending across the room.

Tyler fist bumps my shoulder, then opens his fist to show me there's folded paper inside his palm. Today's my lucky day to receive correspondence from Tyler. I quickly snatch it from his fingers.

Whoever it's from has attempted to fold the paper into an unsuccessful heart but it is a very convincing check mark. Despite Tyler's chaotic behavior with everything else in life, his last letter had been immaculately folded and creased. I know this note isn't from him.

I open the letter on the desk this time. The history teacher has gone lax. He's aware of the carrier system that's infiltrated his third period, but since it's run by Tyler he doesn't have the energy to care or do anything about it. Fighting Tyler was like fighting a cactus. If you touch it, it pokes you back.

I know this handwriting instantly. It's Ben's.

Tyler says you can come over to his house after school so you can avoid the creepy neighbor. Meet me at the gym after cheer. ♥

The heart he drew at the end instead of his name makes me smile.

BENNETTE IS SILENT ALL THROUGHOUT PRACTICE. I'M GLAD SHE hasn't tried to approach me, but I'm also worried for her. She hasn't spoken a word to Corky since the cassette tape exposé. I follow her lead and treat chitchat like it's landmines on the floor. I stay in my place and give people the do-not-approach-me look while I cheer. I still need time to work through how I want to respond to all of this drama, so I remain silent and to myself the rest of practice.

Staying silent gives me a lot of time to anticipate the reunion at Tyler's house. I snuck it into my conversation with Ben the night before, hoping I'd get a chance to return the newspaper clippings before the Jacobsons noticed their missing files—and just as Ben had said, it was an excuse to hide out from the neighbor cop. Ben already spent most of his afternoons working and studying over there. It would take some harder digging for Officer Berrett to find me at the foot of the mountains.

Although I've avoided the underground floor mines of chitchat for an entire practice, that all feels completely ruined when Ben shows up and sits on the whiskey-orange-stained bleacher steps. I feel even more exposed to the issue everyone seems to have with us.

Ben smiles as if I'm the only one he can see in the gym radius.

"You finished?" He invites me to sit next to him with the pat of his hand against the bleacher step. I feel the other's eyes on me, and I become shy as soon as I sit down next to him. If sitting down next to him with a bunch of knowing cheerleaders watching wasn't fear-inducing enough, he begins weaving his hands through my hair with gentle, slow movements as if he'd been fantasizing about it all day. I shove a choke back down my throat at our public display of affection.

He's oblivious and happy. It's cute and I can't help but feel special. From the side, he wraps his arms around me, dangling a small chain of keys in front of me.

"You fixed your bike?" I say in an embarrassingly high-pitched voice.

"You ready to ride?" He confirms his bike's revival with the dangerous glint in his eye. "I promise you my ride will be better than any ride from a cop."

My mouth hangs open wide at his playful jab. He knows what he's doing. He's getting back at me for leading the cop on and asking for a ride in the first place. He wants to be the one to give me the thrilling experience on the back of his bike. I can't wait.

Ben's primary vehicle as an agent was his motorcycle. I would be lying if I hadn't thought he looked so effortlessly cool on it, that I felt the need to wave off the heat escaping from my body, seeing him off every day after work. In that world, as his colleague, I made sure my hands stayed at my side though, holding the excitement in, and instead waved him off nonchalantly with a supportive, partnerly wave.

Here in the gym, this audience means nothing to me versus the thought of me and him on his bike together. He's proud that the two of us are together, so I relax as they watch me sling my drawstring bag full of shoes, newspaper clippings, and a handful of crossword puzzles over my jacket so that it stays secure during the ride. None of these people except for Ben really mean anything to me in the future anyway.

Outside, my left leg lifts to straddle the bike in my heather-gray practice sweats. I slide into the snug space tucked behind Ben's thick leather jacket and admire his Converse and my red cheer socks bunched over my Keds paired at the footrest together.

The charge of the wind firing against my arms as I squeeze Ben's midsection is worlds away from the feelings I got on my last motor-bike ride. That last ride with Officer Berrett was akin to unstable teenage curiosity—the kind that takes over and leaves you unsure of yourself and everything around you. A direct result of feeling lost from the time hop and desperate for answers.

This ride with Ben is peaceful and scenic and I feel at home for the first time in 80s-Landia. Trees become blurry cones and car tires spin circles racing in competition with the others on the highway, and the smell of gravel hits me as rocks spit from the tire turning into the mountainside.

This radiant feeling that's overtaking me is like the sun within our solar system next to a tiny pea. I know the pea's there, but it's abso-lutely insignificant in comparison, just like my concern for my situa-tion here in the eighties is becoming insignificant.

I should be concerned about the fact that I haven't trained in weeks; I can feel the firm federal agent version of me slipping away to a softer version of myself. A version that would shrug my shoulders if you told me I should go back to Non-80s-Land and fix the mess that was created there.

But I wasn't.

Not concerned at all about that little pea.

I had the whole sun in my hands and nothing could bring me down, not even the sharp snake lines Ben carves in the gravel, mucking around with unnecessary turns to make the ride more fun. I'd normally feel a little uneasy, but because he was finally mine, apathy for anything other than him takes over.

"So you're basically family to the Jacobsons now. This is where you spend all your afternoons after school right? Tyler's house?" I say as he hands me a glass of juice and a hostess cupcake from the Jacobsons' kitchen, making me feel like a kid again. "I assume the brotherly beef between you comes from living like brothers."

"Something like that," he says. "Though there's actually not that much beef between us. We're closer than you think."

"Really? That's kind of a surprise considering you don't want Diana to date him. What if they try to go on a date all by themselves?" I playfully mock his concern.

"She can't. I won't let it happen," he pauses. "He's all mine." Ben starts with a weighty tone but ends with sarcasm.

Following behind Ben up the narrow stairwell, I open the plastic cupcake wrapper on the way. The cake looks squishy and juvenile but tasty. We find ourselves back at the top of the stairs in the nook of the sun window atrium combo, in the very place he'd recommended Joe Walsh's "Inner Tube" song the night of Tyler's party. I had since then found the tape and listened to it. If galactic surfing was a thing, I might find that an occasion to listen to it again.

I land on the swivel chair next to Ben who's laying his study material out on the wooden desk by the atrium window. Early evening stars fall into our laps through the glass sky ahead. He organizes his things, but I can tell my presence makes him want to sort through the never-ending collection of cassette tapes within the wall instead.

My swivel chair takes a one-eighty turn with the push of my foot and I end up facing the apothecary wall filled with small drawers, reminding me of the newspaper articles stuffed in my drawstring bag that need to be back in those shelves ASAP.

"Have you gone through all these shelves yet?" I ask, referring to the beloved cassette tapes.

"Tyler's parents consider it their junk drawer. I think Tyler has a baseball card collection in there somewhere." Now's my chance to return the folder to its drawer.

"Can I take another look?"

"Only if we listen to the tapes while doing it," he says nodding toward the boom box at the corner of the desk where the telescope also sits. "Find some good stuff."

I leap out of the chair and walk over to the apothecary wall just as a crisp, cool breeze of fresh air flies in through the loose window vent. I grab the drawer, believed to be the one that previously held the folder of stolen newspaper clippings, and open it, then neatly place the papers back. As I'm doing so, a newspaper headline at the top of the open drawer catches my eye. I hover over the drawer to read the head-line: "Robert Schills Golf Pro Projects His Future." The article was written by Sandra Osmeyer, July 10th, 1983.

Schills' long-time assistant and golf Caddy sat down for an inter-view about Schills' golf tips and plans for the future. Located in down-town Denver, Schills & Sons has declared investment the next big thing. Though Robert Schills still enjoys the beauty and wonder of the golf course, he's stepping into the coffee-in-hand world of stocks, trades, and multi-million dollar business ventures to expand his hori-zons. His assistant Deanna Hurley says his excitement for the future exceeds his last year's PGA tour trophy win. She sips her coffee and gives me a sharp wink.

I feel my hands shake as I fight the thought to pull the full article out of the drawer and slip it into my drawstring bag like I have some sick addiction to pilfering newspapers. I decide against it since Tyler's parents are back from their trip and might check on the clump of papers someone in this household discovered and pieced together.

Schills and Sons. I recognize that name from the business card Officer Berrett handed me at our second encounter. The name Deanna too. He had asked me if I knew Deanna that day.

His connection with Marigold has come full circle now. He mentioned these people and must have been trying to gauge if I knew them as well.

"Tyler's dad should be here this time tomorrow. We sometimes watch football while I study," Ben says as if he's wanting to let me in on his life routine.

"What time does Tyler usually join you?" I ask.

"Just depends on who's here. Both Ty and his dad have schedules all over the place. Sometimes it's me just wandering around. A few months ago I accidentally spotted his badge in his office one day. Can you believe Tyler's dad is an FBI agent?"

I pause to process what he's just said.

"Really?" I reply. What an odd coincidence. Was Tyler's dad— grandpa in Non-80s-Land—a retired FBI agent this whole time and we never knew?

"Yeah. Of course he hasn't actually told me he's an agent, but the moment I saw his badge something sparked inside of me. At that moment I knew what I wanted my future to look like. So I came to him and told him what I wanted to do with my life. He's helping me study for college and tests with the goal of joining the Bureau—it's kind of an unspoken understanding we have with each other. He's offered to help me." He sighs a happy sigh.

This was all too weird and reversed. Although I'd known him for so many years, I hadn't known his reasons for joining the FBI in Non-80s-Land. I assumed he was qualified and went for it, the way most college students do when they like one subject more than the others.

"You'll be a great agent," I say sweetly, knowingly.

Chapter thirty-three

Ben made it to class today. He came to grab a few kisses in between class periods and catch up with Tyler before Tyler was able to push Diana back against the locker for a public smooch. Evan stops by and hands Tyler a bag of store items—looks like Tylenol and ointment—and says "Hi" to Ben while doing so. They must've made up, though Evan pays me no attention.

Ben and I walk around school together sharing mint leaf gum and holding hands. My sweatshirt sleeve covers my hand, but he grabs onto the cloth covering my hand anyway. We're basically a walking billboard flashing the neon letters: We are an item. Our hand-holding is interrupted when Erica reminds me that our dad, my Non-80s-Land Pops, gets back from his Africa trip today and it's Cornish Pasty Day— a yearly tradition in the Atkinson household celebrating our Scottish roots in the form of salty meat-stuffed pasties. So, with cause for double celebration, I'm supposed to ride home after practice with her, not Ben.

"Call me tonight," Ben says before we part for the day.

Cheer practice has me lost in my thoughts. Things are slowing down and Erica is training and making sure the junior cheerleaders are prepared to move on without the seniors for next year's season. I liked to think of myself as a decorative chess piece that stays out of the way, so that the other pawns aren't ousted from the game.

I follow the routines with mindlessness while my head is completely absorbed with sentiments of a music-filled spring, endless dirt bike rides, dates with Ben. Maybe I'd even step foot in the skating rink again. I'd made it an aspiration to be with Ben from now on. I had him this time. I wouldn't lose him.

I smile thinking about how I'd always assumed our futures would be together in some capacity. I figured we'd be partner agents for another five to ten years, and then our families would stick together because of the friend-family connection. At the least, Diana would invite us over for dinners until we grow old and become too inept to drive.

But then again, sooner or later more unpleasant thoughts fight their way through. I'd have to accept the consequences of choosing a relationship with him over choosing the Non-80s-Land future. Thoughts of how I could pursue the issue of Sheriden and Marigold through the past jump to my mind as I justify my choices.

If I wasn't able to make my way back to the FBI and sort out the Marigold issue in Non-80s-Land, I'd have to keep pursuing it on my own through Robert Schills' historic moves. He'd be in the papers, eventually online, when Google ramps up its knowledge. I would keep at it and tip off the world in my own way as best I could.

Then another strain of thoughts hit me. Why didn't Tyler's dad get anywhere with the Marigold case, holding the information he had with the newspaper clippings within the walls of his own home? The question rocks my brain like a ticking clock that needs to be silenced.

Erica and I spot Corky and Bennette approaching each other after our end-of-practice cheer send-off, which gives me a glimmer of hope for them. I hope they can share a mutual hatred for my quick, rebound-like timing to the start of my relationship with Ben. If that brings them closer I'll be happy, even if the hate is directed toward me.

Best friends should stay best friends if they can, regardless of boy drama.

Erica reminds me for the third time today that I'm riding home with her, as if to warn me I'll reap the consequences if I ride off on the back of Ben's dirt bike to his place instead. Pops is coming home, not to mention our Cornish Pasty Day dinner. It's a non-negotiable event that I'd been threatened with since childhood. The threat being that any inheritance from my Scottish side would be revoked if I failed to bake a meat, potato, and onion-filled pasty on that day. The threat was an empty one, but the fear of deceased ancestral spirits hovering above me with trash cans throwing away that imaginary inheritance kept me doing it year after year.

My current world was so upside down that today's date didn't even trigger a Cornish Pasty Day memory. I was pleasantly surprised when Erica planted the initial reminder in the hallway. Marcie's pasties were precious metal in comparison to my previous pasty creations that meet the standard of fool's gold.

Chapter Thirty-Four

"Stop here!" I shriek as Erica enters our street. I almost forgot the parking risk. I explain my need to stay away from our neighbor cop.

"He can't be that creepy, Atta," she says and slows the car to a stop to let me out. I successfully avoid a cop encounter by entering through the backyard sliding door, but I'm exposed shortly after.

The man waiting inside the house is my grandpa, Pops. He looks so young; it's astonishing.

"Hey, Atta!" Pops says.

"Pops!" I run over to him and he wraps his arms around me in a big hug.

"Pops?" he says and smiles like I'd made a joke. Did you miss me or did you think your old dad would never come home?" Then he whispers in my ear so that the others hovering over the counter next to the oven on the other side of the room can't hear. "Looks like you found my hideout while I was away. You left a trail; your crossword and a phone I've never seen on my desk." A clever grin sits on his face beneath his long nose and wide-rimmed coke-bottle glasses. I'd been caught. Doubly so. I'd called him "Pops," which was probably what I called *his* dad in this time. And he knew I'd been to the secret room behind his closet door and by the way he phrased it, it seemed like 80s-Land me had never been invited in.

At this realization, I'm certain my expression turns apologetic. In Non-80s-Land I'd been sneaking through the coat closet for years, invited in after asking why his closet had a door behind it. He told me I was too curious for my own good but let me treat it as my own Little Narnia ever since, escaping many family board games and awkward conversations, rummaging through his knickknacks, comic books, and memorabilia from hiking across twenty-some countries.

"You're welcome to it any time as long as you keep it a secret, too. If everyone knows your hideout, what fun is it anymore, you know?" he continues.

"I won't tell a soul. I promise," I say with a reassuring smile.

"Start making your dough, Atta! We don't want to be waiting on you at the end," Marcie hollers from the stove. Her hands pick at the sticky, wet dough. Davy and Steven coat their hands in it beside her.

"What's the recipe?" I say taking off my bags and sliding my thick socks gracefully against the hardwood kitchen floor toward the kitchen island.

"You know the rules. You've got to memorize your own recipe. No extra help. This is a contest to see who makes the best pasty."

I'm suddenly annoyed at this added bit of information. My parents had never made a contest out of pasty making. For the few years that my dad was alive, he would add chicken and chilis to half the pasties so they took on the characteristics of an empanada. They'd ask me if I liked the beef, potato, and onion pasty better than the chili pasty peppered with thyme, lemon juice, and parsley, and since I was a child with sensitive taste, I chose the less spicy one every time. After my father passed, my mother continued making them for me, except every single pasty was stuffed with chili and chicken every year thereafter, celebrating his heritage, in his memory.

"I'm collecting the bid. Coming around with the jar," Erica says, wearing an apron over her habanero red sweater. White powder disguises her hands. They look as if they've been dunked in the flour bag. "Starting bid is $15 per person."

Davy and Steven pull out cash from their pockets, dropping clumps of dough in the mason jar as they let go of the cash. Marcie points to the money on the table. When Erica holds the jar out to collect my money, I tell them I forgot and excuse myself to my room. I know there's no cash left in there, but I do recall some paper bills in Pops' filing cabinets.

Pops sits at the head of the table with our names written across his notepad. By the looks of it he must be the judge. I slip past the rest of the family who's migrated to the sectioned-off quarters that Marcie's designated for kneading and punching.

I turn the corner, tiptoeing on shag carpet until I reach the closet door to Little Narnia. I open the door and artfully climb past the hanging shirts, careful to not catch the attention of anyone in the household. Atop Pops' desk is a stack of Tanzanian maps underneath a wedding invite, and to my delight, Marcie's recipe for classic potato, beef, and onion pasties—the little recipe note card is dirty with edges browned from use and oil drops settled across the old paper. Pops must have been prepared in case he was picked for pasty making rather than judging.

It's a miracle really. Even if this is considered cheating, I'm using it. It's better than having Pops taste-test a piece of dough made with the incorrect units of measurement. I quickly memorize the list. On my way out I grab cash from the metal cabinet drawer and head back into the kitchen.

I gather my ingredients as the rest of the crew pinches the edges of their moon-shaped pasties together to keep the contents from oozing out.

One can, out of all the cans on the shelf, calls out to me. Chilis! Marcie has a can of green chilis in the cabinets.

I feel a sense of excitement at the prospect of trying out my Non-80s-Land father's Spanish pasty dupe. But since there's only cooked beef on the stove and no chicken in this kitchen, I decide to try something new—a mix of Spain and Scotland if you will.

After adding the inside ingredients to the dough, I pray that the combination of salty pasty batter, beef, potatoes, and green chili tastes alright once baked. I sprinkle in thyme before pinching the ends together as best I can.

Marcie's pasties are the first to come out of the oven, looking perfectly crafted, each half-moon laying on the tray bed with proportions just as congruent as the next. The boy's pasties are cooling on the island table, and Erica's uncooked pasties are glazed in golden butter, creating a reflecting shine like a broken glass mosaic, on the thinly folded meat pockets. Each one of them is dainty and delicate with beautifully sliced air pockets that make them look like little art pieces next to my dough rocks that would only pass if the judge tonight was an ogre.

Marcie puts my tray in the oven and I begin to second-guess the green chili addition. The air slits are leaking green chili juice and it's being absorbed by the pinched dough, producing a soggy combination that I know I'm not coming back from.

Marcie places Erica's tray beside mine and turns, giving me a pitiful look while I try to clean up the tray of oozing juice with a few scrapes of my spatula.

"Make sure your little monsters keep a healthy distance from mine," Erica says as her mouth twists into a devilish smile. She knows she's already knocked me out of the competition even before the baking's begun.

Marcie reaches for the Minute Minder kitchen timer that sits next to the bulky phone book on the island counter, setting the ticker for forty minutes.

I take a second glance at the phone book—so thick it looks like it covers the entire state of Colorado—then scurry on over to the counter and jumble through its pages until I find the Schills and Sons address. I find it easy enough, then look to see if Deanna Hurley, Robert

Schills' assistant, the woman Officer Berrett asked about on our second encounter, is listed in the phone book as well.

I almost squeal in excitement when I find Deanna. I check the Minute Minder to see how much time we have left. Twenty minutes. The family's engrossed in a card game, drooling over pasties they aren't allowed to touch, so I take the chance to sneak into Little Narnia for the second time this afternoon.

The five-pound book slams onto Pops' desk with a small thud, making a few papers fly to the floor. I hurry to pick them up, not wanting Pops to become suspicious that I've made another mess in his secret area, and notice the gold-laced wedding invitation in the clutches of my hand.

The invitation has the couple's names on it, a reception date, and Coors Brewery listed as the location. Someone must love Coors enough for them to want to exchange vows next to a factory full of tubes, wires, and barrels.

I connect the phone up to the phone cable with ease—I've conducted this operation before after all, jerry-rigging what I thought would be a successful time hop back home.

I give my plan a go with a few punches of my thumb. The phone rings and connects me with a lady who's voice is as raspy as the static from the line connecting us.

"Hello, Schills & Sons speaking. How may I help you?"

I ask if Robert Schills is available for an interview this weekend, claiming I'm a reporter from *The Denver Post* wanting to do a follow-up article discussing his progress since our last 1983 article—the article mentioning his transition from golf professional to business man.

"What time?" She says matter-of-factly.

"Three o'clock on Saturday," I say, throwing out a random time. There is no plan. I'm just shooting my shot where I can. If I felt ballsy enough I might even attempt the interview.

"It looks like Mr. Schills is attending a wedding this weekend at

Coors Brewery around that time. Would you be able to request a different time for an interview?" she asks.

Wedding at Coors Brewery. My eyes hit the fancy invitation on the desk before I answer. The invite announces a four o'clock ceremony for all the attendants of Celia Tigard and Bob Garret's wedding.

I don't need an excuse for an interview at all. I need to tag along with Pops to this wedding!

"Let me ask my team. I'll give you a call back tomorrow to schedule another time," I say before hanging up.

I beam for a moment, feeling like I've made considerable progress, then figure I have enough time to sneak in a short call with Ben. I don't know how long this family competition will last tonight and I promised I'd at least call him, but when I dial his number I'm met with a disconnected dial tone followed by a "We're sorry, you have reached a number that has been disconnected" message.

When I make my way back to the kitchen Marcie is shoveling our pasties off the sheets. It smells amazing. The crisp, flaky, scorched, and buttery crusts smell like baked beef and salted potato. Erica hovers around Pops as he tastes her dish. Her concerns seem to grow as my scorched blocks of burnt green goo threaten to tango with her flawless pies.

"I think we can all agree Atta's should be fed to the dog—if we had a dog," Steven says. The table erupts in laughter. My Spanish-Scottish pasty dreams die in humiliation and Pops chooses Erica to be the winner of the mason jar full of money.

Chapter Thirty-Five

I made sure to set the plastic digital alarm before bed last night so I would wake up an hour earlier to catch Pops before he heads to work. I'm at the table eating a bowl of Raisin Bran—because hunger has won out over abstaining from food that tastes like gravel—when I hear Pops' chunky boots clunk down the stairs.

"Good morning honey. You're up early," he says as he enters the kitchen.

"You wouldn't happen to be going to a wedding at Coors Brewery this weekend would you?" I say setting my spoon down on the table.

"How'd you know about that?" he says.

"I saw it last night, grabbing my crossword out of your closet." A white lie will do for now. Better to ask forgiveness than permission if I plan to get anywhere with Marigold.

He shakes his head as if my actions might divulge his hideout location to the entire family.

"You're mom and I are planning on it," he says, chewing a piece of bacon from a cold ziplock bag.

"Can I tag along? I've been wanting to see the brewery for a while now," I say. I'm almost too hopeful sounding.

"It's a plus-one invite only and your mom is planning on going with me. But if she backs out…" he says with a smile. I nod my head.

"How do you know the couple? They must have paid a bunch to reserve an entire brewery for the day."

"Oh, it's my client's wedding. I worked on a few cases for her last year. Her fiancé's pretty well-off," he says.

"Why'd she invite her lawyer to a wedding?"

"Rich people like to show off their lawyers. It's a status thing…"

Robert Schills must be an acquaintance of the groom. I wonder how many Marigold connections will be at the reception.

If I can't be his plus-one I'd make sure to find a way to sneak in.

"WHAT ARE YOU DOING THIS SATURDAY?" BEN COMES UP BEHIND me in the hallway right after our first period. He wraps his arms around my shoulders, squeezing me like a snake coiling its prey. "Let's go on a date," he says without waiting for me to answer.

"What was wrong with your phone last night?" I ask. "I tried calling you. It said your number was disconnected." We continue walking down the hall as if we're glued together, his arms falling over my shoulders.

"Oh. My mom came back from work yesterday with one of those weird rainbow wire phones and decided to switch out the phones. So I spent some time last night trying to uninstall and reinstall the phones."

"The clear phone with colored wire?" I repeat after him. My heart jumps at the mention of the familiar object. The object that landed me here in the first place. I make the connection between the phone Ben installed last night and the retired phones his grandmother gifted to Diana and Ben to play with when we were young. This phone had to be one of them.

"Yeah," he says as if there's nothing to be too excited about. "But about our date…what do you say to riding with me this weekend? To WonderVu."

"When?" I was a sucker for mountain cafes. Diana and I had spent many weekends in Non-80s-Land trying to find good restaurants hidden in the mountainscape. At places like WonderVu, the taste of the food hardly mattered. We were there for the exclusive mountain dining experience. It's the only place where you can be almost entirely surrounded by trees, deep red, brown mountain soil and have a cool mountain breeze seep through the window beside you as you eat.

"Tomorrow afternoon."

"I can't. I'm going to a wedding reception at that time."

"Whose wedding?"

"Pops was invited. He is the bride's lawyer or something like that."

"You mean your dad? Isn't your grandpa in Montana?"

"Uhh yeah," I say. I'd just have to avoid "Pops" and "Grandma" in sentences from now on. It gets too complicated.

"Is your whole family going?" he asks.

"Not exactly. My dad is taking Marcie and it's a plus-one invite only, so I'm sneaking in." His eyebrows raise in response to my admission.

"I have to see how they pull off a wedding at Coors Brewery," I say in defense.

"You're really something, you know that?" Sparks hum in his eyes when he says it. "You want to weasel your way into this wedding? A wedding that probably has security. You don't have a limit to how far you'll go when you're curious, do you?"

"I guess not," I say confidently.

"Let's go riding before the reception then. I'll have you back before the wedding."

Chapter Thirty-Six

D avy becomes an obstacle course I nearly trip over as I enter the dim-lit living room early Saturday morning. By the way a chip bag is strewn across his body, with five or six blankets piled up behind him like boulders, he looks as if he spent the night out on the floor watching the old boxy television. He grunts when my shoe nearly clips his head.

The light is on in the kitchen and Marcie seems to be set on deep cleaning the cabinets before the crack of dawn. I don't have to look at her face to know what her body language is telling me. My head naturally turns to the maritime blue mood chart on the wall to confirm my suspicion. "Today's Mood" sign has been switched out and "Eat my shorts!" now dangles from the peg at the forefront. I know it's a *Breakfast Club* reference and that it comes from seventies slang but I can't help but think of Bart Simpson yelling the catchphrase out of his car window. I get the urge to use his voice to say it out loud but shut the urge down quickly—she wouldn't be able to appreciate a voice impersonation of Bart Simpson from the early nineties, she's not in the mood anyway.

I turn on my heels and retreat back into the living room before the angry bull thinks I'm the red flag in the kitchen. I bump into Pops at the foot of the stairs. He cautiously tiptoes off of the bottom stair into the hallway, then motions to the closet and we slide through without another word.

"Your mom has declined the plus-one position. It's yours if you want it."

"She said no? Are you the reason she's about to peel the paint off the kitchen cabinets?" I ask.

"It's very possible that I may have said something I shouldn't have, but it could also be Davy. Looks like he stayed up all night watching television again."

"Mmm. Well, I'd love to be your plus-one." I feel a sense of relief knowing I won't have to cross the river and try to sneak in with random guests.

"We'll leave around three. Make sure to wear something nice," Pops says. "Oh and I'd stay away from Mom today. She needs some space."

BEN MEETS ME OUTSIDE OUR BACKYARD FENCE ON HIS DIRT BIKE. To my surprise, his bike looks more polished than I thought possible. He must have spent time cleaning crusty dried mud off of the frame, but the thing that surprises me more is how he's dressed. He lifts his leg off of the bike, revealing pleated tan dress pants and a golden brown plaid shirt reminiscent of the Sahara Desert as if he's just come from modeling for a sand dune themed magazine shoot. He's even wearing a matching red, navy, and ochre plaid tie.

"Why are you so dressed up?" I say as I look down at my casual outfit. I'm in basic jeans and a sweater with bunched-up socks coddling my Keds. "You look really good though." He pulls it off really well. My cheeks flush pink at the sight of him.

"I thought about it last night and I'm sneaking into the wedding with you. I want to be there for this madness."

"What do you mean, you want to be there?"

"I'm coming with you. I want to go. We can sneak in together," he says. I'm at a loss for words, feeling like I have to choose between Pops and Ben for this event. As much as I want him to come with me, I have the invite and he doesn't.

"But I'm the plus-one, I don't need to sneak in anymore," I confess.

"Seriously?" He looks as if he's impressed with my manipulation skills or something.

"Yeah." I feel bad that he dressed up for nothing.

"I'll go anyway. I'll sneak in and meet you there." He says it like it's no big deal that he would do this alone.

"What if you end up getting caught trespassing and it ends up on your record? Wouldn't that hurt your chances to get into the Bureau?" I whisper the last part so that no one can hear us if they tried.

"Wedding crashing isn't going to be the reason they deny me entrance."

THE BACK OF BEN'S DRESS SHIRT FLAPS AGAINST MY ARMS AS WE make our way to the edge of Golden. We ride the next six miles of vast open space admiring the caramel-grass heaven that's laid out on each side of the road leading up to the enchanting landscape of green hill terraces and flatirons. My eyes follow the yellow dotted lines on the single-lane road, playing a game of mile-marker counting as I peek over Ben's shoulder.

We pass gold-sprinkled mountains and stuccoed rock walls, flying by so fast it all looks like an out-of-focus photograph, shot using a fast lens. As the road slithers up, sharp curve after sharp curve, I find myself clinging to the bike in order to keep my balance, helmetless and unable to concentrate on anything but the humming aeolian whistle and the bite of the engine underneath me. If the wind wasn't whipping against my shoulders and shins, I might lull to sleep from the sounds that are fast becoming white noise.

The road is less curvy farther up the mountain and I get to enjoy a new view of red brick buildings tucked between thick trees and train tracks. A sign tells me we're at Black Hawk.

I can taste the grass in the area—the smell is strong from the earlier rainfall. A mile ahead the smell is replaced by burning coal from the train engines as we chase CO-119 to Beaver Creek Road.

"We're here." Ben slows his motorcycle to a stop in front of a dark ginger log cafe with a muted, rusty purple sunset entrance sign carved with trees and a mustard yellow sun that reads Wondervu Cafe. Flower-filled planter boxes greet us with a happy wind-blown wave as we enter the deep door entrance and plant ourselves in a booth by the front window.

"Here's a menu," the waitress says, lacking enthusiasm. She either doesn't want to be here or she's been here so long that everything is done at her own pace. She slaps two sunset-colored tri-folds, matching the exterior entrance sign, on the table with a polite thud. "Would you like drinks or an appetizer?" she asks. She has the charm of sandpaper. Ben hands me the long rectangular plastic menu and waits for me to survey the options.

"What sounds good to you?" He looks happy. His mouth is waiting for an opportunity to smirk, but he's holding a sweet-natured gaze.

"Nachos?" I ask.

"Nachos it is." He charismatically delivers the message to the disinterested waitress.

"I'll be right back." By the way she says it, I know it'll be at least half an hour.

"Thank you, Tina," Ben says, then waits a few seconds and winks at her before she turns to escape through the swinging butler's gate at the island bar.

"You two acquaintances?" is my response to his coquettish behavior toward the woman who is as spry as a block of cheese.

"Nah. I just read her name tag," he says as his eyes turn sharp with amusement.

"Oh, I see, so you do this with everybody, even dull diner ladies? When you hollered at my backside—remember after I'd just gotten my hair permed—that was just standard procedure?" I tease.

"Mmm…you caught me," he says, shaking his head. "That was embarrassing though. I really didn't recognize you with your new hair."

"So you were okay with whistling at some random pretty girl's hair?" His face grows red with embarrassment bringing out the cinnamon in his cheeks.

"Uhh," he looks as if I've put him in a corner. "I plead the fifth." He finds his smile and plays innocently before me. "Actually, I only hit on women with big mountain-woman hair."

We both laugh. The waitress and I both have an unruly mess atop our heads. He's reassuring me and making fun of me at the same since the wind pounding through my hair on the way here has significantly increased its volume.

The smell of greasy chips and melted cheese floats into our dining area from behind the island bar and it's not long before Tina shows up with a plate of oily chips dripping cheese under a mountain of toma-toes and sour cream. We order our lunch, this time crunching chips between our teeth mid-sentence.

Not a lot of talking is required for a diner with bad service and great food. I shovel down my plateful of enchiladas while Ben finishes his plate of carne asada tacos, licking every last bit of the plate clean.

"You should wear dress clothes on your bike more often. You look good," I say as we make our way back outside.

"One day I may even wear a uniform on a bike," he says as if trying to catch my interest. "Do you think you'd like that? Me riding a bike in uniform?"

"Mmm…I do like it." I already know that satisfying scene.

We speed down Coal Creek Canyon Road taking CO-93. The china blue sky is slowly swallowed by thick angry warrior clouds as we descend down the mountain. I will the sky to hold back its tears before a sudden blast of wind rocks Ben's upper body into mine. We stutter for a moment as the wind seems to hold us in place, then pushes us forward again, and out of nowhere a ripple of explosions erupt from somewhere in the mountains. It's a sound only a chemical explosion could create.

Ben slows his speed around the next corner and tilts his head back to check on me before slowing to a stop. I'm off the bike before Ben completes the stop, landing on the asphalt with a perfectly timed run. He turns around to face me on the bike. His bewildered stare tells me he's not sure what's more shocking; the fact that I just landed that with ease or that half the mountain is exploding around us.

"Are you alright?" he says, studying my face. I look for passing traffic.

"Yes," I say, answering as if he meant it like a protective boyfriend rather than out of concern for my G.I. Jane-like actions. In all fairness I might look a bit crazy reaching for a phantom gun where my holster used to lay on the job as I run across the road. Ben runs after me as another set of blasts trickle in.

Chapter Thirty-Seven

At the head of the valley, we watch from the road's edge as spiraling clouds of smoke appear through the fir trees. There seems to be numerous cloud stacks, as if multiple trains are traveling through the small valley at the same time. The fumes grow at different speeds and spread like an uneven graph.

"We'd better head out," Ben says. The smoke that fills the trees climbs in our direction and I nod in response, feeling unsettled about the chemical explosion noises continuing down the hill.

Another explosion hits as we pass the bend, showcasing the floor of the small valley and remnants of a building peek through a gathering of trees. In seconds we reach what looks like a lab explosion in the middle of a forest. Orange kite flames sail into the air between dark mats of black smoke. I feel my armpits sweating from anticipation even with the cool air and light rain pour.

As we lean into the curve of the valley, my gaze focuses on the mouth of the old mine, hollowed into the valley of the mountain, where a log sign burns to a crisp. I know this site to be a popular historic landmark with a view akin to the magical Hobbit shire tucked along the mountainside, but instead of hobbit villages, the structure is small sheds and sections of the mine that are collapsing before our eyes.

We're too far out to see any human activity—if there is any down there.

Another thunderous croak echoes down the mountain and the whole mine entrance falls in on itself.

What did we just witness?

What could cause such an unnatural blow to a perfectly good historical landmark? If such an explosion was planned, it was a sour disappointment to see it happen. But something tells me that's not the case. There weren't any vehicles on location and no sign of anyone controlling the situation around that section of the valley. The fire hadn't yet spread to the trees but it would soon if it wasn't taken care of.

Twenty miles down the road we pass a police motorcycle followed by a small train of police officers. I can't make out the rider's face from this distance but Officer Berrett is one of the few officers in Golden who rides a motorcycle. I try to make myself invisible, tucking my head behind Ben's shoulders to avoid being spotted. The trees light up like a town Christmas festival as red, white, and blue shadows beam across dark green fir tree needles underneath a cloudy sky. When Ben and I complete the mountain loop and enter the legal limits of Golden a throng of fire trucks enter the forest.

THE WHOLE ORDEAL HAS US LOST IN THOUGHT AND SLOW TO make our way back. Ben drops me off at the house with only minutes to spare before Pops threatens to drive off without me. I'm notified I have five minutes to book it to my room, zip the back of my navy cocktail dress, and meet Pops in the volkswagen.

I run out the door with a hook and eye still left to clip, but the bulk from the ruffled over-the-shoulder sleeves—like feathery chickens on my arms—and the fact that my hands are occupied tying my hair into a French braid, prevents it.

"How's your wife?" I ask on the way to the brewery.

Pops chuckles. "I haven't seen her since she lost her marbles and tossed yesterday's good mood to the crows," he says. He looks extra trim in a suit and tie. He even went so far as to part his dark brown hair and gel it so that I can see the brush strokes through his set hair.

"I see," I say, tapping my fingers on the dashboard.

We swing onto Ford Street from the freeway and pass Clear Creek where event security checks our wedding invite and sends us into the fifteen-thousand-acre lot to find parking.

As we close in on Coors' main building, the brewery appears to have taken on a swanky force. The venue is all gussied up and the amount of balloons piled under large white tents increases as we get closer to our seats, eventually spreading across the venue like airborne piano keys with their singular monochromatic helium-filled color choices. By the time we pass through the intricately decorated ceremonial archway and a number of outdoor heaters, I'm no longer surprised by the aura of luxury brand labels dominating the atmosphere. We approach tables with hundreds of flutes of champagne and tables set up just to display beds and beds of peach flowers. Though it was quite intense, I liked the tacky affluence this eighties wedding was brewing.

Amidst all the eighties grandeur and wonderment, I search for my target amongst all of the guests; someone who looks like they might golf, but at the same time be in charge of an average-sized cult. I picture a lean man wearing a red mustache, but who am I kidding? I really have no visual to go off, considering I've never been able to put his name to a face. The newspaper articles never came with a picture.

Robert Schills, what do you look like?

I picture some of the faces from the USB video. Thirty-some years had passed. Would a flicker of recognition even appear?

Pops finds seats with a nice view of the sun highlighting the top of

South Table Mountain just across the road—the same mountain we ditched our class reunion for with the high school crew and Kenny in Non-80s-Land. I cringe thinking about how my conversation with Agent Maser that night catapulted this whole Marigold nightmare.

I take another moment to scope out the audience for a familiar face. And to my surprise I find one—though it's not the criminal I'm looking for. He may be criminally minded, attending a wedding he wasn't invited to. But it's just effervescent Ben. He really managed to sneak in.

He sits at the very back with his leg extended into the aisle—making him easy to spot. I notice his pant leg because it looks like it's been dipped in a pool of water. I catch his gaze and as we lock eyes, the prettiest head of curly black hair pops out from behind his shoulder. Diana gives a princess wave and I smile because she is in the seat next to Ben smiling fiercely back at me. Ben didn't sneak into the wedding alone.

After the vows are exchanged, Pops leads me past the brewery's cooling pond, getting straight to business and wasting no time to find our assigned seats in the dining area. I'm grateful for his no-nonsense, no-small-talk attitude. This way I'll have time to scope out the place-setting cards before most guests find their way to their seats. I can do that while Pops is busy fiddling with his napkin, readily anticipating scarfing down some smoked salmon, veggie croquettes, and a variety of puddings with fancy names, like maple fig, honeycomb, and poached pear.

I weave around the circular tables looking for Robert Schills' place card, keeping an eye out for Ben and Diana who could pop in at any moment, tipping off Pops to their unconstrained wedding crashing behavior. I'd already sent Ben the look—the one that said there would be some sort of consequence if Pops were to catch my friends sneaking into this exclusive event. We'd soon find out whether or not he got the memo.

A few tables in, I begin to notice the glass frames placed in the middle of each table. I'm shocked it took me so long to notice the happy newlyweds, brandishing guns in sexy western corset costumes, in their black and white engagement photo centerpiece. I mean, the groom is wearing nothing but jeans and chaps! I let out a slight chuckle, which turns into an audible gasp, as I read the place card name in front of the sexy western snifter.

"David Schills" it reads. A Schills sits here. I nearly trample over my own feet at the discovery. I find Robert Schills' name just a few seats over. His assistant, Deanna Hurley, is seated between them. In the few seconds that I have before a crowd of guests shovels in, I commit the table to memory.

The table I plan to stare at is the table closest to the cheese fondue display and I'm elated at the discovery. They couldn't have seated them in a better place. Now I have an excuse to test out all eight types of cheeses and listen in on a Schills' table conversation simultaneously, hoping something influential will come of it.

Throughout my meal, my eyes stay locked on the Schills' table. To my surprise, it isn't Robert Schills that I recognize first from the video, but his assistant Deanna, who sparked alarm bells inside my head the second she sat down. I recognize this lady as the blonde, red-jacket-wearing woman closest to the camera in the USB video. My thoughts flash back to the bright conference room and the circle of Marigold jackets surrounding a body struggling to survive as blood pools around him. Why had each of these members participated in this—each of them taking a turn to stab this man?

I'm able to memorize Robert's features from this distance. And though I couldn't see the other half of the table's faces I'm confident I could recognize Deanna and Robert if I happened upon them on the street. Robert. A man who wore a dark beard, not a red one. Who was slim but more built than I'd imagined—definitely not the lazy golfer type.

Recognition was key. I was that much closer to getting answers.

I excuse myself from the table to stock up on cheese fondue and head toward the Schills table where Robert's assistant is meticulously chopping her salmon into small pieces with delicate silverware. She lifts the fork into her mouth, and I watch as her ruby lips stain the salmon as she bites it.

Grabbing a large plate, I begin loading it with brie and stacks of crackers, then run the cheese fountain slowly over my blocks of food so that I can listen in on their table's conversation.

"I haven't been able to get a hold of Jonathan all day, have you?" I hear one of the men say to the man next to him. I could make eye contact with Robert right now but I'd have to turn around to see what the other men speaking look like. The man next to him responds, but I don't catch a word of it. I finish drizzling the white cheeses and move in closer to the table, pretending I need some green olives to go with my pile of cheese.

"It's all destroyed, the mountain-side inventory that is," David Schills says to the men I can't see. "We can try to recover some of it but my guess is it's all contaminated. We won't be able to use it." My ears are completely tuned in. If I stay here much longer I'll be suspected of eavesdropping.

"Well, the BLM handled the cops when we arrived and Berrett took care of the loose ends. Nothing was leaked," I hear one man say.

"That is why we chose the Bennett Mine. JD Hammer, the BLM State Director, is a friend of mine and he handles the area. It's all about our connections, you know. That's how we keep it safe in the event something like this happens," Robert says, joining in on the conversation.

"Are you sure we won't be able to recover any of it?"

"Not likely, when it comes into contact with Nixonab, it becomes explosive—the reason it wasn't approved by the EPA until now," Robert says with an air of superiority to his tone, as if this information is exclusively his and he knows it well.

"How did the Nixonab find its way up to the mine? It's not used in much, is it?" Deanna takes a break from her unfinished plate to comment.

"Not much. Nixonab has been used to flavor resin and gum, a sort of natural sweetener if you will. A natural sweetener that turns out to be explosive if combined with random substances, including ours. The last it was used was in a gum brand that hasn't produced anything since 1928. They banned it, as well as the substances that it interacts with, after the discovery in 1925," he says with a sigh.

"So you see just how unfair it was?" Deanna's comment seems to be directed to everyone but Robert.

I can't help but shake my head. Her tone came with natural entitlement. So unfair that someone would want to prevent a reaction like the one we witnessed? The explosion in the mountain was theirs. The sign burning to a crisp was Bennett Mine. I was sure of it.

I feel a body approach me from behind, waking me from my green-olive-searching-stupor. It appears the Marigold table can feel my concrete stare, and three of the men at the table turn in their chairs to see my mouth agape, white cheese dripping from my round plate onto the brewery floor.

"Come with me. Time to go." Ben's familiar voice closes in on my ear as he grabs me with both arms and whips me aside.

"Didn't you see Officer Berrett at that table?" he says with a tinge of anger, dragging me into the stairwell entryway.

"He's here?" I panic internally.

"I can't believe you were standing there for that long. I walked upstairs to see if you could sneak away, but the first thing I saw was that ratty mullet scumbag at the table near you."

Ben peers into the dining area. The hallway remains empty. Just the two of us alone.

"Diana's at the bottom of the stairs," Ben says.

We find her sitting at one of the round table tops with her long legs swimming in the air just inches from the ground. She's dressed up in a drop waist ruffle dress that sits below her knees and her makeup makes her eyes pop like dark obsidian.

"The nut mix is good. Try some!" She spins the seasoned cashews, peanuts, and breaded crisps around so that they clank against the almonds as Ben and I make our way down the last of the stairs. I want to match her welcoming energy but all I can do is give her a blank stare. Nothing comes out and it's as if I've been swallowed up in thoughts over Officer Berrett's close proximity.

"Officer Berrett's here," Ben expresses his concern to Diana. "Atta, why don't we hide out down here until it gets dark. If you go back up he might see you."

I nod my head in agreement, then turn my head back to Diana, finally able to form a response.

"How did you two sneak in here?"

"Ben scoped out the layout from Lookout Mountain yesterday to make sure you'd be safe while trying to crash this wedding. He had the whole route planned."

"You planned everything beforehand?" I say.

"He did. He even checked all the entrances and made the decision to hop the creek," Diana says, her tone carrying a mixture of gratitude and annoyance. "He carried me over the river. Such a good big brother!" she teases. Ben stays quiet at the revelation, as if he would've liked his careful planning and efforts to support my reckless ideas to remain a secret.

"Why is he here? Did he know you'd be here?" Ben asks.

"There's no way Officer Berrett could've known I would be here. I didn't even know, myself, if I'd be here. He came with them. The people at that table," I say.

"Who are those people?" His tone becomes wrecked with concern as if Officer Berrett is really starting to trouble him.

I know who they are, but I don't know how to answer him truthfully without raising questions I cannot answer. Explaining this situation would be like trying to explain quantum physics while skydiving. It's next to impossible and the thought is nauseating.

"I don't know," I say withholding the truth. "Whatever caused the explosive reaction is theirs though, and the BLM was protecting it, so they managed to avoid getting caught."

"What? Are you saying Officer Berrett was up in the mountains with a girl again? Did he do something to cause a fire near the mine?"

"I think he went with the group of cops who raced up there to control the fire. I think he knew what was up there and helped hide it."

"So that group at the table, they're hiding something in the mountainside. Something that's reactive?"

"Yes. Have you ever heard of Nixonab?" I ask.

"No. What's that?" His face shows a look I haven't seen for a month now. It's that investigative concern. The look Ben wore most of the work day at the Bureau.

"I was hoping you would know. I gather it's an old sweetener they don't use anymore. Do you think the Bureau would investigate this if you brought it up to Mr. Jacobson?" I ask.

"I'm not sure I can bring it up to him. Maybe." He stands stiff, contemplating the option.

"Because he hasn't actually told you he's an agent? Since there's an unspoken understanding between you two about what he does, do you think you could do it?" I press him.

"I can try. He could see it as me taking an initiative, I suppose. You think by starting an investigation on Officer Berrett he'll stop bothering you. Is that it?" He analyzes my face, looking for my motivation. "It's not just because you're overly curious about the explosion?"

"Officer Berrett is up to no good and the explosion at that mine is partially his fault. It should be looked into."

"I'll try to talk to him," Ben says. Diana nods. She seems to be taking the whole Officer Berrett issue quite seriously, especially because she probably thinks I'm his next target to take up to the mountain.

"We should be good to go back up soon. The sky is getting dark and he won't be able to see you. Plus I want to dance. With you," Ben says. His eyes light up, revealing fireworks of excitement behind his invitation.

I feel more hopeful, walking back up the stairs toward the music with my two best friends, than I've felt since arriving in 80s-Landia.

Maybe this is my opportunity to put a squash to Marigold and the Sheriden Foundation through Tyler's dad. His household held the newspaper clipping connections. He was already warm to the case. What if the mine explosion was the missing key this whole time? It had been hidden from history by a BLM director and Officer Berrett.

Marigold did one thing well. They had connections to the BLM state director, connections to my own department within the FBI. I can't help but think the newspaper article announcement for Sheriden Foundation's acquisition of the cleaning product company Clean Wave had something to do with the new EPA director's approval. And the death of the old EPA director.

When I had read the article about the new EPA director's approval of something called the MaG compound, I thought nothing of it. But now I can't help but think this is all Marigold's doing. They forced the approval of the MaG compound for Clean Wave. I've read hundreds of newspaper articles over the last few weeks while attending classes and this is one puzzle piece that seems to fit. There's something highly reactive that Marigold has tucked away in a mine, possibly in multiple mines and undisclosed locations.

If Ben and I hadn't driven by, it would remain a silent mark on history. Was it possible that Ben and I could resolve this through Mr. Jacobson thirty years before we even discovered it?

BEN BUMPS INTO A MAN AT THE TOP OF THE STAIRWELL.

"Ben. Nice to see you." Pops' voice surprises the three of us.

"Hi, Mr. Atkinson," Ben replies, holding out his hand to see if Pops will shake it. Pops refuses, instead turning his head back to me.

"I see you invited some plus-ones to your plus-one invite?" He sounds amused but strict, and I'm not sure how scared of this situation I should be.

"Something like that," I manage under my breath.

"I'm heading out now. Don't exactly want to dance with Bob from my table. Since you've been with your friends this whole time, how about you get a ride home with them and we'll talk when you get home," Pops says and gives a quick send off wave. I feel a sense of guilt. He seems to be in a sour mood. I fear I have some kind of scolding waiting for me when I get home.

The view outside is limited to a few spotlights on the dance floor. South Table Mountain blocks the light from the city, making the night pitch-dark with low visibility of anything, even three feet ahead. We choose the dark corner behind the historic brew kettle as our safety net. I was sure the danger had subsided; even if Officer Berrett was the type to stay for dancing he wouldn't have the night vision to see me anyway.

The small clump of stars, which look as if someone had taken a handful of powdered sugar and sprinkled the night sky with it, serve as our only light as Diana breaks into the cabbage patch. She kicks off her heels midway through, then opts to vogue the rest of the song. Ben stands to the side observing our best-friend-energy and waits while Diana steals me for the first couple of slow dances.

Eventually, Ben slips in between the two of us, unable to third-wheel any longer. He rocks me left and right and holds me close as we dance together.

I feel a tap on the shoulder, unphased with the expectation that Diana would intervene not even a song later—as if she still hasn't quite accepted our pairing. When I turn to give her a friendly shove back I notice the shadow of a man and set off running.

I make it to the edge of the cooling pond before Officer Berrett catches up to me.

"Agent Suarez, slow down," says the man I've been trying to avoid for well over a week. "Let's talk."

I make out a long fence in front of me. I hear two sets of feet running toward us. If it's Ben and Diana they've taken a right a tad too early. Officer Berrett is now within an arm's reach. I stop and turn to face him and find his hair is pulled back into a ponytail and he's dressed in suit and tie.

"Uh hi, hello," I stutter, feeling as if I'm sinking into a floor of quicksand. There is no escape, I can only feign ignorance until I've been submersed underground, no longer breathing. The fact that he had been searching for me for the past few days makes what comes next that much more frightening.

"You're more connected than you let on. I didn't need to take you to the flowers. You already know one."

"Excuse me?" I say, feigning ignorance, although truthfully I am a bit confused at his statement. How am I connected to a supposed one?

"This whole time I was wondering who your connection was. How you knew about Marigold. It's the groom, isn't it? Most of the wedding guests on the groom's side are members of Marigold."

"The groom?" I hold a confused stare.

"That's how you know Marigold. You recognized my Marigold tattoo a few weeks ago. I know a look of recognition when I see one." He pauses for a second to read my stoic eyes. I don't break my vacant stare. "You're an Atkinson. You're not an FBI agent. You're not even listed on their payroll."

"What makes you think that?" I say.

"You're not the only one with connections." He spits the words out as if they carry a significant amount of importance. "But whoever your connections are, they have you running operations with that fake FBI badge. I'm right, aren't I?"

I don't say anything. I don't have a good explanation for why I'm not on the payroll—also dumbfounded that a Golden police officer of only two months has access to the Denver Bureau's payroll.

"Atta, secrecy is only important with outsiders." He dares rest his hand on my shoulder. "You can discuss it within the foundation. You don't have to be so unwilling to discuss it with me. Unless you're with someone at the top. If that's the case, well then I understand why you're so hesitant."

"The top?" I manage, taking a deep breath in and out trying to regain my composure.

"Who's your contact?" he prods me. He has me backed up against the corner of the fence, giving cause for the belligerent feelings inside of me to burst. I hold them in. An unperturbed officer is going to be easier to deal with over a suspicious, agitated one. He's unconvinced, no matter how oblivious I pretend to be. He's adamant I know about Marigold.

I weigh my options. Pretending to be one of them would be better than to have him think I know about Marigold, use a fake agent ID, and yet have no intention to join Marigold—marking myself at variance with them and thus a potential target. Or is it?

"Jon," I say quickly, giving the generic name I heard mentioned earlier at their table. If he thinks I know of Marigold and have the guts to pretend I'm an agent, he might consider me a threat.

"Makes sense. Jonathon likes to keep things quiet. There's a reason Robert trusts him at the top." Officer Berrett slides his fingers down my arm so that they now rest on my elbow. "I shouldn't share this with you but not all of us are bent up on the secrecy of it all. We're a group. A network of confidants. I'll teach you there's fun in sharing Marigold news." His eyes light up with a dangerous glint. "Since you're with Jonathan you may or may not have heard about the explosion in the mountain." He waits for my expression to change. When I shake my head to confirm I hadn't, he continues. "Someone who knows about the reaction between resin and MaG compound set out to sabotage us. How they got ahold of resin that hasn't been used since the 1920s beats me. We've taken the necessary precautions to ensure it doesn't happen again. I thought I should mention that in case it holds any weight in deciding whether or not you're up for taking a ride into the mountains with me."

"You think someone wants to sabotage Marigold?" I ask, ignoring his invitation.

"Yes, but those who try will always fail." Another dangerous glimmer flashes across his eyes. "You really should take me up on the offer. I can show you headquarters. Jonathon's so private he'd never be so bold as to show you the benefits that come from knowing someone at the top."

"Headquarters is in the mountains?" I ask, knowing full well by the way his lips curl when he talks that he just wants to feel me once again at the back of his bike.

"Yeah. It's where the MaG is stored before they take it down to the Clean Wave factory. I've taken a few other members up there. The substance is beautiful raw, the brightest orange-yellow, like looking at a field of marigolds. Come with me. Passing up the opportunity would be like passing up a chance to see the aurora borealis, if you have the opportunity it's something you shouldn't miss."

At this he winks. His tenacity to flirt explains the success he had in getting the other women to ride into mountains with him. That or it's quite possibly they're sold on his deceiving good looks before he's had a chance to flash that dangerous smile.

I suck in a deep breath and almost choke on the cool night air. They store MaG compound in the mountain near headquarters. MaG compound is used in Clean Wave products and becomes explosive with an old resin—Nixonab. They killed a man for EPA approval of this stuff. And he wants me to see it.

A flood of emotion pulses through my veins, igniting a hunger within me. My blood is humming. I can't deny the curiosity flowing within me knowing I might have the chance to see headquarters.

"When can I go?" It's dangerous to lead him on like this. But a large part of me wants to scour the site—the head office that hosts people walking through a fog of past and potential crimes. The irresistible impulse sinking me so far deep in quicksand I'm not sure anyone can pull me out.

"I have time next weekend," Officer Berrett replies. A satisfied smile settles under his golden brown mustache.

"I'd love to take a ride with you," I manage to squeak the words out, hating myself as they leave my tongue. "But if you'll excuse me I have to get back to my friends who know nothing of Marigold but have lots of questions about why an officer keeps following me. In fact, your presence is making it difficult for me not to keep my business with Jonathan a secret from them."

"I see. I will give you space in exchange for an evening on the back of my bike," he says.

"Looking forward to it," I say, waiting until he leaves to exhale. My body's lodged in the sand. There's no way out now. I've secured a way to investigate Marigold at its core at the risk of my name being dragged through Marigold's circle by no later than the end of the week.

Chapter Thirty-Eight

I find out real quickly the next morning that the relationship between granddaughter and Pops is quite different from the relationship between Pops and daughter. He sits me down and lectures me about Ben and Diana's not-so-successful wedding crash attempt. I respectfully listen as he gets the message across that he's disappointed and I'm now grounded from Little Narnia. We end the conversation and I'm just grateful I haven't been grounded from dating or leaving the house because I have plans.

Ben invited me to the drive-in as we crossed the freezing creek water last night. I happily agreed after extinguishing any concerns they had about Officer Berrett chasing me in the dark, assuring both of them he'd be giving me a lot more space moving forward.

Thursday night, Ben and I pull into the drive-in's gravel parking lot in my grandparents' station wagon. He's driving. We thought it would be a bit uncomfortable to show up on the dirt bike, and Diana and Tyler are using her car. We find them parked next to Corky and Bennette as we drive past the second row of parking and land ourselves in the open third row spot behind them.

Bennette pokes her head around at me. She and Corky sit on the top of the truck wrapped in thick bunched-up blankets, and she's looking at me as if I've stolen her candy. To be fair that's exactly what I had done. Ben doesn't notice. He's too busy handing me a heap of blankets and adding cream soda to the space in between us—which was quite a lot of space considering 1970s station wagons were built with three rows of leather hotdog seats, void of cup holders, that could easily fit three people in just the driver's row.

Ben reaches down by his feet, then pops back up brandishing a two-and-a-half-foot-long tube that's covered in Tootsie Roll logo wrapping. It's basically the jumbo size version of the Tootsie Roll can in my bottom dresser drawer.

"Tootsie Roll?" he asks. I nod. He pops the piggy-bank-style lid open and at least fifty filled wrappers disperse across our blankets as the screen projector begins playing grainy commercials on the giant screen. My insides warm as the words TOP GUN appear, so large they could be read by the cars driving by on the highway.

"Such a classic," I say impetuously.

"Yeah, it's good. I don't know about classic yet. It's only been out for a year." Ben tugs on the blanket I'd been keeping to myself.

"Trust me. It will be," I say, handing him one of the three quilts he'd given me.

"You've seen this already, but have you seen *Risky Business*?" Ben asks.

"The dancing socks scene only." I leave out the fact that it was a three minute video on YouTube.

"*The Outsiders*?" he asks.

"I've seen that." And many other Tom Cruise movies: *The Mummy, Mission Impossible, Rock of Ages*. All movies this Ben hasn't seen.

"Who's your favorite actor?" he asks as Maverick guides Cougar to the landing strip.

"Chris Farley." It's an easy answer, requiring absolutely no thought. It slips out automatically, like car oil from a worn-out gasket. Non-80s-Land Ben knew this better than anyone. He knew my fascination with the SNL Chippendales skit actor stemmed from the memories I had watching it with my father as a child. He'd understood what Chris Farley truly meant to me other than quick laughs and automatic smiles, even when he and Diana forcibly set limits on how many times I could mention the "fat guy in a little coat" and threatened to destroy a few of my VHS tapes. It was all a tease, a suggestion to help me to branch out, but they'd never actually destroy the things that held most of my sentiments.

"How come I've never heard of him?" Ben says. "What's he in?"

His response gives me pause. The largest difference between Non-80s-Land Ben and this Ben becomes more clear-cut. Ben and Diana knew Chris Farley was one of the only memories I have with my dad. Chris Farley was my way of keeping him in my life.

"*Tommy Boy*," I say as if I've mixed something up and I am suddenly unsure.

"Hmm…I haven't seen that either. We should watch it together."

"We should. I'm not sure how you'll feel about it." When it comes out eight years from now that is.

"You don't think I'll like it?"

"I'm not sure what you'll feel about it," I say, knowing my partner agent Ben was so considerate of these memories that his seventeen-year-old self dressed up as Chris Farley motivational speaker just to sway my mood and bring the comforting memory out for my sixteenth birthday—a situation of bonding over a scenario found in only one time—one universe. The Ben sitting beside me couldn't know this.

I let some deeper thoughts sink in and then resolve to completely shut them out for the night.

"If you love it, I will love it too."

I nod and smile back at him in response.

"You know the moment I think I realized I loved you was when Kelly kicked you in the face." He laughs.

"Oh, it started out so romantic," I say sarcastically. I replay his words again in my head. "Wait, did you just admit you love me?"

"I did." A smirk sits on his face. "I think back to that moment a lot actually, how concerned I was about you after you joined cheer just to mess with Corky. I made it worse and I felt so bad. I couldn't stop thinking about how your injury was because of my prank on Tyler, but then you acted so cool about it."

"I think I've always loved you," I say automatically. At this he seems to realize his ongoing chatter isn't necessary.

"If I kissed you right now would you be sad you missed out on the movie?" he says, leaning in so his face is just inches away from mine and a spark of excitement builds pressure and radiates from his eyes.

"Not even a little bit." At that, he scoots closer to my side and lowers slowly until he reaches my lips. We tangle up in sweet kisses for the rest of the movie. I've already seen the last half of *Top Gun,* and I've missed out on these kisses for ten-plus years. I'll be enjoying every last second of them.

"WERE YOU ABLE TO TALK WITH TYLER'S DAD YESTERDAY?" I ASK, as we sit, stuck in the gravel line, waiting for the cars to move from out of their parked rows.

"Yes," he says, focused on following the next car in line as they speed up and shoot out onto the street.

"Do you think he'll pursue it?"

"I think so."

"What was his response?" My words come out with the same resolute weight as when I'm questioning others on a case.

"He said he'll bring it up with his department." He smiles at me and slowly inches the car forward.

"If you're able to bring it up again, make sure to mention the name Marigold. When I spoke with him the other day I learned Officer Berrett is associated with a group called Marigold," I say, hoping just the mention of the mine explosion itself will be enough for Tyler's dad to connect his Marigold findings—aka newspaper clippings—with the mountain explosion.

The newspaper articles held information about an EPA director's death, a new installment and the subsequent MaG compound approval—a series of events that likely coincide with the fact that they can now sell Clean Wave products containing that chemical. I figured Mr. Jacobson knew enough to assume what was being held up in the mine. Prior to our discovery, what he lacked was evidence and a location.

"I might not get to mention it for a while," he says.

"Why is that?" I say, noticing Ben seems to be far away. Somewhere deep in his thoughts as he stares at Tyler and Diana's car in front of us.

"He's going to be at St. Joseph's for a while." He pauses. "Tyler starts chemo tomorrow."

Chapter Thirty-Nine

"Tyler has cancer?" What? Tyler was always healthy. I spent his seventeenth birthday with him and Diana in a boat on the lake. His head was shaved but he did that every other summer. Did this actually happen in Non-80s-Land as well or is this alternate universe throwing me for a loop?

"Wait. Is this why you didn't want Diana to date Tyler?" I ask.

He nods, affirming my suspicion. "He's been sick for a couple of months now, refusing treatment. Tyler's dad confronted Evan and I to try and convince him to go through with it. We're the only ones who know other than his family and it didn't help at all. He wanted to act like nothing was wrong. He's afraid of showing he's unwell in front of everyone else."

"He refused treatment?" I don't even try to mask the shock on my face.

"Yeah. He became even more resolute after we got involved. Said he wanted to live the rest of his life without regrets, acting the way he always did. He refused to give up basketball season. Even threatened once to end his life even earlier if we said anything—still not sure if that was a poorly timed joke or not. I was already on the fence when my mom asked me to step up and help support the family, but when I found out what Tyler was doing I just couldn't play knowing he was in bad shape.

"Wow," is all I can manage.

"While Tyler's living his life without regrets, Evan and I were trying to convince him to get treatment. That and trying to convince him not to pursue my sister. At least while he was acting so irresponsible."

"I can't believe I never knew this," I say.

"You weren't supposed to know. I was angry because I told him not to do this to Diana. He'll just break her heart when she finds out that he could be gone in a few months, maybe a year. Knowing him, he'll probably try to hide the fact that he's sick from her. At least he's finally given in to chemo."

"Maybe he started chemo so he can stay for her," I say, trying to give Ben a new perspective.

My thoughts stretch in vast directions the rest of the week. One day I'm swept up, musing over Tyler's condition—his chance at recovery, grueling eighties' cancer treatments, who's to be the bearer of telling Diana the bad news. And the next, I'm being beaten with every grim outcome of possibility that comes with fraternizing with Marigold—or running from them—either option is likely to leave me blighted by the end of the week.

Because truthfully riding off into the mountains with Officer Berrett puts an end to the guise that is this eighties refuge, an end to my temporary state of innocence. But not doing so grants me automatic questioning from the entire Marigold foundation.

It's Saturday morning. I sift through the Marigold notes in my crossword turned planner another five or six times, just to be sure that I'm giving what I'm about to do my best shot. It's a plan with about a five percent success rate—five percent might even be too generous a number —but if I time it right and if fate is compelled to grant me a favor I just might be able to pull this off. And in the likely event that it fails, I have Tyler's dad, Mr. Jacobson, who's already hot to the case and hopefully now aware of the mine explosion. If I'm being honest, I entrust him to do all the Marigold investigating from the past with the hopes that Marigold won't be around in the future. My role in 80s-Landia prevents me from having the authority to shut them down myself and he's the most promising solution, now that he can recover evidence at Bennett Mine.

I grab the wristwatch off of my dresser and join Pops at the table for breakfast. The sunrise matches the color of the orange juice in my hand and the teal of my oversized t-shirt, reminding me of an eighties postcard—the kind that paints the eighties as an overly-saturated, neon rainbow paradise. When truthfully, the eighties was a lot more like living in every single shade of orange and brown. The oversaturated sunrise palette almost feels like a sign.

Pops chews on his refrigerator-chilled bacon as I focus hard on the *Calvin and Hobbes* comic strip in front of me. I read a few of them aloud to see if he'll crack a smile. He quickly realizes my objective, sets down his newspaper, and scoots his chair closer to mine so that he can enjoy the paper with me.

He leaves for a day hike soon after, leaving me with Marcie. Her mood wall hanging has been changed to "Feeling Silly." I'm almost relieved when she greets me in the kitchen, excited to share the news that she gets to spend the day making jam at a neighbor's house while the boys are at a wrestling tournament. I ask for the keys to the station wagon and send her off with a smile.

The change of moods amongst both grandparents encourages me, giving me the strength to carry on with today's plans.

My first stop is the track field—a little pit stop before I confront my choices for the future. It's Diana's first meet of the season and I wouldn't miss it for the world. The last time I had watched my best friend fly through the air like this was around 2011. The fact that I was able to witness her doing one of the things she loved the most again was a gift. A gift from time.

It was also an opportunity to gauge who would be at the Browns' home this afternoon.

As I enter the platform, a tall, bony-framed, blonde girl sprints past me with her ten-foot pole at her side. She plants her pole in the box just before reaching the mat and heaves her body forward so the pole bends like a pool noodle in the process. Everyone watches as the pole drops to the runway floor and she flies over the bar with success. Hoots and hollers erupt from the bleachers.

I look over to see Ben, Mama Robyn, and Grandma Harriet amongst the loudly cheering crowd, tucked away at the side of the stands. Ben can't see me from where I stand and I prefer it this way. I have the perfect view of him, the perfect way to gaze at him and admire him without him knowing. I don't plan to catch him today. It's too hard to confront him knowing what I'm about to do.

Diana's next in line. She seems to be in a calm, zen-like state, waiting for her turn. She doesn't look nervous, just focused, like an eagle looking to spot its target from a distance. She holds so much composure I can't help but wonder if she is still unaware of Tyler's condition. I survey the pole vault bleachers for Tyler. If he was here he'd surely be watching, but I don't see his face anywhere. If she doesn't know, I can't help but wonder what she'll do when she finds out.

She pats down a few unruly curls and adjusts her teal sweatband so that it sits at the top of her forehead. Diana spots me and smirks before her vault attempt. I give her an obnoxious wave as a rush of excitement pulses through my blood.

She starts the vault, rocking back and forth on her heels before ascending to a high-knee power run. At the end of her sprint she plants her pole in the box and launches herself into the air. She sails over the bar using a twist motion before gravity pulls her down onto the cushioned mat where she lands with a soft poof.

A few rounds pass, leaving three girls, including Diana, left in the competition. They attempt the eight-foot vault, all barely inching over the bar.

I look at the time on my watch and notice I'm running a little behind schedule. Officer Berrett told me to meet him at the house around noon. The event's taking longer than I expected and it would be wise of me to leave now, but I'm inclined to see Diana's performance all the way through.

We all watch as the first and second competitors fail the eight-and-a-half-foot vault. A snarl hits Diana's bare lips as she preps for her sprint. Her steps are higher this time and powered with even more strength. She hits the target and wins the event, but our eyes stay glued to her as she attempts to beat her personal record on a second run.

For a moment I feel as if I'm watching the same exact scenario that happened during track season of 2011 play out, except this time she wasn't using iPod earbuds to blast Rihanna's "What's My Name" before her final PR attempt. She catapults herself into the air and bends over with centimeters to spare, making the vault and hitting a new personal record. I'm overcome, overjoyed, and reveling in excitement a few yards away, but I can't stay for the celebration.

I hurry back to the station wagon, feeling grateful to experience one of Diana's happiest moments all over again. I let this memory of young Diana embracing her family as they pelt her with congratulatory pats sink into the permanent spot in my brain allotted for core memories.

The drive across town alone in the family car is quicker than usual thanks to less midday traffic. I open Ben and Diana's front door with ease. In the few weeks I'd been here I'd learned locking the door wasn't something the Browns cared to do—along with most households in the eighties. Back at it again, I am running the habit of breaking and entering.

So far the plan is going swimmingly. With no one home I'm able to get what I need from the Browns without cause for disturbance. Though my time is limited and chances are slanted percentage-wise, at the end of this, I will still have a lot of explaining to do.

I run to the kitchen looking for the Browns' new transparent phone with colored wires that Ben spoke of connecting recently—the same phone he'd gifted me in Non-80s-Land when we were young, possibly even the same phone that had brought me here to 1987. I hold the phone cord up in the light to take a closer look at the coil. A slit in the coil exposes the copper wire, confirming my suspicion. This is the same phone I'd held in my hand before leaving Non-80s-Land. I disconnect the wire from the wall jack and hold the phone like a precious baby in my arms, jogging back to the station wagon.

I check my watch again for the time as I drive off. I have thirty minutes to get across town before Officer Berrett knocks down our front door in search of me.

I'd used what little door of opportunity I had to collect Ben's transparent phone, my old Non-80s-Land possession, while my best friend's family was preoccupied and now I'm strapped for time. I need to be early to Officer Berrett's. I must be the first to walk across the street. The first to knock on his door. And no one can witness it. I need to keep this little escapade a secret from everyone, in the likely chance everything doesn't go as planned.

Every couple of seconds I get the urge to glance at my wrist for the time. The more I lean into the impulse the more my chest fills with anxiety, the more my mind races with uncertainty. I take the moment to think over the concerns that had sprouted during my night at the drive-in with Ben.

Ben's lack of knowing Chris Farley's significance in my life brought a new perspective to mind. A perspective of the future and the consequences that would emerge if I were to continue living in this eighties universe. Consequences that might erase substantial realities from my past—like my relationship with my father.

The relationship I had with my father would simply not exist to anyone but me. It wouldn't be acknowledged or spoken of. Eventually it would become an ever-increasing, distant memory of a life I once had. Erica would likely meet my father down the road, giving me the opportunity to see him again sometime in the next decade—a miracle

I would've given up everything for over the last twenty-six years of my life to see, even if it was just to see him one more time—however I can see it all with clarity now. Staying meant my father would marry my mom and have a kid, a kid that wasn't me.

The fact that my Non-80s-Land father knew me as his daughter throughout his time alive bonded us together and I wasn't willing to give that up. I wasn't willing to give up the meaning behind those Chris Farley references—the root of all my core memories with my father—or the reality that they exist only in the Non-80s-Land universe unless I had to. When it came to those memories there was pain in accepting this alternate universe as anything other than temporary.

When I park the station wagon next to Erica's car in the driveway, I hop out of my seat firm in my decision, despite knowing that if I succeed in all of this I'm about to give up my one and only opportunity to be with Ben.

I walk into the house with a few minutes to spare. Upon entering, I quietly sneak into Little Narnia—despite being grounded from it—to drop off the transparent phone. I do a double take to make sure I have everything properly laid out on Pops' desk, ready to test as soon as I get back from the mountain. A feeling of optimism shoots through me as I stare at my future time travel experiment. Optimism is all I have in this huge moment of uncertainty.

❋

"GREG BROKE UP WITH ME," ERICA SAYS FROM THE COUCH, when I make my way past the accordion TV in the living room. I pause at the front door and look at her. Her green eyes coil with anguish.

"Oh, no. Are you okay?" I ask, noticing the bangs left out of her ponytail have woven around the hinges of her reading glasses and she's still wearing her baggy sweats and the tee from the night before.

"No," she says. A tear trickles down past her lips and then another follows in its path. I tell her I'm sorry and capture her in a hug.

I can feel the clock ticking on my wrist as minutes pass, but my arms squeeze around her as our memories as "sisters" flood through me. The nights we spent in front of the TV laughing and stretching, the mornings before school spent doing my hair, and the time we spent together blasting eighties music out of the car window flash through my mind—memories I'd never forget no matter which century I landed in.

I knew everything would work out for her. She would fall madly in love. She'd experience joy and loss and she would be grateful for the experience of knowing my father. It would all work out the way it was supposed to for her in our other universe. The thought of seeing it all play out again in this universe was tempting, but I'd be sacrificing my father-daughter relationship in doing so.

I ask her if I can do anything and then I remember the last phone conversation I had with her in the present day.

"I have to head out and I'm no expert in love, but someone wise once told me this." I pause, repeating the words she spoke to me over the phone in Non-80s-Land. "You may not have his love now but you'll always have my love." I squeeze her one last time and hurry out the door.

Chapter Forty

The second I step foot out the door I bump into Ben. He stands on the porch steps with hands outstretched for the door. His ball cap almost hides the wrinkles of confusion now grazing his forehead.

"Atta! I saw you leave my house and run off with my mom's new phone! I went into the house to make sure I wasn't seeing things. I wasn't. You ripped the phone cord out of my kitchen and took it with you! What are you up to?" Ben asks in bewilderment. His long arms flail at his side before a smirk escapes his face as if he's expecting this all to be a prank and that I'll have an earth-shattering yet satisfactory explanation for him.

I don't have time to form a response when I see Officer Berrett dragging his motorcycle across his driveway. He stops at the edge of his lawn to take a good look at us, drops his bike, and begins making his way across the street.

"I can't talk right now, I've…I've got to go," I say to Ben, reaching behind me for the brassy doorknob.

"Miss Atkinson, are you ready to ride?" I hear Officer Berrett holler from the middle of the street. The words leave his mouth but I already have the door open. In a flurry of panic I scramble through the door simultaneously shutting it in Ben's face. Then I twist the lock before Ben or Officer Berrett have the chance to follow in behind me.

I know I'm being inconsiderate, but I can't risk Ben witnessing me riding on the back of Officer Berrett's bike. Or even having a conversation about it. They'll probably have that conversation locked together outside. The thought makes my insides itch. But my reflex instinct has me reeling to take the next step instead, skipping over the mountain ride entirely and I don't think I'm wrong to do so.

I can't just hop on Officer Berret's motorcycle with Ben in plain sight and then ride off into the mountains with the homewrecker. At least, not without betraying Ben's trust more than I probably already have at this point.

I have no time to deal with either of them right now anyway. I've already decided to give time travel another shot and this was my chance.

Time travel would solve my current Marigold predicament. Whereas my trouble was once in Non-80s-Land, it was now about to reach the same kind of precipice here. The best I can do is deal with the Marigold repercussions as they come and if my test fails, like it did the first time, Tyler's dad has key information that could solve the Marigold issue in the future.

I'll be stuck here forced to choose between joining Marigold or living on the run from them. But as long as I had Ben and Mr. Jacobson's trust I'd deal with everything one step at a time.

The hallway greets me with an ominous glow, as if magic is seeping out from under Little Narnia's closet door. The apparition is likely due to my overflowing sense of hope. A mere delusion.

I approach the closet door, checking my surroundings to make sure Erica's not snooping in the hallway. There's no evidence of Erica near but the sound of banging at the door is met with a clamor of crashing dishes in the kitchen.

I slide into the closet with haste, hiding behind the brood of hanging shirts as Erica makes her way into the living room with flustered steps and a kitchen rag in hand.

"Who is it?" she yells, expecting an answer to reverberate through the solid oak door. "Why is this locked?" I hear her say as she twiddles with the door handle.

When she answers it I have Little Narnia's top lock undone and I'm fumbling for the bottom one with a racing heart.

"Ben!" I hear Erica say. "Atta didn't say you were coming. Did you come to pick her up? She said she was heading out."

"She's riding with me actually. Don't mind if I come in, do you neighbor?" Officer Berrett's voice joins the conversation.

"I thought she talked to you about keeping your distance," Ben chimes in. The closet door is still open and I can hear them through the enclosure. They're in the living room at this point, as it seems Erica has gifted them both the opportunity to barge into our house.

I manage to disconnect Pops' phone from the phone jack and fiddle with Grandma Harriet's colorful transparent cord.

"Keep my distance?" Officer Berrett asks, sounding quite amused with Ben's obvious frustration, not at all concerned about blowing my cover. "She's the one who asked me to meet today."

With my pulse racing, I connect the phone to the wall jack. My fingers can't move fast enough. Their voices grow louder as they enter the hallway. They aren't wise enough to look for me in the closet, right? They'd find it locked anyway if they tried.

I still had time to make this work.

I hear movement just outside the door in the hallway followed by Officer Berrett calling out my name while Ben prods him with questions. I can hear the concern in Ben's voice.

Ben knocks on Erica's bedroom door and then mine, likely hoping to find me before Officer Berrett does.

"How about you both leave? I'll have her contact you when I find her," Erica cuts in. I can tell she's concerned, now that two men are becoming combative while searching for me in the confines of my own home.

"When you find her, tell her I'm waiting outside," Officer Berrett says, abandoning his effort in the house raid.

I keep quiet, holding the Clean Wave spray in hand, listening to them search the stairs right outside the door. I quietly pop one of the cement bubble gum balls in my mouth and begin to chew. It takes everything in me not to try to conjure a chalk flavored bubble—the gum is old but it still chews.

"Ben, how about you walk with Officer Berrett back outside? I'll let her know you stopped by," Erica continues.

"I'm not leaving. That little thief left my house just as I was pulling in and ran off with my mom's new phone for who knows what reason. She ripped the phone cord out of my kitchen and took the whole phone system with her," Ben says adamantly, though there's a lightness to his voice as if he finds it equally amusing as he does irritating.

"She stole your *phone*?" Erica asks, confusion setting in hard when she utters the word.

"Is there a phone jack upstairs?" Ben asks.

"No."

"Atta, if you can hear me, why didn't you just ask to borrow my phone?" Ben shouts up the stairs. "She's up to something. I just know it."

I grab the chewed gum from my mouth, delicately with two fingers, then I stick it on the side of the phone speaker just as it was when I held it in my hands in Non-80s-Land.

My heart breaks a little knowing that if what I'm trying to attempt works, I won't get to answer Ben or say goodbye to the version of the man who loved me. The version who's questioning my bold actions and sanity at the moment.

I was choosing Non-80s-Land Ben. The Ben I had built most of my memories with, the Ben who wouldn't pursue a relationship with me. The Ben I hoped would be saved by my actions in the eighties.

I was banking on the fact that by sharing our mountain mine explosion discovery with Mr. Jacobson I would be able to eradicate the

Marigold threat of the future. Everything was in Mr. Jacobson's hands. I only hoped everything would work out in the end.

I stare at the speaker of the phone in my hand and give it a spray with the Clean Wave solution using the same motion I tried the last time I attempted time travel. Then I think about what I'd said a month ago in Pops' closet with Ben right next to me.

"Atta Mae, where are you? I bet you're hiding because you know what I'm going to say to you when you try to explain why you ripped my phone out from the wall." I hear Ben shout with lightheartedness.

My eyes close with regret, and I dial a pattern of numbers just the way I did the first time when the last four digits ended in 1987.

00-02-02-2023

Chapter Forty-One

I t was the same nauseating experience as the first time. Blacking out. My eyes become weighted and too heavy, as if I'd need a crowbar to pry them open. The feeling continues until the spiraling and dizziness stop and I'm able to glance at my surroundings.

It's Pops' closet, but I immediately know I've left an era and I'm back to his modern-day hideout.

When I slip out from behind the curtain of dress shirts, I'm met with a vista of plush white carpet that happens to be more modernly aesthetically pleasing than before. I feel my sneakers sink into the soft-ness of the floor as I set out in search of the others. Has anything changed? How long was I gone?

I survey the hallway wall hangings and framed photos and find that the living room seems to be in the same form as it was before I first departed Non-80s-Land.

"Atta! Is it really you?" Marcie runs toward me as I enter a more modern version of my grandparents' kitchen. She has peppered-hair and a face full of wrinkles. I don't know who is more shocked, me or her. The look on her face, as she about tosses her breakfast rolls up into the air, tells me we both weren't expecting to run into each other.

"Hold on, stay right there. Do not move. I must call your mother. There's been a missing person report filed on you. Where have you been all week?"

She's shaking and frantically moving her feet, so much so that she looks as if she's running in place. Her expression says she's just seen a ghost but relief washes over her quickly when she pulls me into a hug.

It's only been a week in Non-80s-Land?

"I'm calling her now," she says mid-hug, squeezing me tighter, dialing behind my back and resting the phone between her ear and my shoulder.

Ben shows up thirty minutes later on his bike in uniform ready to fire a week's worth of questions at me. The news of my reappearance has spread quickly within the family-friend circle and Ben was able to get here the fastest. He volunteers to drive me out to see my Mom in Fort Collins.

He approaches me with his arms at his waist, one hand gently grazing the gun at his holster. Goosebumps travel up my forearms as his eyes drag from my face, down my body, and back up to my face. His gaze is different from Eighties Ben, more intense and his chocolate-brown eyes burn with a murderous glare.

"Where have you been?" He lays into me and I expect him to use the sparring move he uses during friendly tiffs but instead he wraps me in his arms, squeezes me tight and looks at me as if I'll disappear in his arms any second. "Thank heavens, Atta. I was convinced Agent Maser had done something to you. Your family and I…we searched for days." His hold feels different than Eighties Ben. He's not emanating that boyfriend warmth and despite our bodies touching, I can feel his brotherly distance. Yet somehow I still covet this version of him even more. "The department helped too. I hounded Kenny every day you were missing and every day he questioned me about your disappearance as if he was trying to play mind games with me. I was so scared he…they…that Marigold had taken you."

"They didn't take me," I say. Disappointment floods through me hearing Marigold's name mentioned in this time period.

This is not the news I want to hear.

He pauses to take another look at me. "Where were you this whole time and why is your hair like that?" he asks. By the way he says it I can tell he's not impressed by my voluminous waves. I peek over his shoulder at the mirror to find a familiar set of oncoming crow's feet around my eyes and I manage a smile back at the living room mirror taking in my oversized teal t-shirt, bold lined biker shorts and frivolous curls that come with an ample amount of bounce—my outfit hasn't changed at all since the track meet in Non-80s-Land. "And what are you wearing?"

"I tried to come back to you," I say, then pause. I'm not sure how to explain what I'd undergone and I wasn't sure I should try. The shock of actually having a successful time travel experience shakes my ability to attempt even a fake explanation for my outdated appearance or my time away.

"What happened in your grandpa's closet? I passed out after the wall socket burst and you were gone when I woke up." He releases me from his hug. My lack of explanation is only met with more questions from him.

"I don't know," I say. It's the only explanation I can give.

"You must know. You've been gone for an entire week. All of Denver's been looking for you and you left your mom and grandparents without an explanation. You wouldn't do something like that unless you were coerced." His beautiful brown eyes stare into mine, accessing the sincerity of what I'm about to say next.

"I don't know where I was or how I got there to be honest," I say.

If I was going to tell him, I'd have to wait for the right time and ease into it slowly. I wasn't about to reveal time travel to the man who called me crazy after a brief stint of believing Bigfoot was real—I mean who am I to say he is or not? If that was my explanation for leaving this world for a week he'd think I'd happened upon a field of psychedelic mushrooms and copiously partook during my time away.

"Where is there? If you think you can't say because you're being threatened you still have to tell me. Who took you?"

"No one took me. I just left. For a week. Let's focus on something else. Is Agent Maser still a part of Marigold?" I ask. If I'm to acknowledge that my plan—to have Mr. Jacobson learn of the mountain explosion and solve the Marigold issue from the past—has failed, then I must confirm it one more time.

"You would do that to all of us? Just leave without telling anyone. No contact to the point that we would have a search and rescue team out looking for you? I know the Marigold thing is taxing but you have to be out of your mind to do this to us and yes, Atta…he's very much still a part of Marigold."

I'm not sure how to get back into Ben's good graces. After all, lying is the best option with time traveling cases. But my whereabouts over the last week are lesser in comparison to the issue that Marigold is still around. This affects everything. Our safety. Our futures.

I was naive to think I could change history through time travel—naive to think our discovery in the mountain would be enough for Mr. Jacobson to resolve the Marigold issue from the past.

Nothing has been solved from my eighties-alternate-universe efforts. I breathe a heavy sigh of defeat and begin pacing the room deep in thought about how to proceed from here.

"Are you safe? Has Agent Maser been threatening you while I was away?" I ask, focusing on the questions I want answered.

"No Atta, he's been busy wondering where you took off to. He probably thinks you up and ran after being threatened with the USB knowledge. I'm not sure what he'll do now that you're back." His face bleeds frustration but he seems to be pushing a calmer tone, likely because he's concerned for my mental state. I only shake my head in agreement.

***

Ben does the responsible thing and notifies the authorities that I've resurfaced before driving back to Diana's place in Fort Collins where my mother is waiting for me.

"I had an emergency therapy session scheduled! You're here and I don't need it anymore. But look at you honey! You're going to need that emergency therapy session," Mom says using a drip of humor to subdue a week's worth of panic when we arrive.

Diana and my mother embrace me with impressive force, well before I have the chance to hop off of Ben's bike. Once they grab hold of me, they don't let go of me for the rest of the night. I'm pestered with hugs and questions too difficult to answer until early in the morning.

A few hours later, I'm awoken by Ben who wants me to get dressed and ride with him to the east side of the state.

"I have something to show you," he says. I know he's hoping for me to explain more about my whereabouts but the sun hasn't even made its appearance at this hour. My work mode has been turned off for about a month—my time, not theirs—and I find it difficult to open more than one eye.

An hour later we arrive at the site of my last investigation. The same chemical plant explosion site that Ben blasted through the week before I'd left this universe. He'd chased a man through my tape, uncovering a mutilated body in the process. I hadn't been back to the site since it had been placed under review.

"I discovered something about the chemical substance left behind at your scene," Ben says as he slows the motorcycle to a stop. The sun has just begun to rise and we hop off the bike taking in the narrow mountainside scenery. "It's a MaG compound."

Ben knows about MaG? If so, does he know about the MaG compound and its relationship with Marigold?

"I haven't been able to figure out exactly which MaG compound it is since there are many different types. But I discovered something." This must be his attempt at trying to give me some hope that we have a chance. That he hasn't gone all week without trying to find something that could stand against Marigold.

We walk a few steps onto the site when he says, "A Marigold

member owns this land. There's gray powder here and I also found DNA on the corpse that belongs to a local officer."

Gray powder? That's not the color of the MaG compound I know.

"How were you able to find all of that out?" I ask. His emphasis on the MaG compound being gray and therefore not the only compound of that nature but a compound under an umbrella of MaG compounds takes up most of the space in my mind.

"After you disappeared, Maser switched his focus to trying to find you. I've been able to get away and search this site."

If what he said is true, I've happened across not one, but two sites that have held a MaG compound, both of which exploded. The orange powdered MaG substance in the mountains where we witnessed Bennett Mine explode on the west side of Denver and now the gray MaG substance on the east side of the state.

In the short amount of time I was able to work the chemical plant case I had only discovered a barrel full of copper wire. But Ben identified a MaG compound on site?

Ben points out the various landmarks where he was able to collect evidence before testing the DNA and powdery substances. I follow along but become lost in thought over the fact that both MaG compounds become explosive around certain elements.

The gray MaG compound must have been the cause of the explosion in my last case—the one under review, the scene Ben and I are currently discussing. And it was clear the orange powdery MaG substance was, in part, the cause of the explosion at Bennett Mine.

The question now pestering my mind is did Marigold intend for the sites storing MaG compound to explode? Were they keen on sweeping both explosions under the rug because they couldn't control the dangerous substance from unexpected chemical reactions?

Ben proposes the connection of Marigold and the containment of this case as the sun continues to rise in the distance, lighting the sky with an icy blue glow. An orange sphere floats above the desert floor and a few glowing pink shadows dance behind it. I'm convinced it's debris from the morning sun until the glowing orbs turn into flashing siren lights.

The siren's blare envelopes us swiftly. Ben turns toward the oncoming officers as they park their vehicles just a few yards away. He steps forward and motions for me to stay put.

Ben seems to comprehend something I don't and starts sprinting toward the shadows. I follow behind, acutely aware of my slothlike speed in comparison at this unholy hour.

Before I'm able to get a good look at the three obscure faces approaching, I feel something hit me from behind. My heart lurches into my throat and I'm temporarily knocked off balance so much so that it's impossible for me to take a defensive position. When I attempt to, I feel the stab of thin metal at my wrists, a long piece of cloth being wrapped tightly around my eyelids, and I feel my freedom being stripped from me in an instant, fifty miles outside of Denver in the middle of nowhere east towards Kansas.

I WAKE UP WITH MY BACK AGAINST TWO STURDY SHOULDER blades to find that Ben and I are alone in a room leaning against each other. I feel his finger continuously tapping the side of my neck.

"Atta, Atta, wake up. Are you okay?" he says. Panic racks his voice.

"There's a strap over her mouth. She can't answer you," a voice that's not Ben's says. Recognition makes my insides churn. That voice is eerily familiar.

The covering is removed from my face and I'm able to see my captors. Agent Kenny Maser and a man with a familiar set of eyes stand in front of us. It's not hard to recognize him even with the dark wrinkles and peppery-hair.

Unlike Ben, I'm able to recognize most of the people in the room. At the edge of the warehouse stand Robert Schills and his assistant Deanna Hurley. Their backs are turned so that I receive only a partial view of their profiles and a man—recognizable from that unnerving

USB video—stands to the side, a few feet away from them, on the phone.

I'm not sure how scared I should be of that man but the man next to Agent Maser, the man who stands just an arm's reach away, strikes a terror in me that no amount of calming exercises could cure.

An older delineation of Officer Berrett is rendered before me. And though I know he's not a painting, I wish he was. Everything about this picture terrifies me. He stands next to Kenny with a wad of duct tape and zip ties. *The* Officer Berrett, the Golden police officer from my eighties universe who prodded me to come chase the flowers with him all while sporting an aggressive eighties mullet and a much younger complexion.

"We have some things we need to discuss," Agent Maser begins. They've yet to remove the strap from my mouth, blocking my ability to speak out.

"Let me introduce you to Officer Borgin Berrett, my father." Officer Berrett nods as if to welcome us kindly. It doesn't matter his approach, handcuffs and zip ties make this a terrifying ambush. I jog my memory thinking about how this family relation was more than just a coincidence.

The little boy at our family dinner with Officer Berrett in 80s-Landia. Was that Kenny?

"Let's start with an introduction. Back there we have Marigold's founder Robert Schills, his assistant Deanna Hurley, and Jonathan," Kenny continues. "All of whom wanted to meet with the two people who've recently come across Marigold. You see, within Marigold we like to keep things under wraps and you both know more than you should. Do you have any intention to share the things you've seen?" Agent Maser asks.

I shake my head no. My mouth can't betray me but my eyes might slip. I want to scream at them. Swear at them. Tell them we will fight them head on. Agent Kenny Maser *had* made an appearance in my alternate universe. Agent Maser and Officer Berrett's relationship made this even more frightening than I thought possible.

Ben doesn't make a sound. Is he shaking his head in silence as well? My worry trails to the person in front of me. Does Officer Berrett recognize me? Is that even possible across the weird barrier between these two worlds I've been traversing?

Nothing had changed at all with the Marigold situation, despite my efforts to tip off Mr. Jacobson about the mountain explosion near the Marigold Company's headquarters. Throughout the course of a week in Non-80s-Land, the only thing that had been altered was the level of danger I was in. Did that mean there's no overlap between the eighties universe and this one? If no progress could be made from the eighties then it would be far-fetched to think Officer Berrett could recognize me from the eighties. Wouldn't it?

"Good. Now that you know your place, you have some explaining to do," Officer Berrett chimes in. He ends it there and waits for his son to continue.

"Agent Brown recently made some discoveries. Discoveries I cannot ignore," Agent Maser continues.

"I told you both there would be consequences if you spoke of what you saw on that USB. I told you your lives would be at stake if you dug any further. Did you know Ben continued looking into your chemical plant explosion case after it had been put on pause, Agent Suarez? Did you also know he's now knee-deep in another one of Marigold's operations. You get involved in one of our murders and you get one of two choices. Ben, I think you know which one I'm talking about. As for you, Agent Suarez, it's time to decide your punishment. We need to talk about why you've been missing."

Without a glint of recognition in his eyes, Officer Berrett walks over and rips the cloth strap from my mouth.

"Start talking," he says.

The End

Epilogue

Ben

The Atkinsons' station wagon is parked in front of my house when I park my bike to the side of the long row of bushes. Robyn asked me to ride home to grab her and Mom some snacks and a blanket when the wind picked up. I was trying to make it a quick trip, so that I wouldn't miss Atta whenever she decided to show up to see Diana run the 4x400 meter relay, but here she is parked at my house.

Did she think we were meeting here?

She must have completely forgotten that both Diana and I told her pole vaulting started at 11:00.

Our front door slams shut and I have to do a double take of the scene in my front lawn.

Atta is walking out of our house holding Mom's new phone and its wires are slapping her shorts, the way a house burglar would smuggle a treasure trove of jewelry on their way out from their escapade.

I watch from behind the massive bush, completely disregarding the reason I came here in the first place, and instead of grabbing what I need, I hop back in the car and follow Atta as she peels out from my house.

This is weird.

I sit in my car outside her home thinking about how I should approach this. She didn't even take the neighboring back road to be cautious of the neighbor cop.

Let's add this to the list of unconventionally weird behaviors she's exhibited lately. The most recent one being the fact that she asked me to ask Tyler's dad to investigate the mine explosion. I brought it up to Mr. Jacobson and despite the implied trust we had with each other about what he did for a living, he'd given me an awestruck expression before assuring me he'd look into it.

I went into it feeling slightly awkward to bring up one of Atta's petty concerns but I did it because I didn't want to disappoint her. I did it this time but I couldn't go on making this a habit. I can't do everything Atta wants me to do just because she has an intrusive mind.

She's made up of curiosity. And that fact right there is going to get me into a lot of trouble if I don't set my own boundaries. "No Atta, I will not fulfill your request to have law enforcement look into why the neighbor gardens in the dead of the night." I laugh at my parody of what *would* be one of Atta's logic-defying concerns.

I could deny her absurd requests before we started dating, so I can do it now. Her curiosities were as extensive as the stars, her mischievousness—I'm learning—might be just as boundless.

It was times like these that I found it exhausting to like my sister's best friend. She's just gone and jacked my family's main line with no explanation, but she's pretty, so I guess I'll put up with it.

That's what I plan to do, but first I must find out what she plans to do with my landline.

This girl.

When I find her, I will wrestle with my sister's best friend until she confesses that she has a problem and then I'll wrap my arms around her and kiss her, because regardless of the circumstance, it's the first thing I want to do when I see her every day.

Acknowledgments

As I alluded to in my dedication, 'Little Narnia' was, in fact, a real place found in my grandparents' home next to their garage. I experienced a little slice of magic everytime I passed through my grandpa's nest of shirts, opening them like curtains and twisting the knob to his hidden lair that was full of treasures from all over the world. Bringing that experience to life again for this book was super satisfying. The Colorado backdrop with its national parks and majestic red rocks, as well as a box of my mom's old eighties photos and watching SNL characters with my father at a young age served as inspiration for this novel. A big thank you to my family for influencing me in all the best ways.

To Shelby Woodland, my first reader. I'm glad you got to experience the story with me in its original form. The ending was hanging in the balance and you are the reason one of the characters has a bigger role than intended. Thank you for being enthusiastic about this story from the beginning.

To Michael Cluff, my incredible editor, thank you for being so meticulous with your edits and caring about the world and characters I've created even though this isn't a genre you'd typically read on your day off. You give incredibly sound advice and did a great job trying to match my writing style when making suggestions. Also thank you to you and your wife for your friendship. Here's to more sushi outings in the future.

To Julie Reush, who did an incredible job proofreading this book, noticing even the smallest grammatical errors and giving me the feedback I needed to finish this book.

To Authortree for formatting this book and making these words and pages finally look and feel real.

To Rena Violet, whose book cover art I am completely obsessed with. You are sunshine in the form of emails. I tend to judge a book by its cover and yours are chef's kisses.

And thanks always to Glen, who is my biggest supporter even though I haven't been able to properly describe this book to him in over three years. Thank you, thank you, thank you for all you do.

If you're reading these acknowledgements, I want to thank you as well—for giving this book a chance, for supporting my writing, and for stepping into Atta's complicated universe to experience this story and these characters with me. I hope to share more with you soon.

About the Author

STEFANI TANNER has a bachelor's degree in business—though these days her creative writing hobby is put to a lot more use. Playing on the same side of the court as her husband in a game of competitive volleyball might be the most exhilarating thing she's ever experienced and when she's not chimerically plotting out ways to sneak off to Ireland or Japan for a week, she spends her time making memories with her boys E and T. Sometimes they let her write.

CONNECT ONLINE

steftanner.writesbooks

www.ingramcontent.com/pod-product-compliance
Ingram Content Group UK Ltd.
Pitfield, Milton Keynes, MK11 3LW, UK
UKHW040932110225
454851UK00027B/182/J